Praise for Beth Gutcheon

"Humor and suspense in equal measure make for a delightful read in this second outing . . . for the well-heeled duo of Maggie Detweiler and Hope Babbin."   —*Booklist* on *The Affliction*

"Maggie and Hope aren't like the biddies of old English mysteries, picking up clues over tea and stuffing them for safekeeping in their knitting baskets. They're sharp and youthful, and the good news is that they're even sharper in *The Affliction*."

—HeadButler.com on *The Affliction*

"I have been a Beth Gutcheon fan forever, since a smart librarian put Gutcheon's first novel in my hands and said, 'You'll love her.' I do. And now this wonderful addition: a murder mystery, with all of her talents vividly displayed. What could be better: intrigue, murder, a New England inn, food, celebrities, and an endearing local cop that Agatha Christie would envy. Brava, Beth Gutcheon! And thank you."

—Elinor Lipman, author of *The View from Penthouse B* on *Death at Breakfast*

"Gutcheon tries her hand at crime fiction and brings all of her talent for creating engaging characters to the task. . . . The dialogue is witty and crisp, and the story moves at a good clip. . . . The delicious prose and exploration of the intricacies of human nature recommend this series to fans of Alexander McCall Smith, Louise Penny, and the late master of the form, Ruth Rendell."   —*Booklist* (starred review) on *Death at Breakfast*

THE AFFLICTION

THE AFFLICTION

Beth Gutcheon

WILLIAM MORROW

An Imprint of HarperCollins*Publishers*

P.S.™ is a trademark of HarperCollins Publishers.

HarperCollins books may be purchased for educational, business, or sales promotional use. For information please e-mail the Special Markets Department at SPsales@harpercollins.com.

A hardcover edition of this book was published in 2018 by William Morrow, an imprint of HarperCollins Publishers.

FIRST WILLIAM MORROW PAPERBACK EDITION PUBLISHED 2018.

Library of Congress Cataloging-in-Publication Data has been applied for.

ISBN 978-0-06-243200-1

18 19 20 21 22   LSC   10 9 8 7 6 5 4 3 2 1

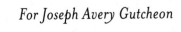

For Joseph Avery Gutcheon

To say *that things were tense* on the Hudson River campus of the Rye Manor School for Girls would be to understate the case fairly recklessly. Its evaluation by the Independent School Association five years earlier had been a near-death experience; the school was in peril of losing accreditation, which would be the same as a bullet to the brain. Today, for its progress review, the very young head of school, Christina Liggett, was so anxious for things to go well as she waited for the visitors who would decide her fate that she had spent much of the time since lunch in the ladies' room, her intestines in an uproar.

Her entire board of trustees was also in town, currently meeting in executive session. Unbeknownst to anyone outside the room, their discussions had become uncivil when the treasurer revealed that he had on his own started "exploring" with bankers and others the nuts and bolts of selling the campus and merging what was left of the school with a third-rate boys' academy in Connecticut. The president of the board, whose daughter was the fifth generation in her family to attend Rye Manor, was weeping with anger at this betrayal, especially egregious since the treasurer was a real estate developer himself, and thus had a shocking conflict of interest. A third trustee had made an emotional speech about protecting the loyal faculty who in some cases had spent their entire professional lives at the school. A fourth noted his daughters' opinions that the longevity of the faculty was a very large part of the school's problem.

"It's a school, it's not a nursing home."

"They live in school housing! They have no equity! Where are they going to go?"

"They should have thought of that themselves. They should have been saving."

"On what we pay them?"

And so on.

The school had once mattered very much in certain privileged circles of the United States. Prudence Milbank Culbertson, a society suffragist who had been force-fed like a goose during her famous prison hunger strike, was actually buried on campus in a grove of weeping birches. But by the time redoubtable educator Maggie Detweiler and her evaluation team set foot in Rye-on-Hudson, the days of commencement addresses delivered at Rye Manor by sitting vice presidents or justices of the Supreme Court in honor of their graduating granddaughters were long gone. Maggie had yet to measure the attitude of her two colleagues but was herself torn between sympathy and annoyance that such a valuable institution, a beacon in the history of women's education, should have been allowed to flounder so spectacularly. As one who had for years faced the challenge of leading a famous school in a changing world, she was no sentimentalist. She saw Rye Manor as a textbook case of privileged people thinking that excellence was a birthright, not something that must be earned over and over. Now with scores of jobs and careers at stake, it would be up to Maggie either to give the place another chance or to recommend a final merciful shove. She expected to be about as welcome on campus as an Ebola outbreak.

* * *

Maggie and her colleagues made their way along paved paths across green lawns under ancient specimen trees and toward the administration building, observing everything from the trim of the grass to the slightly tattered edge of the American flag flopping fecklessly from the central flagpole, while in the board meeting the arguments raged. There was a faction that wanted to change the focus of the school entirely by recruiting heavily in Asia.

"There's plenty of money in China and Japan. Korea. The oligarchs want their kids to speak English like Americans. They want them to go to Harvard. They'll send them as young as nine."

"That's never been our measure of success, sending everyone to Harvard!"

"Nine? Who would send a nine-year-old to boarding school?"

"My parents did," said Hugo Hollister. All heads turned to him. "It saved my life. Wonderful school. If I'd stayed home, with *my* family, I'd be, I don't know. In prison by now." He smiled beatifically. Hugo was a new trustee who had a tendency to throw the old guard off balance. Whether or not that was a good thing was another divisive question among them.

After a brief silence, Emily George, the board chair, asked, "What school was that?"

"Cummington. Closed now, I'm afraid."

After another pause someone else said, "And did *you* go to Harvard?"

Hugo smiled again, as if abashed, before saying, "I did, actually."

Emily George felt that she had completely lost control of the meeting and was more relieved than distressed when Ms. Liggett's secretary stuck her head in the door to say, "Excuse me, Mrs. George—the visitors are here."

The visitors were early. Emily George looked around at the chemistry lab where the board was holed up, at the Bunsen burners that were far from new, the shelves of beakers and Petri dishes and bottles of chemicals with peeling labels. She saw how dingy it would look to outside eyes, little changed from when she'd been a student here herself. The smudgy white board at the front of the room, the sepia photograph of Madame Curie hanging between two windows that overlooked the infirmary. On the top shelf, the room was ringed by jars holding specimens in formaldehyde. Rattlesnakes. Fetal pigs. Large mammal brains of unknown provenance. Hanging from a rack in a corner was a life-size skeleton made of yellowish plastic with which she felt a helpless sympathy.

"Motion to adjourn?" she asked with resignation. Adjournment was moved and seconded. "The reception will be in the library at six o'clock. Best feet forward, everyone." She stuffed her trustee portfolio into her carryall and swiftly left them.

*   *   *

Christina Liggett looked to Maggie Detweiler barely old enough to drive. But in a situation like Rye Manor's, the board would have to hire someone who didn't know what she was doing. No experienced leader wanted to preside over the death of a school that had once been a legend. From what Maggie had seen in the school's self-study, Ms. Liggett was making actual progress. She'd replaced the business manager, an elderly great-great-nephew of the founder, with a young woman who at least knew how to use a computer. Enrollment was up—slightly, but still. Christina seemed to have the support of the faculty, and everyone agreed that the food had gotten better. Maggie's initial response was an impulse to protect her.

In her office, Christina was passing a plate of shortbread cookies to Maggie's team and making brittle chatter about the schedule for the visit. Meanwhile Maggie was taking note of the office itself. The room was a testament to past glory and august by any measure, which made Christina look even slighter and younger than she really was. There was an oil portrait of the founder in a massive gold frame over the desk. The walls were lined floor to ceiling with worn editions of Shakespeare and Wordsworth, Tennyson and Scott, Trollope and Dickens. Maggie studied what looked like the full set of the Loeb Classical Library in the shelf next to her, the Ovid and Virgil showing particular signs of use. Real scholars had worked in this room and led this school.

Mrs. George arrived. She was a stout woman in a cherry-colored pant suit, her blond-gray hair in a pageboy held back by a tortoiseshell band. Her purse was hanging from one shoulder, her heavy-laden carryall from the other, and the carryall slipped and crashed to the ground as she moved to avoid knocking into the cookie tray. Everyone stared at it splayed on the floor. Mrs. George said to the group, while trying to pretend the crashing bag wasn't really hers, "So nice to meet you, I'm Emily George," and offered her hand first to Maggie, and then to her colleagues. "Our board chair," said Christina, sounding as if the cavalry had arrived.

Maggie's team consisted of Sister Rose, who was a senior math teacher from a Catholic girls' school in the Bronx, and Bill Toskey, head of the upper school at a small coed academy on Long Island. The sister wore neat black shoes, a navy skirt and white blouse with only her title to indicate she was a religious. Her glasses had clear plastic frames and she wore no makeup, which made her look deceptively severe. Bill Toskey had a lanky body and bruised-looking liverish half circles under his eyes. He wore an unfortunate beard, something like a Van Dyck but mostly emanating from the underside of his chin, which made him look like a goat.

Afternoon sunlight from a tall French window slanted across the blue of the room's worn Isfahan carpet. Through the window, Maggie had a view of sloping lawns, of huge oaks and beeches arched over pathways in the late afternoon light. The famous weeping birch grove could be seen in the middle distance. Beyond that were the tennis courts and playing fields and the New Gym, which was now sixty years old. Here and there a girl could be seen hurrying across the campus.

"Have you settled in all right?" Emily George asked. "Christina has found you a room for your work?"

"They're using the Katherine Jones room in the library," said Christina.

"Lovely," said Emily, who didn't actually seem to be listening. Maggie could see that her nerves were like an electrical system with an intermittent short circuit. "They haven't toured the campus yet?" she asked Christina.

They hadn't.

"Well, shall we?" They agreed they should. Emily led the way.

*　　*　　*

The new indoor swimming pool was first stop on the tour. Landscaping around the building still looked raw, the plantings like little girls at dancing school, their skinny bare legs insubstantial, as they hopefully dreamed of the mounded bosomy flowering shrubs they had it in them to become. Maggie wondered what Sister Rose was thinking of the expense of this facility, knowing that she taught at a school that would be lucky to find space in their overcrowded building in which to nurture a chess team. Maggie privately thought that the money spent here would have been much better applied to improving teachers' salaries, but she knew the problem from experience. Donors wanted to give what they wanted to give, and they particularly liked it to be concrete, with room for their names carved in stone in large font above the front door.

The vast echoing space for the pool itself was warm and thickly humid and reeked of chlorine. There were bleachers and a scoreboard and high and low diving boards, everything you would need for training Olympic hopefuls. Emily led them through the locker rooms, a far cry from the grim metal lockers and detested communal shower room that Maggie remembered from her school days in Ambridge, Pennsylvania. There had been showerheads around the walls of a tiled room that was too large to be heated by the water, as a shower stall might be. Cold and miserably self-conscious naked adolescents had dashed in and gotten just wet enough that the P.E. teacher wouldn't send them back to do it again, and then made a long wet run across the cold slippery room to their towels and clothes. Here, by contrast, all was bright and squeaky clean, designed for comfort and privacy. Emily chattered somewhat desperately about her hope that the pool would become a draw for young athletes as well as a boon to the wider community. They were already opening it to local groups for after-school and weekend programs.

Back outside, they were invited to admire the outlines of the library where they would meet for the evening reception. They toured the dining hall, lined with portraits of previous heads of school, dour ladies in wire-rimmed glasses. They moved stealthily through a classroom building to avoid disturbing afternoon study halls.

Shadows of the late afternoon were beginning to lengthen as Emily led them up the hill toward the arts building.

"What's that?" Bill Toskey asked. He gestured toward a sandstone building from the Gilded Age, with a vast arched door in the facade, large enough for a carriage to drive through.

"Well that," said Emily, puffing slightly, "is either the stable, or a bone of contention, depending on your point of view."

Bill Toskey looked at her.

Mrs. George soldiered on. "Many feel that the riding program has always been a part of the school's history, and should remain, but others feel it's an anachronism, and one we can't afford. We do have some serious dressage students at the moment who chose us because they could bring their horses, so for now . . ." She flapped a hand to finish the sentence.

"Handsome building," Bill Toskey commented grimly.

She looked at her watch. "Would you like to see it?"

The answer was unclear, so Emily assumed a yes and led the way.

"Back in the day, many of our girls would hunt with the Rye hounds," said Emily. "And some of them drove, too. Little carriages, whatever they're called." She was trying to play to Bill Toskey's apparent interest, but Maggie sensed, and was pretty sure Emily could too, that the whole subject was instead annoying him. Too late to change course, they had reached the entrance to the stable, a great high-ceilinged shell with box stalls along the sides and haylofts above them. Barn swallows swooped across the upper spaces. The empty dirt-floored central space held a mounting block at one end, and a post and rail jump in the middle with a single bar on the lowest pegs, for practice by beginners. The air was filled with floating dust motes, thick in slanting beams of light from high dusty windows. They breathed the rich dense smell of hay, sweat, and horse manure.

As they took it in, none of them sure what to say, they heard raised voices, an argument reaching full throttle suddenly audible. A man and a woman, voices layering each other, the tone strident and angry. A door behind the mounting block crashed open and a man strode out, followed by a woman who paused, silhouetted against light, watching him go. Silence fell as these two saw the little group standing in the great arched doorway.

The man was middle-aged, in khaki pants and a bomber jacket. He had a large, mostly bald head that bulged forward at the top giving it the shape of an upside-down butternut squash. The woman was younger, with hair pulled into a disheveled knot at the back of her head. She wore slim jodhpurs and a hacking jacket.

Emily said, "Oh, honey, there you are. These are our visitors, you know, our visiting committee. I just thought I'd show them your operation."

The surprised pair were now moving smoothly toward them, as if they'd come in expressly to be introduced. The jodhpur woman went straight to Bill Toskey and offered her hand. "Welcome," she said. "Honey Marcus."

Maggie realized that Honey was her name, not a term of endearment. And also of course that Ms. Marcus had assumed that Bill, the one with the Y chromosome, must be the leader of the team.

"Honey is our horse master and riding instructor," said Emily. She turned then uncertainly to the butternut man, and Honey said, "Ray Meagher."

After a second Emily said, "Oh of course, Florence Meagher's husband. Florence teaches history of art. She's one of our stars."

Ray Meagher claimed to be glad to meet them.

"The Meaghers are dorm parents," said Emily. She evidently didn't quite know how to extricate her charges from this unwanted encounter. "Some of our teachers live in the dorms with the girls. It creates a sense of family, gives the girls a place to go when they need advice or comfort. Florence is famous for her brownies, isn't she? Makes little tea parties for the girls, if I remember right?"

Ray said, "Banana bread. We're up in the Cottage in the Woods, now."

"Ah," said Emily. "That's a lovely place." She turned to the visitors. "A dear little house that a neighbor couple left to the school when they passed on. So. We'll let you two get on with your day, we're just on our way to the art studios."

*   *   *

Christina Liggett was waiting in the lobby of the library at six o'clock sharp. She had changed into a long skirt and ballet flats and stood with her hands clasped before her, looking like someone giving a party while facing a firing squad. Behind her in the open-stack reading room, white-jacketed waiters passed trays bearing wine or water, while prettily dressed students trailed them with platters of hors d'oeuvres. Maggie could see that the room was already well filled with people wearing name tags. How many of these bunfights had she been through in her time? Scores, she guessed, if not hundreds. They were all the same and all different.

In Washington, Maggie had grown accustomed to trustees with Secret Service details. In New York City, the glamour factor was different, with the expensively dressed captains of industry serving as the little brown wrens of the gathering while people tried not to notice the network TV anchor, the movie star couple, the famous rapper, and the ice hockey star. Maggie had met her late husband at one of these, unlikely though it seemed. He had had children in the school where she'd taught before she was hired away for her first headship. Maggie had been the star English teacher, the woman who made all the children love Shakespeare. He was the recent widower, the only one who got the joke when Maggie described a politician's fall from grace as "Exit, pursued by bear."

"I'm Florence Meagher," said the woman beside Maggie, unnecessarily as her name was written in large letters on a white tag stuck to her navy wool jacket. The weather was too warm for wool; Maggie deduced that the jacket was Florence's Sunday best. Florence had an eager smile, a slender figure, and a face that just missed being beautiful. There was somehow too much space between her eyes and her mouth, and her eyebrows were shaped like McDonald's golden arches, giving her an unusual look of constant surprise.

"You're the history of art teacher," said Maggie.

"Oh, somebody's done her homework!" Florence studied a tray that was thrust between them. "Now what are these, Marnie?"

"Tapenade pizza," said the girl.

Florence took one and thanked her. After a bite she said to Maggie, with manic energy, as if the force of her flood of words alone could forestall disaster, "Oh! It's olives! I wasn't sure. I like olives by themselves, but not so much in food. Do you know what I mean?" She could even talk while swallowing. "Last summer when I was in Spain, doing my research, my hotel served a breakfast buffet, I think they call it a continental breakfast, or we call it that, probably they don't but anyway, I was, well you know how it is when you travel, so I was *so pleased* to see there were prunes there with the cheeses and other things I don't eat for breakfast so I put a big spoonful of them on my cereal and it was good I was sitting alone, because of course they weren't prunes at all they were *olives!* Then I didn't want to spoon them out because the waiters would think I was a fool, so I ate them, but they were very odd in cereal. Have you been to Madrid?"

"I have," said Maggie.

Emily George materialized and said, "Good evening, Florence. That's a lovely pin you're wearing."

Florence looked down to see what pin she was wearing and before she could reply, Emily added, "I'm just going to spirit Maggie away, because I know you'll meet with her in the morning."

She guided Maggie toward a group who were deeply engaged in their conversation. They were clearly trustees, more expensively dressed and shod than the faculty. When they saw Emily, they moved a little apart from each other. Maggie wondered what exactly they had interrupted.

Bright smiles turned to Maggie. Introductions were made. Emily said to one of the men, "Lyndon, could I have a word with you?" They stepped away for a tête-à-tête. A waiter appeared at Maggie's elbow with a tray of glasses, mostly filled with ruby- and topaz-colored liquids. A shortish man at her elbow wearing a blazer with nautical flags embroidered on the pocket asked the waiter, "What is the red?"

"Ummm," said the waiter.

"The color says pinot noir, do you mind?" The man put one hand on Maggie's arm and with the other took a glass and held it up to the light. He had coarse ash-colored hair and was sturdily built, somehow reminding Maggie of a Shetland pony. He plunged his muzzle into the glass just short of actually touching the wine. After a solemn inhalation of the fumes, he declared, "It's a little chocolatey for a pinot." He took a sip and rolled it around in his mouth a long time before he swallowed. "What do you think?" he said to Maggie and held the glass toward her.

"I think I'll stick to water," she said pleasantly. "We're working."

"I'm getting a little hint of petite sirah," said the man. Apparently this was a good thing, as he did not, as Maggie feared he might, return the glass to the tray. Instead he took a long thoughtful pull at it and said to Maggie, "Hugo Hollister."

"Yes," said Maggie, since they had just been introduced and he was labeled.

"You ran the Winthrop School in New York, I think," he added.

"I did. For several eons."

"I wish we'd sent my stepson there." He smiled at her, as if he felt they were beginning a conspiracy.

"Do you have children here at the Manor?" she countered.

"My stepson went on to Andover and then Princeton, and now he's at Goldman." Hugo rolled his eyes. "He could have done so many useful things besides mint money." A platter of hors d'oeuvres commanded his attention.

"Roquefort cheese puffs," said the girl with the tray.

"Oh," said Hugo, as if she had said "dog dirt on toast."

"Tell me about this," said Maggie, indicating the emblems on his blazer pocket.

"Oh, that's a yacht club burgee, and this is my commodore flag. You don't have to salute or kiss my ring or anything though."

"Commodore of . . ."

"It's a tiny club in Massachusetts. On an island."

"Which one?"

"You wouldn't have heard of it."

"Try me."

He named the island.

"That's owned by the Caldwell family, isn't it?" said Maggie.

Hugo beamed. "You do get around! Yes it is. I'm from the cadet branch. The ones who went with the buggy whip side of the business when the brains of the family bet on petroleum."

And made a vast fortune when they sold out to Standard Oil. Maggie knew this from having had two of those Caldwells in her school and being quite good friends with their mother.

"So you're a sailor?"

Hugo laughed happily. "Well that's . . . that's, that's the funny thing, I'm absolutely paralyzed on boats. My back goes into spasm. It's not uncommon; I'm told it was epidemic in the submarine corps in World War II. Related to claustrophobia somehow. But I'm very useful on land. The rest of the family goes to sea in all weathers and comes in from the races starving and soaked to the bone, and they're very happy to find me in charge of the roaring fire and the cocktail table."

Emily George joined them. Across the room Maggie could see her colleague Bill Toskey in deep conversation with the head of the math department, and Sister Rose was more or less pinned against the wall by Florence Meagher.

"Hugo's daughter Lily is having a wonderful year, has he told you?" Emily asked.

"Tell me," said Maggie to Hugo.

Emily said, "I'll just . . ." and left them, tacking across the room to liberate Sister Rose.

"She's a little . . . *distrait* tonight, our leader," said Hugo, watching Emily.

"I know," said Maggie.

"Lovely woman, though."

"Tell me about your daughter's wonderful year."

"The light of my life. You know there are so many kinds of intelligence in this world."

Maggie did know that. Hugo went on. "My daughter has a vocabulary of two hundred words, and a hundred of them are *awesome*. And yet she is a physical genius. She was Optimist sailing champion of our club when she was eight. And you should see her dive. Her coach thinks she should train for the Olympics, she just amazes me. It takes lightning calculation. Velocity, distance, trajectory—she can do it like an angel. And has no idea how."

"She's an optimist, then?"

Hugo chuckled. "An Optimist is a class of boat. A tiny little single-hander for beginners. But yes, I'd say she *is* an optimist . . . oh, would you excuse me please? I think the excellent Mrs. Meagher is closing in on my wife." Maggie watched as he moved smoothly through the crowd to slide his arm around a pleasant-looking woman in an emerald-colored evening jacket wearing a string of enormous freshwater pearls.

At this point, a tinkling on a spoon against a wineglass alerted them that Ms. Liggett was going to make a speech.

Maggie's room at the Manor House Inn was bare-bones but clean, with an ample work desk and a comfortable chair with a good reading light. She'd had a working supper with her colleagues and Christina Liggett, and now, finally alone, had unpacked and changed into her nightdress. Comfort at last. She answered her e-mail, made notes on the people she'd met and impressions she'd formed, and had gone over the schedule for the next day, which would be packed.

Workday done, she got a beer from the minibar, settled herself in the armchair, and texted her friend Hope Babbin: *Are chocolate notes wrong in pinot noir?*

The reply came in moments: *who on earth have u been talking to?*

And then her phone rang.

"You don't even drink red wine," said Hope. "Where are you?"

Maggie explained.

"Rye-on-Hudson," said Hope. "I guess they've already heard the sandwich jokes."

"So I believe."

"How is it going to go?"

"Hard to tell. We'll know more tomorrow."

"Who's we?"

Maggie explained her colleagues. "Sister Rose is very good and pure but she has a sneaky sense of humor I like. Bill Toskey has a chip on his shoulder about something, I'm not sure what yet. What are you up to?"

"Trying to finish the book we're reading for book group, but I hate it."

"Oh too bad. Who chose the book?"

"I did."

"What is it?"

"*Silas Marner.*"

"I could have told you you'd hate that. Not your thing at all. Does that mean you have to lead the discussion?"

"It does."

"Everything else all right? How are the twins?"

"Molly has an earache."

"Lucky her mom's a doctor."

"Yes. Remind me, why did I join a book group?"

"Lauren was worried you were addicted to mah-jongg."

"There are worse things. And I'm reading one of them."

Maggie said, "I'd better leave you to it."

She finished her beer while polishing off a double-crostic, then brushed her teeth and got into bed. When she turned out the light and settled herself for sleep she found the night was quiet, eerily so to one accustomed to the nighttime hum and sizzle of New York City. The high beams of the occasional passing car sent blades of light through the gaps at the sides of the blinds and sliced across the blue-gray wallpaper. She had a vague but tenacious sense of unease that she eventually put to rest by reciting "The Charge of the Light Brigade" until she fell asleep.

The visiting committee's business of the morning was to observe classes. Maggie went first to Marcia Goldsmith, the head of the French Department. Actually, at this stage Ms. Goldsmith was the entire staff of the French Department, Maggie knew from the school's self-study report. A student guide delivered Maggie to the right classroom and hurried off to her own class. Maggie tapped on the door and opened it, about to announce herself, when she realized that the woman sitting alone at the massive desk in the front of the room was crying.

She was a long boney woman with her sleek dark hair pulled back and held with a barrette. She was plainly dressed in a skirt and sweater set such as might have been worn by a teacher or student on this campus at any period since the 1940s. She jumped when she realized Maggie was in the room.

"I didn't mean to alarm you," Maggie said as Ms. Goldsmith rose and came toward her, mopping her nose, then poked her handkerchief into her sleeve.

"I lost track of the time, I'm so sorry," said Marcia Goldsmith, producing a strained smile. She shook Maggie's hand. "I'm having a bout of allergy, pollen, or something, not contagious, just ignore me."

There was a slight accent, not French. Scottish, maybe?

"We didn't meet last night, did we?" Maggie asked her, giving her time to compose herself.

"No, I had a . . . thing that came up. Family issue." Maggie saw now that the woman was older than she had thought at first. Mid- to late forties, she guessed. She had a very long neck, and with her hair skinned back as it was, Maggie could see that her ears were pierced, but she wore no earrings. Something had distracted her or delayed her as she was dressing? Or she just wasn't much focused on her appearance?

"It was very pleasant," Maggie offered. "I met a number of your colleagues. Mrs. Maltby, and Jody Turner. I had a nice talk with Florence Meagher."

Marcia Goldsmith turned her hazel eyes to Maggie's. "You know she's really a lovely woman."

"I could see that."

"In spite of The Affliction."

Maggie looked questioning.

"She cannot shut up," said Marcia Goldsmith.

Maggie smiled. "Yes, there's that."

"She's a marvelous teacher, though. Passionate about her subject."

"May I ask you something, off the record?"

Marcia tensed a little before she said, "Go ahead."

"In my experience, teenagers aren't very kind about that kind of thing in their teachers."

Marcia's tension dissolved. "No, they do terrible imitations of her. They don't mean any harm though. They just don't really understand that teachers have feelings."

"Well, that's true enough. Now tell me, if you will, what is the thinking behind doing away with AP language classes?"

Marcia was now quite composed and fully inhabiting her teacher persona, and she turned to the task at hand, which was to try and convince Maggie that failing to offer advanced placement courses was actually an enrichment of the curriculum. She was spared having to carry on long by the noisy arrival of adolescent girls streaming into the room, tossing their cell phones into a box on the teacher's desk, banging around the room stowing their backpacks and taking their seats.

At the end of the class, when Maggie's student guide failed to reappear to lead her to Florence Meagher, Marcia said, "I'll take you. I'm free until eleven." Maggie had a sense that for whatever reason, Marcia Goldsmith welcomed a chance to not be alone this morning. Marcia locked the door of the classroom behind them and led off down the hall.

"Is that personal choice, or school policy?" Maggie asked as they clattered down the echoing tiled fire stairs. "The locked door."

"Both," said Marcia. "We had a cheating episode last year. Someone got one of the teachers' grading sheets for the final exams." She paused. "Maybe I shouldn't have said that."

"It's all right. It can happen anywhere."

"The kids are under so much pressure to perform. To be absolutely honest, these days we tend to get the warm fuzzy students, terribly nice but not in the top academic tier, and some parents just can't get the message. They see their kids the way they see their cars and jewelry, advertisements for themselves. They think raging at these girls, or at us, will change what they got in the delivery room."

Marcia pushed open a door to the outside in spite of a sign that said DO NOT OPEN; ALARM WILL SOUND and they stepped out into the sunshine. No alarm sounded. "I'm sorry," Marcia went on, "I shouldn't have said that either. I don't know what's wrong with me this morning."

"It's all right."

"It's not, but I feel so strongly about it, parents who can't just accept the children they have, instead of . . . well you must have seen a lot of this."

"The way of the world, these days," said Maggie. They were

crossing a sun-washed quadrangle, with streams of girls full of animal high spirits clattering around them.

"Do you have children?" Marcia asked.

"Three steps," said Maggie. "All in their teens when I got them, and long grown up now. They were a handful, though. Do you?"

"Two boys. I'm surrounded by hormones."

"You are. Do you mind my asking, where are you from? I'm interested in accents."

"I grew up in Cape Town."

"Ah. You're far from home, then, or is your family here now?"

Marcia seemed to appreciate the personal interest. This was not part of the job Maggie had come to do; she just couldn't help herself. If she hadn't been so sincerely curious about people she wouldn't have been the gifted teacher she was.

"No, my mother and brother are still there; I came here for college and never left. And you?"

"I'm from Pittsburgh. Outside of. My sister is still there, and two of her children. Two more nieces are in New York now, so I've captured them. Tell me, since I've got you, how do you think Ms. Liggett is getting along?"

There was a pause. They were now waiting at the light to cross the tree-lined street to the other half of the campus. Students burbled around them and the sun shone on the bright yellow-green of spring leaves.

"She's young. But she's doing her best," said Marcia.

"I'm sure of that. How did she handle the cheating episode?"

Marcia looked around to be sure they were out of earshot as they hurried across the street with the light. "It was complicated, of course."

"Of course."

"Parents were angry that their girls had to take their exams over, even though they swore they hadn't cheated. Christina can't tell us much more than that, because of the lawsuit . . ."

"Oh dear," said Maggie. "Did she identify the culprit?"

Marcia considered her answer. "We all think she did, I mean we think we know, but the girl wouldn't confess, and no one would turn her in."

They had reached one of the original classroom buildings, a handsome faux-Georgian brick house set on a knoll, with broad stone steps leading up to a veranda, and white pillars flanking the front door. It had certainly been a private residence in the Gilded Age, and it still had beautiful bones, if it made sense to say that of buildings. "Through here," said Marcia as they entered the parlor floor. The front and back reception rooms to the right of the foyer had been opened up to form one large teaching hall. Already the room was nearly filled with girls sitting in rows, notebooks open, textbooks out and ready. Some girls were reading, or doing homework; most were happily gossiping and laughing.

"Good morning," said Marcia firmly over the noise. The girls instantly quieted and composed themselves to signal attention. "We have a visitor. This is Ms. Detweiler. Mrs. Meagher isn't here?"

There were murmurs. She wasn't. Mrs. Goldsmith looked at her watch, then went to the front of the room and said, "I'm sure she'll be here any minute. What are you working on this week?"

Silence.

"Shaundi?"

A tall girl in the front row mumbled, "Northern Renaissance."

"Who has done the reading?"

About half the class raised their hands.

"Well, please take these few minutes to get yourselves caught up. If you're up-to-date, read ahead. I'll find Mrs. Meagher. Alison, what are you doing?"

A girl in the back row did something magical with her hands under the desk and said, "Nothing."

"Where is your phone, Alison?"

"In the basket right there." A large basket on the teacher's desk was full of cell phones of every size and color.

"What is your number?"

Alison gave it, and Ms. Goldsmith dialed it on the phone she brought out from her own pocket. In the basket a hunting horn sounded. Ms. Goldsmith fished it out, an oversize new model iPhone in a lime-green case with rhinestones.

"This is your phone?"

"Yes."

"Please come here."

Resentfully, Alison, wearing stretch jeans and a pair of docksiders with no socks, slouched forward, tugging at her pouchy gray sweater. It reached to her hips, which was not far enough.

Ms. Goldsmith surveyed her. Alison looked into space.

"Please show me what you have in your right-hand pocket."

After a pretense of being unable to understand the direction, Alison produced another cell phone, black and smudgy.

"And what is that?"

"It's not mine."

"Is it a cell phone?" Ms. Goldsmith asked, louder and with impatience.

Alison neither moved nor spoke.

Marcia looked at Alison for a long minute while the class watched somberly. Finally she said, "Please go to Ms. Liggett's office. Give her that phone, and tell her why I sent you."

"What if she's not there?"

"Then stay there until she is," said Marcia, sounding really cross. "The rest of you, please work quietly until Mrs. Meagher gets here."

The visiting committee met for lunch in the Katherine Jones room in the library. It was an intimate room with a fireplace, walls lined with books, with overstuffed chairs for reading, and a round IKEA table with matching chairs in the center of the room. There was a portrait of Miss Jones over the fireplace, a pretty girl with a blond pageboy wearing a pale blue sweater and a string of pearls.

Sister Rose looked at it and said, "If there is anything, anything at all, you would like to know about Katherine Jones, just ask me."

"Who wanted the BLT?" asked Bill Toskey, who was pawing through the tray of sandwiches, chips, and soft drinks that had been left for them. Sister Rose raised a hand, and he tossed her the sandwich and a bag of Doritos.

"I'll bite. Who is Katherine Jones?" Maggie asked. She reached for the sandwich remaining on the tray and began trying to penetrate its triple-wrapped caul of plastic film.

Sister Rose took a breath and began talking rapidly. "She was a student here in the late 1940s, killed in a car crash after a debutante ball in 1951, a week after she graduated. She was going to Vassar. Her parents were devastated, they were from Philadelphia, and they gave the money to build this addition in her honor. The portrait was posthumous from a photograph, it's a good likeness, not Velázquez, but really very good. You would think that her school days were the happiest of her life but no, she hated Rye Manor and was a very bad girl when she was here, but her mother was a passionate alum, so there you have it, mourning or revenge, you're sitting in it."

Bill was staring at her while tearing wolfishly at his roast beef sandwich with his long yellowish teeth.

Maggie said, "Sister Rose, you are a very bad woman."

Sister Rose said, "Fortunately, mine is a loving God, so I know I'm forgiven in advance. I do have a point to make though. What on earth do the students make of that?"

"Will someone tell me what we're talking about?" said Bill Toskey resentfully, chewing.

"I had a séance with a teacher named Florence Meagher at the reception last night," said Sister Rose. "She asked me where we were meeting."

"She has The Affliction," said Maggie.

"What affliction?" Bill was still not amused.

"She cannot shut up," the two women said, almost together. Bill looked at them as if they'd both just come from a party to which he hadn't been invited.

"Did one of you meet with her this morning?" he asked rather aggressively, as if to remind them that someone in the group had to behave like a professional. Maggie recognized him now. He was the kid who had spent a lifetime being the one who didn't get the joke.

Maggie said, "I went to observe her class, but she didn't show up."

Bill stared at her. "Didn't show up?"

"No."

"That's not good," he said, as if Maggie couldn't have worked that out herself. Mrs. Meagher was the leader of the group that had written the school's all-important interim progress report.

"I tackled the business manager instead. We all meet with Mrs. Meagher's committee this afternoon. Bill, why don't you tell us about your morning?"

When they'd finished eating, they went over their schedules for the afternoon and parted. Sister Rose was next meeting with the admissions office, Bill Toskey was going to talk with the building and grounds staff, and Maggie would be meeting with the trustee Long Range Planning committee, which in her opinion had some explaining to do.

The door to Christina Liggett's office was closed when Maggie arrived in midafternoon for a scheduled talk about the school's budget. She moved on to the open office beside the front door, noting reflexively that there was no security here, unless the secretaries were armed. The imposing front door of the main building opened and closed many times a day with no one keeping track of who came and went. No schools in New York City ran that way anymore. There had been too many school tragedies in the news in the last few years.

She stepped into the bright busy room, which was flooded with sunlight from the large double-hung windows facing the street. "Is Ms. Liggett in her office, do you know?" she asked a cheerful woman at the nearest desk, whose name plaque read SHARON COMFORT.

"She will be *right* with you," said Sharon with a smile that revealed a set of murderous-looking braces on her teeth. "You could have a seat in the hall." Maggie had seen the stiff-looking sofa just outside the office door, of a kind last seen by her on a tour of a house museum outside Pittsburgh in 1958. It had a heavy brown wooden frame and was covered in some dark Victorian textile that might have been horsehair and looked as if it belonged in the Lincoln White House.

"Or stay right here," Sharon added, seeing Maggie's expression. "Could I get you some tea?"

Maggie sat in the chair beside Sharon's desk, feeling totally at home and rather nostalgic in the bright and bustling room as Sharon went to microwave a cup of tea for her. At the next desk a trim little woman typed letters on fancy school letterhead. Beyond, a teacher Maggie recognized from the reception was doing a massive copying job at a giant machine. The machine whined and snicked, the background music of so many years of Maggie's life. Making illegal handouts of copyrighted material, Maggie couldn't help thinking, not that she'd ever known a school that didn't do that sometimes. On Sharon's desk, open in the middle and left facedown by her keyboard, was a black and yellow paperback called *Excel 2002 for Dummies*.

Sharon handed Maggie her mug. She moved the book out of her way and said, "Don't ever let anyone know you can work with spreadsheets."

"Words to live by. What have they stuck you with?"

"Exam schedule. The assistant head used to do it, but she had to take over geometry when Mrs. Fuller went on maternity leave, so . . ."

"I understand."

Down the hall, Ms. Liggett's door opened and she came out with a man whose head was shaped like a butternut squash. Maggie watched the two say their good-byes. A moment later, Christina came to the office door to say, "I'm so sorry to have kept you waiting."

Settled back in her office, formalities dispensed with, Maggie asked Christina, "Is this your first evaluation?"

"As head, yes. We went through it when I taught at Groton, but of course that wasn't . . ."

"Yes," said Maggie. The unspoken words were "a life or death matter." She added kindly, "Try not to worry. We're here to help."

Christina said she appreciated that, whether or not she believed it.

"So we better get right to it. You are spending down your endowment."

"Yes. Have been for some time, as I'm sure you know. We've made changes and you can see that we're headed in the right direction—" She pointed to figures in her copy of the school's financials.

"You're doing all the right things," Maggie said. Though it didn't change the fact that for many years, out of indolence and habit, the board and the school had done all the wrong things, and all that the new regime had accomplished was a decrease in the ship's momentum toward the rim of the world and the date at which it might well go over the edge, accompanied by tears and screaming.

Maggie turned a page in her folder and said, "Let's talk about the swimming pool."

Christina sighed. "The board had been kicking that can down the road for a year or two when I got here."

"How, exactly?"

"A life trustee wanted to give us the pool in honor of his wife."

"Life trustee?"

"I know, I know. We've changed the governance rules. There was no chance he would just give us the money. He had a theory that girls' schools were losing out because their athletic facilities weren't as good as the Andovers and Exeters of the world. He wanted to prove it."

"Not a bad theory."

"So it was take the pool or take nothing."

"How is it working out?"

"In a competitive move, another trustee decided to upgrade our tennis courts."

Maggie laughed.

"And it may be moving the needle a little in our admissions. Steph Ruhlman and Lily Hollister definitely chose us for the pool, and we got a very good trustee along with Lily."

"I met him last night," said Maggie. "The Commodore."

"Yes. They're very generous, the Hollisters, and they don't want their names on anything. And he's got a hundred percent of our trustees giving money to the school; the first time that's happened since . . . ever."

They talked about the other items on Maggie's agenda. As an afterthought, she said, "This is my question, not the Association's. What, if anything, do you do about security?"

"You mean the stolen exam sheets?"

"No, no. That I understand. I just was noticing that there's nothing to prevent any person off the street from marching into the building."

Christina said, "We're trying to raise money now for a video system. We upgraded the locks on all the dorms to coded keypads last year. And we have Ray Meagher, Florence's husband. He's a retired air marshal and on the auxiliary police here in town. He's on call for us if we have trouble during the day. At night, the auxiliary police patrol."

"Wasn't that Ray Meagher who was with you just now?"

Christina looked surprised. "Had you met?"

"Yes, briefly, on our campus tour."

"He just got the message that Florence isn't in school. She was gone when he got up this morning. Her handbag and her tote bag are gone, as they always are on school days. Her house keys and car are gone too. He hasn't a clue."

Maggie pondered this for a moment. As she stowed her notes and papers, preparing to meet her colleagues in the library, she asked, "Does Ray Meagher carry a gun?"

"He certainly has one from his marshal days, and I know it's licensed. One of the reasons we moved them out to their own cottage was that Florence didn't think it was safe to have a gun in a school dorm. I agreed with her. Whether he's armed when he's on patrol for us I have no idea."

After a very full afternoon of meetings, Maggie and her team had dinner with the student council, then retired to write up their notes and prepare for finalizing their report. In her room, when she had finished, Maggie went straight to bed without even checking her e-mail. She'd be home by early afternoon, time enough to pick up the strands of her life and get back to living it.

The morning brought rain, and with it the humid smell of spring earth, spongy and promising. The visiting committee met in the Katherine Jones room to try to come to one coherent conclusion about the school's health and prospects. They were all signed in to the same Google Docs file, and were soon at loggerheads about many things, from endowment and admissions to word choices and the proper use of the hyphen. Bill Toskey, a reflexive contrarian, was coming down with a cold and hadn't liked his dinner the night before; overnight his posture had hardened into the dogma that the school deserved one more year to accomplish impossible changes, and then the pink needle. Sister Rose was quietly equally adamant; she saw hard work and improvement; she thought the school should have at least another five years and could even see voting for ten. Maggie was in the middle. They argued, typed, negotiated, and finally settled on their findings, which Maggie would polish and send on to the Independent School Association for its decision. Bill Toskey and Sister Rose left together in his car, and Maggie began to think about lunch and her train to the city, when Emily George, the board chair, appeared at the door and uttered the sentence that used to punctuate her workday about every half hour: "Maggie, do you have a minute?"

*   *   *

The rain had stopped and the streets of the village were washed and drying in the sun. Maggie asked for a sidewalk table at Le Bistro on Rye's charming Main Street, where she was delighted to find a mâche salad with crostini and warm goat cheese on the menu. If she was going to be here a while, it was important to know there would be someplace to eat. She ordered her lunch then texted her friend Hope. Hope was long divorced, and she and Maggie had discovered that they traveled well together and greatly amused each other. At any stage in life it was important to have at least one person who was always delighted to hear from you.

The spring sun was warm on Maggie's face and she could see the Hudson River far below, wide and blue and glittering. She had sailed this river with her husband, Paul, on a chartered sloop called *Curlew* one summer just after they were married. It was a beautiful wooden boat, just right for two; Paul called it their "sleek teak single-sticker." Later that summer they'd sailed her Downeast, before the wind, to Nova Scotia. She particularly remembered an August evening when they had picked up a mooring in Yarmouth Harbor. They had sat in the cockpit, relishing the slight sway and bob of the water beneath them, drinking single malt scotch out of paper cups as the sun, huge and bloodred, slipped silently into the sea like a giant coin into an unseen slot in the horizon. They got talking about the Dry Salvages on the way in, so after dinner, Paul read the *Four Quartets* aloud to her by lamplight. You had to love a man whose nautical library included not just charts and *Lloyd's* and Samuel Eliot Morison, but also P. G. Wodehouse and T. S. Eliot.

Her food arrived, along with a glass of lovely pale gold Sancerre, and at the same moment, her phone rang.

"Greetings from the home of the cod and the bean," said Hope. "Are you done dissecting that poor school?"

"We are."

"Did you push it off the edge of the cliff?"

"Bill Toskey badly wanted to, but he wasn't a match for Sister Rose. We recommended they get another five years."

"I'm glad," said Hope. "So you're on your way home?"

"I am not. I'm having my lunch at a rather charming joint on the main drag, and trying to decide what to do."

"About what?"

"The art history teacher has disappeared."

"How disappeared?"

"Unclear. I was supposed to observe her class yesterday morning but she never arrived. The husband says her car and purse and her school bag, everything you would expect her to have with her, are gone, and he has no clue."

"Suitcases missing? Passport? Money?"

"Everything right where it should be."

"What do the police say?"

"So far, they shrug and quote statistics. The husband serves on the local auxiliary force and they all go bowling together. The husband's not worried, so the police aren't worried."

"But?"

"Her colleagues say this is completely unlike her. She was very wound up about the evaluation and chaired the committee that wrote the self-study. She loves the school. But there's more, of course. This morning Christina called the woman's sister in Virginia. She expected the sister would laugh it off, since Florence could be a little scatterbrained. She didn't. She burst into tears."

"Wait a minute, I'm going to take notes."

"The last time the sister saw her, Florence said, 'If anything happens to me, don't assume it's an accident.' The sister has been in a swivet about it ever since."

"Oh Em Gee," said Hope. She'd been told by her daughter to stop saying that but she couldn't help it. "What did she mean?"

"I don't know yet. There's a lot of gossip, about her husband, and the marriage. So here is this incredibly fragile institution, just inching away from disaster."

"Got it."

"Whatever is going on will probably shake out on its own in a couple of days, but . . ."

"The child school head asked you if you would stay and see what you can do."

"The board chair did," said Maggie. "She'd heard about what happened at Oquossoc last fall. The board wants me to guide Christina through whatever comes next."

"You mean they're hoping you can figure out what happened to Florence before they have to call the police."

"I'm sure they wouldn't mind that. Of course she'll probably call from the Virgin Islands in a day or two, or from Reno, in which case I can go home."

"What's the address of that place where you're staying?"

"Why?"

"I need to program my GPS."

"You're coming?"

"Of course I'm coming. This is an answered prayer; my book group meets tonight."

"You never finished *Silas Marner.*"

"I didn't even finish the CliffsNotes. Look I'm clearly much too busy to belong to a book group; this just proves it. I'll see you for dinner."

Maggie thought best while in motion. The afternoon would have felt like early summer, had it not been for a sharp breeze off the river, and she had a warm jacket with her and Fauré's symphony in her iPhone. When she'd finished her coffee and paid her check, she put in her earbuds and began to walk. She wanted to think about Ray Meagher, but first she wanted to know exactly where she was. What was this town, who lived here, how did the town think about the school, what kind of neighbor was the school to the town?

Main Street gently sloped downhill. Just past the line of buildings on the west side of the street there was a sharp drop. Far below, beside the river, perched a small train station where the commuter line went through on its way to Poughkeepsie. You could reach the station either by a flight of very steep steps, or by following Main to a gentle switchback that led eventually to the level of the water.

Across from Le Bistro there was a restored movie theater, the Royale, that now served as a concert venue for live performers, as well as showing films selected by the Rye-on-Hudson Cineaste Society. Advertisements for coming events were posted on the facade and on sandwich boards in front of the theater. Next door was a vegetarian café and deli, and next to that was the Wooly Bear yarn shop. Its logo was a caterpillar in shades of yellow, green, and scarlet. Maggie went in.

The shop was warm and bright, with one entire wall given over to cubbyholes filled with yarns of every hue in many weights and fibers. The opposite wall held small skeins and spools of thread on pegs for embroidery and quilting. There were racks of pattern books and magazines, and in the back a mini classroom was set up with a small maple table and folding chairs, now accommodating a group of eight-year-olds wielding fat knitting needles and balls of oversize wool. A girl of about sixteen wearing a Rye Manor sweatshirt was helping a little boy to cast on stitches.

"Can I help you?" a pretty woman with a buzz cut and cat's-eye glasses asked Maggie. She was sitting beside a cash register in front, her hands knitting furiously as if by Braille, with slender needles and fine forest-green yarn she never looked at.

"I'm just sightseeing," said Maggie. "Pretty shop."

"Thank you. Are you a knitter?"

"More of a purler. I learned once, but that's all I remember. I don't suppose you have a darning egg?"

The woman laughed. "You can try up the hill at the Trash and Treasure, and good luck to you."

"Nobody darns anymore, do they?"

"My mother used to, but by the time I asked her for her eggs, she'd given all her sewing stuff to the Goodwill. Macular degeneration."

The girl in the back of the shop called, "Mom? Can you come show us the cable cast-on? I can't remember it, and Jude's first rows are always too loose."

The woman looked doubtful. "That's a hard one for little fingers."

"I think he can do it."

"I'll be right there."

Maggie said, "Your daughter goes to the Manor?"

"My alma mater," said the woman with a smile.

"Really," said Maggie. "You must have liked it, to send your daughter."

"It was a whole new world to me," said the shopkeeper. "I got to study Latin. I got to ride horses."

"There wasn't any tension between the day students and the boarders?"

"Well sure, there were some snobs back in the day. But I don't think Ellie feels it. Nowadays the boarders are allowed off campus more, and they aren't so cliquish. They like being friends with the day students because they like coming to our houses, getting out of the dorms. Oh hello, Alison."

As if to illustrate, the door to the shop opened, and a girl of Ellie's age came partway into the store and stopped. She looked at Maggie and apparently recognized her as the stranger from yesterday morning, when she got caught with the burner cell phone.

Alison held up her lime-green cell phone toward Ellie, who nod-ded and made texting motions with her thumbs. Alison backed out and closed the door.

"One of Ellie's BFFs," said the shopkeeper.

Interesting, thought Maggie.

Continuing her walk, she stopped in at the Frigate, a mostly sec-ondhand bookshop with a few bestsellers in the window. A bell tin-kled as she opened the door and stepped in. The long narrow space was like a mirror image of the wool shop, except that here the walls were lined with books rather than yarns, and the proprietor was in the back. In front as you came in there was a table full of volumes labeled STAFF PICKS.

The choice of books in the shop surprised and interested Mag-gie. While the strongest part of the collection was vintage travel books and cookbooks, there was a carefully curated section of belles lettres, fiction, and poetry. Maggie liked that the owner, or clerk, whichever he was, didn't try to chat with her as she examined the shelves. No one, in her view, wanted to chat while reading, even if all they were reading was book titles. In under a minute she had found a copy of a Molly Keane novel she'd been looking for, and took it to the desk in back, wallet in hand.

The clerk opened the book to the endpaper where the price was noted in pencil in the corner. Maggie saw that a previous own-er's name, Barbara Wellby, was inscribed along with a note: From Patrick, Christmas 1982. A lifetime of walking between students' desks during exams and study halls had left her skilled at reading upside down.

"Wonderful book," said the bookman. "Do you know it?"

"I do," said Maggie. "I foolishly lent my copy and never saw it again. I've been looking for a replacement. Did you know Barbara Wellby?"

"Very well. She taught up at the Manor until they forced her to retire. She *had* gotten awfully deaf. Educated at Oxford. She used to buy from me, and then, later, she would come in with a few books to sell, especially toward the end of the month."

"She stayed in town when she retired?"

"She wasn't the type for golf in Florida. She rented a little apartment over the Gourmet Shop. I worried about the stairs, but she said they were good for her. Must have been; she lived to ninety-three."

"Well, thank you. I'm glad to have found this copy. If I'm here long enough I'll come in to do a more thorough inventory of your shelves."

"I'll be here," said the man. He chuckled, as if the idea he might be anywhere else was very droll. The little bell tinkled again as she opened the door to let herself out.

On the street, she felt the wind begin to freshen and was sorry she didn't have a scarf. When she had put her head in at the Gourmet Shop and looked at the window of Manor Hardware, she had pretty much done the whole of the commercial district, seeing no need at the moment to visit the drugstore or the banks, all three anodyne excrescences from huge chains familiar all over their part of the country. Instead she turned east, and slightly uphill, toward the church steeple just visible beyond what she took to be the town park.

The park was partly lawn, partly patches of bare earth. There was a sandbox and forlorn swing set, and a few benches. One young woman, a babysitter Maggie guessed, sat on a bench punching at the screen in her hand while her little charge sat in the sandbox looking blank. Now and then the tot hit the sand with a yellow plastic shovel. Beyond was a fenced dog run, empty at the moment, sporting a sign requesting that residents pick up after their pets and hose down the run after use. The evidence was that the residents didn't care or couldn't read. Maggie walked on to the church, which was Episcopalian, built of rusticated brownstone and sporting a squat square bell tower. It looked as if the stained glass in two of the windows might be of interest if seen from inside, but the door was locked. A small sign gave the name and telephone number of the sexton, who could be applied to for admittance. The message board announcing the coming Sunday's services led with the sermon title: COME LABOR ON.

Beyond the church there was woodland. She walked on, thinking about Barbara Wellby, an honored teacher in pinched old age who had sold her library off in pieces while she waited for her next month's insufficient infusion of cash. She compared that with the fairly grand salaries she had been able to pay her faculty at Winthrop, and thought about the trustees at the Manor school she had met. She wondered how much they cared about what happened to the school's most important assets. She thought about the ancient chicken-and-egg question: Did society undervalue teachers *because* they were underpaid? Or did it underpay them because what they did seemed less valuable to a civil society than running a hedge fund?

She was just about to turn back when she came to another tract of open land, somewhat sheltered by a stand of poplars from the wind from the river and the view of the road. An arched metal entrance gate said RIVERVIEW CEMETERY. Maggie loved cemeteries. The Protestant Cemetery in Rome was one of her favorite places on earth along with Père Lachaise in Paris, Green-Wood in Brooklyn, and especially the cemetery in Key West with its memorial to the destruction of the *Maine*. Did anyone Remember the *Maine* anymore? And elsewhere in the same graveyard, the tombstone that read I TOLD YOU I WAS SICK.

The cemetery had been sited to give best possible views of the river, and she could tell by the moss and eroded edges of the headstones that the oldest graves were above her, at the very top, with the best view of the Hudson and the huge blue country beyond. There were vast old trees here, oaks and beeches and elms, and venerable dogwood, azaleas, and rhododendron. There were two nineteenth-century mausoleums, one carved with weeping angels and a plaque explaining that it held the remains of a young girl drowned in a boating accident, and of her mother who died of grief on the anniversary of the disaster. GOLDEN LADS AND GIRLS ALL MUST, AS CHIMNEY SWEEPERS, COME TO DUST was the epitaph. Perhaps the only lines from *Cymbeline* that everybody knew, Maggie thought.

There were many headstones with biblical quotations, especially for veterans of the Civil War. She found the family plot of the founder of Rye Manor School, and on the shoulder of the hill a family plot in pie formation, with the founding couple in the center, their children and children's spouses in a ring around them, the grandchild generation in an outer ring, and on the fringes, pets and two ladies born in Ireland who had died at great ages in Rye-on-Hudson, who Maggie guessed were family servants. The founding couple's graves were placed so that on the day the seventh seal was cracked and the graves flew open they could sit up and see the river. All their descendants and dependents were buried with their feet toward the center of the pie so that they would arise facing their progenitors. She was just as glad that she would not be present to see this reunion. Unless it had been a most unusual family, there could be problems.

Maggie had just taken out her Moleskine to sketch when she heard from over the brow of the hill a loud splash. That was interesting. There must be another pond up here. Which made sense; if you drove up here on a summer's day before the advent of the automobile, it would be a long hot climb for the horses. Perhaps it was also a collect pond for the use of the cemetery groundskeepers. She made her way upward.

The pond came into view as soon as she crested the hill where the town's founders were enclosed within low iron railings. There were graves here from the very early nineteenth century and not a few from the eighteenth. The railings must have marked the original boundaries of the parcel, since they would have kept neither intruders out nor the dead in. The pond beyond looked like a typical farm pond. Clearly man-made, oval, and from the color, not deep. A walkway around it had been laid out in local stone, and a pair of carved granite benches tilted on the near side of the pond, with a weeping willow planted between them for shade. It looked like a Victorian sampler.

A small motion drew her eye to either a young teenage boy or short-haired girl, kneeling beside the willow. The author of the splash. He had a fisherman's net and a knapsack full of gear on the bank beside him. She watched as he took up the net and sat still as stone until he saw what he was looking for, then dipped swiftly into the water among some reeds. He brought the net up, dripping. By the pull of the netting she knew that he had caught something, and soon, by a familiar glunk sound, that it was a bullfrog. Quite a big one, and it wasn't happy.

Maggie had spent plenty of long afternoons in the creeks and streams of western Pennsylvania catching pollywogs and watching water bugs and dragonflies. She watched with a memory of that pleasure as this lone naturalist held his catch in his hand and studied it. She could see his profile now. He had blond-white hair, frizzly like Little Orphan Annie's in the comic strips of her childhood. His skin was surprisingly pale. He looked as if he spent more time in the cellar or under his bed than outside.

He was busy now with his prize, whether examining or doing something to it she couldn't tell. She hoped he wasn't hurting it. The boy stood up suddenly and posed as if to pitch a baseball. Then he hurled what he was holding in a high arc over the pond. He had timed his pitch exactly right this time, for at the apogee of the arc, there was a powerful bang, and the frog exploded in a spray of guts and rusty goo as the boy emitted a high-pitched giggle of excitement.

"Hey!" Maggie shouted. The boy didn't even turn around. As if by a conjuring trick, he and his gear had disappeared into the shrubbery.

The bell tinkled as Maggie reentered the Frigate.

"I'm back," she declared to the bookman, panting slightly.

"You are," he said.

"I just saw something disgusting."

"I'm very sorry to hear it. Can I help?"

She hesitated, just then realizing that it might be slightly odd in a moment of crisis to head for the nearest bookstore. *Could* he help?

"There was a boy up in the cemetery. I saw him catch a bullfrog and blow it up with a firecracker."

"I'm Mattias, by the way," said the bookman.

"Maggie." They shook hands. "Is there a policeman in town, or a—I don't know, a game warden?" Not that frogs were game. What did she mean, animal control officer? The man who comes to help when there's a skunk under your porch? Or truant officer? Shouldn't that boy be in school?

Mattias said, "We call the big city if something serious happens. Otherwise it's just us and the social contract. Some of the volunteer firemen are auxiliary police. You might go to the firehouse."

"Where is it?"

The firehouse was a brick building on the uphill side of the village a block from Main Street. The truck bay door was open, and a gleaming red engine stood facing out, ready for action. It was squeaky clean and lovingly polished. In the dark recesses of the bay behind the truck, she could hear voices.

Sitting around a battered table at the rear of the building she found three men playing Texas Hold'em. One was small with a belly that looked as if it needed a cantilever to hold it in place above his pants. One was young and fair-haired with a toothbrush mustache. The third was Ray Meagher. They all stopped their play to turn and look at her.

"Help you?" asked the man with the belly. Ray Meagher was looking at her as if he couldn't place where he'd seen her before.

"I just saw a boy up in the cemetery blow up a frog with a firecracker."

The men looked at each other.

"It's very serious," she added, in the voice that had made captains of industry snap to attention when their children were on the carpet in her office. "Torturing animals is part of a dangerous pattern . . ."

"Ma'am? Me and Ray are only auxiliary. We can't intervene unless we actually see a crime committed. And I don't know if this would even count. Ray? Would it?"

Maggie knew little of the requirements to qualify for auxiliary police, but evidently they didn't involve a very rigorous study of the statute books.

"Aren't fireworks illegal?" Her tone was steely.

They thought about that. It looked to her as if the young man with the mustache was trying not to smile. Right, she thought. Even if he wouldn't blow up a frog himself, he'd think it would be cool to see it happen.

"Look. That boy is disturbed. Fireworks are illegal, and cruelty to animals is a crime. His parents and his school need to know that he's in serious trouble."

All three men looked solemn. Like boys acting contrite in the principal's office when you know they'll be giggling and imitating her as soon as they're free and out of earshot. Hope would have done this better, Maggie thought. Hope would have sat down and played a few hands with them and then persuaded them to let her ride shotgun as they went to arrest the felon.

"Whad'ee look like?" the man with the belly asked. "The firecracker kid."

She described his pallor, his frizzy bush of freakishly light hair. She saw the men look at each other.

"You know him."

"It's a small town, ma'am."

"So, who is he?"

"Sounds like Jesse Goldsmith," said the belly.

The name startled Maggie. "Does his mother teach at the Manor? That Goldsmith?"

"Yeah. They're doing the best they can with him," said the man with the mustache. "We all seen him grow up."

"How old is he? Shouldn't he be in school?"

"Sixteen? Seventeen?"

Maggie was surprised. He looked younger.

"Think he might be homeschooled."

"Or done," said Ray.

"Yeah, he might be done," said the belly. "He's a little . . . what's that thing where you can't stop washing your hands or folding your sweater?"

"OCD," said Maggie

"Yeah, OCD. He's different, but he's harmless."

*　　*　　*

It was just three-thirty when Maggie started back to the school. She had a lot to think about. First on the agenda was to spend some time in the faculty lounge when the girls were at sports or study hall and the teachers were off duty. She needed to know who Florence's friends were, and now for different reasons she wanted to know more about Marcia Goldsmith and her family. She remembered Marcia's tears the previous morning. It was good that Hope would be here soon. Hope would help Maggie think her way through the underbrush just by listening, but she also had an uncanny way of reading people. Plus she was fun to be around, and Maggie felt she could use a serious dose of that right about now.

She was walking briskly back toward the school on the side of the road, not yet knowing the footpaths around the village, the shortcuts the locals knew. Rounding a bend, she saw emerging from the woods a slightly dumpy young person in jeans and a baseball cap. In a flash of cold alarm, she feared it might be young Mr. Goldsmith but quickly realized it was a girl, and one she knew. She quickened her pace and caught up with her.

"Alison?"

The girl, huffing along, looked up and said warily, "Yeah?"

"I'm Mrs. Detweiler. We saw each other at the yarn shop earlier. Do you mind if I walk with you?"

"Wait, were you in our class the other morning?" With the words wafted a strong scent of cigarettes and mouthwash.

"I was, yes. With Mrs. Goldsmith. Are you due somewhere?" The girl was setting quite a rapid pace, designed, Maggie suspected, to wear her out.

Alison checked the time on her phone and said, "Yeah. I have riding at four and I have to like get my boots and stuff."

"That's your athletics?"

"Yeah."

"Are you one of the dressage riders?"

"No. Just, you know. Walk, trot, and canter. I think we're going on a trail ride this afternoon though."

"That sounds like heaven."

Alison looked as if she thought Maggie were out of her mind.

"Tell me about Miss Marcus." Maggie knew she was perilously close to the kind of conversation kids hate, with the aunt who tells you how much you've grown and wants to know what your favorite subject is.

Alison shrugged. "She's an easy grader."

"Riding goes on your transcript?"

Alison shrugged again. "I guess."

"How about Mrs. Goldsmith?"

Alison looked up at Maggie as if she didn't understand the question, and Maggie didn't know exactly how to phrase it without leading the witness.

"Do you have classes with her?"

"Oh. No. I take Spanish."

"I just met Mrs. Goldsmith but I liked her. Do you know her son?"

Alison perked up unexpectedly. "Not well, but . . . you know."

"I don't know, actually."

"He thinks he's the shit, because he can sing and everything. He was nice to me, though, so I like him."

"Nice to you how?"

"I messed up my lines all the time and he always knew them, he'd feed me my cues. He knew all our lines."

"I'm sorry, I'm not following."

"When we do plays, we have to have boys from outside. Obviously. He's hot, and he doesn't have much choice, since Mrs. Goldsmith makes him, so he was Birdie last year in the musical. My roommate was, like, *so* into him."

Maggie was astonished. "Jesse Goldsmith?"

Alison surprised in turn. "*Eric* Goldsmith. Mrs. Goldsmith's son."

"Does Eric have a brother?"

"Uh—don't know. Maybe. This is my dorm."

"Run, then."

Alison was already jogging away, no doubt wondering what tedious thing *that* was about.

The faculty lounge was below grade, downstairs from the entrance, in the main building of the school. Windows high in the wall mixed lemony afternoon sunlight with the rather synthetic aura from the fluorescent bulbs that hummed from the ceiling. From inside, through the windows, you could see feet and ankles pacing by on the walkway to the quad. Running shoes. Sandals. UGG boots, though it was warm. A pair of bedroom slippers, all framed in the window, like an avant-garde film that told its story exclusively through footwear.

The room held a couch and some armchairs, worktables, a copy machine, a microwave, coffeemaker, sink, and a small undercounter fridge. When Maggie came in, instead of the hive of school hubbub she had been hoping for, there was a sole woman unknown to her rather fussily washing coffee mugs and wiping spilled crumbs from the counter. Her hair was crimped into orange waves that had the burnt look of a home permanent, and she wore a wrap skirt and sneakers.

"I don't know who they think is going to clean this up, if they don't clean up after themselves," the woman said. "It's not as if the ladies' maids are going to do it. Would you like some coffee?"

"Thanks, I'd love some."

The woman banged around in the cupboard, finding filter papers and whatever else she needed. "No matter when I come in to read the paper, it's always a mess."

Maggie observed a used-looking newspaper on one of the chairs.

"We used to get three papers and some magazines but we're down to one copy of the *Times* now. Are you here for the science job?"

"Me? No, I'm just doing a little consulting for the board. Maggie," she added, offering a hand.

"Pam," said the other.

"You teach?"

"Yes, by negative example. I'm what we used to call a housemother. When I was in school, it was our joke, the worst thing that you could think of, to wind up back here as a housemother. Dorm parent, being the current locution. So here I am, and you know what? We were right. It's pathetic. But . . . life doesn't go the way you expect. Milk? Sugar?"

Pam gave Maggie a mug with a picture of Snoopy on it, dumped three heaping spoons of sugar into her own cup, and sat down across from Maggie.

"Well," said Maggie, "start at the beginning and tell me everything."

"No. We'd be here until next week."

"Okay, we'll start small. What can you tell me about Florence Meagher?"

"*That's* not starting small," said Pam.

"What do you mean?"

"Florence and Ray used to live upstairs from me in Sloane House," Pam said.

"And?"

"And," said Pam. She let it hang, then added, as if it should go without saying, "you learn a lot."

"Like what?"

Pam's rather small hazel eyes, with colorless brows and lashes, narrowed as she considered her answer. Maggie was preparing an explanation of why she wanted to know, when Pam apparently decided that it wasn't her job to shut the barn door after the horse was gone.

"It's a wooden floor, and they didn't use rugs. You hear everything, shoes, click clack click clack. Things breaking. Voices."

"Raised voices?"

"*Oh* yeah."

"His? Hers? Both?"

"Mostly his."

"And what was it about?"

"Different things. One of the big ones was children. They don't have their own. She wanted to, he didn't or couldn't. She got more and more into mothering the girls. She'd have big breakfasts for them on Sunday mornings. She has favorites. The runts, the ones from divorces, the ones who'd been raised by servants. Ray doesn't like her having groupies. Or friends, really."

"Are *you* a friend of hers?"

"Try to be. To tell you the truth I find the verbal diarrhea hard to take, but that's just because I'm not a very nice person. Florence is. And she rattles on like that because she's frightened. She didn't used to."

"Frightened. Of Ray?"

"I assume."

"And the girls were hearing all this as well?"

"They must have heard some. But our apartments are down at the end of the corridor and there's a fire stair between us and the student rooms. Sound may not travel through the walls as much as through the floor. My girls never mention minding the music I play, and believe me they would, if they heard it."

Maggie at once wanted to know what kind of music Pam played but asked instead, "Is it just because of her student pets that Ray gets angry?"

"Oh, he just uses that as an excuse to bully her. He's one of those big babies. I can't help it, whenever I see him I picture that great hairy body in diapers with his big forehead bulging out of a frilly little bonnet. Having a tantrum."

The door opened, and a man and a woman came in, both teachers Maggie had met the first night. Unhelpfully no longer labeled. The woman filled the electric kettle and plugged it in.

"Anyone else want tea?"

No one did. "But don't use that mug, Mary Jean," said Pam. "It's cracked."

Mary Jean looked at it and back at Pam, as if to ask, if it's cracked, why is it still in the cupboard, then dropped it into the wastebasket.

The man, who had the Arts section of the paper open and had

just sunk into an armchair, cried, "Oh bloody hell. That crafts closet dingbat filled in the puzzle again."

"You don't know who did it, Andy," Mary Jean said without turning around. Maggie recognized that this wasn't the first time this scenario had been played in this room.

"Yes, I do. She uses green ink," said Andy with disgust.

"And half the answers are wrong," said Pam, who had gone to the cupboard above the microwave, and reached up to a high shelf. She produced a photocopy of the blank puzzle and passed it across to Andy.

"For you, from the puzzle fairy."

Andy looked at her with surprise.

Pam said, "I figured out if I get here before the morning milk break I can get to the puzzle before the dingbat does."

"A grateful nation thanks you," said Andy, his mood much improved as he propped the photocopy against the folded newspaper and took out his pen.

"Do you have another one?" Mary Jean asked as she sat down with her tea.

Pam got her a puzzle.

"Is it a hard one?"

"Typical Thursday. The trick is in thirty-three across."

"Don't tell me unless I beg."

"This is Maggie. I was just telling her about Florence and Ray," said Pam.

"Where *is* Florence, by the way?" Andy asked.

"Gone to her sister's. Somebody's sick."

"Oh too bad. Something serious?"

"Couldn't tell you. What I was saying was, that Ray makes a huge rhubarb about how much time she spends with the girls, but I think it's just something to complain about. To keep her in line."

"I heard that what really sets him off is Marcia Goldsmith's kid," Mary Jean said.

"Eric?"

"No, the younger one. She spends a *lot* of time with him. Tutoring, playing Scrabble, that kind of thing."

"Better her than me," said Pam, making a face.

"I know," said Mary Jean. "They latched onto each other somehow, I think it was last year during the play. Jesse would come with Eric and spook around backstage and other places he wasn't supposed to be and Florence lured him into her Havahart trap."

It took Maggie most of that evening to get Hope up to speed on what she knew so far. Since their successful work together on the death at the Oquossoc Mountain Inn, Hope had taught herself a form of shorthand, not Gregg or Pitman, and not all that fast, but she diligently transcribed what Maggie told her in a handsome notebook with a green leather cover. Hope was in favor of any endeavor that required the purchase of new equipment.

"What are you doing?" Maggie asked, peering across the dining table at Hope's squiggles.

"I learned it from a book in the library. I wish I'd done this when I was in college, it's changed my life."

"Is it hard to learn?" Maggie was one of those rare people who could take complete notes on the sentence she just heard while also fully understanding the sentence she was hearing, so she had not found the need of quicker notes.

"Not at all," said Hope. "I can write it like the wind."

"But can you read it?"

"Oh no, but I remember things if I've once written them down."

They had decided to have dinner at the inn where they were staying, since it was nearly empty midweek, and they could talk without being overheard. Meals were served in a drafty room with many windows, all leaking night air. The one waitress on duty had to be summoned from the pantry whenever they needed her, as it was warm in there. They'd been given a little bell for the purpose.

"We'd like to try a bottle of the pinot noir," Hope said to the girl when she appeared. "We need to see if it has chocolate notes."

"Wait—it isn't a dessert wine," said the girl.

"It'll be fine," said Maggie, and the waitress rushed off. "You frightened her," she added to Hope.

"I'll make it up to her."

Maggie returned to telling Hope about Florence Meagher and the olives on her cereal.

"You said she was in Rome doing research?"

"Madrid."

"What kind of research?"

Maggie stopped chewing and looked at her. "I don't know. She blew right past me with the prunes and I didn't ask the obvious question."

"Is she working on a thesis, maybe? Taking an advanced degree?"

"We'll talk to her friends. I'm sure they know all about it. The way she talks, they could hardly help but know. That will be our first order of business tomorrow."

FRIDAY, APRIL 24

B*ut it wasn't.* Maggie was downstairs for breakfast at seven-fifteen, where the same waitress was presiding over the untouched breakfast buffet. Maggie was wondering whether the girl slept here, chained to a leg of the sideboard, when her mobile began to buzz and vibrate. It was a text from Christina Liggett.

Cd u come asap?

She answered *Yes. All ok?*
The answer: *no.*
Maggie drove so Hope could put on her makeup in the car, and they reached Christina's office in eight minutes. Christina was waiting at her door, which she shut behind them once she'd herded them inside. Maggie introduced Hope, but Christina hardly seemed to hear. She went to stand at the window, which looked down the slope to the playing fields and the New Gym. Her breathing was rapid and shallow, her skin the shade of putty.
She said, "They've found Florence Meagher."
"At her sister's?"
"No. In the swimming pool. The coach works with a couple of

our girls in the morning before classes. This is Lily Hollister." For the first time they noticed a small figure in sweat clothes, pale as a newt, sitting huddled in upon herself in the farthest corner of the room, half hidden behind a large globe in a mahogany stand.

"She found the body," said Christina, still looking out at the glowing spring morning to the cloud of pear tree blossoms that had just come out that week.

She turned to Maggie and said, her voice a throttled whisper, "I don't know what to do."

Hope went at once to the administration office down the hall and returned with a mug of strong tea for Christina and a coffee for herself. "I've told them to route all callers to me," she said, holding up her cell phone. "I am now your press officer."

Christina looked at her as if her processing unit had just rattled a cascade of unrelated facts into a semblance of meaning. She said, "This is the end."

"No, it's the beginning," said Hope.

"I mean, it's over. All we tried to do."

"I knew what you meant. It's the end for Florence Meagher, but not for anything else. At least not yet. Drink your tea."

Christina sipped, then looked at the mug. "I don't take sugar." Hope saw a fragile child, who could function heroically up to a certain level of stress and chaos, and beyond that, stopped dead.

"Today you do. You're going to need the energy." Her cell phone rang. Hope answered, "Rye Manor School, Ms. Liggett's office." She listened briefly, then said, "I'm sorry, she's not available. She'll have a statement for you later in the morning. You're welcome," and hung up.

Christina looked amazed, as if to say *You could do that?* Just refuse to talk? She'd been trying so hard to answer to everybody, at all hours of the night and day, for so long, that she'd forgotten she had any right to act rather than react.

While Hope debriefed Christina, Maggie settled onto the sofa beside the huddled girl, Lily Hollister. "Tell me," she said.

Lily's long, thin, rather elegant feet were in flip-flops. She must have rolled out of bed and into her swimsuit and sweats. Maggie saw that she had to swallow several times before she tried to speak; she was salivating as one does when battling nausea. She was a pretty thing, with full lips and very large blue eyes.

"Coach meets us at the pool, Tuesday and Friday mornings. Me and Steph. We're training for Junior Nationals. Steph's suit was at the pool, in her locker, but I had taken mine home to wash out the chlorine, so I dressed in my room."

"Are you and Steph in the same dorm?"

"Yes. No. She's in Sloane One, I'm in Sloane Two."

"So you went down together?"

"No. We always meet at the pool. It's just easier."

Maggie noticed the earbuds hanging out of the pocket of Lily's sweatpants and understood. One or both of them preferred music to talking in the early morning. She would herself.

"Tell me exactly what you did this morning. You met in the locker room?"

Lily shook her head. "I went in the front door, straight through to the pool, because it's warmest there."

Maggie could picture her hurrying through the chilly early morning, into the lobby of the new building lined with as yet mostly empty trophy cases, and pushing open the heavy door into the high-ceilinged echoey humidity of the pool room.

"The front door was unlocked?"

The girl nodded. "Coach opens the building for us. We're not allowed to swim if we're alone, but I like to do my stretches in the pool room. I was a couple of minutes early, by the clock . . ."

"What time, exactly?"

"Six-fifty."

"So you . . ."

"So I started with some sun salutations." Maggie remembered how literal children are, especially in crisis. "I must have had my eyes closed for a while. Coach says you have to hear what your body says, where it's tight, what hurts."

She was stretching this out. Was it because she wanted to avoid the thing that she didn't want to see again? Or because she was stalling, thinking. There was something hard to parse in her manner. Maggie waited.

"But—at some point, I was like . . . I saw there was something at the bottom of the pool. Something big, and dark. Like someone had thrown a coat or something in there. It seemed weird and I didn't really want to look at it, but Coach still didn't come and it was there."

She stopped again. Maggie waited. "So—there's a net with a long handle? Like a thing you can use to fish things out with? Or skim things out of the water, I don't know what. I guess we track things in on our feet or something. So I took it and I . . . sort of poked the thing at the bottom. It was right at the deepest part, under the diving boards. Over the drain. I thought if I moved it, I would see what it was, and then . . . it turned over."

She put her hands over her mouth and Maggie thought she might be going to vomit. Moving surprisingly fast, she crossed the room and returned with a wastebasket, but Lily took deep breaths and got through the moment.

"The water's a little cloudy," she added. "I guess from all the chlorine. I wish they wouldn't use so much it really hurts your eyes."

"But you could see well enough."

The girl nodded.

"And then what did you do?"

Lily thought for a long minute. Her eyes skittered, like someone dissociating. Or lying. "I can't remember," she said. "Coach came."

"She screamed," Greta Scheinerlein said.

She was called Coach because it was easier than teaching the girls to pronounce her last name. Greta had explained this to Maggie after the police were finished with her and Steph, the other swimmer. Lily Hollister had by now been taken to the infirmary to wait for her parents in private, but Steph was sticking close to her coach as they settled into the Katherine Jones room, which was once again Maggie's headquarters.

"Where were you when you heard the scream?" Maggie asked now.

"In my office," said the coach. She was a stocky brunette, all muscle by the look of her, with a short gamine haircut and enormous sloe eyes.

"What did you do?"

"Took off running," said Greta. "I thought—I thought maybe Lily had tried a dive and hurt herself, I thought broken neck, broken back . . ."

"And this was at . . ."

"Right before seven."

"And you, Steph?"

"I was in the locker room with my suit in my hand. I was naked and there was this scream like in a horror movie. I pulled my sweats on and ran toward it."

"Did you notice the time?"

"No, but I was right behind Coach. I still don't even have my underwear on."

"She was right behind me," Greta confirmed. "We ran into the pool room and Lily had both her hands pressed to the sides of her face, like this, screaming and staring into the pool."

Steph began to cry and shut her eyes, as if she was now really seeing what they saw, but for the first time. The coach reached over and took her hand. She squeezed it hard.

"And did you see at once what it was?"

"It was Florence," said the coach. "She was wearing a flowered dress. The skirt had floated up but her face wasn't covered. Her eyes were wide open. Staring. Her legs were bare and her . . . She had her shoes on." Here Greta Scheinerlein stopped. She was at a remove. Soon the effects of adrenaline would wear off and she'd feel how hard she'd been hit. Steph was feeling it already. Her narrow face was parchment white.

"Were any of Mrs. Meagher's belongings there in the room? Or in the pool? Other than what she was wearing? Jacket, handbag, car keys?"

Greta shook her head. Steph, her eyes behind a thick lens of tears, shook her head. Her lips were pressed tight together to keep them from trembling.

"Not anywhere in the room?" She had already asked Lily this. Lily said she'd seen nothing but the body, but Lily was so clearly in shock that Maggie knew not to trust her answer.

"And the body. Could you see if it was . . . intact? Any wounds or injuries?"

Greta looked as if she might gag. She shook her head no. She had not seen. She had not looked.

"All right. I'm sorry I had to ask that. Tell me what you did next."

"I took the girls back to the office and called Christina. She said she was coming and told me to call 9-1-1. She came and took Lily away, but Steph decided to stay with me to wait for the ambulance."

Maggie said to Steph, "You're a tough young lady."

Steph shook her head no. She still wasn't outright crying, but her eyes brimmed, and she bit her lips hard. Maggie could guess that Steph wanted to stay with her coach because they'd just been through something terrible together and it seemed wrong to leave in the middle.

"So . . . the EMTs arrived. We went outside to meet them and showed them the way into the pool."

"But you didn't go in with them."

"No. The police from White Plains came too, and they sent us back to my office. A detective went with us and took our statements. After a while we saw them wheeling a—" She gestured with her hands in frustration at missing the word . . .

"Gurney . . ."

"Thank you, outside, with a white sheet over—Florence. It was wet. Sticking to her. I don't know how they got her out of the pool. They put her in the ambulance and took her away. Then when he finished taking our statements, they said we could go."

"Is there anything else at all you can tell us about the scene?"

Greta shook her head. "They asked about when I locked up last night, and when I unlocked this morning."

"And you said . . ."

"There was a town meet here yesterday evening. It was all over by eight-thirty. I locked up the way I usually do. I was home by . . . nine . . . ?"

"That's a guess?"

"Yes. Nine-ish."

"You live alone?"

The coach hesitated, then said, "No, but my partner was out. I fed the cat and turned on the TV, and the show had just started. That's everything."

There was something in there that Ms. Scheinerlein didn't want to talk about, at least not right now, and Maggie decided to leave it for the moment. The coach placed her broad strong hands on her knees, fingers splayed, as if to indicate she was about to stand and go.

Steph said timidly, "Car?"

Greta Scheinerlein, suddenly dazed to be shown how poorly her mind was working, bopped the side of her head in embarrassment. "The car! Thank you, Steph!" She turned to Maggie again. "Steph noticed as we were leaving the building. Florence's car is parked outside the pool house. I'd seen it when I arrived this morning but I didn't know it was hers so I didn't think anything of it."

Steph said, "I was like, 'There's Mrs. Meagher's car.' Mrs. Meagher was Lily's dorm mother until they moved up the hill. The car was always parked behind the dorm."

"Both the Meaghers lived in Sloane, didn't they?"

Steph's mouth made a slight sign, of dislike or something else Maggie couldn't tell. "Yes," was all she said.

"What kind of car is it?"

"A Subaru. Gray station wagon. My grandma has that car."

"And does Mr. Meagher drive the Subaru as well? You called it Mrs. Meagher's."

"No, he drives a snot."

Greta gave a surprised bark of laughter and then looked embarrassed, as did Steph, who hadn't meant to be funny.

Knowing that inappropriate laughter often occurred with shock, Maggie merely looked a question at Steph.

"Smart car. The first time we saw it, Mr. Meagher drove by, all crouched in this tiny thing like a clown car, and my roommate tried to read where it said 'Smart' on the back and she thought it said 'Snot.' It did look a little like it said that. So." The unseemliness of this sentence seemed to grow upon Steph with every word and her distress made Maggie want to tell her that it was all right to go on being human.

There was no point trying to keep news of the death from traveling like shrapnel from an explosion. By the time Maggie reached Christina's office, Hugo Hollister had arrived; by chance, he'd been on his way back to the city from the family's country house in Hatfield. Hope was on her mobile in the corner of the room. Reporters for the *Poughkeepsie Journal* and the *White Plains Daily Voice* plus a stringer for the *New York Post* were in the outer office, corralled for the moment by Sharon. Christina was on the phone to the trustee who served as the school's lawyer.

Hugo was impeccably dressed, in a double-breasted suit and a tie, crisply knotted, that might as well have been spun from money. His handsome lined face was tense and focused, and Maggie found herself unexpectedly relieved to see him.

Maggie said, "You've seen Lily?"

"Yes, she's packing."

"You're taking her home?"

"At least for the weekend. We'll see after that."

"Have classes been canceled yet?" Maggie asked him, after giving Christina a signal that she needed to talk with her.

"Not yet," said Hugo.

"They should be, pronto."

"Yes."

Christina got herself off the phone and joined them.

"What is your crisis plan?" Maggie asked.

Christina looked at her, her eyes wild. Crisis plan?

"Right. Tell Sharon to get the word out that classes are canceled as of now. There will be an all-school meeting at"—she looked at her watch—"noon. Where do you meet when you are all together?"

"The Delano Theater," said Hugo.

"Shouldn't I talk to Mrs. George first?" Christina asked.

"No," said Maggie and Hugo together. Christina picked up her phone to buzz Sharon but got a busy signal. All eight lines on the phone were alight. Christina left the room. After a moment's hesitation Hugo hurried after her through the throng in the hallway and reached her just as the reporters landed on her like ants on a jelly sandwich. Maggie heard him explaining with gracious firmness that Ms. Liggett would have a statement for them as soon as she could. Then he gave Sharon the message and escorted Christina back through what looked like a wall of curious faces, students, kitchen staff, teachers, and neighbors of the school who had seen the police cars and had a few questions. Maggie then ran the gauntlet to Sharon and told her to hold all calls and let no one through to Ms. Liggett's office except Lily Hollister, if she came, or Mrs. Hollister, or Ray Meagher.

Inside the office, they sat in a circle. Hope had silenced her phone at last. Maggie said, "All right, Hope will talk to the press. What do you want her to say?"

"Our lawyer told me to say 'No comment.'"

"That's wrong, makes it sound like you're covering something up," said Maggie. "What kind of lawyer is he?"

"Family law," said Hugo.

"I rest my case. Hope, you'll tell the press that there has been a tragedy in the school family and we ask them to respect our privacy at this time. Then they'll all start to chew on you. Tell them that's all you're at liberty to say for now, then shut your mouth and keep it shut.

"Now. The statement to the school. Christina? It will be best if it's in your words, dignified but from the heart. Why don't you try to talk it; Hope can take notes." Hope beamed and whipped out her handsome notebook.

In a quavering voice, Christina said, "I am sorry to tell you that our . . . honored teacher and . . . dear friend Florence Meagher . . ." And then she began to cry, great desperate sobs of unfeigned grief. Her friend, her school, her job—she wept, she was handed tissues, she wiped her eyes, she blew her nose, and then she began to hiccup.

"Hold your breath," said Maggie, patting her and looking over Christine's shoulder rather desperately at Hugo. Christina took a deep breath and held it but kept hiccing painfully until she had to let it out.

"She should hold her breath and drink a glass of water at the same time," said Hugo.

"I can fix this," said Hope. "Christina, stand up." Maggie and Hugo watched as Christina stood and Hope placed herself practically nose to nose in front of her.

"Look me in the eyes and don't blink," ordered Hope, and Christina, surprised, obeyed. After they stared at each other for some moments, Hope said softly, "Go ahead, hiccup. Don't blink. Don't look away. Go on, hiccup."

Maggie and Hugo looked at each other as this went on for another minute. "Good girl," said Hope, suddenly smiling.

Christina's crying jag was over and her diaphragm had abandoned its rebellion. "That's amazing," she said weakly.

"Next, the press," said Hope, and she left them.

Looking after her, Hugo said, "I want to know how to do that."

"I've found," said Maggie, "that most of Hope's gifts are nontransferable. Let's get to work on the statement. First question, Christina, I assume you've notified the family?"

Christina said, "There's only her sister. I've told her. That was terrible."

"I'm not surprised. And Ray?"

"Not yet. No one's been able to find him."

The school nurse escorted Lily Hollister, carrying her weekend bag, to Christina's office. Lily was wearing a long-brimmed pink baseball cap and dark glasses, but when she took the glasses off, her face was blotched and mottled. She and Christina said good-bye to each other and both started to cry again, so Hugo put his arm around his daughter and said, "Brace yourself, kiddo. Here we go."

"Go out through the kitchen," Maggie said.

"Smart," said Hugo, shooting her an appreciative look. He opened the door and exposed them briefly to a line of faces craning to see into the room without seeming to. Then they headed toward the dining room, away from the crowd, and the door closed behind them.

Christina unraveled once or twice during her speech to the school, but so many in the audience were undone that she was in good company. She remained enough in control to convey a sense of being buffeted but steady at the helm, and that was really all that was required. For most of the girls, Mrs. Meagher's death was their first experience of the sudden extinction of someone they knew personally. For virtually all it was their first brush with death by misadventure.

Lunch following the meeting was subdued, and after it girls could be seen in small groups, talking intensely, sometimes weeping, wandering the campus. It was lucky that the weather was warm and open; it gave those who mourned a chance to be out under the sky.

Not everyone was mourning, of course. There were those who had threatened to kill Florence themselves if she didn't shut up. There were faculty members who grumbled that Florence's death would add to their workloads. There were teachers who resented the disruption of the schedule when they were trying to prepare their girls for exams, and students who agreed, especially among the grade-conscious juniors, ever mindful of the ordeal of college admissions rolling toward them in the fall. And there was that faction of the board that quite looked forward to the demise of the school as they knew it and the opportunities that might present themselves in the dismantling. In their view, the present unsavory tragedy could only hasten the moment.

One of the true mourners was Marcia Goldsmith, or so it seemed to Maggie when she encountered her sitting on a bench outside the library with a boy whose face was preternaturally pale, with a bush of white-blond hair and eyes like marbles. Whom she had, of course, seen before.

Marcia looked up at Maggie and said, "I *knew* something was wrong, that morning when Florence didn't show up. I felt it. I wish I'd . . ." Then she sniffled and stalled.

Maggie gestured toward the empty end of the bench. "May I?"

"Of course, oh excuse me. And you haven't met my son Jesse, have you? Jesse, this is Mrs. Detweiler."

Jesse raised his eyes to a point about at Maggie's chin, and flopped his hand in a wan greeting.

"Could you say hello, honey?" his mother asked.

He shrugged and looked at his shoes. His expression was stony. Maggie took that for a "no."

"What do you think you could have done?" Maggie asked Marcia.

"Can I go?" the boy whined, twisting his body and speaking to his mother, his hand held up to conceal his mouth from Maggie as he spoke. It was a gesture Maggie associated with fifth-grade girls intent on signaling that whoever was looking on was being pointedly excluded. She found it surprisingly offensive.

Marcia said after a beat, "Sure, honey." Jesse took off without a farewell or a backward glance as his mother gazed after him.

"He's so upset," she said finally. "Florence was very good to him."

"That's hard. A big loss for him."

Marcia added, "I think it's worse because he'd had a fight with her the last time they met."

"Really?"

"Yes. He had just told me about it that morning, when you came to my classroom."

Maggie thought again of Marcia's tears that morning.

"Jesse doesn't have many friends and it was so sad that he'd . . ."

"What?"

"Well I don't know the details. He does drive people away sometimes, even when he doesn't want to. I wish I knew why. I'm sure she would have forgiven him but, you know. It seemed like such a good sign, that they liked each other. I used to hear them laughing together when they played Scrabble. Even when they weren't together, they used to play Words With Friends. I'd hear him laughing in his room, and I knew that he and Florence were online together."

"Even you?"

Marcia didn't follow.

"Does Jesse even try to drive you away?"

Marcia hesitated. She looked at her hands, and said, "I'm his mother. He knows it's safe to lash out at me."

"I've been told that Florence liked to adopt the young," Maggie said carefully.

"She does. Did. She was very kind."

"How did she and Jesse find each other?"

Marcia said, "I have another son. Eric. All the things that are hard for Jesse come easily to Eric. Eric was always sunny and happy, an easy baby, a happy little boy. Jesse was the opposite. Touchy, intense. He feels things very strongly, he was born like that. He had terrible tantrums when he was small. I think he may have had pain he couldn't describe—stomach, headaches, something. But doctors couldn't tell what, and neither could I, and by the time he had language it was just part of him, the screaming. Eric didn't like it. My husband hated it. He thought since Eric was so easy that all children should be easy. He's always treated Jesse as if there's something wrong with him. So Eric does too. And of course, that's a perfect way to make sure there *is* something wrong with him."

They sat together quietly for a minute. Eventually Maggie said, "And you?"

"It's been hard."

"I can imagine."

"You just have to love them. There are difficult people in the world. It's a fact. Loving them can help, and not loving them certainly doesn't."

"Your husband disagrees?"

After a long pause, Marcia said, "Yes. He disagrees." There was another pause and then she added, "We're separated."

"I see," said Maggie. "Is that recent? Forgive me, it's none of my business, but I remember you were upset the day we met."

Tears started in Marcia's eyes. She said, "Todd moved out Tuesday. I didn't think he'd go." She looked in her bag for a packet of tissues and found it.

"And Eric?"

"Eric's in college."

"Does he know about the separation?"

"He does now. When he comes home—I don't know if he'll come to me, or go to Todd, or stay away from all of us. And I don't know what to hope for. I love Eric, but when he's home, Jesse's worse."

Maggie could well imagine it. She thought about how she would counsel this family, if they were her problem. "I assume," she said, "that Jesse's been evaluated?"

"Endlessly. He's normal, he's not normal, he'll grow out of it, he's got this syndrome or that disorder. When he was in fifth grade his school insisted on some drug, and I wasn't allowed to give it to him, the school nurse had to do it when he got to school. I took him his lunch one day and found him so doped up he was practically drooling."

Maggie could hear in this litany an undertone of anger at the people who hadn't helped, or hadn't loved.

"What happened?"

"I took him out of there, of course. My husband wanted to send him to a psychiatric school of some kind. Just to get him away, so things would be normal for Eric. I don't know how he thought we were going to pay for that, and how can you do that anyway, sacrifice one child for another? I mean, Eric will be fine, no matter what."

"What happened?"

"I homeschooled. We live close to campus. It hasn't been ideal. I'm not a specialist and Jesse has reading issues, and he's alone too much. But it's better for him than being bullied, or having a drug lobotomy."

Maggie was thoughtful. The two women sat side by side in

the bright afternoon, thinking their very different thoughts. Then Maggie noticed that a blue-and-gray Smart car had stopped at the streetlight that protected the crossing where the girls went back and forth from the upper to lower campus. Her view of it was blocked by a parked car, but when the light turned green and the car moved forward, she saw that it was driven by Ray Meagher.

The phone was ringing as Ray Meagher walked into his house. He had to go to the john something wicked, so he let it ring. In his own good time he went into the kitchen, popped the top on a lite beer, sat down at the kitchen counter, and dialed his voice mail code into the phone. The mechanical woman said in her quacking voice *You have . . . fifty . . . three . . . new messages . . .*

There were seven hang-ups before he got a live one. It was from Christina Liggett. She said, "Ray, please call me when you get this message. It's urgent. I'll keep trying you." He called the school without listening to the rest.

He finally got through the wall of busy signals and said, "Sharon, it's Ray Meagher."

She said, "Oh god—where are you?"

"Home. I just got back."

"Have you talked to anyone?"

"No. What is it?"

She said, "I think you better come down here."

"Can it wait at all? I need to charge my phone and check my e-mail. Is Florence back?"

Sharon said, "Could you come down now? Please." He guessed it wasn't really a request.

*   *   *

In days to come, Maggie and Hope would recount their impressions of that meeting many times, to many people. They were with

Christina when Ray walked into her office. He was wearing slacks and a sweatshirt and looked liverish, as if he'd drunk too much or slept too little.

When Christina told him about Florence, he put his hand to his mouth and dropped into a chair. Then he covered his whole face with his hands and barked a sob. Maggie had an instinctive reaction, that he'd accepted it too fast. He should have been more surprised. He sat with his face in his hands for a long stretch until Hope crossed the room and handed him a handful of tissues. He carefully wiped his eyes and nose, then looked up at Christina.

"I don't understand what happened."

"She was found in the pool at seven this morning," Christina repeated.

"Did she—I mean she was a strong swimmer, what was she . . . did she have a heart attack? A stroke or something?"

Hope was diligently writing her squiggles in her notebook in the corner, slightly behind his line of vision.

"No," said Christina. "She hadn't gone swimming. She was dressed."

Ray gawped, as if he couldn't make his mouth work right.

"You mean . . . somebody . . . ?"

"The police assume so. We've been trying to reach you all day. Where have you been?"

"I should call the police, shouldn't I?"

"Sharon has called them. They'll meet you here."

Then there was a silence. Ray looked at Christina, who looked steadily back at him. Then he looked at Maggie and at Hope. They watched him.

Christina said, "I'm very sorry for your loss, Ray."

"Yes, I'm—I'm sorry for yours too. I mean . . . we all loved her." He looked as if he was going to cry again.

"It's been a very hard day," said Christina.

The silence stretched. After a while, Ray said, "I had theater tickets. I was going to surprise her. Then when she went off to her sister's, and wouldn't answer my calls, I thought, 'I'll just go anyway.'"

Maggie spoke for the first time. "So you were in New York last night? At the theater?"

"Yes," said Ray, as if appealing to them to see the pity in it. There he was, not suspecting a thing while his wife was in trouble, and he would never see her again. Maggie thought, this was a man who was used to playing the poor helpless soul who needs to be comforted and rescued. Just Florence's type.

"What did you see?"

"*Jersey Boys*. Floro loves the music, she plays it all the time."

"Was this for her birthday or something?"

"No, it was. . . ." Ray made a gesture of appeal with his hands. "Just a present. You know. We'd had a little rough patch and I wanted to give her a treat. Then when she went off in a snit, I . . ."

"Did you go by yourself?"

"No, I took a buddy from my air marshal days. Happened to be in the city."

"Name?"

"Guy Thompson. He called, so." Hope scribbled. Christina and Maggie sat quietly, eyes on Ray. He grew uncomfortable with the silence and went on. "There's a hotel way over on the West Side that's clean and cheap, the Clinton. I used to go there when I was flying, I flew out of Newark. I was based in Florida before I met Floro. I checked in there and met Guy for dinner and then I tried one more time to call her—that's when I realized my phone was out of juice."

"And what time was that?" Maggie asked. Ray looked at her, suddenly sharp, but couldn't find the harm in the question. "About ten of eight. Something like that. We were walking toward the theater. It was such a pretty night . . ."

"Where was it you had dinner?"

"Little place on Ninth Avenue. I don't remember the name. Red something."

"And how was the show?"

"She would have loved it." He looked down at his hands, his face a mask of bewilderment and sorrow.

"I love that opening number," said Maggie.

"Yes," said Ray. "It was great. Florence used to—"

The phone buzzed and after a word from Sharon, Christina said to Ray, "The police are here."

The two White Plains detectives were shown in. They introduced themselves around the room. Charles Bark, the lead, was short and grizzled, with a large nose and a pitted face. He had small sharp eyes, brown verging on black. His partner was younger, a thickset blonde named Evelyne Phillips.

"Could you come with us, please? We have some questions," Bark said to Ray.

"Now? I just got home. There are things I have to . . ." He trailed off, looking from one of the officers to the other. He was used to being the muscle in the room himself. "Or could we do it here? I'm just trying to digest . . ."

"I know it's a difficult moment," said Bark. "We can go with you to your house, if there are things you need to do. But then we'd like you to come with us."

"For how long?"

"That depends."

"What about my . . . my car's out back, should I . . . ?"

"Detective Phillips will ride with you. I'll follow."

After a beat Ray said, "Okay, then. Yes. Sure."

"Lead on," said Phillips, and the three went out.

Maggie, Hope, and Christina, who had stood to greet the newcomers, sat back down and looked at each other. "Does he have pets of any kind?" Maggie asked Christina. "Goldfish? A cat? Anything that needs to be fed?"

"I don't know," said Christina. "Why?"

"I don't think he'll be home tonight."

"Why not?"

"Curtain for *Jersey Boys* is at seven on Thursdays."

* * *

Mattias Benes was in the back of his store on Friday afternoon, reading a fat book of essays by Clive James, when the bell over his shop door signaled arrivals. It was the suddenly ubiquitous Mrs. Detweiler and an urbane blonde he hadn't yet met. He offered tea, which they accepted. While he fussed over the electric kettle, Maggie said, "I expect the village knows all about what's happened up at the school."

"We think we do," Mattias conceded, "though I'm sure we've got it slightly wrong in the details. The word down here was that the Hollister girl was *in* the pool when she noticed the body. And so forth." Then he held up the book he'd been reading. "I just found such a good sentence. Here, I'll read it to you. 'The true political monster insists that, apart from a few hand-picked satraps, there shall be no individuals but himself.' Isn't that good?"

"Brilliant," said Maggie. "Kim Jong Il to the life."

"He was writing about Hitler, but yes, you make his point."

Hope said, "He could just as well have been writing about my ex-husband."

Mattias turned from where he was arranging the teacups and saucers and gave her a look. "Exactly," he said.

"So. Ray Meagher?"

"All happy tyrants are alike."

Maggie looked at Hope and said, "What on earth made you think he was talking about Ray Meagher?"

"Isn't he what we're *all* talking about?"

"Were you?" Maggie said to Mattias, who shrugged.

"The shoe fits."

"Ray is not your favorite?" Hope pressed.

"Let's just say we were not destined by nature for a warm personal friendship."

"Well, I'm not talking about Ray," said Maggie. "I have a pure and open mind and Ray wasn't the only person angry at Florence. So, speaking of unhappy families, we'd be interested to meet Todd Goldsmith. I assume you know him?"

Mattias handed teacups around and produced a pint carton of milk from a tiny fridge under his counter.

"Of course. Why, may I ask?"

"I've met his wife and one of his sons, and way leads on to way."

"Which son?"

"Jesse."

"Ah. Well you won't find it hard to locate Todd. He seems to be more or less living in his office at the moment. It's right down the street, River Realty. If he's not there, ask in the Wooly Bear. When things are slow he likes to chew the fat with Kate Curtin."

They found Todd Goldsmith in his office. He was a tall man with messy gray curls, wearing a jacket and tie and a crisp white shirt. Maggie noticed that he wore a thick wedding band on his left hand. She was about to introduce herself when Hope stepped forward and said, "I've just discovered your charming town. Beautiful views, right on the train line—how many minutes into the city?"

"Fifty," said Todd, smiling his salesman smile.

"If I wanted to see a house with a view, at least three bedrooms, in walking distance of the station, what could you show me?"

"Well! That would depend on your price range, of course . . ."

"What about that Colonial?"

She waved in the direction of the photographs that crowded the front window.

"It's a little far for walking to the station, but that's a beautiful home . . ."

"Does it have a garden?"

"Not as such, but it has a big yard and plenty of room to put one in."

"Can you show it to me?"

"Certainly. When would you like to . . ."

"How about now?"

After a moment of pleased surprise, he said, "I'd be happy to." He rooted around in a desk drawer, came out with a set of keys with a big orange label on the ring tag, and stood. "The owners work in the city, but the dog knows me. You won't mind if it isn't neat as a pin, will you? They usually get some notice before a showing."

"Couldn't care less," said Hope.

"Will your friend . . . ?"

"Thanks, but I have errands," said Maggie, improvising.

To Maggie, Hope said over her shoulder as she followed him out, "That Bistro place. One hour."

Maggie pushed open the door of the Wooly Bear and found the shop empty. She tapped a little round bell on the counter, and the woman with the cat's-eye glasses emerged from a back room with a toothbrush in her hand. She waved at Maggie and held up a finger, meaning I'll be with you in a second. And she was.

"Sorry about that. I was just getting ready to fold my tent and go home. I had chili for lunch and it was loaded with garlic. Ellie says she can tell all the way down the hall if I had garlic for lunch."

"It's very good for you, though."

"I know, but she's sensitive. Born that way. Anyway. Welcome back, are you planning a purling project?"

"You know—why not? I might even branch out into knitting."

"I like to start people with socks. They don't take forever, and just when you get bored doing one thing, like ribbing, it's time to do something else, like turning a heel."

"That does sound like fun," Maggie said. "I'm Maggie, by the way."

"Kate." The two then spent some time looking at pattern books and perusing different colors and weights of yarn. When Maggie had made her selections, Kate offered to help her wind the skeins into balls, showing her how to do it without stretching the yarn. This led them, as Maggie had hoped, into the age-old occupation of women sitting together doing handwork.

"The girls told me what happened up at the school this morning. Terrible," said Kate.

"Terrible. Did Ellie have classes with Florence?"

"No but her friend Alison does. Did. She used to—" Kate interrupted herself. Maggie mentally finished the sentence: *she used to do a great imitation of The Affliction.* Knowing Alison, Maggie could bet she did.

"How are the girls taking it?"

"Shocked. But fascinated. Ellie's never even seen a dead body."

"She didn't actually see the body, did she?"

"No, but Steph Ruhlman is a friend. They've made her tell the story over and over."

"Girls sort of like being horrified."

"They do."

A silence as the wool wound swiftly.

"I ran into young Alison yesterday," said Maggie. "She told me about Eric Goldsmith. I gather he's a heartthrob. Do you know him?"

"Since he was a toddler. Both those boys. His father and I are colleagues, of course, on the village Merchant's Guild. I know Marcia too, but not as well."

"Marcia seems quite broken up over the separation."

"Yes," said Kate drily. "Well."

"I'm sure there are two sides."

"Marcia thinks it's all about Jesse. But really, it's her. Jesse is what he is. No one can change that. But she can't accept it. And in the meantime, she's got another son, and a husband who . . ." Kate shrugged, as if the rest of the sentence was too obvious to utter. Maggie made a mental note. Todd seeking consolation elsewhere? Here?

"Marcia told me that Florence Meagher was very good to Jesse."

Kate shot Maggie a look, as if to see how much she knew.

"Much good it did her."

"What do you mean?"

Kate stopped spooling the yarn from Maggie's hands and readjusted the fingers around which she was forming her ball. Maggie had the impression it was costing her some effort not to tell her everything she knew about the Goldsmiths.

"Sad situation," she eventually remarked as her hands resumed their practiced movements.

They wound wool in silence, minds as busy as their hands.

"Marcia said Jesse fought with Florence," Maggie offered. "Or, what she said was 'he drives people away.'"

"That's the truth. That's been true since he was in the cradle."

"What was it about, between Jesse and Florence, do you know?"

"Of course. Florence gets very involved in the spring musical. She helps with props and makeup and that sort of thing. Eric was in the play last year, and Jesse came with him and got in everybody's hair as usual. This year *he* wanted a part. A particular part, one of the leads, like Eric had had. They let him audition, and it was pitiful. Plus, he hardly had the right look, they weren't casting Fagin's pickpockets or anything. Ellie was there. She was in the play."

"And he blamed Florence?"

"He said he was going to *kill* Florence. Not that she had any say in the casting, but he must have thought she could fix it for him. He was so angry he was foaming at the mouth. Ellie said."

"I take it this was in public?"

"I think Ellie was the only one still there. Florence went to put some props away and found Jesse had waited backstage to attack her."

"You don't mean physically?"

"No, just words, but it was frightening. Thank god Todd showed up to take Jesse home. Ellie was horrified. Well, you know how it feels when someone is spewing hate at you, it's like being shot. Names can never hurt you, my aunt Fanny."

*   *   *

Maggie had a bottle of wine and a plate of crostini waiting on their table when Hope found her at Le Bistro.

"You're a devious one," she said as Hope sat down. "Why didn't you tell me you were going to vamp Mr. Goldsmith?"

"I didn't know until I saw him. I thought, This guy is never going to unbutton to two old broads he doesn't know if they're sitting and staring at him. One on one, and side by side, that's how you find out what people are thinking."

"And tell me, doctor, how did you arrive at this technique?"

"Driving my children to the airport at the end of college vacations. Or, you know. Reform school, in Buster's case. The whole time they were home they were in their rooms or out with their friends; on the way to the airport was when I'd find out that Lauren had a boyfriend or Buster was moving to Nevada. Besides, I liked the look of that house."

"And how was it?"

"Just gorgeous. Huge trees, ravishing views of the river. The kitchen alone was the size of your apartment. Attached garage, mammoth televisions in every room."

"Any books anywhere?"

"You really want egg in your beer, don't you? There were book-*shelves* at least. And the neighbors might be a little mobbed up, but that means the street is very safe. Not that the owners are taking any chances. Their dog is the size of a young steer. He lives in the basement, where they're letting him eat a couch."

"Did you actually see the dog?"

"Yes, he stopped roaring when he heard Todd's voice. He was

very welcoming after that, we let him out and he clopped around with us."

"I'm sorry I missed it. What else did you learn, Miss Divide and Conquer?"

"Well I told him you were doing some consulting for the school, and that I was keeping you company. I said I had accidentally moved to Boston but was missing New York and might move back."

"Is that true?" Maggie asked happily. She was slightly surprised at how much the thought pleased her. She had scores of friends in the city, and she and Hope were in fairly constant touch as it was, but it would be more fun having her closer.

"Yes. Mostly. Sort of. Anyway, I asked him to give me a tour of the neighborhood so I could see what was available. We got chatting about Rye Manor, about his wife and poor Florence. He talked a lot about Eric. He's on the dean's list at college, he's joined the photography club, he may major in journalism. I asked if Eric was an only child."

"And?"

"We'd been having a high old time. There's nothing like being the client's new best friend when you're trying to sell them houses. But he went very cautious all of a sudden."

"Interesting."

"He said he had a special-needs son named Jesse who was living with his mother. I asked if that was the Jesse who Florence Meagher was so fond of, and he said he guessed so, but he and his wife were living apart so he wasn't the one to ask."

"And?"

"And he suddenly thought I might be interested in a ranch-style house we were passing. Made a hairpin turn and there we were in the driveway. I said *not* my taste, but it took some work to get him back to the subject. I told him that I'd had a son who wasn't a walk in the park to raise, and that it's hard on a marriage. I said my son had turned out wonderfully, on track to be a detective with the sheriff's department, and that Jesse would probably be fine. And that it was so helpful when a child who is difficult at home has someone who isn't a parent take an interest in him, and did he know that Jesse and Florence had quarreled?"

"And?"

"He said he didn't know anything about that, and asked if I'd want to join the country club because he had a nice bungalow out by the golf course he could show me."

Maggie told Hope about what she'd learned in the yarn shop. "Todd walked in on the fight. Kate was clear about that."

"So," said Hope.

"Yes. Jesse's father thinks he actually could have killed her."

*C*hristina Liggett *was looking better* after a night's sleep. They found her at home the next morning, in the pretty brick Georgian house that had been the home of the founder. She was just finishing her breakfast. Once again, Maggie was struck by how very young Christina looked. Wearing slacks and loafers, she met them at the door and led them through the imposing drawing room, the formal dining room, and into the kitchen, which was clearly where she really lived. The table was stacked with papers and files, and the bulletin board was stuck with family photographs. In the middle of the table was an enormous cream-colored cat, curled on what looked like a pile of bills.

"And who is this?" Maggie asked, eyeing the cat.

"This is Nimbus. She's hypoallergenic."

"I didn't know there was such a thing."

"There isn't. But light-colored female cats of breeds that are missing a certain protein in their saliva are the least allergenic and she mostly lives back here, where the students don't go. Unless they are staying with me."

"What kind is she?"

"Siberian."

"Do students stay with you often?"

"When they live too far away to go home for vacation. Or are recovering from something. I had an appendectomy case here for a couple of weeks in March."

"She's beautiful," said Maggie. Received wisdom was that you couldn't have dogs or cats on campus these days any more than you could cook with nuts without huge warning labels on everything.

"She's a very one-woman girl," said Christina, at which point the cat majestically rose, stretched, and stepped daintily off the table into Hope's lap. "Oh, Nimbus, you slut!" said Christina.

"Don't worry, this always happens. Hope is a cat-whisperer."

"I've never seen her do that before! The trustees let me keep her because she never goes near anyone but me."

"We won't tell them," said Hope.

"What's the program today?" Maggie asked.

"The grief counselors will be on campus all day. Florence's sister arrives this evening. Can you come for dinner?"

"We'd love to. Have you heard from Ray?"

"Not a peep. I assume they'll be keeping him in White Plains, don't you?"

"I do," said Maggie. "What I was wondering is, could we have a look at the Meaghers' cottage this morning?"

Christina moved the folded newspaper from a stack on the table and found a butter plate with a half-eaten bagel under it. Maggie wondered how long it had been there and whether this child was remembering to eat.

"Don't you need a warrant or something?" Christina asked.

"We would if we were police but we're not. You are Ray's landlord, are you not?"

"I guess I am."

"You have a right to enter at any time, to check on your property. You or your duly appointed agents."

"Are you . . . I mean do you think . . ."

"We don't think anything at the moment except that Ray was not at *Jersey Boys* on Thursday night. I'd like to know where he was, but I imagine the police are on that case. We need to get to know Florence better. Her home is the best place to start."

"I'll get the keys," said Christina.

Ray Meagher's blue-and-gray Smart car was parked in the driveway when Maggie and Hope parked on the street in front of the house. The house looked lifeless. A window on the second floor was slightly open, but no lights were on, and no creature stirred.

Maggie walked around Ray's car slowly.

"Wouldn't you have thought they'd impound this, or whatever it's called?" Hope asked her.

"I guess not if they haven't charged him yet." She reached for the door handle, when Hope cried "Wait!"

This morning Hope was carrying a capacious handbag in the shape of a chicken. She produced a ball of latex gloves and handed Maggie a pair, then donned her own.

"Well, look at you, you're prepared," said Maggie.

"Buster taught me a lot. So useful, having a son who's in law enforcement. I've got my whole forensics kit in here. If they *do* impound the car we don't want our fingerprints all over it."

"We do not, it's very true."

The car was unlocked and the keys were on the floor beneath the steering wheel. They found receipts, snack wrappers, and take-out cups on the floor of the passenger seat, as if he was using that side of the car as a wastebasket. There were unpaid parking tickets in the glove box, all local. Clearly Ray Meagher felt that rules didn't apply to him, at least on this turf. Maggie wondered how Detective Phillips had felt about riding in this mess. There were also used paper napkins, road maps of New England, New York, New Jersey, and Pennsylvania, some cough drops fused together in their half-squashed package, and a white poker chip with the name TURNING STONE CASINO on it.

"I wonder what that's worth," Maggie said.

"Not much, if he didn't bother cashing it in. Where is Turning Stone?"

"See if you've got a signal," Maggie said.

Hope poked at her phone and said, "Yes."

Poke poke poke. "Near Syracuse."

"How long a drive is that?"

"Three hours and forty-nine minutes, according to this."

Maggie put the chip back in the glove compartment, along with the maps and detritus. They closed the car. Hope produced a tiny flashlight, got down on her hands and knees, and peered at the undercarriage.

"What are you looking for?"

"I have no idea." She staggered to her feet again and brushed gravel from her skirt. "I guess if there were long grass or something caught under there it would mean something."

"Is there?"

"No. Why do you think the detectives didn't take all that stuff from the car with them?"

"They'd have needed permission or a warrant. Probably didn't want to start their questioning on that footing."

They went to the house. Hope picked up the copy of the *White Plains Daily Voice* that lay in its wrapper on the mat, and Maggie unlocked the door. They stepped carefully inside. All was silence. "You take the living room, I'll do the kitchen," Maggie said.

The cottage was lightly built, as if more for summers or weekends than for year-round use. There were two rooms downstairs in addition to the kitchen, a living-dining room, and a small study. The whole thing was clad in knotty pine.

Maggie methodically opened the kitchen cupboards one after

another. They were well stocked, but with a schizophrenic quality. In one cabinet were bags and jars of beans and lentils, barley and quinoa, and at least four different kinds of rice. In another, vegetable stock and broth, pastas, nuts and dried fruits. Beside the toaster oven was a well-used copy of the newest Ottolenghi vegetable cookbook. Maggie thumbed through it and found multiple margin notes and cooking stains. On the endpaper was an inscription: *For Florey with love from Sooz, Christmas 2014.*

That would be the sister, Maggie thought.

In the refrigerator she found drawers full of limp carrots and celery, a head of romaine and another of cauliflower, both well past their sell-by dates. There were also tubs of hummus, Greek yogurt, and a jar of preserved lemons. In the freezer, stacks of frozen pizza and lasagna, sausage and hamburger meat and oversize Hungry-Man frozen dinners. She pictured mealtime at the pretty little maple table in the next room, with Florence at one end serving an elaborate dish of lentils, walnuts, and braised kale, and Ray at the other end tucking into a heap of kielbasa and mac 'n' cheese.

Hope came in.

"Anything?" Maggie asked her.

"Parallel lives. The living room is Florence's domain, I'd say. The other room is a man cave. Socks in the seat cushions. Paperback thrillers. TV set to the sports channel. A stash of porn under the sofa."

"No."

"Yes."

"Show me."

Maggie followed Hope into the den, where she produced a stack of magazines from under the sagging seat of the sofa. The manly forest-green slipcovers were homemade, Maggie noted. She looked at the magazines and thought of the woman who had troubled to try to make this room inviting for her husband.

"That's just rude," she said.

"And old school. Doesn't everyone use the Internet for that?"

"Did you look through it?" Maggie gestured uncomfortably toward the stack of magazines.

"It's plain vanilla. No whips or chains, no children. Lots of huge Kardashian bottoms."

"Well, that's a relief. I guess." They headed upstairs.

The bedroom was oddly impersonal, as if here, where the couple couldn't avoid each other, there could be no individuality at all. The double bedstead was maple, very 1950s, probably from a thrift shop. The bed, unmade, had pale blue sheets and mismatched blankets. There was a clock radio on each side of the bed, one set ten minutes faster than the other.

"I'm finding this very creepy," said Maggie.

"Really?" said Hope, opening the closet door. "I once thought of getting a real estate license just so I could do this."

On what she took to be Ray's side of the bed, based on the racing form beside the lamp, Maggie opened a drawer in the nightstand. She quickly closed it again.

"What's in there?" Hope asked.

"Mint-chocolate sex oil." Maggie looked as if she'd smelled something fetid. "Definitely Too Much Information."

"I tell you what, I'll do the bathroom. You take the other bedroom."

The second bedroom, at the back of the second floor, was dark, with its one window shaded by an overhanging maple tree. It was however as full of personality as the master bedroom had been unreadable. There was a daybed covered with a patchwork quilt that Maggie guessed was Florence's handiwork; the fabrics were modern and the colors bright. It was in a pattern that Maggie knew in her reptile brain—though not how she knew it—was called Wandering Foot. Her sister in Pennsylvania was a quilter. The pillow shams were made to match the spread, and Maggie inferred from the sleep mask and tube of lorazepam on the side table that Florence slept in here more than occasionally.

The desk under the window was a cheap hollow core door supported on two file cabinets. The power supply for a laptop was plugged into a power strip on the floor, its business end held on the desk by a dictionary, like a snake with its head pinned down, so it wouldn't slither off to the floor when the computer was absent, as it was now. Under the desk was a portable sewing machine in its beige case, a wastebasket, and a shredder.

Maggie went to the bookshelves next, and here she found a richer picture of Florence's life of the mind. There were many shelf feet of art books on everything from the kimono to Josef Albers. An expensive recent volume on Mark Rothko had pride of place. Maggie pulled it out.

"To Mrs. Meagher, December 2012. Thank you for everything and Happy Holidays, from Mairi. XOXO" was printed in an earnest schoolgirl style.

Florence's first love was painting of the Renaissance, Maggie inferred from the number of monographs on Velázquez, Leonardo, Michelangelo, Rembrandt. Most of the books and pamphlets had stickers from the Strand bookstore in New York, where remaindered copies of expensive books could be bought for much-reduced prices. Most of the volumes were underlined and their pages bristled with colorful stick-on flags marking pages with quotes or pictures of interest.

Hope came in.

"There's a whole history of art symposium going on in here," Maggie said, turning to show her a page in a study of Vermeer, pocked with notes and queries in the hand she now recognized as Florence's. "All these voices yammering away in here across centuries without making a sound. I'd have hired this woman."

Hope looked at the desk, and said, "She clearly had a laptop and a smart phone. I wonder where they are." She picked up a little thumb drive and looked at it, as if trying to read it.

Maggie found a letter used as a bookmark in a volume about the lives of Francisco Pacheco and Antonio Palomino.

"What have you got?"

Maggie, skimming the letter, said, "It's just a bread-and-butter note from a student who came to dinner. But it makes me think we should turn out all of these books to see what else is tucked in the pages."

"You do that, and I'll get into these drawers."

Maggie was sitting on the floor paging through a book on Bernard Berenson and Hope was deep in one of the desk drawers when a voice from the doorway said, "What the *hell* do you think you're doing?"

Maggie's heart moved so violently in her chest that it took long moments to return to normal rhythm. Hope slammed the file drawer so fast she caught one of her fingers and swore.

"Holy crow, you nearly gave me a fit!" Maggie said.

"I asked you what the hell you're doing," Ray Meagher said, menacing as he stepped into the room. He was wearing the same clothes as when they'd last seen him being escorted away by the White Plains detectives. He looked as if he regretted that the fright he'd caused them had not been fatal.

"We were just—" Maggie began, wondering how she was going to finish the sentence when Hope interrupted.

"I don't *wonder* you're cross," she said with warm sympathy. "You've had a long night."

"I've had a long night, a long day, I'll be having a long rest of my life. What the hell are you doing in my house?"

"We'll get out of your way. Have you had anything to eat? Would you like me to make you tea or coffee?"

"I'd like you to answer my fucking question!" he yelled. "You've broken into my house, you're pawing through my *dead* wife's stuff, and I'd like to tear your fucking hair off!"

Maggie looked at Hope and said, "I know just how he feels, don't you?"

Ray took a step toward Maggie, as if he was going to drag her to her feet and beat her up, but Hope stepped between them.

"Oh gosh, I'm sorry, did I step on your foot?" she asked, sliding by him. Before he could answer, they had both gotten around him and were racketing down the stairs.

Once they'd gotten outside and safely into their car, Hope slammed it into gear and took off, not quite burning rubber. She pulled over to the curb when the house was out of sight and took deep breaths.

"Ohmygoodness," she said.

"How did you think so fast? I was paralyzed. I kept trying to think how to answer the question," Maggie said.

"Instinct. There wasn't anything we could have said that wouldn't have made it worse, was there?"

"There was not."

"In a case like that, I've learned, it's better to go for knocking them off balance. I got caught going through Hank's pockets in his closet once, and it worked then."

"But you lived there."

"And he was guilty, which was the ever-important subtext. He couldn't push me too hard, because he didn't know what I might have found."

"What a useful dodge," Maggie said.

"Yes."

They were both beginning to feel their pulses return to normal.

"Have you got everything?" Maggie asked. "Your bag?"

"Yes. Am I bright red?"

"You *are* a little pink."

Hope tilted the rearview mirror so she could see herself, and said, "Well. I guess I'm safe to drive." She tilted the mirror back, put the car into gear, and inched back into the street. Actually, Maggie didn't think Hope was ever really safe to drive, but there was no point mentioning it.

"Did you find anything helpful in the drawers?" Maggie asked.

"There was a travel file with receipts and brochures from museums and churches. Italy and Spain, mostly Spain. I was just getting into it. Did you?"

"Similar. Grocery lists. To-do lists. A boarding pass. It's all in here." She indicated the chicken bag. "And did you mean to say you think Ray Meagher is guilty?"

"I'm sure he's guilty of something. Maybe a lot of things. But what I really meant was that after a night of being questioned by the police he for sure is *feeling* guilty and that would give us a little chink of advantage. Also he hasn't had any sleep. I didn't think he was at his best, did you?"

"Very much not. I wonder where he was on Thursday night though."

"Me too. How can we find out?"

"Make ourselves useful to those detectives, I'd say."

Marcia Goldsmith's house was on a cul-de-sac called Violet Circle. She and Todd had bought it in the early 1990s with a dream of happy children able to play outdoors in safety and ride their bikes and skateboards around the neighborhood. No through traffic, a neighborhood watch against strangers. All seemed to be going according to plan; then Jesse was born, and their family origin myth began to darken. By 2008 the economy followed suit, and neighbors, unable to pay their mortgages, moved farther out into the country or in with relatives as the banks took over and tried fruitlessly to find new buyers. The lawns of many of the houses where friends had once lived were tended fitfully by an irregular rota of day workers, if at all; the blinds were drawn, the garages were empty. As Violet

Circle unraveled, Marcia's older son Eric found ways to spend less and less time at home. He was a happy sociable kid and he preferred the more stable atmosphere at his friends' houses. But Jesse liked the decimated neighborhood fine.

The houses on the circle were all of a pattern, some identical except for paint colors, others the mirror image of the basic layout. Marcia's house was painted slate gray with white trim and was tidier than most on the circle. She and Todd had added a screened porch at the back. Marcia tended the lawn herself, or persuaded Jesse to do it. Bribed him, really, with new video games, or trips to the firing range, his latest passion. He was doing extra chores these days, saving up for a gun for shooting trap. A membership at the gun club was to be his birthday treat.

Marcia was sitting at her desk at an upstairs window grading French dictations when she saw a late model Buick tiptoe down Violet Fairway and, after a pause, turn into the circle. Maybe a buyer for the Johnsons' house? If Eric were at home she might have thought it was one of his pals coming to visit, but Eric wasn't, and no one came to visit Jesse. She watched as the car slowed, stopped, reversed briefly, and then parked in front of her own front walk.

Out climbed Maggie Detweiler and that friend of hers, whom Marcia had met briefly but not memorably enough to recall a name. She put down her red pencil, checked her face in the hall mirror to be sure she didn't have parsley in her teeth, and was downstairs and at the door by the time the doorbell rang.

"Is this a terrible time for us to be disturbing you?" Maggie asked.

"Not at all, I'm grading papers. Always happy to be distracted from that."

"I know the feeling."

"Come into the kitchen. Have you had lunch?"

"We have."

"Coffee then?"

"Love some," said Hope.

The kitchen was large and yellow with a brick fireplace at one end. On a table beside it was an empty cage with a wheel, a bedding of wood shavings and a few petrifying shreds of lettuce.

There were dishes in the sink from lunch, and an open Westchester paper on the table in the breakfast nook, which was designed like a booth in a diner, a place for a happy family of four, beside a window overlooking the back lawn where there was still a rusted swing set and a sandbox, long unused.

"Is Jesse at home?" Maggie asked as Marcia measured coffee into a cone of filter paper. She was fairly sure of the answer, since she could hear the explosive noises of a video game coming from somewhere.

"He's upstairs. He's playing one of those games where you're on a team with other players who are in Hawaii or Dubai. He had to eat his lunch upstairs because he didn't want to let the team down. They're fighting their way out of a booby-trapped gorge, guarded by a golem. Unless that was last week."

"My daughter is a fanatic about electronics," said Hope. "She won't let her children play them."

"How old are her children?"

"Going on four. But you see babies who can barely hold their own heads up clutching their tiny screens in their fat little hands these days."

"I'll talk to her when they're sixteen," said Marcia. "For my son, they've been a godsend. He has learning differences. Those games provide him with challenges he can master. He's learned to focus intently and he knows what it feels like to succeed at something. And it's social for him. He's homeschooled, so this is his team. I try to get him to go to bed at a decent hour and he says 'Mom, I can't . . . the Lizard King just got up and he needs me, I'm his bodyguard.'"

"Where does the Lizard King live?"

"Somewhere in Eastern Europe. It's made for some very good

units on geography. Time zones. Modern European history. And medieval, of course. For the dragons."

She brought her Chemex to the table with three mugs and went back for spoons and a carton of cream. She slid into the seat beside Hope, and when it was ready, poured the coffee.

"How are things going down at the school?" Marcia asked.

"Ray Meagher is back. He spent the night being questioned by police, but they let him go."

Marcia tore a packet of sweetener and stirred it into her coffee. "It's so hard to believe. Florence gone is hard enough, but murdered . . ."

Hope and Maggie briefly looked at each other. No one official had yet said Florence had been murdered.

"What can you tell us about Florence's frame of mind in the past few weeks?" Maggie asked. "Was she worried about anything? Depressed, upset?"

Marcia got up and began rooting around in a cupboard. She found an open package of Fig Newtons and arranged some on a plate. Maggie watched her carefully, trying to decide if she was stalling.

"I'm trying to think if there was anything unusual," Marcia said when she came back to the table. "She was busy with the play, and she always loved that. As far as I know she was happy with her classes. She was very concerned with the evaluation. Christina depends . . . depended . . . on her a lot. Of course the end of the year is stressful, with exams coming, and the curling parents pressing you to raise grades, and overlook term papers cut and pasted from Wikipedia."

"What are curling parents?" Hope asked.

"Like the ice sport. The parents sweep along in front of the children removing obstacles from their paths."

"How was her marriage?" Maggie asked.

"Well—you know. Poor old Ray. He's kind of mean, and he's kind of a dope, but otherwise, what's not to like?"

"Did Florence like him?"

"She must have at one time. They rubbed along, like a lot of people. I don't think they had much in common, but she'd reached a certain age and she wanted to be married. She especially wanted children. When that didn't happen, I guess the whole thing made less sense to both of them. And he gave up his work. Gave up or was fired, I don't know which. So that didn't help, she was so busy and very good at what she did, and she had a community. Ray doesn't have much except, frankly, Florence, and those louts on the auxiliary police force. I think he's one of those people whose personality is formed in opposition to something else. His was disrespecting Florence."

"That doesn't sound like much of a marriage."

"Oh, I don't know," said Marcia.

There was a silence.

"I see you have a hamster," Hope said, indicating the cage. "My son, Buster, had a couple of those."

"We had a pair of dwarf ones," Marcia said. "I didn't realize when we got them that they're nocturnal. I thought it would be so cute to watch them running on their wheel, but they mostly slept all day. Jesse begged me for them. He really wants a cat or dog but he's allergic to everything."

"Where are they now?"

Marcia shrugged. "I don't really know what happened to them. I came home a few days ago and the cage was empty."

"What does Jesse say?"

"Not much. He doesn't like to talk about things when he's upset. I think he probably took them out to play with them and lost them. They're tiny, they could scoot under something in a heartbeat."

"Be careful when you put on your shoes," said Hope. "The voice of experience."

Maggie decided, remembering her first view of Jesse in the cemetery, that she didn't want to pursue the question of the hamsters' fate any further.

There was another silence. Then Marcia added, musing, "The oddest thing was that he seemed very upset that first day. He was sniffly and his eyes were red, although he said he wasn't crying. Then the next evening while we were sitting right here at supper, he said 'Right now is when Calvin and Hobbes wake up. I don't hear them though.'"

Maggie and Hope looked at each other.

"What did you say?"

"I reminded him that we'd talked about them being gone the day before and he said 'Oh,' and went to his room."

Hope said, "Has he met Christina Liggett's cat? It's supposed to be hypoallergenic."

"Nimbus hides from him. She's a one-woman cat. And Jesse comes away from Christina's house with his nose all stuffed up anyway."

"But the hamsters don't bother him?"

"He takes a Benadryl if he's going to play with them."

"What day was that?"

"What day was what?" Marcia said. Maggie instantly sensed something change in Marcia's posture, a stiffening. This woman had a sixth sense for anything sensitive to do with Jesse.

"What day did the hamsters disappear?"

"Why?"

Maggie thought for a moment. She wasn't official; no one had to talk to her. Her only play was to keep things personal and social.

"You were upset on Wednesday morning, when we first met. Remember?"

"Oh. Yes," said Marcia. "I *was* upset. So it must have been the night before that they disappeared. That's why I wasn't at the reception Tuesday night, I didn't think I should leave Jesse alone, in case he needed to talk. His father had just left us, so . . ."

"This sounds hard," said Hope.

Marcia, suddenly teary, looked down at her mug and nodded.

They all let the silence stretch until Hope produced a packet of tissues from her bag and pushed them to Marcia. Maggie said, "We were wondering if we could speak with Jesse for a minute or two."

Marcia's face was concealed behind a wiping of eyes, and blowing of nose. When she raised her eyes again, her expression was cold.

"Yes? Why?"

"We'd like to ask him about his—disagreement with Mrs. Meagher."

"It was nothing."

"That wasn't the impression you gave me."

"What I told you was it was hard for Jesse, one of those accidents of timing. They'd been close but then they briefly weren't and then he never got a chance to make it up."

"I understand that, but I'd like to hear it from him, if you wouldn't mind."

"Look. My son has a hard time with a lot of things that are easy for other people. I tried to explain that to you because I mistook you for someone who would care. I would mind very much if you talked with him; he's busy and engaged and he's going to stay that way." All three listened to the sudden explosive sound of something in a computer game upstairs coming to a violent end.

Marcia stood up to let Hope out of the booth. Maggie took the hint. Marcia walked them in silence to the front door.

Outside, when the door had closed behind them, Hope said, "That went well."

"This was easier when we had Buster to help us. Maybe I should get a PI license."

In the car, Hope set the GPS to take them to Christina's house, while Maggie drove.

"What creeped me out was Jesse forgetting the hamsters were gone."

"Were dead, if you ask me," said Maggie. "That's about as serious a case of compartmentalizing as I've seen."

"It would be convenient, wouldn't it, if you could take terrible things and put them in a closet in your brain and truly forget that they were there?"

"*Convenient* is one word for it."

"Were you serious about getting a private eye license?"

Maggie was at the intersection of a highway and a country road, waiting for a long enough break in the traffic so that she could make her turn without being T-boned. As she finally zipped across the oncoming lane and swung into her own line of traffic, she said, "Oh I don't think so. I can't imagine that we're going to keep finding ourselves in situations like this."

Hope was thoughtful. She was going to be seriously depressed if she had to go back to reading *Silas Marner* and playing mah-jongg full-time.

"On the other hand," said Maggie, "I seriously want to know what happened to Florence."

Hope exhaled. "I think getting licensed might be kind of fun."

Florence's sister Suzanne was small and plump and very sad. She had driven up from Leesburg, Virginia, where she lived with her daughters and her husband, who was an IT guy with the State Department. There would be a memorial service for Florence next weekend, in the Congregational church in Rye-on-Hudson where Florence had been married and where she had worshipped. Suzanne had come to talk with Florence's minister about the service, and to make herself available to the police. She was staying with Christina Liggett.

Hope and Maggie arrived for dinner at the appointed hour, and Christina led them into the overstuffed formal drawing room, where Suzanne was drinking sherry with tears rolling down her cheeks. After introductions and more pouring of sherry into little cut-glass thimbles, the four sat in a half ring looking out at the sunset over the Hudson, and Suzanne tried to stop crying.

"She was my big sister," she eventually explained, in apology. "We're both adopted. Our parents were older and they've passed on. We were a team."

Christina reached across to her and clasped Suzanne's hand. Suzanne had surely shed many tears already, but it had all started again for her here in this place where Florence had done her life's work. Down on the river, the sun glowed red and scattered pink, maroon, and magenta shards on the water. Suzanne talked heartbrokenly of their childhood, about what a tender and loving aunt Florence was to her daughters, about how much her sister loved teaching, about her kindness to their confused and difficult parents at the end of their lives.

Christina led them into the dining room, where a woman from the school kitchen had decanted lasagna and salads from aluminum trays onto the founder's Victorian china. When they had served themselves and settled around the table, Maggie said, "Your sister spoke to me about her research. What was she working on?"

"She was so excited about her book," Suzanne said. "She'd shown a chapter to an editor in New York and she was sure it would be published."

Maggie and Hope exchanged a look. A book? A book that might have something in it that someone wanted suppressed?

"What was it about?"

"Velázquez. She loved him, it was a thing. Knew every picture, knew the names of his models. He used the same ones over and over, you can recognize them easily. She knew his whole life story, from a Portuguese immigrant family in Seville to the court of Philip the Fourth. Believe me, I feel as if I'd had a past life in seventeenth-century Spain."

"A scholarly study, then?"

"Oh no. That wasn't Florence. She was a teacher always. This was a novel for the girls, my girls and the girls she teaches. Philip the Fourth once had a contest to find the greatest painter in Spain.

Velázquez won. He was a young man in Madrid at the time, and Philip made him a courtier."

"Wait, that's Florence's story, or that's true?"

"True."

"What was the painting that won?" Hope asked.

"The Expulsion of the Moors from Spain."

"Where is it?" Hope got out her phone and started poking it while Maggie looked disapproving. They had an ongoing disagreement about screens at the table.

"It was lost in a fire. In Florence's book, it's a girl who wins the contest. A girl painter who trained in the studio with Velázquez in Seville. Velázquez helps her by pretending the painting is his, and then gives her credit when she wins. I was so looking forward to reading the rest of it." She started crying again.

Before they parted, Suzanne had admitted that she didn't want go alone to talk to the police the next morning. She was afraid she'd weep through the interview and not properly hear anything or say what she wanted to say.

Maggie said, "We'll go with you."

"There's no need for you to do any of this alone," Hope added.

They *picked Suzanne up* after morning prayers at school and headed for White Plains.

Detective Bark was waiting for them at an IHOP on Hamilton Avenue. He was in civvies, off duty and ready for a big breakfast.

"Detective Phillips will be here in a minute," he said. "I hope you don't mind this place. It's close to my house and the food's better than at the police station."

The waitress, suddenly at their elbows, said, "You folks ready or do you need a few?"

Detective Bark said, without looking at the menu, "A Rooty Tooty Fresh 'N Fruity and a large coffee."

"Three of those," said Hope, handing the waitress her menu and Maggie's.

"And for you, hon?" the waitress said to Suzanne.

"Just coffee, please."

Detective Phillips arrived and asked for coffee as well. Bark introduced her to Suzanne.

They sat in silence for a time until Suzanne said to Bark, "I understand you've talked with my brother-in-law."

"We have."

"Well, don't believe everything he tells you."

"Do you mind telling me what you mean?" Bark asked.

"Florence was afraid of him. He was up to something. She didn't know what it was, but when she asked him, he got angry. One day last winter he tried to kill her by throwing her laptop down the stairs. And there were strange gaps in his schedule, days when he'd disappear and wouldn't explain where he'd been."

"What do you mean, tried to kill her? Was she holding the laptop or something?"

"I meant, he did the angriest thing he could do to her. With no provocation."

Phillips asked, "What do you mean he'd disappear?"

The waitress was back with the coffees.

"She didn't know if there was another woman, or what it was, but he was defensive and mean and suspicious of her, the way people are when they're guilty of something themselves. And she could tell he was snooping around in her computer when she was out."

Bark had taken out a notebook and a pencil and laid them on the table. "And how did she know that?"

"She could see that he'd been looking at her search history, and was pretty sure he was reading her e-mail. She confronted him about it and he began to scream at her."

"Do you know what kind of things he said?" Phillips asked.

"Why couldn't she understand how angry it made him to be doubted. That was always the mantra. Then he picked up her laptop, ran to the stairs, and threw it over the banister. She was terribly upset. She ran down to the kitchen. She planned to go out the back door and drive to a friend's house, but her car keys weren't in the bowl where she always left them. That was when she got really terrified. He had known in advance he was going to fight with her and had taken her keys so she couldn't get away."

Detective Bark made some notes, and the waitress arrived with their Rooty Tootys. Maggie stared at hers. It was a stack of pancakes half a foot high with sliced peaches and whipped cream on top. She picked up her fork.

"Then what happened?" Bark asked Suzanne with his mouth full.

"The house was quiet for a while. She stayed in the kitchen, near the door in case he came at her again. After a while Ray came down the stairs and then she heard the TV come on in his study. He had turned on the hockey game. She went to the door, and he didn't even look at her, he just said 'What kind of new computer do you want?'"

Bark emitted a chortle and made a note in his book.

"You sound as if you saw it all."

"It happened right before Christmas. They always spend Christmas with us. The girls love Aunt Florey, and Ray doesn't have any relatives he speaks to."

"Really?" Hope looked up from her Rooty Tooty. Her unlamented ex-husband had family he didn't speak to.

"He has a sister who came once when he thought he'd had a heart attack. She spent a half hour with him in the hospital. Then they learned it was just a panic attack, and the sister went home. He has two brothers Florey never even met."

"They live far away?"

"Yonkers, I think."

"Huh," said Bark. You could drive to Yonkers from White Plains in twenty minutes.

"So at Christmas, she kept describing the laptop thing to me. Over and over, the way you do when you're trying to . . . you know, the way you do."

"Perseverating," said Maggie.

"That's the word. My husband took Ray off to a computer store so we could talk. That's when she told me that if anything happened to her, we shouldn't think it was an accident. I asked her why she didn't leave him, and she said he didn't have anyone but her,

and she hoped he'd get over whatever it was that was making him
so angry. She claimed the marriage had been really good in the beginning and she was holding on to that. She was such an optimist.
And way too kind."

"What kind of computer did he get her?" Bark asked.

Suzanne, who had been about to cry again, recovered herself
and squinted in an effort of memory.

"You know, I can't remember. It was a little one. Very light. He
wrapped it up and put it under the Christmas tree. I can see her
opening it. She was so pleased, as if it was just so sweet of him."

"Where is it now?" asked Bark.

Both Maggie and Hope stopped eating.

"You don't have it?"

"We do not. It wasn't in her car, or in her classroom or the house."

"How about her phone?" Maggie asked.

Bark shook his head. "Nope. We got nothing but what she was
wearing."

"And what about the cause of death?"

Bark shuffled his feet under the table and poured some creamer
into his coffee. "Do you mind telling me, again, what your interest
is in this case?" He was looking at Maggie.

"The board has hired me to consult with Christina Liggett
through this difficult time for the school."

"The school where Florence worked."

"Yes."

He nodded, thinking, then asked, "Is that common?"

"Yes, especially for a first-time head."

"So you're what, a professional coach or something like that?"

"Just a retired school head."

"Don't they call them principals?"

"Sometimes."

She could see him thinking, hoity-toity private school people,
and hoped he wouldn't decide to shut them out.

"My nephew got sent to some boarding school in New Hampshire," Bark remarked. "I didn't see the point myself, but it did him a world of good. I'm actually hoping he'll join the force."

Hope said, "My son is a deputy sheriff."

Bark looked surprised and held out his fist. Hope gently bumped it with hers. Buster to the rescue again. They exchanged some data about the department Buster was with in Maine, his hope of making detective.

Detective Phillips had her phone out and was working with it under the table.

Maggie said to Suzanne, "Does Ray often have panic attacks?"

"He's had a couple, but with the first one, they didn't know what it was. The EMTs came and took him away on a stretcher. He had to stop flying after that. The air marshals put him on disability."

They had all finished eating. The waitress came back to offer more coffee and Hope asked for some fruit for the table. Maggie was thinking that if she ate any more she'd have to have her stomach pumped but they hadn't quite gotten what they'd come for. They made small talk until the waitress came back with a plate of cut-up fruit and a pile of forks.

"You didn't say," Maggie ventured, watching Bark spear a chunk of pineapple, "if you've got a cause of death."

Bark looked at her as if to say, you know I'm supposed to be asking the questions. He seemed to decide *What the hell,* since so far they'd helped him more than he'd helped them, and besides, it was the woman's sister sitting across from him.

"She was strangled. Hyoid bone broken, no water in her lungs."

Suzanne put her hands over her mouth.

"Sorry," said Bark.

Before they went their separate ways, Bark gave Suzanne a business card. CHARLES N. BARK, DETECTIVE FIRST CLASS. On the back he wrote his mobile number. "If you ladies think of anything else that might be helpful, give us a jingle," he said. He and Phillips watched the three walk off to Hope's car.

"What've you got?" Bark asked Phillips.

"Margaret Detweiler ran the Winthrop School in New York City until her retirement last year. As stated. No record of any kind. Hope Babbin has had quite a few moving violations. She was married to someone called Henry Babbin Jr., a hedge fund guy, divorced many years ago, decree sealed, but she must have been left well fixed, judging from real estate records. Lives in Boston now, has two kids, a doctor in Boston and the deputy sheriff in Ainsley, Maine, Henry Babbin the Third. I wouldn't want to drive with her, but there's nothing suspicious."

"That's a relief," said Bark. When civilians inserted themselves into criminal cases, "just trying to help," it was all too often the case that it was themselves they were trying to help by muddying tracks, or interfering with the flow of information. And if it was just random nosey-parking, they could still do plenty of damage while making themselves important to the press or on the Internet.

"There's more. They were involved in solving a murder in rural Maine last fall. Sheriff's department had the wrong suspect, these ladies smoked out the right one. They got a confession, tied it all up with a bow. Pretty interesting case. Sheriff had to retire, I gather."

"No kidding. Got a conviction?"

"Hasn't gone to trial yet. Looks good, though. I sent you the link."

"Thanks."

Lily Hollister returned to campus Sunday night. Both parents accompanied her, anxious to be sure that Lily was really ready. The three were in the Manor House Inn dining room when Hope and Maggie came in to have their evening meal. Hope took one look at Lily's mother and exclaimed, "Caroline!"

Mrs. Hollister looked up in surprise and then jumped to her feet, her face alight with pleasure. The two embraced each other, exclaiming over how well each looked, and how small the world was.

"This is your husband?" Hope was asking, as her old friend tried to introduce her to Hugo. To Maggie, Hope said excitedly, "This is Caroline Westphall, I used to . . ."

And Caroline said at the same time. "So nice to meet you, Hope used to run with my older brother . . ."

"Her much older brother . . ."

"We all hoped she'd married him."

"I should have."

"There's still time," said Caroline. "He's single again." Then they both laughed at this ridiculous serendipity, although, to be honest, in their world this sort of thing happened all the time. Meanwhile, Hugo was politely standing with his napkin in his hand. Lily, eyes cast down, was picking at the crust of the toasted cheese sandwich she wasn't eating.

"I'm so sorry, we're letting your dinner get cold," Hope exclaimed as Hugo said, "Won't you join us? They can put together some tables . . ."

"No, please sit down. You should be together tonight." Before Caroline would let her go, she made Hope promise they could have breakfast together in the morning.

"Well, tell all," said Maggie as the waitress/maid of all work, whose name they now knew was Lenore, led them to their usual table.

"I haven't seen her since I broke up with her brother. She was about the age Lily is now. She looks as if she's thriving. Married to Hugo Hollister, well well well."

"Why do you say it like that?"

"If I remember right, and of course I may not the way things are going, she married young, a guy the family couldn't stand, so when he went bad she stayed much longer than she should have, just because they had warned her."

"What kind of bad did he go?"

"The usual. Other women. Oh, and I remember, he thought he was a genius in the markets and lost vast piles of money. Hers."

"I know she'd had previous children. Hugo mentioned a stepson."

"Two children, if I remember."

"Does she *have* piles of money?"

"She does, poor thing. It makes you such a target."

Lenore came back and announced there were no specials, it being Sunday. They ordered and Hope asked for a bottle of Sancerre.

"So what happened with you and the brother?" Maggie asked.

"At the time, I thought we just outgrew each other, but hindsight says it was actually the piles of money. His parents were so sure they understood how the world worked better than anyone else, and how everything should be done, and how lucky I'd be to be one of them. There was just no chance that he was ever going to come home and say, 'Let's move to Wyoming and live in a tipi. Let's go to Crete and dig up Minoan ruins.' At twenty-four he had the exact same receding hairline as his father and I just couldn't face it."

"But Hugo can."

"Face the piles of money? Well it's ugly work, but someone's got to do it."

K*nowing she wouldn't see Hope at breakfast,* Maggie rose early and went for a walk. She had gotten all the way to the cemetery and the pond where she had first seen Jesse Goldsmith up to his repellent tricks. The morning was mild and fresh and the view sufficiently inspiring that she decided to pause there and ponder the mighty Hudson below, and the mighty mess the Rye Manor School was in. She had just chosen a carved stone bench beside the grave of a little girl who had died in 1947 on her sixth birthday, and was trying not to think about the heartbroken parents coming to sit in this spot, watching the light on the river, watching themselves grow older as their child never would, when she saw two figures in the distance strolling toward her, deep in conversation.

As they drew closer, she recognized Hugo Hollister. The other was a short man in running gear. His doughy physique suggested that the exercise outfit was more atmospheric than functional. He had a very round head and dark thinning hair, and she was fairly sure he'd been at the reception for the visiting committee. The treasurer? Lyndon something? He was talking with great intensity to Hugo, who asked brief questions, then listened intently to the man's voluble answers. When the two were so close to her it would seem like eavesdropping if she didn't declare her presence, she stood, and Hugo at least finally saw that they weren't alone.

"You're up early," he called, smiling as his companion fell silent in midsentence.

"School folk have that habit," said Maggie.

"Have you both met? This is Lyndon McCartney, the treasurer of our board."

"Lyndon McCartney," said the other, offering his hand and talking over Hugo. "I saw you at the reception when the appraisal began, but I don't think we met."

"Appraisal?"

"Evaluation. Sorry. I'm in real estate."

They shook hands. "I understand you've stayed on to counsel Christina," said McCartney. He would have been part of the executive group that made the decision to hire her, Maggie knew; if she had to guess, she would infer that he'd been against it.

"Yes."

"How long will you be here?"

"That depends. Two weeks at least, and then we'll see where we are."

"Big expense for a struggling school," Lyndon said.

"Not really," Maggie said calmly. "A promising young school head is worth some investment."

Hugo and McCartney looked at each other. "Investment being rather a hot topic for our board, these days," Hugo said. "You find us having an impromptu meeting of the Finance Committee. Since my wife had a breakfast date, we thought we'd get some work done. I think better on my feet."

Maggie, who had been practicing lip reading for years, knew that in fact McCartney had been talking to Hugo with some urgency about something else entirely. She said only, "I imagine the vista is helpful as well."

"For the long view, yes. Certainly better than the science lab," said Hugo.

McCartney said, "I better be moving along. Nice to see you, Mrs. Detweiler." And he departed.

"Is that where the board meets? The science lab?" Maggie asked. She took her seat again on the bench and made a gesture with her hand. Hugo sat.

"We do when we're all together. Committees meet wherever. This is my chosen venue." He gestured to the astounding sweep of scenery before them.

"I see the point. Are many of the board members local?" Maggie asked.

"No. McCartney's a little unusual in that he asked to join the board. Usually we have to beg people, especially when they find out there's a financial commitment."

Maggie looked after the departing McCartney. In her experience, if a person asks to join a school's board it almost always meant the candidate wants some kind of control or power that did not in fact properly go with the territory.

"What's his interest in the school?"

"He's fairly new here, as I understand it. I just think that, that, that he saw it as a way to get involved with the community."

When he stammered, Hugo would spread the fingers of both hands and bounce the tips together, as if trying to get some gears to mesh. When he got traction and made it to the next word and then on into the sentence, the hands would slide together and clasp before him. It was a rather fascinating phenomenon. She wondered if he was aware he was doing it.

"And has he been a good trustee? McCartney?" She already had an opinion on this subject, after a talk with Emily George during the evaluation, but wanted to hear Hugo's view.

"He's been helpful to me. And he doesn't try to interfere in internal matters, since he doesn't have kids in the school."

"What *is* the financial commitment for a board member?"

"Oh, it's not bad. Ten thousand a year, give or raise."

If Maggie could have whistled inwardly, she would have. Glad *he* didn't think that was a big commitment. But, of course, he had Caroline and her piles of money.

"McCartney said he's in real estate. Does that make him a competitor of Todd Goldsmith?"

"Todd Goldsmith," said Hugo, as if trying to place the name.

"Married to Marcia Goldsmith, the French teacher? He's a Realtor here in the village."

"Oh, Goldsmith. Yes, no, he's he's he's a retail broker, isn't he?" He did the finger meshing thing again. "Lyndon is more of a developer, I believe."

"What brought him to this area? You said he was new here."

Hugo looked at his watch.

"You're right," said Maggie, standing. "We should be getting back."

"I just want to be sure Lily is settling in all right."

"Of course. How does she seem to you?"

"Shaken. But she's strong, like her mother. She wanted to come back. She wanted to get back in the pool."

"Brave girl."

They walked for several minutes downhill in silence, each with plenty to occupy the mind. Then Hugo said, "Oh! To answer your question about the McCartneys, they had friends in the area. They decided to move here when Lyndon gave up flying."

"Flying?"

"Yes, he was a pilot. He flew for American Airlines, I think. Maybe Delta. I can't keep the airlines straight, I don't fly myself."

"You mean you're not a pilot?" Maggie asked, thinking it was an odd thing to say, since so few people were.

"No, I mean I, I, I"—fingertips bouncing at each other—"don't get into airplanes. I don't get off terra firma in any way if I can help it. I tried to rise above it when Caroline and I went on our honeymoon, but they had to carry me off the plane on a stretcher in London, stiff as a board. It was agony."

"Forgive me for laughing."

"No, you're right. It's ridiculous. I hadn't wanted to tell Caroline, she was so keen to go to Europe. I thought I could overcome it with force of will."

"How did you get home?"

"*QE2.*"

"But you told me when we met you can't go on boats."

"Good memory. It was the biggest boat we could find, and I was on heavy drugs the whole way. I wasn't very good company. And now I go no more a-roving."

*   *   *

"Come in, it's open," Hope called in what Maggie thought was a slightly strangled tone, when she knocked on the door of Hope's room back at the Manor House Inn.

Maggie pushed the door open and found Hope upside down, doing a headstand against the wall of her sitting room. Hope had taken the corner suite, not very grand but the best the hotel had to offer, because her investments had done well, and her accountant had told her that she should travel first class, or her children would.

"I'm impressed," said Maggie.

"I'm very glad to see you, I forgot I don't know how to get down without my yoga teacher holding my legs. Come help, would you?"

When Hope had gotten right side up again, which she managed with surprising grace for an old bag, Maggie asked, "How was breakfast?"

"Loved it. She's not a beauty, Caroline, but all wool and a yard wide, as my father used to say."

"What a great expression. Meaning?"

"The real goods and exactly what she claims to be. She reassures me that I made the right call about her brother, much as she loves him. He bores everyone cross-eyed. What have you been up to?"

Maggie told her about her chance meeting with Hugo and Lyndon.

"Hmmm," said Hope. "Hugo's a funny one."

"What do you mean?"

"I don't know what I mean. I just don't quite see Caroline as his type. But she seems very amused and happy, and he's devoted to Lily. I'm just going to get dressed. What should we do today?"

"I was thinking we should have another talk with Greta Scheinerlein. Whoever dumped Florence's body in the pool knew how to get into the gym. Let's find out how."

Maggie was pleased to see that school seemed to be humming along with an appearance of normalcy as she and Hope entered the administration building. Groundskeepers were mowing the lawns, loosing the shimmering green smell of spring grass into the warm air. Classroom windows were open. Flowering pear trees along Main Street looked as if their branches were full of warm snow. Somewhere down the slope, someone was whistling.

"Good morning, Mrs. D," said Sharon. "Are you here for Christina?"

"No, I'll see her this afternoon. We wondered where we might find Ms. Scheinerlein at this hour."

Sharon reached for the phone. After four or five rings, she said, "She's not in her office. Let's see, it's Monday," she said, pulling up a spreadsheet on her screen. "Unless she has private coaching sessions that aren't on my schedule, she's probably down in the faculty room, or at home."

"We'll check downstairs. If that fails, could you tell us where she lives?"

"Right up Woodland Road there," said Sharon. "She shares an apartment with Honey Marcus above the stable."

"I know how to get there. Thank you."

On the way downstairs, Hope said, "Does that surprise you? Have you met Honey Marcus?"

"Yes and no. I'll tell you later."

The faculty room was empty except for Pam the housemother attempting to photocopy that day's crossword puzzle on the room's ancient copy machine.

"I see you're performing your public service," said Maggie.

"Oh, hello. Yes. Except this thing jams every three pages. Not that I bother with the Monday puzzle, but there are those who love it."

"*I* love it," said Hope. "I like challenges I know aren't going to defeat me."

Pam gave her a look. "Well I see the point of that," she said. "Soothing at bedtime."

Maggie introduced them to each other.

"We were looking for Greta Scheinerlein."

"Coffee?" said Pam.

"Love some," said Hope just as Maggie had been about to decline. Hope, much more than Maggie, believed that the interesting things in life arose in the interstices between plans and appointments.

Pam poured three mugs and offered milk and sugar, and they settled into chairs. Down the hall, someone was attempting Mozart's piano variations on the tune we know as "Twinkle Twinkle Little Star."

Maggie asked, "Are music lessons given in this building?" She knew that there was a dedicated music building for lessons and practice on the other side of campus. It had once been the cottage of the founder's kennel man, however, and was not very grand, or very convenient.

"No," said Pam. "That's the spinet in the staff dining room. The chef plays for relaxation. She doesn't usually need relaxation so early in the week, though."

"I guess the stress has gotten to everyone."

"Yep. There was way too much salt in the oatmeal this morning. Always a bad sign. And we're supposed to have Field Day on Wednesday, but now no one knows if we will, how would it look with poor Florence still lying in a drawer in a morgue somewhere? Field Day is a secret, by the way. The girls aren't supposed to know when it's coming until it's announced the morning of. Girls are supposed to enjoy surprises. I think they'd rather know what's going on, myself, but that's why I don't run the school. Or anything else. Apparently."

"Does Field Day mean the kitchen has to turn out box lunches instead of the normal meal in the dining room?"

"Exactly." The piano down the hall abruptly fell silent. Pam asked, "What do you want with Greta Scheinerlein?"

"Tell us about her," said Hope.

"I don't know much," said Pam. "She was one of Christina Liggett's first hires. She and Honey Marcus came here together. They're both Olympians, I know that. Honey medaled in dressage. *Medaled.* Is that a verb?"

"It is now," said Maggie, who rather enjoyed the language of sportscasters. She'd been collecting neologisms since a moment long ago when she heard Howard Cosell, broadcasting a boxing match, announce that the judges were total-upping the scores.

"Christina saw that if we were going to have that pool, we needed a first-class coach," said Pam. "On the salaries here that wasn't easy to find, but Greta and Honey were looking for a place where they could both teach. It was some kind of package deal."

"Interesting. When?"

"Three years ago? I think that's right. Old Mr. Cadbury, the last head, was carted off after the evaluation disaster five years ago. Then we had an interim head, who did nothing, then we got Christina. I feel like one of those Apache historians who remember the tribe's history by memorizing famous battles and terrible winters."

"What a gorgeous building," said Hope as they approached the horse barn. "I love that Richardson Romanesque."

"I'm told the horses prefer it as well," said Maggie. They stepped into the warm loamy half-light of the interior. The same training jump Maggie had seen before was set up in the middle of the vast dirt floor. Light filtered down from dusty windows high above them in the haylofts, and beamed through a huge circular window above the wide door. Far down the row stood a large garden cart, into which someone was pitching mucky straw from inside a box stall.

"Hello!" Maggie called.

A figure in jeans and a T-shirt appeared from the stall. Small and wiry, with lean, well-defined muscles in her bare arms. Honey Marcus. She was holding a pitchfork. Her auburn hair was tied back with a blue bandanna.

She waited for them to approach her; no need to point out that they had interrupted her work.

"We met the other day," said Maggie. "This is Hope Babbin."

Honey took off her work glove and shook hands with each in turn, her expression impassive. Her eyes were large and hazel with yellowish flecks, most unusual, Maggie noted. "We were hoping to talk with Greta."

"That looks like great exercise," Hope said, pointing at the pitchfork.

"You think?" said Honey wryly, and handed Hope the pitchfork. Hope, wearing a starched white blouse, a linen skirt, and a pair of pale blue espadrilles, went immediately into the stall and dug the long tines into the straw. She came up with a forkful of stall bedding and horse apples, pivoted gingerly, and managed to shake her load into the waiting garden barrow without losing any of it on the floor. Proudly returning the pitchfork to Honey, she said, "My goodness, that's wonderful! I feel it all down my spine. May I come back after lunch and help when I'm dressed for it?"

Honey said, "Lady—be my guest." She added, "Greta's up in the apartment. Go out that back door and you'll see the stairs."

"You never cease to amaze me," Maggie said as they climbed the outside staircase to the apartment above the tack rooms.

"Well doesn't it make more sense to do something useful than spend an hour on the StairMaster?"

"It does, indeed."

"Especially since we don't have a StairMaster here."

There was no doorbell, so Maggie knocked. Then she knocked again. Before the door opened, they heard the sound of heavy locking braces being shifted on the other side of the door, followed by a second smaller bolt being turned. Greta opened the door to them in a bathrobe with a towel wrapped around her head. She looked surprised.

"I'm sorry, is this a bad time?"

"No, it's . . . Just give me a minute, would you? Come in. Sorry about the mess. Sorry. I'll be right out." She showed them into the small untidy sitting room, which was dominated by a massive and very out-of-date television set. There was a heap of back issues of *The Chronicle of the Horse* in a basket beside one tattered armchair, and a spaniel-mix taffy-colored dog asleep in the other. Dog hair was everywhere, and by the look of the stuffing coming out of the shredded fabric on the arms of the chair, there was at least one cat here somewhere too.

Maggie sat down on something she thought was called a davenport and studied the room. Hope was on her feet examining the framed pictures on the shelves. There were snapshots of Greta with a boy who must be her brother on a beach as teenagers, in a tin washtub on a lawn as small children, and with an older couple and Greta in cap and gown, a high school graduation.

On the far side of the television was the Honey wall. A newspaper photograph of Honey in top hat, tails, and white breeches, with a huge smile and a medal around her neck. Many pictures of Honey on horseback, her mount in some balletic pose with leg flexed, neck arched. Sometimes Honey was in full regalia but often just in jeans and jodhpur boots and a hoodie. Testament to the hours and hours of practice that went into her sport. There was one snap of Honey and Greta together, sunburned and smiling with the Golden Gate Bridge behind them.

Greta returned, wearing khakis and a work shirt, her wet hair slicked back to keep it out of her eyes. Her feet were bare, and her toenails were painted a metallic color of blue-black that made it look as if she'd slammed her toes in a car door.

"Can I get you something? Tea, coffee, water?"

"No, thank you," Maggie said before Hope could ask for a mint julep or toasted scones, or anything that would take Greta away to the kitchen again. "We just wanted to see how you are. That was an ugly thing you went through."

"Kind of you." Greta scooped the dog off its chair and sat down. "I'm all right. I haven't been sleeping very well, but it's getting better."

"And Steph? Is she holding her own?"

"Seems to be. Both Steph and Lily are back in the pool. Kids surprise you, they can bounce like rubber."

"Particularly athletes," said Maggie. "The grit it takes to excel serves them well in life, I've noticed."

Greta gave a quick smile that flashed and disappeared. Her face in repose was handsome, but seemed troubled. Sad, or anxious, unless it was just the way her features were arranged; it was hard to tell which.

"You're sure I can't get you anything?"

"I'd love some tea," said Hope. "But stay here, I'll get it." Greta half-rose to protest, but then subsided. Hope was already in the kitchen, banging around, and how hard could it be to heat some water and find the tea bags?

Maggie said, "I noticed that when you described your thoughts when you first heard Lily scream, that you thought she might have hurt herself diving."

"I don't remember saying that. But it sounds right."

"Even though she wasn't allowed in the water when no one else was with her."

"Yes."

"She's given to risky behavior? Lily Hollister?"

Greta hesitated. Then she said, "You know kids. They don't think anything bad can happen to them."

"I do know. Menaces to themselves, all of them. But Lily, more than most?"

"Well," Greta conceded, "yes, more than most. She wants to practice when she needs to rest, and to try things she's not ready for. She's driven."

"By what?"

Greta ran a hand through her drying hair and tousled it. Her eyes flicked to a corner of the room. Remembering something, or briefly dissociating, Maggie thought.

"Lily has found the thing she's good at. She's had years of being the pretty little rich girl who couldn't read. Now she's Lily the athlete and she's going to show them."

"Who?"

"Them. Us. Everybody."

"Ah," said Maggie. "And you, you coach both swimming and diving?"

"Yes, I was a diver first. But when my dad realized I had a shot at being competitive, he made me specialize. My build was better for the butterfly, so."

"You and Honey are both Olympic athletes, I'm told."

"We met at the summer games in Beijing."

"And you've been together ever since?"

"Not always together-together. A few months after Beijing, I ripped up a shoulder, diving when I wasn't warmed up. Showing off, really. Stupid. During rehab, I decided it was time to grow up. I'd been swimming six hours a day since I was nine."

Hope came in with a teapot and three mismatched mugs on a tray.

"I'm making Greta tell me her life story," said Maggie.

"Excellent. How far have we gotten?"

"I was just saying that I turned pro in 2008. I took a teaching degree back home in Minnesota. Then I coached in Minneapolis for a couple of years."

"And where was Honey?"

Greta shot a look toward the door. Probably didn't even realize she'd done it. She said, "Honey doesn't like anyone speaking for her."

"Fair enough," said Maggie. "Let's talk about the pool. How many people have keys to the building?"

Greta pondered the question. "The maintenance crew, of course. The front office. Me. Security. I told the detectives this."

"I know. Do you mind telling us again?"

"I guess not. I mean—no. I don't mind."

"Who provides security?"

"That's a fancy name for not much. Ray Meagher during the day. At night, or when he's not here, his buddies on the auxiliary police keep an eye on things, but I don't think they have keys. There used to be a night watchman but I guess it was a budget item they thought they could cut. It's such a quiet town."

Maggie and Hope were careful not to look at each other. Or at the massive lock on the apartment door.

"Where do you keep your keys, Greta?"

"When I'm in the building, they're on a hook in my office. When I'm here, they're in a drawer in the kitchen."

"In other words, they are basically wherever you are."

"Yes."

"Do you ever lend them?"

"Yes, sometimes. No one ever told me not to. Some evenings

when there's nothing else on the schedule, faculty families or school staff will use the pool. If I know them, I leave them to lock up, and they bring the keys back to me when they're done."

"Have you ever lost your keys?"

Greta bristled slightly, a little defensive. "No. I thought I had once, but I'd just dropped them on the floor." Maggie was looking at her steadily. Maggie had a way of gazing without blinking that most people found unnerving. Greta added, "One afternoon when I went to lock up, the keys weren't on the hook in my office. I went up and borrowed the office keys, but when I got back, of course there they were, on the floor. They'd slipped off the hook and some-how I'd missed them. Dumb." She looked at her watch. "Look, I'm sorry but I have to take a lunch table down at school today. If I can be any help, another time . . ."

Hope and Maggie rose to go. "Oh, I meant to say," said Maggie, "that's some pretty impressive hardware on the door. Is it a Fox Lock?"

Greta looked at the door, where a second dead bolt and massive double-brace affair spanned from doorframe to doorframe in addi-tion to the standard double cylinder lock set into the door.

"A new brand, but yes. Basically."

"Show me how it works," said Hope. Greta demonstrated. A knob in the center of the mechanism was pulled toward you, then turned to rotate the braces outward into steel brackets bolted onto the doorframes, barring the door with steel beams from frame to frame. A key in the center of the lock on the other side of the door could turn the whole arrangement from the outside.

"Was this here when you got here?"

"No. We put it in a couple of months ago."

The three women stepped outside together. "Can I try it?" Hope asked.

"Sure," said Greta, after a beat. She handed her key ring to Hope. "The one with the blue marker." Hope locked the door and handed the keys back, remarking with surprise that it worked so smoothly.

Greta left them. On the walk back down the hill, Maggie said, "Well, Auntie Mame, are you really going to go back to muck out stalls?"

"I can't wait," said Hope. "Do you think Greta is afraid of Honey?"

"I wouldn't be surprised if Honey had a temper; in fact I think I've seen it in action. But somebody in that household is afraid of *something*. I haven't seen locks like that since Southeast Washington in the 1970s. What did you find in the kitchen?"

"*Lots* of vitamins and protein powder. The only kitchen appliance is a blender the size of an outboard motor. It looks like they live on smoothies and power bars."

"Or else they make a killer margarita."

"Thought of that, but I couldn't find any tequila."

Hope had to nip into the village to buy a pair of suitable boots for the barn, but she presented herself, stylishly turned out, at the stable at two o'clock. A sullen rain had begun to fall, and Honey had two students who'd balked at working in the outdoor ring, tacking their horses for an indoor class. The garden cart was where Hope had last seen it with the pitchfork still leaning against it. If Honey was at all surprised that Hope was as good as her word, all she said was, "Got work gloves?"

Hope pulled out the soft gloves she'd bought at the hardware store in spite of the fact that brown was not her color. Honey gestured toward the cart and pitchfork, then turned back to the girl whose horse was cross-tied in the grooming area.

"Linda—start at his knee and run your hand down to the fetlock. He'll give you his hoof. Good. Be careful with the pick, don't hit the quick." The girls curried and brushed the horses while Honey brought them their tack, and Hope bent and forked, spun and carried, until her stall was clean. She was just about to ask what to do next when an enormous thud right behind her made her jump. She looked up to see that Honey, in the hayloft above her, had just tossed a bale of straw down to the stable floor. "Bombs away," she called as she threw down a second one. This seemed to startle the horses not a whit, although Hope could see that you could break a person's neck or maybe a horse's back if you hit him. Had she thrown the first one without warning on purpose? Testing Hope's nerve, or just acting out of habit?

Honey slipped swiftly down the ladder affixed to the stable wall and came with her wire cutters to unbind the nearest bale so that Hope could fork off slabs of clean horse bedding and scatter it in the stall. Hope finished the first stall and moved on to the next as the girls warmed up their horses. Eventually they worked up to a slow canter and practiced changing leads while Honey stood in the middle of the ring and called corrections. With her back and arms aching, Hope thought it was as pleasant an hour as she'd spent since she left home, absent the falling straw bales.

Near the end of the hour, as the girls were cooling their horses and the rain pelted against the slate roof high above them, Honey came to join Hope, who was finishing a stall and actually dripping with sweat.

"How was that?" Honey asked.

"Heaven," said Hope. "I'm so tired I feel as if I've been beaten up."

Honey smiled. "You know your way around horses?"

"Just enough to know that those flying lead changes are no easy tricks."

"They're coming along well, those two. Helps to have good horses, of course. Thanks for the work."

"You're welcome. You wouldn't have a beer upstairs, would you?" Hope asked, knowing there was a six-pack of Sam Adams in the fridge.

"Happen I do," said Honey. "Is that your price?"

"Yes, I'm nonunion."

Honey said good-bye to her girls and led the way upstairs. She unlocked the door with a key from a ring she kept clipped to a belt loop, the keys tucked into a hip pocket. Inside, she produced and opened a beer bottle for Hope, and handed it to her without a glass. She herself drank half a bottle of smartwater standing up, and put the rest back in the refrigerator. She leaned against the counter, her muscles loose, looking as if she were trying to figure Hope out.

"You know, if you could open a chain of stables as exercise studios in New York City you'd make a fortune," said Hope.

Honey snorted. "That sounds like a great business plan."

"Did you grow up with horses?"

"I did. Maryland. My father took care of other people's horses to finance his habit; he rode steeplechasers. My brother still does."

"I went to the Maryland Hunt Cup once."

"So you know," said Honey.

"The horse I bet on fell and broke his leg. They put him down right there on the course. I never went again."

"That's why I went into dressage."

"Expensive sport."

Honey laughed bitterly. "Tell me about it. Most of my competition had three or four horses, I had one. I bought him as a colt and trained him myself. He was a genius. I called him Baryshnikov."

"I don't like the past tense."

"Oh he's fine, he's still in the game. But London was as far as I was going to go, without a rich backer. I sold him so we could buy this place."

Hope startled. "*Buy* it?"

"Yes, a really talented dressage horse goes for a lot, and the sport is growing. There's less and less open land for fox hunting or point-to-point. If you want to ride seriously and you can't go cross-country, you do dressage."

"That's not what I meant. I was surprised that the school doesn't own this. This building, do you mean?"

"I own the building and about an acre around it. They needed a swim coach and were thinking about phasing out the stable. I needed a place I could live and teach. The long-range plan is I'll train young horses for competition here and sell them, but I'll also teach at the school as long as they want me to."

"You didn't want to train and teach in Maryland?"

There was a minute pause. "It wouldn't have been as good for us. Nothing there for Greta to do. And other reasons."

"Does your father still own the stable there?"

"He died. Broke his neck in a fall."

"I'm sorry."

"It's exactly how he'd have wanted to go. Maybe not quite as young as he did, but— He left the stable to my brother and me, and my brother bought me out. That's how I could afford Baryshnikov in the first place."

"Do you have horses in training now?"

"I do. The pretty chestnut mare in the first stall on the left as you come in. She's still flighty but I think she's going to turn out." Honey checked the time on her phone, and Hope took the hint.

"I won't keep you. Thanks for the workout."

"Any time," said Honey, though Hope couldn't exactly tell if she meant it or not.

*   *   *

Alison Casey had a roommate, but they hated each other. Alison was from an extremely rich Connecticut suburb and the roommate was from small-town Texas, and forget what you heard, folks, those are *not* in the same country. Willie Nelson records? Oh please. Her parents probably went line dancing on Saturday night. Her mother probably served dinner wearing an apron. Alison's parents had a cook.

The roommate's name was Pinky. Hee-haw! Stinky Pinky. Alison had thought she'd be with her two roommates from last year, Becky and Jill, who had shared the coolest three-room in Sloane II with her, but just at the last minute, when it was too late for Alison to find someone else, Becky and Jill told her they'd made a plan with another girl and she was out. So the school stuck Alison with Stinky Pinky, who was new this year. Nobody came new in junior year.

Stinky Pinky rode western style. She was a 4H-er. She had a Justin Bieber poster. Alison's dad did NetJets, so Alison almost never flew commercial. Pinky didn't even know what Alison meant when she said NetJets; she thought it was a sports team. Pinky didn't fly commercial either; Pinky had come from Texas by bus.

EEeew. So, Alison didn't have a cohort in Sloane this year. In fact, since the thing last spring, she was just as happy to keep to herself. Her parents would fix it. Meanwhile, Ellie Curtin wasn't really that pathetic. The cool kids didn't normally hang with the day students, but Ellie's mother worked, so they had her house to themselves in the afternoons. Ellie's mom wanted to teach Alison to knit, which was *not* happening, but she made them penuche fudge, which Alison was totally going to get their cook to make at home, and they could smoke in Ellie's backyard, or in the basement when it was cold. They took an electric fan down there and opened the little dirt-level window high up in the basement wall, and by the time Ellie's mom got home, the smell was gone, or gone enough that Ellie could say they'd been toasting marshmallows over the stove burners and Mrs. Curtin believed her.

Before Alison came into Ellie's life, Ellie's best friend was Gussie Spoonmaker, who also lived in the village and also transferred to the Manor when Ellie did. Gussie really *was* pathetic; she didn't seem even to have hit puberty, and she was, like, sixteen! In the beginning she used to show up at Ellie's house when Alison was there, wanting to study with them or watch the Apple TV, but Alison put a stop to that.

Alison's Christmas present to Ellie had been a pair of gold studs for pierced ears. Eighteen karat gold, from Alison's mom's favorite jeweler in Greenwich. They were practically the cheapest thing in the store and cheap they were not. Alison had bought them when she was home for her suspension. A week before Christmas vacation, when they were at Ellie's house supposedly working on their Modern European History papers, Alison produced the package, wrapped in shimmering green paper that looked like taffeta, and said, "This is half your Christmas present."

Ellie was moved practically to tears, but not entirely because she was at the same time horrified that she had nothing for Alison. She hadn't even thought of getting something for Alison. She had almost no pocket money, and what she had she'd been saving to get her mother a faux fur hat she knew she wanted because her head got cold now that she had the butch Peter Pan haircut. She and her mother always only did Christmas presents for each other.

When Ellie unwrapped the little box, which *looked* like a fancy jeweler's box, and then saw what was inside, she really did almost weep. They were exactly, but *exactly,* what she had wanted. And thought she would have to wait years for, and then get fake gold ones with silver posts, because she knew the posts had to be real or you'd get infected but she didn't expect real gold ever. She was so undone at Alison's generosity, as her eyes teared and her nose started to run, that instead of saying "but I don't have anything for you," she said, "but my ears aren't even pierced." Which Alison very well knew.

"I said it was half your present," Alison said, with her trademark cackle.

"Oh! . . ." Ellie's mind darted, trying to guess what that meant, as she searched her pockets for a tissue. Was Alison going to take her to New York to a piercing place? When? How?

"*We* are going to pierce your ears! Right now!" Alison produced a cork with a long needle stuck into it, and a bottle of rubbing alcohol.

Ellie didn't know whether to cry "Oh thank you," or just to cry. She hated pain, and it was hard to believe a sixteen-year-old would really know what she was doing, making a hole in a body part, and she'd promised her mother she wouldn't. On the other hand, she knew instinctively that saying no to this would be to fail a very important test and it wasn't a very important body part, healthwise, and she had been like literally dying to have pierced ears.

"You know how to do that?" she finally said weakly, thinking suddenly, also, of how angry her mother would be.

"Of course," Alison said, as if to say "doesn't everybody?" In fact, she had had her own ears pierced by their family doctor and it didn't seem to be a big deal, and she had read about it on the Internet. "Don't worry. You don't really have many nerve endings in your earlobes. We need some ice."

First, they went to Ellie's mother's bathroom and decided where on the earlobes the holes should go.

"Not too low, or when you get older your earlobes will stretch like Mrs. Moldower's and you'll have Ubangi ears. You want to be able to support those great big rocks your husbands will shower you with," and Alison cackled. Avaricious dreams of marrying astoundingly rich men was one of their fantasies that Alison at least maybe wasn't kidding about.

Alison marked Ellie's ears with a red felt-tip pen after a lot of elaborate measuring to make sure the ears would match. Then she got a bowl of ice from downstairs and gave Ellie an ice cube to hold against her ear to numb it. When the cold of the ice was hurting more than Ellie feared the needle would, Alison dried the ear, put the cork behind it with her left hand, and with her right, tried to push the needle through what she'd expected would be a mere veil of yielding flesh, like firm butter.

It turns out there is cartilage in earlobes. Or can be. After a pause in which Alison ran down to the kitchen for a rubber glove with which to keep her fingers from sliding down the resisting needle, she succeeded in ramming the point through the lobe to lodge in the cork. So apprehensive was Ellie by now about the detergent smell of the gloves and worried images of where those gloves had been lately, that she agreed with a flood of relief that the pain hadn't been as she had feared. Alison mopped the lobe front and back with alcohol, then drove the post through the angry little hole she had just made. This stung like blazes and when Ellie asked, frightened, if she was bleeding, Alison said, "Not much," but sounded as if this weren't the whole truth.

But when she let Ellie look in the mirror, there she was with an only slightly red-looking ear, and a gleaming ball of fine yellow gold right in the middle of the lobe. Alison stood behind Ellie and winked at her in the mirror.

Ellie was cool. Ellie was bad. Ellie was totally in. Alison handed her another piece of ice and they went at it again

When she arrived at prayers the next morning, instantly the center of whispered fuss, Ellie didn't know which was better, saying "No, it really didn't hurt much" or "Alison gave them to me for Christmas, aren't they pretty?" or "Oh, Alison did it. No biggie."

Of course, the business with her mother was a good deal less gratifying. Kate Curtin had stared when she got home from the Wooly Bear and encountered Ellie in the kitchen, a sullen surprised anger settling into her expression behind the cat's-eye glasses. Mrs. Curtin didn't fight with her daughter. She didn't feel she could afford to. Nor, really, did she need to. A long cold stare said more to Ellie than any flood of words could have, and hit deeper, since it couldn't be contradicted. It was a bad moment for both of them.

"I thought we said when you were eighteen," Kate said finally.

"They're a Christmas present," said Ellie, knowing that it didn't sound like much of an excuse.

"From Alison Casey?"

Ellie nodded. Her mother looked at her steadily for another long minute, then turned and wordlessly began unpacking groceries. The quickness of her movements expressed how hurt and disappointed she was, but she never said another word about it.

And when school had resumed after the New Year, and Gussie Spoonmaker appeared in class with cheap gilt hoops in her ears and one swollen lobe bright red and badly infected, Alison Casey was beside herself with amusement.

*　　*　　*

Sloane House was not a house, as some of the student residences once had been, but a brick dormitory built in a vaguely Georgian style in the early years of the last century. In plan it was shaped like a long shoe box with a corridor running down the middle, like an alimentary canal through a body, with student rooms aligned along both sides. There were two of these residential corridors stacked one on top of the other, known as Sloane I and II. The ground fell away from the back of the building where the campus sloped down toward the weeping birches and the sports fields, so that the classrooms in the basement of Sloane House, though institutional, were light and bright, or at least had windows, except the two rooms immediately beneath the front door, which were used for storage.

Maggie Detweiler was accustomed to architecture that made use of hillsides, and was charmed by it, since the town she'd grown up in was dug into the steep bank of the Ohio River northwest of Pittsburgh. When she was young the steel mills along the river had belched flames and smoke of gray black, red and yellow, very beautiful against the evening sky, however poisonous. It pleased Maggie to know that Charles Dickens had described the area as looking like Hell with the top taken off.

The air in her hometown had been cleaned up and the plants were mostly closed now. Every civic benefit seems to bring with it necessary evil. Maggie thought of that as she walked silently down the long institutional corridor of this quiet dorm high on quite another riverbank in midafternoon. Most of the bedroom doors were closed. Within, girls might have been typing on soundless keyboards, or listening to music in their earphones, but no noise seeping from beneath the doors gave such occupations away. Most students were out at sports, or in the library, or down in the village on afternoon passes.

When the dorm was built the bedroom doors had been fitted with slots for the inmates' calling cards, but young ladies no longer paid that kind of call or possessed such cards and most were too young for business cards. Though not all. One door sported a card printed in turquoise that identified the owner as the publisher of a webzine called NotYourDoormat, with Internet addresses and a cell phone number. Most of the doors bore signs created by the girls, with their names written in imaginative scripts and adorned with stars and rainbows. One added the title Bardolatrix. A sign on another door identified the inhabitants by way of speech balloons in a four-panel comic strip, skillfully drawn in the style of Alison Bechdel.

At the end of the corridor and past the fire stairs, a central door in style more like the front door of a house than the bedroom doors of the girls' rooms announced the apartment of the "dorm parent." Maggie tapped on the door, and a voice called, "Come in, it's open."

The door gave into a living room or parlor, square and bright with large windows looking toward the sports fields and the river, amply equipped with cozy sofas and chairs to accommodate gatherings large or small. Pam Moldower was in the galley kitchen that was tucked into one corner of her domain. A door on the other side led, Maggie guessed, to the bedroom. Pam appeared from the kitchen with a tray carrying cookies on a plate and a pitcher of iced tea.

"Sit ye down." She gestured with her head toward the sofa with the coffee table in front of it. "Welcome to my little all."

"Thank you. You've made this really very homey."

"Since it *is* my home," said Pamela. "Did your school give you housing, or did you have your own apartment?"

"The latter," said Maggie.

"Well, you played that card right. Are you okay in that chair?"

"I'm fine for now, but I may need to be hauled back out of it. How long have you been here?"

"Eight years. The school provides furniture if you want it but I brought my own. For a while, after the explosion, I kept a houseful of stuff in storage too but—what's the point? I sold it all last year. Didn't even go back to empty drawers or check for change under the seat cushions. And with my luck, there was probably a fortune in stocks or diamonds in there somewhere. But what the hell. It's a relief to stop pretending, to myself if nobody else, that this is temporary."

"Do you mean literally an explosion?"

"Oh thank god," said Pam. "Someone who literally knows the meaning of literally. No, no actual boom. Or I wouldn't even have the couch you're sitting on." She took a cookie and ate it.

"What happened? Do you mind talking about it?"

There was a silence. "No, I have to talk about it every once in a while," Pam said at last. But she didn't begin.

"You were a student here."

"I was a student here during the last ice age. I grew up in a country club suburb of Pittsburgh. Sweetwater. Do you know it?"

"I do," said Maggie.

This might have led to surprise, or a diversion into discovering what they had in common, but in this case, did not. "The public high school wasn't very good," Pam said, in all likelihood referring to the very high school Maggie had attended, "so everyone went away to school after eighth grade. My mother wanted me to go to Miss Pratt's but I didn't want to work that hard. My father thought I'd meet a better class of girl here. He was probably right. They had to press hard to keep up with the Joneses, my parents, so it was important to him." She gave a laugh. "Oddly enough, I never seem to be able to be here when my fancy classmates come back for reunions. Winding up here, doing this, really *was* our idea of the worst thing that could happen to us. We thought we'd all—well, never mind. My classmates aren't all world beaters either and they wouldn't be unkind, I just don't want to have that conversation." After another pause for thought, she went on. "I had way too much fun while I was here," Pam said, choosing a new tack away from the shoals she'd been heading for. "We broke a lot of rules with a lot of Yalies who weren't much more studious than we were. I was pregnant at my own deb party."

"That must have been complicated."

"It was and it wasn't. My parents never knew. My brother was furious. I got an illegal abortion in Puerto Rico and went on to some preppy junior college that doesn't exist anymore. Oh, stop me," she said, picking up the pitcher of iced tea and pouring more into Maggie's glass. "I didn't invite you to tea to bore you blind."

"If you hadn't invited me, I'd have asked to come. I'm interested."

"People who live alone talk too much," said Pam. "Which is not a good idea in a small community."

"But you don't live alone," said Maggie. "You have adolescent life boiling in and out of here."

"That's true." She repeated it, thinking some private thought. "That is true. But it's not like having real friends. Or family. Unless I'm everyone's least favorite aunt." Pam picked up the plate of cookies and thrust it toward Maggie, who took one.

"Do you still have family in Sweetwater?" Maggie asked.

"The brother. We had a falling-out when I got married. He called my fiancé an asshole at the rehearsal dinner, and I took it badly."

"I don't wonder."

"The thing is, he wasn't an asshole. My husband. He was a crook, but that's different."

"A crook? Really?"

"Amazing, isn't it? We know there are a lot of them in the world. Stands to reason they get married to somebody. You don't expect it to be you, though. This isn't a story I ever tell people."

"Maybe you should. Might save someone else some trouble."

Pam said, "I'm done trying to save other people trouble."

There was a silence, into which they could now hear distant noises of girls clattering down the hall outside the door, laughing, yammering, calling to each other. Neither woman needed a clock to know it was the interval between sports periods.

"How did you get from junior college to marrying a crook?"

Pam said, "Oh, I can't skip lightly over that part? I got a job in New York and shared an apartment in Murray Hill with two other girls. After a while they each got married, and two others took their places, but I went on and on. And it wasn't like I had a career. I had jobs, and help from home. It didn't occur to anyone, least of all me, that I would do anything but get married and join the Junior League and raise two point five perfect children. Then, just when it was getting embarrassing to be unmarried with no prospects, along came the asshole. Pardon me, the crook. He was fun, at first, and handsome enough, and he wanted the job. You know what I think now?"

"What?" said Maggie when she perceived that Pam was really waiting for an answer.

"I think I was out of my mind. I think from the day I got that abortion until the day my daughter was born, I was clinically nuts. People think you get pregnant, it's inconvenient for you, you have an unpleasant half hour on a table somewhere, and get on with your life. That is *not* what happens. I don't care who you are, what kind of a flibbertigibbet, you do not get an illegal abortion and come out without something like PTSD. It's a terrifying thing to go through, on so many levels. I functioned well enough to hold a job and go through the motions, but that's not the same thing as being well. It was *years* before I could speak of it without crying. I was a lot of fun on dates."

Maggie sat quietly, listening.

"So. I married the crook, without somehow noticing what was wrong with him. Our daughter was born, I joined the Junior League. We lived in a nice house, he went to work every day. He did seem to change jobs more than other men we knew, but he always had a story. Finally one day when I was talking about what a hard time my husband had with his current boss, one of my *friends*"—she made air quotes—"told me that my husband didn't have a boss, he had been out of work for eight months. I said 'Don't be silly, he goes to work every day.' She said, 'He gets dressed and leaves the house every day.' I just stared at her. And then I thought, Jesus Christ, how would I know?"

"And was she right?"

"Of course she was right. But I didn't want to know because I had no idea what I would do next if it was true. I didn't admit to myself that I knew until the day he was arrested."

Maggie sensed that any response would be wrong. They sat in silence for a bit. Finally Maggie asked, "How long ago was this?"

Pam waved her hand, as if to minimize the enormity of what had happened. "Long time, now. Fifteen years. More. The rest is my fault. I'd gotten used to being a wife, doing what I did, what all the other rich wives did. It took me much too long to admit to myself that no one was going to rescue me and that I *could* end up a bag lady. Don't we all have that terror, that when you look closely at some creature sitting on a stoop with all her belongings in a shopping cart, that it will turn out to be someone you knew?"

Maggie agreed that she did, and thought of one or two she particularly worried about.

Pam went on, "When my neighbor suggested that living here or at Miss Pratt's or somewhere would be a solution, I was so offended I stopped speaking to her for a year. But—here we are. I'm a value-added housemother, since I dispense cookies and tampons, and present a cautionary tale, all at once."

"Do the girls know what happened to you?"

Pam rolled her eyes. "All they have to do is Google. I don't invite the topic, but believe me, they know."

There was a knock at the door. Pam stood and brushed a crumb from her skirt, saying, "Well, that's enough of that."

The girl in the hall was Steph Ruhlman. She was about to speak when she looked past Mrs. Moldower and saw Maggie.

"What can I do you for?" Pam asked her. "You've met Mrs. Detweiler, haven't you?"

With a nod, Steph agreed that she had.

"Have a cookie," said Pam.

Steph came into the room, and sat down on the edge of a Windsor chair. She accepted a cookie from the plate Pam held out to her. The women waited for her to speak, which she eventually did with the air of one who has rehearsed what she's come to say.

"Someone's posted another awful thing on the message board and there are already six 'up' votes. Lily's crying."

"Another awful thing?" Pam asked. "About Lily?"

"Yes!" said Steph. "And it scares her but she doesn't want her parents to take her out of school again."

"She should tell Ms. Liggett immediately," said Pam impatiently. "Who is doing it?"

"We don't know! Nobody knows, that's the point," said Steph angrily. "I didn't mean to interrupt, but . . ."

"But we can find out. Danny the tech guy can trace the address . . ."

"Is this TickTalk?" Maggie asked the girl.

"Exactly!" cried Steph.

"It's a message board where the posts are anonymous," Maggie said to Pam.

"But—why would that be allowed? An anonymous bullying board?"

"It's not supposed to be available in high schools but it's nearly impossible to wall out," Maggie explained. This fresh hell had been a bane of her existence in her last two years at Windsor. "Steph, what do the messages say?"

Steph showed Maggie her phone. On the screen was an image like a virtual Post-it note, saying *The girl who finds dead bodies gets away with everything. Why?*

Maggie scrolled to the next. *The girl who finds dead bodies hated the art diva. Just sayin'.*

And then to: *Ask the girl who finds dead bodies about her key to the pool.*

"There has to be a way to trace this," Pam snapped, furious.

"There is," said Maggie. "But we'd have to call the police."

"Well, let's do that."

"Hold on. Would you e-mail those screenshots to me, Steph?" Maggie said. She gave Steph an address, and Steph tapped with her thumbs. "The first thing we need to do is make sure Lily is safe. Steph, you're sure she doesn't want her parents notified?"

"Totally," said Steph. "*N-O.*"

Maggie, surprised by the vehemence, waited for more. Steph noticed she had a gingersnap in her hand and began to eat it. Maggie had thought Lily's parents had seemed so nice, but you never knew.

"Steph—is everything all right at home, for Lily?"

"This is good, Mrs. Moldower, did you make these?"

"Steph," said Maggie.

"Fine," said Steph. "You know. Just normal weirdness."

"I don't know," said Maggie, who could see Steph was lying.

"I really have to go. Study hall."

Maggie tried to leap up to match her, eye to eye, but she didn't make it all the way out of the downy fastness of the chair. Pam took her hand and pulled her up. Her grip was surprisingly strong.

"Please don't tell Lily I told," Steph said to Mrs. Moldower.

"Of course not," Pam said.

With a diffident nod, Steph scuttled out the door.

Looking after her, Pam said, "TickTalk? As if kids bullying kids on Facebook wasn't bad enough? What the hell?"

"You have no idea. You squash one of these things and three more pop up."

"Do you really know how to get at this thing without going to the police?"

"No idea. But I may know people who can figure it out. Thank you for tea, Pam. And thank you for telling me your story."

"Thank you for listening."

"And those *are* very good gingersnaps."

"Whole Foods. I haven't baked a cookie since the first Bush administration. That was Florence's bailiwick. Listen, do you think Lily's in some danger? I mean, beyond some opportunist mean girl thing?"

"I'll put it this way," said Maggie. "I am not sure she is *not* in danger."

Pam whistled. "Well. I didn't see *that* coming."

"There was one more thing I was going to ask," Maggie said, pausing at the door.

"Fire away."

"Where is your husband now?"

"Oh *him*. I assume he's in the slammer. He embezzled a shitload of money. But I don't know for a fact. I hope never to hear the son of a bitch's name again."

"Fair enough. And please, keep what Steph told us quiet. I know I don't need to say that."

"Four walls," said Pam.

*　　*　　*

By Monday evening Hope knew that her new stall-mucking exercise routine had resulted in a painfully overworked something or other in her lower back. She had left a message for Maggie that she was skipping dinner, and had taken to her bed with a hot pad and a bottle of gin when Maggie knocked on her door.

"Go away," Hope called. Maggie laughed.

"Are you sure I can't help?" she said through the door. Knowing the inn was virtually empty saved her from being embarrassed to stand shouting in a drafty hallway.

"Not unless you know a good drug dealer," Hope yelled back

from where she lay. In truth, she was feeling a little better and watching an episode of *Foyle's War* on her iPad, but she still didn't want to get up to open the door.

"Text me if you need anything," Maggie yelled, and left her.

Emily George was waiting for Maggie at The Boathouse, a barn of a restaurant and wedding venue down by the river. The view was spectacular, though Mrs. George was sitting with her back to it, frowning and tapping frantically on her phone as Maggie joined her.

"Everything all right?" Maggie asked her employer as she took her seat.

"Yes. Well no. . . . It's just . . . Cleo. My daughter." Emily looked frustrated and put her phone away.

"She's a junior, isn't she?"

"Yes. She needs to shine this semester, but the girls are all over-excited, believing crazy things, egging each other on."

"What dorm is she in?"

"Sloane One. She wanted a coed school, to tell the truth, but she's not the strongest student and I thought this environment would help her focus."

"And has it?"

Emily just looked at Maggie over the top of her glasses and gave a sigh.

A waiter arrived and they made some decisions about what to eat and drink.

"Anyway," said Emily, changing the subject. "I had a visit from Hugo Hollister. He's upset that the police let Ray Meagher go. Ray's on the auxiliary police here in the village."

"I know that," said Maggie.

"And Hugo thinks that they're treating him as one of their own. The police. Is there anything we can do?"

Maggie thought about breakfast with Bark and Phillips, and the detectives' obvious suspicion of her and Hope. Not that she blamed them, but she didn't think they'd welcome suggestions of that nature from her. "Early days. What are your other concerns?"

"Number your paper from one to twenty," Emily said. "Lyndon McCartney is up to something. I thought it would help our relationship with the town when he joined the board, a local businessman. Plus we always need people who can read a balance sheet. God knows it's not one of *my* long suits. But I think he's spreading rumors that the school is going to close."

"That's a four-alarm fire, if true. What's your procedure for removing trustees?"

"I have no idea."

"But they all sign pledges against self-dealing?"

"Yes."

Maggie looked relieved and made a note. "Good. What else?"

"I'm told that several girls we don't want to lose are looking at other schools."

"You've had requests for transcripts?"

"We have."

Maggie knew that given the state of the budget there weren't *any* girls that they wanted to lose, but that wasn't the real danger. You could get a cascading loss of confidence if a critical mass started transferring, and critical mass didn't have to be all that big.

"Florence's funeral is going to make a difference," Maggie said. "She loved the school and wanted it to succeed. Christina will make it a teaching moment."

"Will she?" Emily George asked doubtfully. The woman looked to Maggie as if her stomach lining was dissolving as they spoke.

"She will. She's a good hire, she just needs a little breathing room." Maggie hoped she wasn't lying. Fortunately the waiter arrived with their drinks, and they could take a moment to raise a glass to each other. Or to happier days. Or to something.

After this brief moment of relief, Maggie said, "I'm afraid there's something else." She explained about the TickTalk situation.

Emily said, "Not *again*."

"A culture of bullying really can be fatal to a school, but so far it's a worrying outbreak, not a pandemic." Maggie had once seen a school lose half its fifth grade, when one mean girl dominated an attack clique. So many girls withdrew to escape them that then the clique left too, because there weren't enough girls in the class. The boys stayed but were plenty confused and unhappy.

"What can we do?"

"Plant your flag on your principles, and your history. Persuade the girls themselves to act as antibodies against the virus. Beyond that there may be something *I* can do, but I don't know yet, so stay tuned. I do have some good news. I think I've found you a replacement for Florence Meagher," Maggie said.

Emily looked at her as if she'd just heard the sound of the cavalry's bugle and thundering hooves beyond the rise.

"A master teacher who retired last year because her husband wanted to travel. Three months later he died. She's seeing Christina this afternoon. The girls will love her."

W*hile it was far from the only mess* of pottage on their burners, Detective Bark and Detective Phillips had made some interesting discoveries about the Meagher case. They had known before they sent Ray Meagher home on Saturday that he hadn't been at *Jersey Boys* the night before Florence's body was dumped in the pool. They knew he wasn't registered at the Clinton Hotel, although he was known there; the desk clerk recognized his picture. The hotel knew Guy Thompson as well; he *had* stayed with them Thursday night. By Monday afternoon, Detective Phillips had reached Thompson through his airline. He was in Denver. He said he had called Ray to see if he'd like to get together on that Thursday but Ray told him that he'd be out of town. He and a pal were going somewhere to play the slots, he said. Where? Detective Phillips had asked. Guy Thompson said he had no idea. He himself had ordered takeout and spent Thursday night in his room.

"What's our next move?" Evelyne asked. "We could start calling the casinos within a half day's drive . . ."

"You got an idea how many there are?"

"None."

"Or how many crappy motels there are around them where gamblers stay?"

"No . . ."

"Me either. Let's try the easy way first, go see how hard it is to get Ray Meagher to spoil his own day."

Ray was sitting at his kitchen table Tuesday morning in the mangy sweats he slept in, eating a microwave pizza for breakfast and drinking a lukewarm Coke, when he saw Bark's sedan pull into his driveway. He watched through the kitchen window as Bark and Phillips got out and started for his front door. With the piece of pizza still in his hand, he opened the back door and called angrily, "Do you mind? I haven't even brushed my teeth yet!"

"No, we don't mind," said Bark cheerfully, changing course for the back door. "That your breakfast? Got any coffee?"

They pushed past him into the kitchen, making the little room feel full to overflowing.

"If I had coffee, would I be drinking Coke?" Ray asked rudely.

"I have no idea," Bark said, gazing around with interest.

"Someone left something on your front stoop, looked like a casserole," said Phillips. "You haven't been out?"

"Uh. No, I was going to—this morning."

"You want me to bring it in?"

"I guess."

She went out the front door and was soon back with a Pyrex dish full of macaroni and other less-identifiable matter. There was a note taped to the aluminum foil that covered the top. It said, "Deepest sympathy. Marcia and Jesse. PS, leave the dish outside when you're done. I'll come for it. M."

"Marcia and Jesse," said Phillips. "Would that be Marcia and Jesse Goldsmith?"

"I guess it must," Ray said, ungraciously.

"This looks like it's been rained on. I wonder how long it's been out there," she said, lifting more of the aluminum foil and poking a finger into the casserole.

"Do you *mind?*" said Ray again, looking at the food. He hadn't eaten anything in days that hadn't come from his freezer, and not all of it had been in the best condition.

"I wonder if there's mayonnaise in there," said Bark. "Mayonnaise or cream. Isn't that the stuff that gives you food poisoning if you leave it out of the fridge?"

"Bound to have one or both, from the look of it," said Phillips. "It's thick, and it's white. Up to you, Ray, but I'd throw that right out."

"Is there something I can help you with?" Ray asked, with ill-concealed anger.

"Go on with your breakfast, we already ate. We just have a few questions." Bark sat down in the chair opposite Ray. Phillips squeezed by and opened the refrigerator.

"What is your problem?" Ray suddenly roared. "I'm not running a restaurant here. I don't have to pass inspection, do I?"

Phillips stood with the refrigerator door open, contemplating. She leaned over to open the vegetable drawer, made a face, and closed it again. "You're going to have to empty that and soak it, that does *not* smell good. I hope you have some bleach—"

"Don't you need a warrant or something to come in here and jack me up before I even . . ." He was sliding into bullying mode, something that Phillips had already suspected was habitual with him.

"You invited us in," Bark said pleasantly.

"I did not!"

"I thought he did, didn't you, Phillips?"

"I did not invite you in!"

The detectives looked at each other.

Ray said, "Look, just tell me what you want, then get out of here. It isn't the best of times for me, you know?"

"We do," said Bark.

"We know, it's been a very confusing time for you," said Phillips, straightening and turning to face him. Her tone was suddenly all-business. "Lot of confusion. Yes?"

Ray put down the piece of pizza he'd been holding and said to no one, "Oh, fuck."

Phillips went out and came back with a side chair from the dining table, and sat down beside Ray. The effect was like plugging a bottle's neck. Ray was trapped with his back to the kitchen door and nowhere else to go.

"We talked to your man Thompson," said Bark. "He said he wasn't with you Thursday night."

Ray just sat, stone-faced.

"He was in New York on Thursday, at the Clinton, but not with you."

"He said you were off somewhere, gambling," said Phillips.

There was a silence. What had he thought, that they wouldn't check?

"Is that what happened, Ray?"

"You went someplace to play the slots?"

"All by yourself?"

"Or with a *friend*?" Phillips made the word friend sound like the already failed gambit of a notorious liar.

Silence. Ray fidgeted, and his eyes darted briefly from the ceiling toward the door into the living room.

"Or did you murder your wife, Ray? Is that what happened? You strangled her, maybe on purpose, maybe by mistake, and then you had to take her somewhere, to figure out what to do with the body?"

"Of *course* I didn't murder my wife!" he yelled.

"Why of course? You lied about where you were. You have no alibi. You were known to have fought with her repeatedly—"

"Who told you that?" he snapped.

The detectives both stared at him. They didn't move or blink.

"Who told you that? Those little cunts from the dorm?"

"Language, Ray," said Bark, tipping his head toward his partner.

"Or her sister. That pious *bitch* . . ."

Phillips raised an eyebrow. She was good at that, she could move one eyebrow up to speak a question while the rest of her face stayed still, and the question the eyebrow asked was "Really? Is that the tack you're going to take?"

There was another long silence as Ray stared defiantly and the two detectives waited. Finally Ray said, "I have to go to the bathroom."

Phillips and Bark looked at each other. Finally, Bark twitched a shoulder toward the door, and Phillips went out. There was a half bath behind the kitchen, hardly bigger than a broom closet, with a toilet and a tiny sink, stained and chipped, fitted into the corner because there wasn't room for a full-size one opposite the flush. There was a tiny window high up in the wall; no possibility of escape that way. She checked behind the toilet and took the top off the tank to be sure there was nothing hidden in there that he could use to make trouble for them. She made sure the small smudged mirror was attached flat to the wall, not concealing a cabinet. Then she went back to the kitchen and made a gesture to Ray: be my guest.

Ray stood and made his way past the kitchen table and both detectives followed him. He went down the brief hallway and into the tiny bathroom, where he closed and locked the door. Bark and Phillips stood outside the door. After several minutes, Ray called, "Look, you know I can't go anywhere. Could you please move off?"

Then they heard the taps turned on to muffle whatever noises might be produced during his mission.

The two detectives moved several feet down the hall. Phillips called, "Is that better?"

They got no answer. After several more minutes, the taps were turned off, the door unlocked, and Ray emerged, drying his hands on his sweatpants.

Instead of going back to the kitchen, he went into his den and sat down on the sofa that concealed his porn stash. Phillips and Bark followed him and sat down as well, Phillips in the plaid armchair facing the TV, Bark on an old office desk chair that he rolled out from a corner.

Ray said, in a new man-to-man tone he'd thought through in the bathroom, "Look. I'd been under some pressure, okay? We'd had a couple of rough days. My wife went off in a snit, and I thought I'd give her a dose of her own medicine."

"So you went off in a snit too?"

"I just decided to go off and let her see what that felt like."

"Your wife disappears on a day you know she'd been preparing for, for months, and you weren't worried about her?"

"No! She'd been . . . I mean we'd . . . I mean no, I wasn't worried. I thought she'd gone to her sister's."

"Because this had happened before?"

"Once. Yes. I mean, sort of."

"She disappeared on a school day without telling anyone where she was going?"

"Stop putting words in my mouth! Once before she went off to her sister's and we had a time-out."

"Sounds like *Romper Room*," said Bark.

Ray swung his whole upper body toward Bark, as if he were trying to loom over him, threatening, without getting up.

"What about this pressure you've been under, Ray?" Phillips asked.

"It's business. I have a business deal going down to the wire, and it's a lot. Of pressure."

"What kind of deal?"

"Real estate. We're putting together a package to develop. We have expensive options that will expire if we can't . . ."

He stopped and looked confused, not sure if he should be talking about this. Suddenly he changed course. "Look. I'm bereaved, here. I'm in mourning right now, I lost my wife, do you mind? Why are you sitting here in my house, why aren't you trying to find out what happened to her?"

"Who's this 'we,' Ray?"

"What?"

"'We're putting a package together.' You and who else?"

"My partner, Lyndon McCartney."

"And what is this package?"

"Look, am I under arrest?"

"Not at the moment. Why?"

"Then I don't have to answer your questions and our business is none of your business."

Bark and Phillips looked at each other. Then they each took out a notepad.

"So, you went off in a snit to gamble on Thursday night, is that right?"

"I was *not* in a snit!" Ray yelled, in a snit. "I like to gamble. It relaxes me. It's harmless."

"Really? You win all the time?"

"Not all the time. But enough."

"So why did you tell us you went to the show?"

"My wife is a prude about gambling. That was what I was going to tell her. She'd never have checked. Then when . . . when she died and you were all 'Where were *you* last night,' I just . . . it was what came to mind. It just came out. *Look.* I went to a casino with a friend. I *have* an alibi. I didn't do *anything wrong.* Why the hell are you messing me over, why don't you go talk to that creepy little shit Jesse Goldsmith, for instance? There is a real fucking whack job, for you. He said horrible things to my wife! She was terrified of him!"

After a pause, Bark said, "Jesse Goldsmith who leaves you casseroles?"

Ray made an annoyed gesture. "Marcia Goldsmith is a friend of Floro's. Her creepy son is so weird they had to take him out of school. So of course Florence had to make a pet of him. She *would.*

He even scares *me,* that kid. You know what he did this week? He was up at the pond at the cemetery, blowing up frogs with firecrackers!"

"Really? You saw him blowing up frogs with firecrackers?" Phillips asked.

"Not me, that Detweiler woman did, she came down to the firehouse to try to make us do something about it. Who the hell is *she,* by the way?"

"A kid blowing up little animals? I'd tell somebody if *I* saw that," said Phillips.

"What did you do about it?" Bark asked.

A pause. "Nothing. We're auxiliary, what could we have done?"

"How about tell the boy's mother?" Phillips asked.

And Bark said, "Ray—who did you go to the casino with?"

*   *   *

For anyone but Hope, it would be a misfortune to be stuck in an elevator, especially when feeling fragile after a painful visit to the chiropractor. Lenore, the young slave of all work at the hotel, had recommended a practitioner in the village who had fixed her brother when he had his frozen shoulder. Hope was in the man's treatment room by eight-thirty Tuesday morning.

The practice was in the village's office and medical building, a newish square yellow brick edifice upstream from the movie theater. The chiropractor, pudgy and pink-faced, wearing a white jacket and crepe-soled shoes, was called Dr. Aker. He spoke to her at an uncomfortably high volume, as if anyone with misaligned vertebrae must by definition be hard of hearing, even though she mentioned that she was not. Hope found his technique terrifying, but after forty-five minutes of being prodded and leaned on and given sudden and violent jerks of various body parts, she had to admit that her pain had transformed from piercing to semibearable.

The fourth-floor office had a lovely view of the Hudson, she discovered while giving the receptionist her credit card. She'd been too miserable when she arrived to notice, so she must be better. In the hallway, she deliberated between the elevator and the stairs, deciding in the end that the elevator presented less challenge to her spinal rearrangement, and pushed the button.

A lady was already in the cab when it arrived. Hope nodded to her as she entered, and then mentally returned to her plans for the day, now that she could move without screaming. Hearing about Maggie's visit to Pam the angry housemother was at the top of her list, right up to the moment the elevator gave a lurch and stopped.

Hope and the other woman looked at each other. Her companion was of medium size and age, with shining dark hair pulled back in a ponytail and full unpainted lips. Her dark brown eyes were adorned with stylishly redesigned eyebrows of an alarming severity.

"Tell me you're not claustrophobic," said Hope.

"I'm not," said the other.

"So far so good," said Hope. "What should we do?"

"Push that red button?"

"Let's give it a minute," said Hope, pushing the button marked L just to be sure the elevator knew where it was supposed to go. It apparently knew and didn't care.

"I'm Hope Babbin, by the way."

"Margot McCartney."

"Nice to meet you. Sort of. What do you think, red button?"

"Let's do it." Margot pushed the red button and an alarm began shrilling.

"I can't say that's much of an improvement," said Hope. The alarm rang and rang and nothing else happened. Then it stopped.

"Oh, I feel so much better," said Hope. "What now?"

Margot began pounding on the walls of the cab. Hope joined her and then both added shouts.

"Hello?"

"Hello?"

"Hello, can anybody hear us?" Whap whap whap.

Somewhere far below them, they heard a muffled male voice. He was not inside the elevator shaft, wherever he was, and they could hear only the interrogatory in his voice, not actual words.

"We're between floors! We're stuck! There are two of us!" they cried in overlapping answers, trying to guess what question had been asked. Then they stopped and listened. Far below there was some feckless banging, much like the noise they had made themselves, then the voice called up to them again.

"What did he say?" Hope asked.

"I think I heard 'Fire Department,'" said Margot McCartney. Then there was silence.

After a long moment of stasis, Hope sat down on the floor of the cab. Margot joined her. Hope said, "If you have to use the loo, please don't mention it to me. Not that, or running water, or faucets, or Kegel exercises."

"Gotcha," said Margot.

"Also, please don't make me laugh."

"No," said Margot.

They sat in silence. After what seemed an eon, Hope said, "Well at least the lights are still on. How about rock, paper, scissors?"

Margot stuck out her fist and Hope counted to three. Hope threw scissors, Margot threw rock.

"Damn," said Hope. "Let's keep score."

Margot was down by five points and Hope was at twenty-three when the lights went out.

Hope waited for her eyes to acclimate. They didn't. The darkness was thick and total, like a black hood over your head.

"I close my eyes and open them and it makes no difference," said Margot.

"None," Hope agreed.

They sat listening to each other breathe.

"So," said Hope at last. "Do you come here often?"

Margot let out a bark of laughter.

"Fairly often. You?"

"My first visit. I was at the chiropractor. Dr. Backache."

"I was with my accountant."

"Do you live here?"

"Yes. We've been here for about four years. My husband was with the Trump organization in New York and he decided to go out on his own."

"As what?"

"Developer. Real estate."

"So you moved here from the city? Was that okay with you?"

After a brief pause, Margot said, "I've adjusted. The school district is pretty good, and I'm making friends."

"Are you? How?"

"Oh you know. Parents at my kids' school. That sort of thing. No soul mate yet, but people to have coffee with. What about you?"

"I know just what you mean," said Hope. "I moved to Boston last year to be near my grandchildren, but it's dawning on me, I'm not really the hands-on granny type. My daughter is crazy busy, and I meet people my age, and they're perfectly nice, but they want me to join things. To tell you the truth, I'm here hiding out from my new book group. What do you do with your time? Do you work?"

"I manage my husband's office. Keep the books and so on."

"How did you choose Rye-on-Hudson?"

"A business opportunity. But now a terrible thing has happened to his partner's wife."

Hope felt a prickle on her arms. Or thought she did; she'd been reading a lot of detective fiction and was a fan of the inexplicable intuition.

"You don't mean Florence Meagher?"

"Yes! Do you know her?"

"No, but the friend I'm traveling with met her at the school. Rye Manor."

"My husband is on the board there!"

"Are your children at Rye Manor?" Hope had registered that she'd mentioned the good school district but wanted to know where Margot would take the subject.

"No, we have boys. And we couldn't afford it anyway. But as I said, Lyndon and Ray Meagher have this real estate project, and Lyndon thought joining the board would be good PR in the community."

"This is so interesting. Ray Meagher. He must be devastated, poor man."

"He must be. I haven't seen him since she died, but Lyndon has. Says he's like in a fog. Can't seem to put one foot in front of the other."

"Are they very old friends, Ray and your husband?"

"Not that old. Lyndon's not the kind of man who makes a lot of friends; he leaves our social life to me. Such as it is. But he met Ray in Atlantic City, and somehow, they hit it off, and then Ray had this great idea."

"Atlantic City?"

"Yes, Lyndon was there with the Trump organization, and I guess Ray was a regular."

"Regular gambler?"

"Yes. I don't have the itch myself, but Lyndon enjoys it. He can take it or leave it, don't get me wrong, he doesn't have a problem. But he's under a lot of pressure from business, and it's good for him to blow off steam." She subsided, perhaps noticing that she didn't sound entirely convinced herself.

"You're a very understanding wife," Hope said into the blackness. She wondered if she saw a tiny crack of light between the doors of the elevator, or was that a hallucination, brought on by sensory deprivation.

Margot said, after a thoughtful silence, "Not all that much. We came here because there was an opportunity. Ray said. Complicated, with a lot of moving parts but a really big payday, was the pitch. It's just that it's taken much longer than we expected to put the pieces together and honestly . . . We don't have any cushion. The boys are growing up, they need things. It hasn't been an easy time."

She *did* see light through the crack between the doors. Then a voice from close above them. "Hello?" a man called. His voice was deep, offhand and confident.

"Hello, we're here," both women shouted.

"Took us a while to find out where the car was," said the voice. "Just hold tight. We're going to move it manually and we'll have you right out of there."

Then the lights came back on. Hope and Margot looked at each other and remembered that they were strangers. Except, not, anymore. Margot smiled, suddenly finding the situation silly.

Hope said, "I'm terrified that if I stand up I'm going to soil myself."

"I'm sure you're not," said Margot. The elevator cab began to lurch, and there was a lot of yelling up and down the shaft. Margot grabbed Hope's hand and they braced themselves, hoping they were not about to plummet into the basement. After minutes of jerking, swinging within the shaft, and noise, the doors opened and they were released into the lobby.

Hope finally found Maggie in the Katherine Jones room, after she had changed her clothes and had a club sandwich and restorative pot of Lapsang souchong at their hotel. Maggie had spent the morning with Danny, the school's IT guy, learning all he knew about TickTalk, which wasn't much. There was a block on Wi-Fi access to the site from anywhere on the campus, but you could still get to it easily through a cell tower. And of course Wi-Fi off campus, down in the village, say, was wide open.

For the moment, Hope was more focused on the news that

Lily Hollister didn't want her parents told about her troubles at school. "I'm shocked that Caroline let me think things were ducky at home," said Hope. "Are you sure young Steph wasn't making things up?"

"The TickTalk posts are certainly real. And a sixteen-year-old who doesn't want her parents told something like that is upset about *something* . . ."

Hope felt unsettled. She and Caroline were such old friends. Well, such long-term acquaintances connected by so many cross-threads. Hope after all had told Caroline everything. More or less. Maybe not quite everything about her former husband and his popsy in the marital bedroom, which was too shaming, but.

"Think of it from Caroline's point of view," said Maggie, her thoughts keeping pace with her friend's. "She's had one failed marriage. It would be painful to admit to you she'd made another mistake, if tension in the marriage is the problem."

"I don't see why, I've made enough mistakes myself," said Hope. But Maggie's attention had reverted to the cyber-mean-girl situation.

"How are we going to sort out this TickTalk business without calling the police?"

"Don't you know any hackers?" Hope asked.

"I do, of course. One of my favorite Latin students from years ago developed quite a little sideline at MIT. Now he teaches workshops at Langley called something like 'Coding for Poets.'"

"Why poets?"

"Calling it Hacking for Spies sort of eliminates the element of surprise. But I hate to bother him with this while he's busy defeating ISIS, if he is."

"Do a search on TickTalk, let's see who's behind it," Hope said. "How does it make money?"

Maggie typed and soon said, "Here's a piece from the *Financial Times*. Blah blah blah Bitcoin, no that's not it, blah blah. . . . Oh!"

Hope came around behind her and peered over her shoulder as Maggie read. "Kenneth Liu and Isabelle Marszalak, friends since they met at Wesleyan University, hit on the idea for a digital campus message board. 'We thought there was a need for a place to post anonymously, like you can on a bulletin board in a dorm. Say you want to know if anyone else thought the math quiz was impossible, or if anyone found the sweater you lost. It would be geographically limited, just for communication within a particular community . . .'"

"Tell me one of those kids went to Winthrop."

"That would be handy, wouldn't it? No, but a Rose Liu teaches music at Nightingale-Bamford. We've served on committees together. I'm almost sure that her son's name was Kenneth, and I know he went to Wesleyan, let's just see . . ."

"Why does this not surprise me at all?"

A few taps more brought her to Kenneth Liu's Wikipedia page. "New York City, Stuyvesant High School, Wesleyan University, married to Leigh Anne Johnston . . ." She typed some more and found a wedding announcement for Leigh Anne Johnston and Kenneth Liu, married in New London, Connecticut, a year previously. "Got it," she said. "'The bridegroom is the son of Charles Liu, owner of a restaurant in Jackson Heights, and of Rose Monaghan Liu, who teaches music in New York City. The couple plans to reside in Manhattan after a wedding trip to Bali.'"

"Bali. I guess the TickTalk business is pretty good."

"Danny told me this morning that it's raised a lot of money, but the bullying issue is a problem for them. And well it should be."

"Can you get to him?"

"It might take a few phone calls."

It took two. Kenneth Liu returned Maggie's call as soon as he got back from lunch in the city. They arranged to meet in his office the following morning.

"I need a night at home to do my laundry and pack fresh clothes anyway," said Maggie.

"I'll go down with you," said Hope. "I think I need another talk with young Caroline."

*   *   *

While Maggie wallowed in the domestic pleasures of her own bathtub that evening, her own enveloping bathrobe, takeout from her favorite Vietnamese restaurant, and the satisfaction of dispatching a week's accumulated mail, Hope was waiting for Caroline Hollister at JoJo in the east sixties. It was a favorite of hers, cozy and old school, with a flattering pink light. It was steps away from the Town Club, where she was staying, and they served a devastating butterscotch pudding.

The first to arrive, Hope was surprised to be shown to a corner table set for three. Caroline had made the reservation. Hope had hoped for a tête-à-tête, but this might be just as useful, a chance to study Caroline and Hugo in close quarters.

But when the hostess led Caroline to their table, she was followed not by Hugo but by, unmistakably, Hope's onetime beau, Angus Westphall. He looked almost exactly as he had when she last saw him decades earlier, but thinner than in his self-satisfied salad days, with only a few wisps of his once luxuriant hair combed across his bald pate, and something sad in his expression.

"I hope you don't mind my crashing the party," he said before Caroline could speak. "I heard that Caddie was going to see you tonight and I couldn't resist."

"Of course not, I'm delighted," Hope said with a warm and not entirely fraudulent smile. Angus kissed her cheek and took the chair across from her, as Caroline slid in beside her on the banquette.

After they placed their orders, the talk, predictably, was a fire-hose stream of data from all three, about children, old friends, their parents and siblings as they'd been when they'd all first known one another. Angus had three grown children and four stepchildren from three different wives, and had developed a scholarly as well as personal interest in the Great Camps of the Adirondacks. Caroline's children from her first marriage were both married with children of their own, the son in finance, the daughter an economist.

"Hugo is hell-bent on proving that *his* daughter with Caddy is every bit as much a world beater as her first two children," Angus said, giving Caroline a teasing smile.

"That's not true," Caroline said, throwing a bread pellet at him. "He's terribly proud of Lily."

"It's totally true," said Angus, in a needling move Hope remembered from when they were young. Once a big brother, always one, she thought. "Hugo is so competitive, you're lucky dueling has been outlawed. He'd have Roger Donovan out at dawn with pistols in Central Park tomorrow." Roger being the father of Caroline's older children.

"With my luck, they'd just blow each other's feet off, and I'd end up nursing both of them, like Zeena Frome," said Caroline.

"You're much too nice to your ex-husbands," said Angus.

"Singular. I only have one. And of course I am, I'm a very nice person."

"That's true," said Angus, and turned the conversation back to Hope. How was she liking Boston? Did she text or tweet, and would she friend him on Facebook? Then their desserts were served, and the talk turned to summer plans. Hugo and Caroline and Lily would spend part of the summer on Bride Island, where Lily had a job teaching sailing. When asked if she enjoyed it, Caroline admitted she could do without quite so many of Hugo's Caldwell cousins, but she had to be there to chaperone Lily when Hugo was working. What was his work? Hope asked. Private art dealer, said Caroline. Before Hope could ask for details, Angus announced that he would be at his "place" in the Adirondacks of course, which

Hope didn't need to be told would be on the scale of a medium-size hotel, where he hosted a rotating cast of children and grandchildren all summer. He would love it if Hope would bring Lauren and the twins for a visit. She noticed he didn't show the same enthusiasm for hosting her son, Buster, the sheriff, who lived in a trailer in rural Maine with his unwed girlfriend. Which indifference would be entirely shared by Buster.

Wednesday morning brought Maggie to Kenneth Liu's office downtown, near the majestic old Police Building on Centre Street. The Police Building had been abandoned in the 1970s, hopelessly infested with roaches and rodents; police brass had apparently never been that careful about where they left their food scraps. Naturally, now that "fashionable SoHo" had sprung up on its western perimeter, it had been converted into expensive condominiums, and served as a magnet for the trending and the fashion-forward on the streets around it. The address Maggie had been given was for a loft building just off Cleveland Place with a storefront selling cunning housewares on the ground floor and on the second, a gigantic open space with temporary barriers marking off rental office areas, a shared pair of receptionists opposite the elevators, and in one corner, a sort of private café with bookshelves, bistro tables, a refrigerator, microwaves, espresso machines, and a full-time coffee barista.

The boy on the reception desk took Maggie's name and made a call, and in short order there appeared a man of about thirty dressed in jeans and a short-sleeved button-down shirt. He had thick straight glossy black hair in a ponytail and hazel eyes, and was preternaturally tall and thin, as if he'd been made of Silly Putty and stretched about a foot longer than the original design specs had called for. She recognized his face from his wedding announcement.

Maggie followed him through the maze of partitions, noting the industry and noise level all around her. When they were settled in the "room" from which President Liu conducted his empire, beneath gigantic windows facing north with a view of the Empire State Building, she said, "Explain this place to me."

"Office space co-op. We've bought our own space in FiDi," Ken said, giving the Realtor's shorthand for the gentrifying Financial District. "But it's still being built out. I'll be sorry to leave here, to tell the truth. There's always something going on, and when you need answers, there's usually someone in the coffee room who can answer them. There's a graphic design firm next door, and two other tech start-ups over there, and a bunch of freelance writers sprinkled around." He waved his hands to indicate directions.

"But you're leaving because . . . ?" said Maggie.

"It's what happens next. Got to impress investors. My mom said you need some help with TickTalk?"

"I do." She explained the situation and handed him her phone, with the screenshots Stephanie had sent her. "For the sake of the school and for the victim's privacy, we'd rather not go to the police."

"I would also rather you not do that. We already had to postpone our IPO once after a bullying dustup. Let's see what we can do."

He began to type.

"Do you mind if I watch?" Maggie asked.

Ken gestured to her to move her chair closer to him. She could see his cursor flying around the TickTalk screens, but to be truthful, he was moving too fast for her to follow.

"Do you have back doors into users' accounts?"

"Up to a point. We have to protect their privacy, but we also have to protect ourselves from people abusing the site. We'd prefer that not be generally known, though. There we go. 'The girl who finds dead bodies hated the art diva.' That it?"

"That's it."

"Okay, I've got his IP address and username."

"Hers, most likely."

"Right."

"Do they give you their real names when they register with you?"

"No. Username, password, and e-mail address. The password we can't see, but often the other two tell you a lot."

Maggie peered. The username was Miss305 and the e-mail was miss30567@gmail.com. Neither one told her a thing.

"Let's see if that username is turning up on other sites."

She watched as he typed and clicked. The username did turn up but was associated with other e-mails. Not helpful.

"Let's try sending a message to the e-mail address." He typed a test and pushed send. It bounced back.

"Hold on."

Ken Liu copied some things onto the back of a Post-it note, then popped up to open a door into the adjoining white cube, where a young woman wearing, for some reason, vintage riding jodhpurs and a pair of flip-flops was typing furiously. Maggie recognized her by her mass of Janis Joplin hair as the woman in the *Financial Times* article. "Izzy," Ken said, "are you stacked up?"

"Not really. Just stalking some asshole I met last night." Catching sight of Maggie, she added, "Kidding."

"Could you get onto the ISP for this IP address, and get them to give us a physical address? You are way better at persuading than I am."

Ken was telling Maggie about his wife's medical training when Izzy came in with a piece of paper and handed it to Ken.

"Whoa, you are *good*," he said.

"You're welcome," said Izzy.

"I really appreciate this," Maggie said, tucking the address into her purse.

"Do me a favor and don't tell anyone you know me. Our subscribers would go postal."

"I understand. My best to your mother."

Evelyne Phillips sat in her car for several minutes Wednesday morning, studying the house on Violet Circle. It was dark gray with white trim. The two-car garage at the left of the house was open to the street, and empty of cars. There were three bicycles hanging from the ceiling on hooks, and a smaller bike, a child's, leaning against a wall. The house itself looked asleep, with curtains drawn and no lights on, although it was late morning.

She got out of her car and walked to the front door. Cheerful annuals in little beds at either side of the front steps, purple and white petunias, struggled to keep their heads up. They looked as if they needed water. Phillips pushed the metal gray button beside the door.

She could hear the bell shrilling inside, but through the narrow windows of the entry, she could see no movement inside the house.

"You looking for Marcia?" a voice called from somewhere behind her. Phillips turned to see that from the house across the circle, identical to this one except painted colonial blue, a woman in tennis clothes had stepped out of her kitchen door.

"Looking for Jesse, actually," said Phillips.

"He's in there," said the woman, coming across the paved circle toward her. "He gets up around now. Marcia's at work."

"He isn't answering the bell," said Phillips.

"No, he doesn't," the woman said. "You from Social Services?"

"No. Detective Phillips." Evelyne showed her ID.

"I knew you weren't the last social worker but they keep changing. Come around to the side."

Phillips followed the woman to the garage, where she tried the knob of the back door into the kitchen. It was unlocked, and the two went in.

"Jesse! Jesse—it's Mrs. Keegin," the neighbor woman called loudly.

No sound, no answer.

"Jesse—there's someone here who needs to speak with you. Are you going to come down, or should we come up?"

After a moment a high voice called, "Who?"

"It's a lady. She needs to speak with you. Are you coming down? We can come up if you want."

The door closed loudly and Phillips thought she heard a creak of floor above them. She was about to add her voice to Mrs. Keegin's when the neighbor put up her hand to keep her silent. Then she saw two bare feet, the legs in pale blue knit pajama pants with navy cuffs, appear on the stairs, descending slowly. She could watch their progress through the open kitchen door into the front hall.

Finally the entire boy appeared. He had a weirdly narrow head, as if it had been squeezed in a vise. His fuzzy white-blond hair needed a good washing. His eyes had dark purple-gray half circles under them, and his skin had a yellowish pallor. He was as tall as Detective Phillips, or would have been, if he'd stood anything like straight.

"This is Detective Phillips, Jesse," said Mrs. Keegin. She talked to him with slightly exaggerated volume and diction, as if to someone hard of hearing, or a little slow. "I'm just going now, I have a tennis lesson, but you give this lady whatever help she needs."

"Thank you," Phillips said.

"Oh, you are welcome," said Mrs. Keegin, as if to say, You don't know the half of it.

Left alone, Phillips said, "Jesse, I'd like to ask you some questions."

*   *   *

Hope and Maggie met at Grand Central and boarded the train for Rye-on-Hudson. When they had found two seats together and settled themselves, Maggie showed Hope the address she'd been given.

"Fifty-three Second Street, Rye-on-Hudson. They don't go in for names like Gin Lane in these little burgs, do they?"

"Second Street is the most common street name in America," said Maggie.

"Really?"

"Yes, because the first street is called Main, or Broadway, or something grand like that, but no one worries about what to call the next one."

"Where is it? This Second Street," she said, pointing to the address on the paper.

"Parallel to Main, behind the Bistro and the bookstore. Can you do a reverse address lookup? My phone is out of juice."

Hope could. She got a phone number. "Shall I call it?"

"Do."

Hope dialed, and indicated ringing. Then her eyes met Maggie's; an answering machine had picked up. She listened, looked surprised, and ended the call.

"What?"

"You have reached Kate and Ellen's house. We can't come to the phone right now yada yada."

"Kate and Ellen? Kate and Ellie Curtin?"

"Wouldn't you guess?"

"Wow," said Maggie. And after a moment's thought: "That's a surprise." Then added, "Before I forget, tell me about your date with Caroline Hollister."

"It took a funny bounce; she brought her brother."

"Your boyfriend? Why did she do that? She said he was so boring."

"*He* said he had insisted on crashing. Might be true."

"But is he? Boring?"

"Well he won't be taking over for Jon Stewart, but I've met worse," Hope said. "He made an interesting remark. Angus thinks Hugo Hollister is supercompetitive about Caroline's children from the first marriage. As in, his child with Caroline has to be at least as impressive."

"Even though she can't read. If that's true he may be competitive with Angus too."

"Very likely. Which puts him in a position he may be used to, and not in a good way," Hope said.

"Meaning?"

"He comes from a rich family, but his branch of it doesn't have any money. Now here he is again, in a rich family but none of the money is his."

"Do we know that?"

"No. But you could ask."

"I could not," Maggie said. "Anyway, I like Hugo. Unless he's making his wife unhappy, then I hate him. Speaking of his wife though, do you think she didn't want to be alone with you? Sometimes people don't, if there's something they don't want to talk about. Something they don't want to know or aren't ready to deal with."

"I certainly thought of that."

"It's not important, but if we're going to protect Lily, we need to know where she feels safe and where she doesn't. Does Hugo work, do you know?"

"He's a private art dealer."

"Aha. Now who do we know who will tell us more about that?"

Hope looked at her watch, and said, "I'm going to time you, to see how long it takes you to come up with someone."

"Why? Do I do that all the time?"

"Remember the time I was on a bus in Tel Aviv, and right in

front of me, in the midst of all that Arabic and Hebrew, I heard someone say 'So how do *you* know Maggie Detweiler?'"

There was a silence. Both looked out the window and listened to the rattle of the train. "Anyway, I've thought of someone," said Maggie.

"Ha! Who is it?"

"Avis Metcalf. She has a gallery on Madison."

"And how do you know *her*?"

"I'm not going to tell you if you're going to make fun of me. So, now that you and Angus have been reunited, are you interested?"

Hope turned and looked at Maggie. "Listen. If I ever tell you that I'm thinking of taking up with Angus Westphall, so I can spend my summers playing horseshoes with his friends from Groton at our little 'place' in the Adirondacks, I want you to promise you'll shoot me."

"But I don't have a gun."

"Use mine. It will be in my sock drawer, top left."

*   *   *

McCartney Partners, LLC, had its office in White Plains in a fairly new office building within walking distance of The Westchester, an upscale shopping mall where Lyndon could take colleagues to lunch. Their space was small but glossy, with new-looking office furniture, all chrome and glass and dark wood polyurethaned until it looked like something that had never grown in nature. The furniture was rented, but it had been lightly used, and if it came to returning it they should get the whole deposit back, in Margot's opinion.

Margot worked in the outer office, and Lyndon had a room beyond hers with a sofa and chairs and a big flat-screen TV that was never used. When they first started out here he had rented a suite with its own conference room, but the rent was too high for the amount of use they got out of it, so.

"Good morning," said Margot brightly to the man who came through the door on Wednesday morning. He didn't look to her as if he'd come to invest in real estate. "How can I help you?"

"I'd like to speak to Lyndon McCartney, if he's in. Detective Bark, White Plains Police," the man said, showing his badge, then handing her a business card.

Though shocked, Margot didn't flinch. "I'm Mrs. McCartney," she said. "My husband's on the phone, but if you'll take a seat?"

Bark took a chair against the wall and folded his hands in his lap. He sat quietly, watching her. Most people found that unnerving.

Margot pushed a button on her telephone console. "Sorry to interrupt. There's a detective here to see you." She disconnected before he could question her.

She looked at Bark. See? I'm not rattled. Everyone feels guilty about something, but I know you are not here because I called my husband a bastard this morning and the children heard me. I wasn't wrong, I just should have kept my voice down. Of course this isn't about me. You're probably collecting for something. Policemen's Benevolent. Something.

Lyndon McCartney's door opened and he stepped out of his office, hand outstretched. Lyndon the salesman.

"Lyndon McCartney," he announced with his bluff smile. "How can I help you?"

"I have a few questions, if you have a minute," said Bark, standing.

"Of course." Lyndon waved him into the inner office and shut the door behind them. Whatever the hell *this* was about, he didn't need it, couldn't afford it, and for effing sure didn't want to talk with Margot about it. Maybe the mortgage? Their house was underwater, but Margot didn't know that. Not that they'd send a detective about that, they'd send a banker. Except they *had* sent a banker already once . . . Well, whatever it was about, here it was, like a flu you'd tried not to catch, sitting across from him in a badly cut suit.

Bark had taken out his notebook with some ostentation. "I understand you and Ray Meagher are business partners. Is that right?"

"Yes, that's right."

"And what is your business, Mr. McCartney?"

"We are real estate developers."

"I see. Developing what, exactly?" What would it be? Office parks? Shopping malls? As if Westchester needed more of those?

Lyndon opened a drawer and handed Bark a glossy brochure that said HUDSON ESTATES across the top of the first page. Inside there were a lot of words, and some artists' renderings of town houses in a grassy sylvan setting. On the back page were a lot of figures. Bark only glanced at it before putting it into his pocket.

"And what is the nature of your partnership with Ray Meagher?"

"He's got the local knowledge," said Lyndon. "I'm the real estate professional."

"And did you know Florence as well?"

"Of course," said Lyndon, feeling relieved. Florence, of course. Poor Floro. Of course, this was about Florence, why had he thought . . . He relaxed and felt himself suffused with helpfulness.

"You were friends as couples?"

"We were. Well, both our wives worked of course, and we have children and they don't, which makes a difference, but we socialized."

"Dinners at one another's houses, that kind of thing?"

"Yes. Some. We have a big picnic in the yard on the Fourth of July and they come to that."

"So how often would you see them? In a month?"

Lyndon looked as if he didn't know how to answer.

"I think we—we went to a movie together, I think it was last month; I'll ask my wife," and he reached for the phone. Bark forestalled him.

"That's all right, I understand. You and Ray saw each other on your own, did you?"

Lyndon looked relieved. "My wife is a quiet person. She works, and she has the kids, and she's busy with her own family, they live in Peekskill. Margot's family is close. And, Florence was such a talker."

"I had heard that."

"But Ray and I are pretty good buddies."

"He says he was with you on Thursday night, the night before Florence's body was found."

"That's right. We decided to run over to check out the new casino that's opened in the Poconos."

"Just the two of you?"

Lyndon's eyes flicked to the door of the outer office.

"It was just a quick trip. Florence was working, and Margot has the kids. It's a thing we do, spur of the moment. Margot's fine with it."

It was the second time Lyndon said that his wife had the kids. Bark himself had kids; his wife had been killed by a drunk driver when his girls were ten and twelve.

"But Florence wasn't working," said Bark.

"I meant, I thought she was."

"Ray didn't tell you his wife had gone off in a snit?"

Lyndon looked as if he were mentally trying to get a large car into reverse to make a U-turn in too tight a space.

"I don't remember, I don't think I asked. I assumed, I guess."

"What was the name of the casino?"

"Mohegan Sun Pocono. I'm sure Ray told you."

"And how long a drive is that?"

"Not bad. A couple hours."

"I see. And you went in Ray's car?"

Lyndon snorted. "You ever ridden in a Smart car? They are horrible, those things. Terrible ride."

"I take it that's a no."

"We went in my Lexus. Driving it gives Ray a charge."

Bark, impassive, made a note on his pad.

"He drove your car?"

"He drove down this time; I had some calls to make. I drove back."

"And what did you talk about on the drive? After your calls?"

Lyndon looked puzzled. "You know. This and that."

"I don't know. Why don't you tell me." His tone had dropped a few degrees of warmth.

"Uh . . . well we talked about the school, Rye Manor. I'm on the board there."

"Go on."

"There's a property we're trying to buy, to complete our package. Ray wanted to hear how the evaluation went. At the school. Last week."

"What's that got to do with the price of eggs?"

"Uh . . ." Lyndon was ooching and backing again in his big conversational car stuck in another mental back alley, Bark saw.

"Nothing, really, just . . . he was interested, you know. Because of Floro's job."

"I see. And he didn't mention that she was gone? Since Wednesday morning? Off in a snit?"

Lyndon was beginning to look uncomfortable.

"Look. Detective . . ."

"Bark."

"I think I know what you're trying to ask me."

"Really? What?"

"I won't lie to you. Ray and Florence were having some problems. He isn't the most sensitive guy in the world, and he wasn't always all that nice to her. But it's just . . . marriage, you know? Ups and downs. She's a perfectionist at work, she'd wind herself up and then she couldn't shut up, and it . . . well it would drive *me* crazy, but they just needed a little distance. You are barking up the wrong tree, there."

"What tree do you think I'm barking up?"

Lyndon was closing in on exasperated. This guy in his shopping mall suit was condescending? To *him*?

"You're trying to find out if Ray did something to Florence. And he didn't. He couldn't have. We drove down to the Poconos, we played some blackjack, had a nice dinner, went back to the tables, drove home the next morning. Her body was found way before we got back."

"What time was that?"

"What?"

"When you got back?"

"I don't know. Around noon, something like that? Margot will know," and he reached for his phone again.

"Never mind that, I'll talk to her myself. Let's go on. Did you share a room, at the hotel there?"

"What?"

"With Ray? Did you share a room? Or did you each have your own?"

"We're friends, not fuckbuddies," said Lyndon rather shirtily.

Bark raised his eyebrows.

"Sorry. Pardon my French. I mean we're a little old for sleepovers. Things aren't *that* tight."

Writing in his notebook, Bark said, "So, you drove down. You checked in. Did you ask for adjoining rooms? Rooms near each other?"

"No. We just checked in, one after another, and took whatever rooms they gave us. We weren't even on the same floor, I don't think." Where the hell was this guy going with this?

"So. You checked in, you got your key cards . . ."

"Yes."

"And then what?"

"Jesus! You want the whole thing, minute by minute?"

"Pretty much. Yeah."

Lyndon leaned back in his chair and twirled it halfway around, so he was facing his window, which looked out onto a parking garage. He rotated back slowly, and with an air of resignation.

"We went to our rooms. I wanted a shower and a change of clothes. I knew Ray would be at the slots, and I told him I'd find him. So I found him—"

"What time was this?"

"You know there aren't any clocks in casinos? You know that, don't you?"

"I assume you wore a watch."

"About an hour later. About seven. I found him playing Triple Red Hot 7s. We went to the tables together and played some roulette—"

"You said blackjack."

"Roulette *and* blackjack! I play roulette, he plays blackjack. About nine we went for some dinner. Then we went back to the tables."

"You were winning? Losing? Breaking even at that point?"

Lyndon took a deep breath. "I was winning. Not sure about Ray."

"Where'd you have dinner?"

"What?"

"Those casinos usually have a choice of places to eat. Restaurants, coffee shops, fast food."

"I don't remember the name of it!"

"Well what did you have?"

Lyndon looked at him levelly, trying to decide if he was being toyed with. At last, he said, "Steak. I had a rare steak and a baked potato."

"And Ray?"

"I don't remember. Hamburger. Pork chop. Then we went back and played a couple more hours, then we went to bed, that was it."

"Went to bed at the same time? Decided together to go to bed?"

Lyndon gave him a look, then answered very precisely. "I believe I went over to Ray and said I was turning in. Then I went upstairs."

"And what time was that?"

Lyndon looked at his watch, as if it would tell him. "I'd say, two-fifteen, two-thirty. Right in there."

"And Ray was still playing blackjack?"

"And Ray was playing . . . I think he was shooting craps at that point. It was late, I was tired, I don't remember. Are we done here?"

"Almost. Were you still winning? When you quit?"

"I had a great night."

"And in the morning you had breakfast together? You and Ray?"

"No," said Lyndon with exaggerated patience. "I ordered room service. We met downstairs by prearrangement. I don't know if Ray had breakfast or not. Are we done?"

"One more thing. How tight *are* things?"

"What?"

"When I asked if you had separate hotel rooms, you said 'things aren't *that* tight.'"

"Oh. I just meant, I didn't mean anything. It's just an expression."

"Really. So things are fine with you, financially. Doing great, even in this economy."

There was a silence.

"Well, never mind," said Bark. "It was an idle question." He stood up. "Thank you for your help. I'll just take a little of your wife's time now, if you don't mind."

"Knock yourself out," said Lyndon. He swung himself back to look out at the parking garage. It had floors supported on columns, but no outer walls, so he could watch the attendants zoom down the corkscrew ramps as if they were racing at Daytona, then slow to a sedate pace as they hit the level where the owners waited. Lyndon had worked in a garage like that for three years during college.

———

Ellie Curtin was sitting at the kitchen counter, her laptop open before her, when she heard the door buzzer. She wasn't supposed to open to anyone she didn't know, unless someone was with her. Through the front door's little peephole that distorted everyone's face she saw three people. That wrinkly she'd seen on campus since last week, and also at the shop, another lady like that, same song different verse, that she didn't know, and Danny the IT guy from school. Okay, did this count? Did she know them or didn't she?

Well, she knew Danny, and her mom knew the first wrinkly, and it had started to rain, so it seemed rude to make them stand there. She undid the guard chain and opened the door.

"Thank you, Ellie. We met the other day at the Wooly Bear. I'm Mrs. Detweiler. I'm helping Ms. Liggett with a few things, you may have heard. This is Mrs. Babbin, and you know Danny Chin."

They had all three stepped into the foyer.

"Hey," said Ellie to Danny.

"Is your mother home?"

"She's at work. She'll be here soon, though. Do you need me to call her?"

"Up to you. It's you we came to talk to."

"Okay," said Ellie warily. She meant "Okay, I understand what you just said," not that it was okay with her.

"Good. Could I just ask you, do you have a TickTalk account?"

This was Wrinkly #1, and uh-oh. Ellie did not like the sound of this. Last semester they had had like an all-school emergency chapel about anonymous bulletin boards, and how no Rye Manor girl was supposed to use them, because you could be mean on them, and being mean without signing your name was cowardly and way worse than just being mean. Duh. But she wasn't. Mean. She did like watching what went on on TickTalk, though, and her mom was clueless and probably never heard of TickTalk, so she never told Ellie she couldn't, at home, where school rules didn't count. Sort of.

"Would you mind if Danny had a look at your phone?" Maggie asked her.

What the hell was she supposed to say to that? Of course she minded. "Well but . . . why?" Ellie said.

"Would you feel better if we asked your mother first? We had hoped she'd be at home."

"I mean, yes," said Ellie.

Hope handed Ellie her phone, and Maggie said, "Would you dial her for me?"

Ellie took it and punched. "Mom, it's me," she said. "There are some people here," and she handed the phone to Maggie.

"Kate, it's Maggie Detweiler. The purler. We're at your house, with Ellie. Something has happened at school, and it's a bit of a story, but it has to do with some electronic messages that have come from this address. We'd like to look at Ellie's phone, if you don't mind."

Maggie listened to dead silence for something like half a minute. Then Kate said, "Please wait until I get there. May I speak to my daughter?"

Maggie handed the phone back to Ellie, who said "Mom?" and then listened to what sounded like an extremely directive series of remarks. Then she ended the call and handed the phone back to Hope. (What was it, were these old bags sharing a phone? They didn't both have their own? What was the point of being a grown-up if you couldn't afford your own stuff?)

"She'll be right here," said Ellie. "She says you can sit in there until she gets here." She gestured toward the sitting room beyond the staircase.

"Thank you, dear," said Maggie, unperturbed, though she was pretty sure the tone of Kate's remarks had not been hospitable.

Kate Curtin came through the front door in a matter of minutes and she did not look like a colorful wooly anything unless it was an angry mammoth. She had dashed through the rain without an umbrella or a hat and there was water on her cat's-eye glasses; they must have been hard to see through. Danny stood as she came into the sitting room. Maggie and Hope looked up pleasantly from their chairs while Kate stood over them.

Foregoing pleasantries, Kate said, "I'd have appreciated if you'd spoken to me first," with a certain pressure behind the words. "Before you start questioning my daughter. In our *home*."

"I'm very sorry that we didn't," said Maggie. "It was late enough in the afternoon that we thought we'd find both of you here. And it was raining. We guessed wrong, but I apologize."

"And what is it you want?"

Maggie explained what TickTalk was, and why the school had a problem with it.

"This house isn't at school," said Kate.

"I'm sorry, I didn't put that clearly. There is a rule against Rye Manor students using the site at all. From anywhere."

"I never heard of that."

"I'm not surprised."

"Does Ellie know that?"

"I believe she does. Ms. Liggett made it very clear, I'm told, early in the year. Schools find it difficult to enforce, for the very reason that the posts are anonymous, and it's become an issue at this school because someone is posting quite nasty messages on the board about a vulnerable Rye Manor student."

"Who?"

"Is it important that you know? We're trying to protect her privacy."

"If you're accusing my daughter of something then yes, it's important."

After a thoughtful moment, Maggie said, "We're not accusing your daughter of anything. But I can see your point. It's a girl named Lily Hollister."

She saw an almost undetectable reaction.

"Ellie's barely mentioned her."

"That may be true. But the messages that are upsetting her came from a device connecting through the Wi-Fi in this house."

Kate looked blank, and then sat down on a hard chair in front of the bricked-up fireplace.

"Wait. If they're anonymous, how do you know that?"

"Please take my word, we're not here annoying you for the fun of it."

Danny spoke up. "Digital messages leave trails as they move through the system." It was the kind of remark that a civilian who knew only how to turn her computer on and off really had to take on faith, so Kate did. To Maggie's relief.

"We'd like to have Danny take a look at Ellie's phone, if you will allow it."

"And if I won't?"

Maggie let it hang until she was pretty sure Kate had figured out the answer on her own. Then she said, "We're trying not to involve the police."

After a moment, Kate stood up and made a gesture: right this way. She led them into the kitchen.

The kitchen was awash in yellow, lemon-painted cabinets and sunflower wallpaper lighting the room in the gray wet of early evening. Ellie sat on a stool, typing furiously on her laptop at a program the girl had closed by the time they reached her. She looked up, her expression a mix of wounded innocence and resentment.

Her mother said, "They need to look at your phone, honey." The phone, in a royal blue bumper case, was lying beside the computer on the counter.

Ellie gave her mother a long look, then handed the phone to Danny.

He woke it up and instantly found the TickTalk app. He opened it and saw it had autofilled the username JinglebElle. He handed it to Ellie, who tapped in her password, and handed it back. He scrolled through the threads he found there, poked around in various settings, then locked the phone and handed it back to her.

"Ellie, are you on this tick thing? Do you use it?"

"Everyone *has* it, Mom. I don't use it though."

"Not everyone has it. *I* don't. Why do you have it if you don't use it?"

"I, like, follow it. See what's on it. I don't post."

Kate looked as if this were a topic they would revisit in private.

Danny moved to her laptop. "Okay?" he said to Ellie. Ellie nodded a resentful assent. The three women watched as Danny conducted a series of maneuvers through the operating system that no one in the room understood but him. Maggie and Hope were examining the actual bulletin board on the wall by the refrigerator, covered in family photos, when at last he said, "I don't find it. No one has accessed the site from here."

Ellie said, "I could have told you."

"Thank you for your help, Ellie," Maggie said. "I'm sorry we had to interrupt your evening."

Danny said, "Is this the only computer in the house?" He looked at Mrs. Curtin.

She said, "Well, no . . . my computer is upstairs."

"May we?"

Kate appeared to like this development even less than having her daughter electronically strip-searched. But after a long moment, she waved her hand toward the stairs in the foyer, and they followed her where she led.

At the bedroom door, Maggie understood the many layers of reluctance Kate had to be feeling. When she turned on the light in her room, they saw the bed unmade and days' worth of crumpled clothes draped over a chair. Socks and other items of small clothes lay on the floor around it.

"Sorry," said Kate, "the maid must have missed a day," in a tone that meant *Don't you dare judge me.* She went to the desk that occupied one corner of the room, switched on the table lamp, and woke up her computer. Then she moved aside to let Danny do whatever he was going to do.

Hope sat on the bed. Maggie sat on a Thonet chair in the corner. Kate, as if they weren't there and she might as well use the time, began shaking out discarded garments and carrying them one by one either to the closet, where she hung them up, or to the laundry hamper in the adjoining bathroom. She was thinking that you really haven't lived until you've sorted through your dirty socks and underwear in the company of a couple of judgmental old trouts who probably *did* have maids, when Danny said, "Found it."

The room went quiet. Kate had jerked as if a bolt of current had run through her.

Maggie and Hope were up and going to Danny, both looking as if they had been so sure this was just due diligence that they'd forgotten why they were bothering with it.

"TickTalk was accessed several times from this machine on Friday afternoon, and twice on Saturday."

Kate said, "That's ridiculous. I never even heard of TickTalk before today."

"Do you lock your computer when you're not here, Mrs. Curtin?"

"No—there's no one here except the two of us."

"Is your Wi-Fi password protected?"

After a slightly embarrassed pause, she said again, "No."

"You really should, you know. People nearby can use your signal and slow it down for everyone."

"I know. I meant to do it."

Maggie said, "Would you ask Ellie to come up here, please?"

When Ellie was installed in the chair that more usually served as a clotheshorse, Maggie asked, "Were you in the house at four in the afternoon last Friday? The twenty-fourth."

"I have no idea," said Ellie.

"Think, please. The day Mrs. Meagher's body was found."

"Oh," said Ellie. "I remember. Yes. We were dismissed after lunch."

"I know who did this," Kate said. Maggie held a hand up to ask her to be still.

"What time did you get home?"

"Umm . . . three?"

"And was anyone with you?"

Ellie looked at her mother. Her mother looked back, deeply angry.

"Alison Casey," said Ellie.

Maggie went to the computer, opened a browser, and typed TickTalk. The site came up at once. Maggie typed *Miss305* into the username log-in box.

"Ellie, do you know Alison's password?"

"No," she said, as if she'd like to add *Duh*.

"How about for Snapchat or Instagram?" In Maggie's experience besties were constantly popping onto each other's feeds. She wondered they didn't fall down the stairs on their way to the gym or to lunch, they were so busy passing phones around to share whatever had come through during class while their phones were off, instead of watching where they were going.

There was a silence. On the one hand, Ellie was bound by teenage omertà; you never narc out a friend to a teacher or any other grown-up. On the other hand, she was a little pissed that Alison had been in her mother's room and using her computer. Just because Alison hated her own parents didn't mean Ellie hated hers.

"Ellie," said her mother, in a tone they both understood.

"Try Trixie2012," said Ellie. Trixie was Alison's dog until her brother ran over it. A picture of Trixie was Alison's screen saver. A Jack Russell terrier.

M argot McCartney *had had to lie* to Ray Meagher three times before lunch on Thursday, and she was not enjoying it.

"I don't know what to tell you, Ray, I don't know where he is," she said when he called the third time. "I'm sorry. I promise I'll have him call you as soon as I can." When she'd hung up, she went into the inner office where Lyndon was on the computer with a spreadsheet on the screen.

"I don't know why you won't talk to him, Lyndon. He's trying to plan Florey's funeral."

"I'm busy."

"Everyone's busy."

"I thought the school was planning the funeral."

"Well he wants to talk to you about *something*. He's in mourning. You're his friend. Next time I'm going to put him through."

Lyndon x-ed out of his program and stood up. "I've got to go out," he said.

"For what?"

"Margot, are you *trying* to annoy me?"

"Not yet."

"Good. I'm going out and I'll be back when I'm back." He

walked past her and had just reached the outer office when the front door opened, and he found himself face-to-face with Detective Bark. There was a woman with him.

"Oh good, we caught you," said Bark. "This is Detective Phillips."

After a beat, Lyndon said, "I was on my way out."

"We won't take much of your time."

Reluctantly, Lyndon reversed course and went back into his office. His wife gave him a long look as he passed. He avoided her eyes.

When they had all settled into seats, Lyndon back in his swivel chair and the two detectives facing him, he said smoothly, "Can I have Margot get you anything? Coffee? Tea?"

"We're good, thanks," Bark said. "We just have some things to clear up."

"How can I help?" McCartney produced a pleasant smile and leaned toward them, elbows on the desk, hands folded together.

Bark took out his notebook and flipped through the pages, as if refreshing his memory.

"Detective Phillips here had a talk with Ray Meagher about your road trip."

Lyndon nodded. He had assumed she had, or Bark had.

"Meagher said you picked him up at the firehouse around four P.M., in your Lexus, and you drove together to the Mohegan Sun Pocono resort in Pennsylvania. Yes?"

"That's right," said McCartney.

"After you checked in, he went to get a burger and a beer, and you went to your room, to shower and change. He was playing Triple Red Hot 7s when you joined him at about seven P.M. All right so far?"

"As I told you," said McCartney, nodding.

Bark flipped a page in his book and read some more. "And then, he says, you moved on to the table games. He played blackjack, and you played roulette. At about eight P.M., you both moved on to a craps table, where you were on a roll. The two of you stayed there until eleven, when you went to grab some sushi, then you went back to the same table. He says you both stayed there until two in the morning. You see my problem."

Lyndon McCartney sat very still for about a minute. Then he turned his chair to face the window and the parking garage. Then he spun back to them, looked at his watch, and said, "You know what? I'm starving. I've got to grab a bite, why don't you come with me?"

The two detectives looked at each other. Then they looked back at him and Phillips said, "Sure. Walk or drive?"

"Walk," said McCartney. "There's a taco place around the corner. I'm buying."

"Lead on," said Bark.

The restaurant was mostly empty, since it wasn't yet noon. Lyndon chose a table in the corner, well out of earshot of the other two patrons. The detectives ordered coffee and Lyndon fish tacos from a boy wearing a sleeveless T-shirt and tattoos covering both arms. The boy had a sunny demeanor and sounded to Bark as if he was from the Balkans somewhere. When they were alone again, Lyndon said, "Thanks for coming out."

Bark shrugged. Phillips said, "Shall we pick it up where the train went off the rails?"

McCartney ran a hand over his large round head and nodded.

"I have you and Meagher in sync up to about eight o'clock. Would you agree with that?"

McCartney would.

"He's playing blackjack. You're playing roulette. Right so far?"

McCartney nodded again. "I was on a hot streak. When that happens, there's a kind of ripple, people want to get close to you, as if it will rub off. There was a girl right beside me, and we goofed back and forth. She was into it, you know? Then Ray came over.

The girl said she was really good at blessing dice, and we should all go play craps."

"And was she?"

"She was. I wasn't betting all that much but it was a rush."

After he paused long enough to be called a full stop, Phillips said, "We get the picture. Go on."

"I invited the young lady to have a drink with me, and she said yes. I told Ray I was going to quit while I was ahead. He understood."

"Understood what?"

"That I was . . . that we were . . ."

Phillips just looked at him levelly. His face began to take on a painful-looking flush.

"So you had a cocktail. Where?" Bark asked.

McCartney shrugged. "I don't remember the name. Some lounge right there by the game rooms."

"And after that, did you go back to the tables?"

Another painful silence.

"You took the young lady up to your room, instead?" Bark asked.

Lyndon didn't say anything. The way Phillips was looking at him made him feel worse even than he'd expected to.

"And when I check with the hotel, let me guess. I'm going to find that the security cameras don't place you in the game rooms for the rest of the night, and I'm going to find you ordered breakfast for two, from room service?"

McCartney took a deep breath and turned his hands palms up.

"Do you do this a lot?" Phillips asked.

"Do *what*?!"

She had moved her hands onto the table where Lyndon couldn't help seeing her wedding ring.

The Balkan boy arrived with Lyndon's food and coffee for the detectives. There was a silence until he was gone again. Nobody touched what they'd ordered.

"Your wife doesn't see your credit card statements?" Phillips asked.

"My wife pays the business credit card. She sees those statements. I pay the personal cards."

Phillips nodded and watched him, cool and steady.

"So from nine o'clock on, you actually have no idea where Meagher was," said Bark. "He could easily have driven to Rye and back and met you midmorning back at the casino."

McCartney had been so busy worrying about his wife hearing how he'd spent his night on the town that he'd briefly forgotten this aspect of the situation.

"No, he couldn't, he didn't have a car."

"You told me he'd driven your car down. Where were the keys?"

McCartney went momentarily silent.

"Valet parking?"

"No, we parked ourselves."

"And he gave you back the keys?"

McCartney said, "I'm sure he did."

"Meaning you don't remember?"

The two detectives watched him closely. They could see a worm of doubt inching around in McCartney's mind.

"How about the next morning, when you left," Phillips asked. "You met in the lobby, walked to the car together?"

After a long pause, McCartney said, "Ray went and got the car. I had . . . I was . . ."

Saying good-bye to your new best friend, Phillips thought. She was picturing a lingering kiss in the lobby. What had this asshole told the girl, that it was the first of many? They'd see each other again?

"So Ray had the car keys," said Bark.

McCartney said nothing.

* * *

Christina Liggett's mother had called Thursday morning while Christina was leading morning prayers, and it was almost lunchtime before she could call her back.

"Mom, I've only got a minute. What's up?" Her mother, excitable at the best of times, had sounded, in her message, as if her hair was on fire, which was just about the last thing Christina had time for today.

"I am speaking to you from Planet Martha," her mother announced.

Christina closed her eyes and offered a silent prayer to a god who seemed to have put a spam filter block on her messages some time ago.

"Okay. Tell me."

"They can't keep her."

"I see. Why?"

"Could you just come out here and see for yourself, Chrissy? I have a school to run, and I'm sixty-two years old, and I need a knee replacement and now I have to have cataract surgery, and I just can't deal, I really can't. If you would come talk to them."

Christina's mother ran a day care center for the local Y in Carmel, Indiana. She was sixty-one, and a world-class complainer, which didn't mean she didn't have a list of formidable genuine grievances. Any one of which she could have made a meal of without Martha, her firstborn, her bright witty daughter, now a three-hundred-pound menace to herself and others, given to aural hallucinations and aggression, which could erupt anytime she decided that the nurses were poisoning her meds and she'd be better off without them.

"Mom, I can't come now. It's really a busy time—"

"But you have staff. I'm meeting with them Saturday and I need you."

"Saturday there's a funeral I—"

"For who? This is your family."

"For a teacher in the school who died. I'm giving the eulogy."

After a silence, her mother said, "What time of day is the funeral? Can't you come after?"

Christina's telephone buttons were all lit up, meaning calls waiting, and now Sharon Comfort was at the door, making the time-out sign.

"Mom, hold on a minute." She pressed the mute button.

Sharon said, "The nurse needs you in the infirmary."

"Why?"

"She has a student there in tears with her hair coming out in clumps."

Christina stared, wanting to sputter. She pushed the button to unmute the call. "Mom, I have to call you back, I have an emergency."

"Christina, *I* have an emergency. The emergency is your sister. If they won't keep her it's the state hospital, I can't have her in the house, you know I can't handle her, and I can't afford . . ."

Actually it was Christina who couldn't afford the one private facility in the county that had not yet expelled Martha. She'd been paying her sister's uncovered medical expenses for ten years, and barring some deus ex machina, she would for the rest of her sister's life.

"Mom, just a minute . . ." She pushed the mute button again and said to Sharon, "Who is the student?"

"Pinky Tyson."

Christina unmuted the phone and said, "Mom, I promise I'll call you back, but right now I really have to go," and she ended the call with her mother in midsentence of protest.

"What else do I have waiting?" she asked Sharon, looking at the lit-up buttons on her phone.

"The insurance adjuster, Florence's sister, the minister doing the funeral service, and Caroline Hollister."

"Take messages. I'll get back to them as soon as I can." She was pulling on her blazer as she headed toward the side exit on her way to see the nurse.

The infirmary, built in the style of a cottage from Hansel and Gretel for no reason that Christina could imagine, was hardly a state-of-the-art facility, but it was clean, and the nurse, a motherly woman from the village who had presided there for decades, was reasonably competent. She greeted Christina at the door and ushered her through the small waiting room where a wan freshman sat with a thermometer in her mouth reading a *National Geographic*.

"I've got her in my treatment room; I don't think she's contagious, but she should see the doctor before she goes back to mingling with the other girls."

The treatment room had a table and sink, a medical cabinet full of jars with red crosses on them, a rolling stool for the doctor or nurse, and an examination table on which Pinky Tyson lay sobbing. There were shiny circular patches on her head where her sand-colored hair was entirely gone, and a large area at her crown where the light shone through to the scalp, as with male pattern baldness.

"She's been like that since she walked in here," said the nurse.

Christina sat down on the doctor's stool and rolled herself close to the patient's side.

"Pinky."

The girl opened her eyes, experienced a renewed spasm of despair, and leaped from the table to dash to a box of tissues on the medicine cabinet to wipe her flowing eyes and nose. On the pillow where her head had been lay clumps of hair, as if a frantic long-haired animal had torn itself free of a trap there.

Touched, Christina said, "Your pretty hair."

Pinky shook her head.

"Has this ever happened to you before?"

She shook her head again.

"Can you tell me how I can help? The doctor is on the way."

Pinky waved her hand as if to say, that wasn't necessary.

Christina actually knew more about alopecia than most, since her mother's hair had all fallen out overnight the day after Martha was first hospitalized when she was nineteen. Martha had been found at midnight, barefoot in a bathing suit and a tinfoil helmet, using a toothbrush to try to unlock the Carmel public library under the impression that it was her house.

"Pinky, I hope you feel you can talk to me."

Pinky nodded, looking at the floor, which Christina took to mean she had no intention of talking to her. And why should she? Christina had known when they had admitted Pinky that she would be far from home and that she probably had no idea what a different world she had signed on for, but . . . she hadn't expected the year to be this hard.

The nurse came to the door to announce the doctor, and Dr. Maynard waddled past her into the room. He was retired from private practice but kept up his license so he could continue on call for the school. He was affordable, and that had to be weighed against the possibility, which had just occurred to Christina, that it was creepy that he wanted to stay on.

Christina stood to make way for him but didn't leave the room. Dr. Maynard said to Pinky, "Now, let's see here, little lady," and then went through the same pulse, blood pressure, temperature, ear, nose, and throat routine he would have if the patient had presented with a fever, a broken leg, or a gunshot wound.

When he'd collected all the data he felt he needed, he rolled back a little way and turned to Christina, as if Pinky were deaf and dumb.

"Alopecia," he said, magisterially. "I thought so, just wanted to rule out any underlying condition. Fancy name for 'Your hair fell out.'" He chuckled, then resumed his air of godlike man of medicine. "It can be caused by allergies, or sometimes heredity. Absent those two, we look to stress. You are working these young ladies too hard, Ms. Liggett. Exams coming? College boards, something of that nature? Or . . . ," he said, suddenly entertaining a new thought, and casting a knowing look at Pinky, "boyfriend trouble?"

He finished stowing his gear in his valise and stood. "She has no fever, she's not contagious, there's no reason to keep her from the general population, but she may not feel too perky about how she looks." He turned back to Pinky. "Looking like you've got the mange? May not feel too perky about that." He grinned at her, and threw her a wink.

To Christina: "Might want to let her go downtown, buy a wig at the drugstore. Or a new hat. Women always cheer up with a new hat."

He went out, leaving Christina staring after him. One more thing to put on her endless list of problems to solve today if not sooner.

She closed the door and sat down again, facing the miserable girl.

"Pinky, tell me how I can help you."

"I'm fine."

"Can you tell me what's made you upset?"

There was silence.

"Is there someone beside me you'd like to talk to?"

Pinky raised her eyes to the window, and looked out, as if her thoughts were elsewhere, but didn't speak.

"Would you like to call your parents?"

Pinky shook her head decisively. "I'm fine."

"How about your roommate?"

Pinky shook her head even more emphatically.

"Are you feeling out of your depth in your course work? I can arrange extra help for you if you need it. Your teachers all want you to succeed, that's what study hall is for." Note to self, she added silently, get Pinky's transcript and follow through with this. "Is there *anything* you'd like to tell me?"

Pinky thought about it and said finally, "I have biology right now."

Christina was feeling distinctly in need of counseling herself. Could she call Pinky's parents if the girl didn't want them to know?

Could she *not* call them? What if the child was having a nervous breakdown? What if she ran away?

On the other hand, what if this fell into the Didn't Cause It, Can't Change It, Can't Fix It Category? She stood up.

"If you feel you want to talk, about anything, my door is always open to you."

"I can go?"

"If that's what you want." Pinky was on her feet, gathering up her backpack. She was out the door, eyes downcast, without another word. Christina went out to the waiting room, where the nurse was now reading the *National Geographic*.

"Mrs. Bunting," said Christina, "if Pinky didn't want any help, why did she come to the infirmary?"

"Señora sent her." The Spanish teacher. "She was afraid the girl had the impetigo, or nits. Pinky was crying when she got here because she was missing test prep."

"I see," said Christina.

There was a nail salon in Rye-on-Hudson, but Hope hadn't liked the look of it. She'd gotten a bee in her bonnet about salons that exploited new and illegal immigrants. When she had gone in to ask a few questions about the management's employment practices, the owner had pretended not to speak English beyond waving her toward the nail varnishes and urging her to pick a color. Hope decided to drive to The Westchester mall in White Plains for a manicure and some retail therapy.

The manicure had been satisfactory and she'd enjoyed window-shopping at the mall, wondering if her grandchildren would like little surfer outfits, or Elvis costumes, when she passed a brew pub on an upper level just in time to see a woman seated at a window table pick up her wineglass and hurl the contents into the face of the man she was lunching with.

Too interesting. Hope, who had in truth been looking for a place to have a quick lunch herself, went into the restaurant and was shown to a seat with a fine view of the couple at the front table. The pair still sat facing each other, eyes locked, he dripping, she shaking with anger. Lucky for him she had been drinking white wine, Hope thought, and thought too that if she were the wet man, she'd move that glass of red he had ordered out of reach of his companion.

Instead, the man wiped the wine out of his eyes with his napkin, reached for his wallet, dropped some bills onto the table, and got up to leave. Before he reached the door, the woman called after him, quite loudly, "You *shit*!" Then the man was gone, finally, and the woman, whom Hope had recognized, reached across the table and downed the glass of wine he had left behind.

Hope tore a page out of the handsome green steno book she had always with her in her chicken bag these days, and wrote on it, "It's Hope, from the elevator. Join me." She got her waiter's attention, which took some doing, since the whole waitstaff was breathlessly watching the drama in the front of the house, and had her note carried to Margot McCartney. Margot read it, turned and saw Hope, and came at once to sit across from her while the waiter followed with her plate. Margot said, "Well that was fucking embarrassing. I don't usually make scenes."

"We probably should more often. I once cut off my husband's necktie in the middle of La Grenouille," said Hope.

"Did you really?"

"I did. We were entertaining clients of his and he was boasting about what a soccer star our son was, when he'd never bothered to go to one of his games, and I suddenly remembered I had a pair of scissors in my handbag." Margot started to laugh, but it turned to tears. Hope signaled the waiter again.

"I'll have whatever that is," she said, pointing to Margot's plate, "and we'll have two more glasses of the wine that was spilled."

"Crab Louis and two pinot gris," he said, and whisked off with her menu.

"*Was* that your husband?"

"It was," said Margot. "Is. Was? God—what am I going to do? I thought I knew how many ways he could fuck up our lives."

"I had a feeling that moving here had been harder on you than you let on," said Hope.

"How much did I tell you?"

"Just that you were making friends slowly and the school was good."

"Jesus. I've lived in New York City since I finished college. Nineteen years. My friends are there—I left a job I loved—It's only fifty minutes on the train, Lyndon says, and that's right, it is, but it's still a different planet. My New York friends *never* come up here. Why would they? I have to make dates to talk on the phone with them, they're running here, they're late for there, things I'd be doing *with* them if I still lived there, and my boys are bored at school and they fight with each other all the time, which they didn't used to do. They had their own friends, they had playmates in the building, they were growing up with some street smarts . . ."

Their wine arrived and they clinked glasses and drank.

". . . and I hate working for Lyndon. I hate it. I'm alone in his damn office all day, I never see anyone or meet anyone. He can't afford to hire someone else, but we have to *look* prosperous, or he'll never attract the rest of the money. Plus, there's a holdout property he needs before the deal can go live. The whole thing depends on it, his options on other key parcels are running out. He was so sure he could finesse it, offer more money, make the owners a swap for something more valuable than what they'd give up, but they won't budge. I don't know what we're going to . . ."

She started to cry again.

"So money is a problem."

"You have no idea. The boys need computers, they need sports gear, the cable just got canceled because we hadn't paid the bill—I had no idea we were behind, Lyndon takes care of all that."

"Would it help if I lent you some money?"

"Don't be . . ."

"Really. Simplest thing in the world, I'll give you a couple of thousand, you keep it in cash, pay for everything you would have charged. Lyndon will never know, and you can take care of your boys."

"But why would you do that?"

"Because you're crying on your salad. It's only money."

Margot smiled sadly. "You are amazing. But I can't."

"At least tell me what just happened." She tilted her head toward Margot's previous table.

Hope's salad arrived, and they both picked up their forks. Then Margot put hers down again.

"You know Florence Meagher?"

Hope said she did.

"Everyone knows Ray was a beast to her. He's got to be the prime suspect, and Lyndon is his alibi. Lyndon and Ray were off at some casino together in the Poconos when Florey's body was being dumped in the swimming pool. They claimed they were together, but they weren't. Lyndon can't say where Ray was because he was up in his hotel room boffing some bimbo named Jerilyn . . . unprotected sex with a . . ." She began crying again, this time with rage. "Can you believe it? That he did that and came straight home to me and . . ."

Hope stopped eating out of respect, although she realized she was really hungry. "I *can* believe it. Betraying someone and getting away with it is quite the aphrodisiac to some people. I have discovered."

When she had gotten a hold of herself again, Margot said, "The police came to talk to Lyndon. Twice. He thinks it doesn't look good for Ray. And if they arrest him, then it will all come out,

where Lyndon was that night, so he thought he better tell me first."
She picked up a forkful of food, then put it down on her plate again,
and dropped her face into her hands.

"He promised this had stopped. He *promised* me. What am I
going to do?"

*   *   *

Maggie had spent Thursday morning on personal business. She
was taking a course in Koine Greek at the New School and was
behind in her translation from the Book of Matthew. Also, her beloved former assistant at Winthrop wanted a teaching job in Paris
and needed letters of reference, and she had to find someone to use
her tickets to the opera on Friday night. It was midafternoon by
the time she and Christina Liggett were free to powwow on recent
developments. Maggie found Christina studying a transcript.

Having described the drama of the morning, Christina said,
"Pinky's test scores were terrific when we accepted her but she came
from a terrible school. I expected her to be struggling, but look."
She handed Maggie the transcript. "She's killing it in everything
except math. And a C+ is nothing to lose your hair over."

"She'd have to be unusually high-strung," said Maggie drily.

"Should I call her parents? She doesn't want them to know."

"Is she on financial aid?"

"Some. We don't give full scholarships anymore. As you know.
So they're paying a sacrificial amount, for them."

"And she wants them to think it's all beer and skittles." Maggie
was thoughtful. "It's a risk, but I think I'd respect the student's
wishes. She's got an opportunity here that could change her life if
she makes the most of it. She's trying hard to do that. If you tell her
parents they'll feel helpless, or try to fix it in some way that might
well make it worse."

"But she's suffering. I can't just do nothing, can I?"

"I have a theory. To a hammer, everything looks like a nail, and at the moment the nail I'm looking at is bullying. We found where the TickTalk postings about Lily Hollister came from."

"You *did*? How did you manage that?"

"Don't ask."

"Okay. But what's the answer?"

"Kate Curtin's home computer."

Christina looked baffled. "Ellie Curtin's mother? But she's . . ."

"No, of course she didn't send them. At the times the posts were sent, Kate was at work and Ellie was at home, with a friend from school. Alison Casey."

Christina stared. After a long moment, she said, "Oh it would be. It just would be. Kill me now."

"Why?"

"The Caseys are already suing us."

"Why?"

"Because we accused their daughter of cheating."

"Alison Casey is the student who stole the answer sheets?"

"Whom we *allege* stole the answer sheets. We know she did it and her classmates know she did it, but on advice of counsel, I'm not allowed to talk about it."

"So now she thinks she can get away with murder? So to speak?"

"I'm sure she does. We didn't know it when we took her, but she was accused of cheating at her last school as well, and the parents had sued them too. Which no one had the courtesy to mention in her letters of recommendation."

"Because the school wanted to get rid of her. Understood."

"So the parents will say we're at it again, scapegoating because we have it in for her."

"But tell me this," said Maggie. "Why was she posting from a computer instead of from her phone?"

Christina paused. "Good point. Why?"

"The dates of these posts are last Friday and Saturday afternoons. After Marcia Goldsmith took away Alison's burner phone.

Just a theory, but I'm guessing she kept her TickTalk business and anything else that could cause trouble on the second phone so she could throw it away if she needed to. Do you still have it?"

Christina looked at her, as if trying to work out a very tricky piece of mental math. Finally she said, "I don't know. I can't remember what I did with it." She put her hand to her mouth. "I don't think this has ever happened to me before."

"Stress will do that. Don't worry, by the time you're my age it will be a daily occurrence. Let's set the scene. It was the first day of the evaluation. And the day Florence Meagher disappeared."

"And Honey Marcus wanted to talk to me, Sharon said she was upset about something . . . I don't think I ever did sit down with her. I better . . ."

"That can wait," said Maggie.

"So . . . the phone is important," said Christina.

"Let's just find it. Florence hadn't shown up, my team was on campus, you had people waiting to talk to you . . ."

"I was trying to find someone to cover Florence's classes when Alison came in."

"Good. Then what?"

"I said I would call her parents, and she got this little smirk, as if she looked forward to that. I put her on bounds until Friday and sent her back to class."

"*Did* you call the parents?"

"No, I called our lawyer."

"And he said . . ."

"He said I shouldn't even turn it on. The phone."

"Because?"

"Because if she'd been sexting on it, and nothing would be more likely, there could be dirty pictures on it. I'd be in possession of child pornography. He told me either to destroy it, or to send it to him and he'd put it in the safe."

"What a world," said Maggie.

"Yes."

"Which did you do?"

"Then Ray Meagher came in to say he didn't know where Florence was, then I went out to see if Honey was still waiting . . ."

"And she wasn't, but I was."

"And then it . . . got away from me. I don't know what I did with it."

She was rooting through her desk drawers. By the time she had finished with the bottom ones, with no luck, she was visibly upset. "This is important, isn't it?" she asked again.

"I think of it this way," said Maggie. "Your memory is like a Ferris wheel. Sometimes the thing you're looking for isn't in the bucket at the top; the wheel has turned, and it's down there somewhere. But if you don't worry about it, it gets back up to the top again."

Christina buzzed the front office. "Sharon—did I give you a cell phone last week to send to our lawyer? Ancient smart phone, black?"

Sharon said that she had not, but that Christina's mother was on line two and was determined to wait.

Christina, looking ragged, said, "I have to take this," and pushed the button that connected her to Planet Martha.

F*riday had been a long day for Honey Marcus.* The same argument every day for a week.

"It was a threat. To us."

"It wasn't. It's my property and I have nothing to do with Florence Meagher; I barely ever met the woman."

"But why the pool? Why not dump her in the river, or leave her in the woods? That's a direct message to me, it has to be."

"Greta, stop."

"To embarrass the school and frighten us into selling. No school, no jobs for us. He's not going to stop. It's never going to stop."

"I don't believe it. Ray Meagher is a meathead. He's mean, but I just don't see him being that subtle."

"You don't think he killed her?"

"I don't know who killed her, I told you, I barely knew the woman! But you can't give in to this, you're making things up!"

"You didn't see her."

"I know. And you can't stop seeing her, I get that . . ."

"I've got to go," Greta had said, which was what she always said when she was afraid she was about to be really angry. She had gone out without saying good-bye, leaving the breakfast smoothie that

Honey had made her standing on the counter. Goddamn it. God-
damn it—they had been through so much, maybe too much, but
they had both believed they had found a sanctuary. They had been
talking about starting a family. This was all about Greta's goddamn father somehow. Not for the first time Honey wished she
could drive straight through to Minnesota, yank him out of his
wheelchair, and make him listen to chapter and verse of the damage
he'd done to his beautiful, talented gift of a daughter. And then
drive a golf club through his heart. Then since she'd gone all that
way, she would strangle Greta's mother for protecting her marriage
instead of Greta.

She'd had a long day of teaching, interrupted in the middle by
a drive with one of her clients to evaluate a horse he might want to
buy. (She'd had to recommend against. The mare was still green,
and the owner wanted too much money. Too bad though, she was a
stylish little thing.)

When Honey climbed the stairs to the apartment that evening,
she didn't know whether to hope that Greta was home, or that she
wasn't. She wanted a hot shower and a cold beer, and an evening of
binge-watching *The Americans* wouldn't be bad. She liked her shows
to have really high body counts.

Greta's car was downstairs, but that didn't mean anything; she
often walked back and forth to campus. She might have come home
at lunch while Honey was off with her client, and gone back to
school on foot.

The door was unlocked. So Greta was home. If she'd come wanting to make peace, she sometimes signaled this with flowers on the
kitchen table, or a steak in the reefer. But the kitchen was exactly as
Honey had left it this morning.

She hadn't left the door unlocked. Had she?

She never did that. But she'd been upset, so it was possible.
Something felt off to her in the quality of the silence.

"Greta?"

Nothing.

"Lovey, are you here?"

Honey went to the living room, which looked to her unchanged from this morning. The book she had been reading last night was still open on the arm of her chair. Greta's tea mug was still on the table where she'd been sitting on the couch.

A floorboard creaked. She whirled around.

Standing in the hallway leading to the bedrooms was Lyndon McCartney. He had a braided leather riding crop in his hand. Hers.

"I didn't mean to startle you," he said.

"The hell you didn't! What the fuck are you doing here?"

"I called to say I was coming. Door was unlocked."

"It was not!"

"It was, actually, but let's not fight about it."

"What were you doing in our bedroom?"

"I wasn't in your bedroom. I went looking for a place to wash my hands."

"How about the kitchen sink?"

"Honey. I was using a figure of speech."

"I didn't hear a flush."

"I flushed, washed my hands, and left the seat down. I was just looking at the pictures in the hallway."

"Thanks for letting me know you were here."

He shrugged. "I wasn't hiding."

Honey, her eyes fixed on him, went to the answering machine and pushed the button for replaying messages. Out of the tinny speaker came Lyndon's voice: "Honey and Greta, it's Lyndon McCartney. I'd like to speak with you this afternoon, if that's all right with you. Something's come up. Okay, you're not picking up. I'll take my chances and drop by." She turned the machine off.

"Mr. McCartney, we have nothing to say to you. Nothing has changed. We're not interested."

"You haven't heard my offer."

"And I don't want to."

"Look. I've put a great deal of time and personal capital into this project."

"Not my problem."

"I have—I shouldn't tell you this—I have more riding on this than I can afford to lose." His voice took on an almost pleading tone. "I could lose my marriage. My children. I am willing to offer you an estate worth substantially more than this barn, and this frankly crummy apartment. You'd have sunlight and land and a garden *and* a pool. We'll do an even trade."

"And you are not listening. I don't want any of that. I want what I have. It's not for sale."

Gambit failed, and over. He asked coldly, "Is that how your girlfriend feels too?"

"Why do you ask?"

"I just thought she might like to hear what's on the table."

"Why?"

"We left a message for her. I wanted to hear what she thought of it."

Honey lost her mind for a minute. She stood immobile, staring at him. Message. We left a message for her.

"What message was that?"

"A prospectus. I dropped it by the school for her. The property I'm offering."

"How dare you?"

"Hey! Don't get your panties in a bunch. Couples can disagree," he said smoothly. He even smiled. "I thought there might be a difference of opinion here. That's all I'm saying. I'm asking you as friends to think about it."

"We are not friends."

"But I'm being honest. I have to make this work."

"Not my problem."

He rolled one shoulder, and his right eyelid began to twitch. "If you say that one more time it may become your problem," he said.

"Are you threatening me?"

"What do you think?"

"What if I told you the answering machine has recorded this whole conversation?"

"I would laugh. I saw you turn it off." He took a step toward her. Honey held his gaze and stood her ground.

"Why do you have my riding crop?"

He held it up and flexed it. "Is that what it is? I'm not a horse guy myself. Didn't grow up with the boarding school set."

As if she had. "What are you doing with it?"

"I found it on a shelf in the hall. I was just looking at it when you came in. So you use it to whip your horses?"

He took another step toward her. Then he turned and laid the crop on a bookshelf in front of a handful of photographs from Greta's childhood. He looked at the pictures, one by one.

"Will Greta be home soon?"

"What's it to you?"

"I told you, I'd like to make my case to her. I'm offering you a crazy good deal. Win-win for everybody. I intend to make it work."

"I intend to make you leave. Do I have to call the police?"

"Don't be dramatic."

"I want you to leave."

"But we haven't finished our business."

"Are you deaf? We have. Go away." She picked up the receiver. The dial tone filled the room.

"Are you going?" she asked. For the first time in this encounter, she thought Lyndon looked a little less sure of himself.

When he still didn't move, she punched three buttons.

"Keep your hair on. I'll go," he said, moving to the door. "Hang up the phone."

A voice inside the phone said, "This is 9-1-1, what is your emergency?"

Lyndon said louder, "Hang up the phone."

"A man has forced his way into my house and won't leave. His behavior is threatening and he's scaring me."

Before she could go on, Lyndon turned and said, "You'll regret this."

Behind him as he opened the outer door he heard her giving her address to the dispatcher.

Saturday was a warm day bright with the green of high spring. Attendance at the memorial service for Florence Meagher was not compulsory for the girls, but by 10:00 A.M. nearly all were dressed in their church clothes, heading out in twos and threes to sit in the sun on the dorm lawns, or to walk and talk quietly as they waited until it was time. Graduates had returned to the school in force to honor a teacher who had nurtured them and, in many cases, determined their future careers. All the rooms at the surrounding inns were filled.

Those who had worked with Florence on the school plays had gathered in the grove of weeping birches so they could enter together. Another cadre, her history of art stars, were wearing silk scarves tied in the special way that Florence always wore hers. Many of the girls had labored to write their first letters of condolence to Mrs. Meagher's sister. Or to Mr. Meagher, although there were many fewer of those. For those handicapping the investigation into Florence's death, Ray Meagher was the odds-on favorite.

By ten-thirty, the lovely old Greek Revival Congregational church on the town green was filling. A trio of girls playing piano, violin, and cello had prepared a selection of chamber music that was going pretty well. Those who felt themselves to be chief mourners found seats near the front, while those who were simply paying respects chose seats at the back and sides. The girls from the drama club, with Ellie Curtin among the leaders, filed into the pew just behind those reserved for family. The art history girls took the pew across the center aisle.

Hope and Maggie had been invited to sit with Florence's sister and her family. As one of the pretty student ushers led them down the center aisle, Maggie noted how many of the trustees were in attendance, plus a surprising number of townspeople. Hugo and Caroline Hollister were there. Kate Curtin and Todd Goldsmith came in together, followed by Mattias Benes, the bookseller. Hope gave a squeeze to the shoulder of a woman seated on the aisle as they passed. Margot McCartney. Their usher gestured them into the pew in front of Ellie Curtin and her friends.

Toward the top of the hour, as the musicians were subsiding, Ray Meagher, wearing a blue suit and an unfortunate polyester tie, walked down the aisle with Marcia Goldsmith. He looked neither to right or left, although most eyes in the church were on him. Behind Ray, with one of the student ushers, came a tall woman in a dun-colored pant suit, wiry and businesslike, who took a seat in the pew beside Ray and began fanning herself with the funeral program. Her high bulging forehead was so exactly like Ray's butternut squash head that Maggie guessed this was one of his estranged siblings, come to show some family solidarity. Following her was Lyndon McCartney. He sat by himself in the empty pew behind Ray's, ten rows apart from his wife.

At 11:00 A.M., the side door to the robing room opened, and Florence's sister with her husband and daughters made their way from the minister's study up to the front of the church and into the front pew. Suzanne's eyes were wet and red, and her daughters too had been weeping. An older couple who had been with them joined Maggie and Hope in the pew behind.

"All rise," intoned the minister, and the service began.

The hymns were led by the church choir. The first was "Onward Christian Soldiers," discontinued from the hymnal because of its incorrect martial tone but printed on an insert in the program and sung in all six verses. It has been a favorite hymn of their father's, according to Suzanne. After the minister's invocation, Florence's older niece mounted to the lectern and with a trembling voice read the first lesson. The next offering was a student's performance of "Goodbye England's Rose," as Elton John had performed it in honor of Princess Diana. The girl had been practicing all week, and even though few of the lyrics fit Mrs. Meagher, the church was filled with snuffling as the song concluded.

Christina Liggett, who had been seated at the side with the minister, climbed into the pulpit, laid her notes on the lectern, and looked out over the roomful of faces. Maggie felt protective and anxious as she began her eulogy.

"Florence Meagher was not a perfect person," she said. Her voice was clear and steady. "Few of us are. But she was a wholehearted and loving woman, committed to her students, devoted to her family, doing her best to make the kindest and most helpful use she could of every hour of every day. She . . ."

Christina faltered, and Maggie saw her attention snagged by something at the back of the church. There was a murmur behind them. Hope was already turning toward the disturbance, and Maggie felt Hope's hand briefly clasp her shoulder. What happened next happened so fast that it took many times the seconds in which it played out to retell afterward, and longer than that to fully understand.

A figure with a mangy mat of white-blond hair, draped in a long blue raincoat, was walking down the center aisle. Jesse Goldsmith. Christina's eyes were locked on him, as if she'd been frozen midsentence. One of the main doors to the church stood open behind him, leaving an almost blinding rectangle of daylight in the cool dimness of the rear wall of the sanctuary. As he passed down the rows, people stared and whispered. Ray Meagher had turned to watch the figure come, looking puzzled, his mouth slightly open. At the very back of the church someone was up and moving; they would realize much later that this was Detective Phillips, but it was still in no way clear what kind of scene the boy intended to make, or whose job it was to stop him.

Then it was. Jesse reached the front of the church, turned to face the crowd, and shrugged off the raincoat, which had mostly concealed the pump-action shotgun he carried. There were screams of shock and fear, and bangs and scraping of people ducking for cover as he scanned the front pews. Jesse found his target, pumped the forearm of the gun, and raised it to his shoulder, aiming straight at a paralyzed Ellie Curtin, and then with a bang he screamed and fell to the floor as pandemonium broke out and Maggie realized that Hope had shot him.

Marcia Goldsmith, screaming, was trying to climb over Ray to get to her son. The minister, from the side, and Phillips and Bark from the back, ran to the boy on the floor, the minister looking like a huge black bird with a white neck ring, the two detectives knocking people out of the way as they pelted forward, shouting, weapons drawn. By the time they reached Jesse, the minister had captured the shotgun and unchambered the shell. Maggie was looking at the 9 mm pistol in Hope's hand.

"Well aren't you just full of surprises," she said. Hope handed her the gun and started rooting in her bag.

"I don't want this thing," Maggie said.

"Don't worry, the safety is on. Hold on a hot minute, I have to find my concealed carry license. Tell me it isn't in my other purse."

"You mean you've been packing heat the whole time you've been here?"

"No, I told you, it's usually in my sock drawer. I just had a feeling about today, though. People get so emotional at funerals."

The school nurse was now ministering to Jesse, who was alternately whimpering with self-pity and emitting howls of rage and pain; Hope had shot him in the thigh. The nurse and Ray were rigging a tourniquet, using a cloth from the altar and Ray's unfortunate necktie, while Marcia wept and told her son that everything was all right, which it definitely wasn't, and about two hundred people called 9-1-1 yelling for ambulances. Detective Phillips had Jesse's hands cuffed, in front of him because he screamed so much when she tried to cuff him behind that she feared that the boy's mother would attack her. Detective Bark had made his way back to Hope and Maggie's pew.

"Mrs. Babbin?"

"I've got it here someplace, just give me a second," Hope said. Then she found the necessary paper in a zipped pouch with her lipstick and keys and a clean hanky, and handed it over. After thorough study, Bark handed it back and said, "Pretty good shot. No bones broken, no major arteries."

"If he hadn't been facing me head-on I'd have hit him in the fanny, but I couldn't get my shot."

"They're still going to want to talk to you in White Plains," said Bark.

"Exciting. Will I need a lawyer? I know a lovely one."

"Wouldn't be a bad idea."

Ellie Curtin had gotten past her cowering friends and was now sobbing in her mother's arms in the main aisle. Kate's face was the greenish white of a person in shock. Maggie slid out of the pew and went to join Detective Phillips and the minister in the growing clump of people surrounding Jesse. She spoke to them quickly and briefly. Phillips nodded, and the minister hurried off toward his study.

Marcia Goldsmith was still on the floor cradling her son's head, murmuring to him. She raised her eyes to Maggie's with a look of pure hatred. Maggie went to Christina, who stood now at the foot of the pulpit looking as if she was in the middle of a country where she couldn't speak the language and her GPS had just lost its satellite signal.

Recalculating. Recalculating.

Christina brought her eyes into focus on Maggie standing in front of her. Sounding dazed, she remarked, "I just remembered what I did with Alison's cell phone."

The minister and Maggie between them dealt with the influx of police and EMTs and the process of getting Jesse, still handcuffed and shrieking, now strapped to a gurney, out of the church and into the ambulance. Christina was stationed at the door of the church, modeling composure and dispensing calm remarks. As Marcia Goldsmith passed, rushing to follow the ambulance to the hospital, she turned ferociously to Christina as if she had denied it and yelled, "He *loved* Florence! He *loved* her!"

A few mourners, mostly from the village but also a few of the students, came to the door to murmur that they were out of time and had to be going. Christina murmured back that they should take their seats again. Some did. Between such ministrations, she had time to notice Alison Casey sitting by herself. There were students in front of her and behind, but no one joined her. Christina expected Alison to saunter out, but she sat where she was, head bowed, face blank, pretending to read the funeral program over and over.

Police, having arrived in force from White Plains, wanted to set up interview rooms all over the church and process the crime scene, but by force of personality Maggie and the minister, with Bark's help, persuaded everyone to take seats and allow the ritual of mourning to be completed. Since there were police cars parked all around the church, including on the lawn, with men and women in riot gear standing around talking to one another or muttering into walkie-talkies to who knew whom, no one crucial was likely to slip past them. And in Bark's opinion, the statements they would take when the service was over and everyone had calmed down were likely to be more reliable than if they talked to people whose adrenaline levels were still up to their eyeballs. Meanwhile, the press had gathered in ever-increasing numbers in a parking lot across the street, trying to find someone to interview.

In a surprisingly short time, given the circumstances, they were under way again. Ray, tieless, had returned to his pew, where he sat with his ash-colored sister, whose pinched expression seemed to say that she had known coming here was a mistake. Of course it wouldn't just be a nice normal funeral service.

Christina returned to the pulpit. She was steady now, and focused. She said, "Before we resume the service, I'd like to ask you all to put away your devices. The Wi-Fi service has been turned off to give us all time to recover our best selves.

"We are here today to mourn a tragedy. Unexpectedly, we almost had another. The worst thing we can do, now, is talk to the press or post anything on social media about what happened. To do that is to make this near tragedy glamorous and invite imitation. Please, rise to this occasion. When we are done here, resist the impulse to talk about what we don't yet understand. Florence's family deserves that respect and the young man and his family should be allowed their privacy. Please consider how you would feel if he were your son or brother."

With that, after a moment of silence, Christina resumed her eulogy. When she finished, a senior girl came forward and read an affectionate remembrance, and the congregation recited the Twenty-Third Psalm in unison. For the final hymn, at the nieces' request, they sang "Silent Night." There was something piercingly sweet in the repeated refrain, *Sleep in heavenly peace.* The minister gave a parting blessing and reminded the congregation that the family had invited all who wished to join them to retire to the fellowship hall downstairs for refreshments.

When the church doors were reopened, a wall of reporters with microphones and camera crews outside the narthex set up a roar of questions that joined with the blaring sunlight to create a wall of assault. This had the beneficial effect of driving a surprising number of people downstairs to the fellowship hall instead of out into the barrage of ravening curiosity. From there the mourners would be able to leave in twos and threes from back and side doors.

In the hall, sandwiches and punch were being served. Many of the girls lined up to speak to Mrs. Meagher's sister. Someone realized that Florence's ashes, in a mottled salt-glazed pottery jar, had been left upstairs on the altar along with a vase of lilies and a framed studio portrait of Florence taken right after her college graduation. These were retrieved and brought downstairs to sit on the table with the punch and the visitors' book.

Phillips and Bark stayed to the bitter end of the reception, overseeing the taking of statements from this cloud of witnesses. They were also closely watching Ray. Bark had hoped that Ray's behavior might in some way give a clue to the nature of his inner turmoil, but Jesse Goldsmith had introduced so much outer turmoil that no one's behavior could be said to be normal or otherwise. They clocked who spoke to Ray and who didn't though, the former group consisting mostly of people who knew little about the couple or the case. Certainly, Suzanne and her family treated him as if he weren't in the room.

They were also keeping Hope Babbin in their sights. She was waiting for a junior from her lawyer's office to arrive to accompany her to the station in White Plains. In the meantime, she wasn't exactly in custody, but the detectives didn't want her going anywhere, which she said she understood perfectly. She sat with Phillips while Bark worked the room.

"You don't have to say anything," said Phillips, "but I'm curious that you happened to be carrying."

"I don't mind," said Hope. "My son Buster thought I should be armed."

"He's the deputy sheriff?"

"Yes."

"Any particular reason?"

"He likes guns," said Hope.

Phillips nodded. "He made you take the training?"

"Yes, I did very well. Then he took me gun shopping. We hadn't been shopping together since I bought him his last school blazer in sixth grade."

"In Maine, you bought the gun?"

"Yes, they have a wonderful store near him, where you can also buy groceries or rent a wedding dress. Did you know guns come in colors? There was a very pretty purple one, but I chose gray because I didn't think purple would go with everything." Surveying the room, she added, "I don't know how your case is going, but if Ray's life depended on the court of public opinion it wouldn't look good."

"No," Evelyne Phillips agreed.

"Am I allowed to ask, how *is* your case going?"

"You can *ask*," said Phillips.

After a pause, Hope offered, "I know that his alibi fell through. Ray's."

Phillips looked startled. "You do?"

"Yes." She explained about her lunch with Margot McCartney. "I assume you've checked the cameras in the casino that night."

"We have," said Phillips. "They have pretty good coverage in the game room, but it isn't perfect. A couple of cameras were off-line, a couple badly aimed."

"Did you find Ray?"

"We did not. Not in the elevator going to his room either. But it's hardly proof you can take to court."

"You'd think they'd be security conscious, with all those people wandering around with chips and cash."

"I guess margins are tight in the casino business."

"How about his room key? Do they know who uses them when?"

"The record shows that the key issued to Ray opened his door at two-forty-four Friday morning."

Hope was thoughtful.

"Of course, that only proves his key was used, not that he was the one who used it."

"Right."

"Witnesses in the game rooms remember him?"

"The craps dealer does, but he can't swear to times. Who is that talking to Ray now?"

Hope turned. "That's Hugo Hollister. He's a trustee at the school. His daughter is the student who found Florence's body."

Phillips watched the pair. Hugo seemed to be reassuring Ray. At one point, he gave his arm a squeeze and seemed to be giving him a string of advice. Ray was paying close attention, and both women saw that Ray was mollified at receiving the kindness of this world beater in his flawless linen suit, with the silk pocket square that matched his tie.

Hugo gave Ray a pat on the back and left him.

"Are they friends?" Phillips asked.

"News to me, if true. I'll ask Hugo's wife."

"You know his wife?"

"Yes, historically."

"Is she here?"

Hope pointed out Caroline.

"Let me know what you find out, will you?"

"Will do."

"By the way, could you tell who Jesse was aiming at? Was it you or Mrs. Detweiler?"

"No, it was Ellie Curtin. The girl sitting right behind us."

"That's Ellie Curtin?" The detective sounded alarmed.

"Yes. Why?"

Detective Phillips decided she shouldn't be talking about this with a civilian, but her mind went back to the day she had gone to interview Jesse. He had made a disturbing impression on her, his demeanor unpleasant, refusing to meet her eyes, answering in monosyllables with an air of contempt when he answered at all. Except when he suddenly asked her, "Who told you to come here? It was Ellie Curtin, wasn't it? I knew she'd blame me."

When Phillips had replied that she didn't know who Ellie Curtin was, the boy had finally looked at her, his small eyes blazing. "That jealous slut. She was always hanging around us. She knew how much Florence liked me."

The associate sent by Hope's lawyer arrived, a slender young woman in a pinstripe suit with a pencil skirt and platform pumps that could break your ankle if you fell off them. Hope went off with her to her date with destiny in White Plains, and Phillips went to find a place where she had cell phone service to call the hospital and see if the shooter could yet be interviewed.

When the final stragglers were saying good-byes, and at last Suzanne Cuneo was gathering her family to start the journey back to Virginia, she found Maggie to say, "I brought you the manuscript you were asking about."

Maggie was briefly baffled.

"Florey's novel. It wasn't finished, you know, but I thought you might like to see it."

"Of course," said Maggie.

"It would be so wonderful for Florey, if you thought that a publisher might . . . well, you live in New York. Maybe you'll know someone who could take a look at it."

"Of course," said Maggie again. Suzanne fished a thumb drive out of her purse and handed it over. "Seems ridiculous, doesn't it? So much time and work stored on a thing the size of a piece of gum." Her husband was beside her, holding Florence's mortal remains, while the niece carried the framed photograph to return to the mantelpiece in Virginia. Across the room, Maggie noticed Ray staring at the urn Matt Cuneo had taken, but he didn't move. Suzanne looked at Maggie for a second more, as if trying to ask her something, extract a promise. But in the end she was too undone to translate it into words, and the family started for their car.

After Maggie helped the minister reboot his Wi-Fi router, she walked down to the head's house to wait with Nimbus for Christina to get back from the hospital. She'd have liked to have gone herself, but the point was to take support and comfort to Marcia Goldsmith, now in grievously deep emotional water, and it was clear to her from that moment in the church that her presence would not bring ease to that particular sufferer.

Maggie had a kettle for tea ready when Christina finally came in, dropped into a chair, and pried her shoes off.

"Have you eaten?" she asked the younger woman.

"I can't remember," said Christina, gratefully accepting a mug. "Wait, yes. I had some peanut butter crackers from a machine."

"Would you eat a scrambled egg, if I made it for you?"

"I don't think so."

Maggie didn't press. If Christina didn't know how to maintain her own machinery by now, feeding her an egg wasn't going to help. "How is the boy?"

"He'll be fine. It's a deep flesh wound."

"And Marcia?"

"Terrible. It was her raincoat he was wearing. She doesn't know where he got the shotgun. Her husband came to the hospital but she wouldn't speak to him, she's fending off everybody."

"I'm sorry."

"Yes," said Christina.

They sat in silence until Maggie said, "On the other hand—did you really remember where Alison's cell phone is?"

Christina nodded, swallowing a hot gulp. "I'm afraid to look, in case I'm wrong, but when everyone started screaming I had a memory of coming into this room and getting down my sewing basket. A sense memory of feeling a button in my pocket. I'd pulled it off my jacket at some point during that day and I wanted to deal with it before I lost it."

When you're surrounded with things gone wrong that you can't fix, it's calming to fix something you can. Like a button.

"Where is the basket?"

Christina pointed to a shelf over Maggie's head. Among the books and ring binders there was a round container about the size of a cookie tin woven long ago from sweetgrass. Maggie stood to lift it down. The lid had a pattern of concentric green and tan rings woven in.

"My grandmother's," said Christina as Maggie handed it to her and sat down again. "Mom doesn't sew."

She took the lid off the basket, and there, among measuring tapes and needle papers, pin cushions and dressmaker's chalks, lay a scratched and grimy black smart phone. Maggie gave a small whoop of relief.

"I knew it had to be somewhere," Christina said. She laid the phone on the table between them. "Now what?"

Maggie pushed down the locking button on the top corner that would have brought it to life if it had any juice. Nothing. She peered at the slot where the charger would connect and said, "I assume you have a drawer for mystery cords?"

Christina did, since all such things on campus had to be disposed of in an environment-neutral way, and a campuswide green waste drive was the duty of the ecology club, which had gone moribund when its faculty advisor left to have a baby. She returned from the drawer with a snarl of charger cords, earbuds, ancient stupid phones, and two pagers. Maggie soon found a charger that would fit and plugged Alison's phone into the wall socket. It began to flicker and chirp, awakening from coma.

"Won't it be locked?" Christina asked.

"With old ones, sometimes they don't bother." But Alison had; up came a keypad.

"So we're cooked."

"Not if she's lazy about passwords. Most kids are."

TRIX took care of it. They had a screen of icons. Maggie swiped through, to see what was there. Facebook, Twitter, Vine, TickTalk, Snapchat, Instagram, YouTube. The phone's Message app.

Christina didn't look happy.

"Should you be doing this? I don't want *you* to . . ."

"I'll risk it. I don't seriously think they'd bring a case against me, and I don't have a career at stake if they do."

"Picture roll—no thank you. E-mail—later for that. Texts—wow. It looks as if she never erased a thing. The most recent ones are back and forth with Ellie Curtin. . . . Okay, TickTalk. Here we go."

The app was set to log in automatically. It gave her a sunny home screen, with a couple of cartoon clocks talking to each other. She scrolled backward to see what had been posted from this account. Christina watched her.

"'Does your roommate have mange? Mine does,'" read Maggie.

Christina put her hand over her mouth. Eventually, Maggie handed the phone back to Christina, who read what she had found.

After a few minutes, she looked up at Maggie and said, "Oh my god."

"Yes."

"We admitted Pinky right before the school year started and Alison was the only one in the class with an open bed in her room. I thought—well, I guess I thought since Alison was being shunned that it might help her to shepherd someone else new and alone."

"Might have worked."

"But it didn't." She gestured toward the phone as if it had started seeping noxious goo. Maggie took it back.

"She's pretty horrible to someone called Earlobe Girl too," she said, back on the TickTalk screen.

Christina sighed. "Gussie Spoonmaker. A day girl. She's one of my projects. Can Alison really have hoped these girls would drink bleach? Or jump in front of a train?"

"Who knows?"

They sat in silence for a bit.

"So the pattern here," Maggie said, "is that she targets whoever is vulnerable?"

"Apparently."

"She doesn't have any special animus against Lily?"

"No idea. She's isolated and angry, so she stirs the pot. Now, how am I going to protect Pinky?"

Maggie said, "Why don't you invite her to live here? While she 'convalesces'?" Maggie made air quotes.

Christina brightened. "Brilliant. I'm chockablock with spare bedrooms. Thank you!"

"You're welcome."

"If she isn't allergic to cats. You said the text messages go way back."

"Yes."

"Back before Alison came to us?"

"Let's see. She came here when?"

"Beginning of last school year."

Maggie was scrolling backward. She came to something that stopped her. She studied it. She rapidly scrolled further back, then slowly and carefully read through post after post.

Christina said nervously, "We shouldn't be doing this."

"She shouldn't have broken the rules. When she chose to, she must have known there could be consequences."

"So far, I can't see that she's ever suffered much of a consequence for anything," said Christina.

After a beat, in which she finished what she was reading, Maggie said, "You'd be wrong about that." She scrolled back to the top of the thread she'd been following and handed the phone to Christina.

Christina read in silence. Scrolling slowly. Once in a while looking up at Maggie. Finally she turned the phone off and put it on the table between them.

"Oh, god," she said.

Maggie nodded. "Do you think her parents had any idea?"

Christina thought about it. "More tea?" she asked.

"Sure."

Christina refilled the kettle. At last she said, "I can't imagine they did. If they'd told me—I would have . . ."

There was silence until the kettle whistled and they both had fresh mugs steaming in front of them.

"What am I going to do?" Christina asked. "How could young people—children—say such things to someone they know, someone they see every day?"

"This is something your generation is going to have to solve. She said, with a carefree laugh."

"Oh, thanks," Christina said. Then added, "Poor little thing. I mean, it seems crazy to feel sorry for her, but she *is* a child."

"Yes. As for what you're going to do, it's too late to talk with Alison directly. You might have been able to help her when she first came to you, if you'd known, but it's gone too far for that; these are criminal matters."

"So what do I do?"

"I think you should take this phone to your lawyer. Have him set up a meeting with Alison's parents. Both of them."

"And me?"

"No. You've seen the phone and you don't want them off on a sidetrack about whether you had a right to look at it. Have him tell them where to start and have them read the whole history there in his office, from the boy's posts and the shaming at her last school down to the things she posted about her victims."

"What if they won't read it?"

"They will. No parent can resist knowing their children's secret lives."

"And then?"

"Then your lawyer will tell them that they are going to withdraw their lawsuit. Otherwise you'll go to trial and this will all wind up in the press. He can recommend they withdraw Alison from the school; that's up to you. If she stayed you might be able to help her, but I doubt she will. I'll send you some names of people who can advise them what to do next if they take her out."

Christina looked glum. "When are you going?"

"This evening. I'm sorry, I wish we'd had more time."

Christina nodded. She had five weeks to go until commencement, four of them in May, the month where everything that hasn't yet gone wrong during the school year blows up at once. She couldn't imagine what that would be, given what they'd just been through, but she wasn't looking forward to it.

"Christina, look at me."

The younger woman did so.

"You are going to be fine. The school will get through this, and so will you. You are stronger than you think, and wiser than you think. You did a wonderful job today and it's going to play very well in this community."

The phone rang. Christina punched a button on the landline unit on the table that turned on the speaker, and said, "Yes, Sharon?"

"I'm sorry to bother you," said Sharon's etiolated voice, "but your mother's on the line and she says it's an emergency.

*　　*　　*

"Tell me the truth—why did you bring the gun to the funeral?" Maggie asked. They were in Hope's car, headed for the city. Hope's driving was usually a source of low-grade terror for Maggie, but they had so much to catch each other up on, she had decided to risk it rather than take the train.

"That sounds like the beginning of a moron joke."

"Whose horoscope did you cast? Mine?"

"I just had a feeling."

"Pants on fire."

"Oh, all right. Yours. And wasn't I right?"

"You know, I'm beginning to be sort of impressed."

"As well you should be."

"How long have you had it? The gun?"

"It was Buster and Brianna's Christmas present to me."

"That was a pretty good shot you got off."

"I found a terribly nice shooting range, where the police go. I practice every week. I have my own ear protectors."

"Do they have any idea what to make of you at the Chilton Club?"

"Not really. Tell me about the cell phone."

Maggie hesitated. "I don't want to shock you."

"Go ahead. I was young once."

"Not like this you weren't."

They rolled south through the gloaming of a spring evening. Lights glinted on the river, and there was pinkish-orange light in the western sky.

Maggie said, "Alison is a year too young for her class, plus she'd been at junior boarding school since she was eleven."

"Why?"

"Good question. The father is British. It may have seemed normal to him. Or maybe there was trouble at home, marital split or something. Christina says they are together now, the parents, so we don't know. What it looks like, from what's on the phone, is a boy asked her for a nude picture. She saved the texts, the way you saved notes from a boy you had a crush on at that age."

"Fourteen?"

"She should have been fourteen, but she was younger. The notes from him are sweet. He says she's the prettiest. He says he loves her eyes, and her flirty answers are so full of hope. She sent him a picture."

"What, a naked selfie?"

"Yes. She wasn't very good at it; you can see her arm holding the phone and most of her face is cut off, but you can see her mouth and enough of the rest of her. But for the boy, it was a joke. Or a bet. She was so young, she didn't have much to show off, but he took a screenshot and apparently posted it someplace where all their friends could see, and then her phone filled up with slut-shaming, including from the girls she used to group-text with ten times a day."

"That's all on her phone?"

"Yup. Boys asking for BJs, girls calling her pathetic, and thirsty, and a slut."

"I suppose a BJ is what I think it is."

"I suppose so too."

"Is school always like this?"

"Pretty much," Maggie said. "It doesn't usually all blow up at once, but it's mostly all happening all the time."

"I have no idea why you retired," said Hope wistfully.

They were in upper Manhattan, keeping pace now with New Yorkers on bicycles, hunched over their handlebars, streaming along Hudson River Park in the evening light. There were runners in T-shirts and tiny shorts pounding along as well. When they were passed by two joyously smiling Rollerbladers in nun's habits, rosary beads swinging, Hope said, "God, I love New York."

"Amen," said Maggie.

"To be continued. I'll drop you at home. I'll be at the Town Club for a couple of days, and then we'll see."

Charlie Bark was at home on Sunday morning, waiting for his younger daughter to suit up for Ultimate Frisbee. Her team was playing in a tournament, and he was driving her to Poughkeepsie. She had just gotten her license but he wasn't crazy about letting her drive herself, and anyway, if she took the car, he'd be stranded. His mobile rang.

"Hey, Charlie," said the desk sergeant on weekend duty at his shop. "Sorry to catch you at home."

"You didn't really catch me, I'm out the door with my kid."

"This won't stop you, I just thought you'd want to know, I just got a call from the sheriff's department in Stroudsburg, Pennsylvania. Someone turned in a lady's purse. Money's all gone, but there was some ID in the name of Florence Meagher, address in Rye-on-Hudson. That's your murder vic, isn't it?"

Bark was suddenly all nerve endings.

"Where was this again?"

"Stroudsburg, PA."

"Where is that exactly?"

"Hang on, I'm googling it."

"Never mind, I can do that. When—"

"Here it is, here it is. Northeast Pennsylvania, on I-80, just over the Delaware Water Gap."

Bark was beginning to sweat down his back, a prickling itchy sensation. "When was it found?"

"Well, that's unclear. It was turned in at some visitors' center at Lake"—he paused to sound it out— "Wall-en-pow-pack a couple of days ago."

"Where the hell is that?"

"Hold on, I'll google it—"

"Don't! I'll do it. Just tell me exactly what you know."

"It was turned in a couple of days ago, that's a quote, I don't know how many, at this visitors' center. It's kind of off-season, and no one knew exactly what to do with it, I mean I guess they put it in a lost and found for a while."

"What does it look like?"

"I don't know. The wallet was gone but somebody finally searched the pockets, probably hoping for change, and they found a library card or receipt or something with a name on it, so the next time someone was going to the big city, they dropped it off. Detectives ran the name through the system and called us."

"Where is the bag now?"

"It's on its way, he's having a deputy drive it over. What do you want me to do with it?"

Bark was torn between an intuition that this was the crack in the wall he'd been waiting for, and the knowledge that if he didn't drive his daughter to her game, she'd go with kids who were about as safe at the wheel, when their friends were along, as a carful of guys in beer hats after the St. Paddy's Day parade.

"Log it in and lock it up, will you? I'll be in soon as I can."

"Want me to e-mail you a picture, when it gets here?"

"Yes. Thanks."

"You got it."

*   *   *

Alison Casey had been hanging around the stable the last few days. Ellie Curtin was being a bitch to her. Pinky, her roommate, had moved to Ms. Liggett's house because her hair was falling out, and Alison sort of missed her. Sunday afternoon she had nothing to do except go smoke in the maintenance shed behind the pool building, which wasn't that much fun by yourself. The glee club had gone off in a bus for a concert in Hartford. The jocks were having color war softball and lacrosse games. The grinds were writing term papers or studying for exams. She herself was supposed to be writing a paper on *John Brown's Body,* this long poem, but she couldn't sit still. The TickTalk board was full of chatter, some of it not very nice about her, but she had nothing to add, no one to show off for. She didn't have anyone to talk to.

Honey Marcus was schooling her dressage mare, Ginger Rogers, in lateral movements in the outdoor ring when she noticed Alison sitting by herself on a folding chair she must have carried out from the stable, watching. It was a hot day for early May, and she was sitting in full sun, her eyes behind mirrored sunglasses. Honey danced the horse on a diagonal from one corner of the ring to the opposite end. She trotted with long elegant strides the perimeter of the ring, then she made the lateral move from corner to corner the other way. Over and over, the improvement in style invisible to the untrained eye. When Honey was satisfied that the horse had learned all she could absorb in one session, she turned Ginger and brought her to a halt facing Alison. Then she reversed four steps, as if taking a bow. Alison smiled.

"Do you want to try?" Honey asked.

"Ginger?" Alison asked, sounding startled. Ginger Rogers was a lot of horse, for all her delicacy, young and spooky. Alison had seen her buck like a baby when Honey had her on a longe line.

"No, she's done for the day," said Honey. "But why don't you go down and tack Free Willy? You're ready to start some little jumps, don't you think?"

"I don't have a helmet," said Alison.

"There are extras in the tack room." She slid off Ginger Rogers and pulled the reins over the mare's head. At a gesture, Alison came to hold the horse's head while Honey slid the stirrups up to the top of the leathers. Then she took the reins and started walking toward the stable. After a minute, Alison fell in beside her. She wasn't used to being alone with grown-ups.

In the stable, as Honey untacked her horse, she said to Alison, "Go get Willy," and Alison went.

By the time Ginger was cooled and curried and brushed and back in her stall, Alison had her horse groomed and tacked. She led the horse to the mounting block, and Honey held Willy's head while she mounted and adjusted her stirrups. Alison's fear was palpable, but Honey was unperturbed. She knew the girl only a little, but she knew the horse a lot.

After a warm-up out in the ring, Honey started them trotting over poles laid flat on the ground. Alison tensed and took a hank of mane in her hand, a measure of her fearfulness, but Free Willy could have earned a teaching degree in his own right. He clipped neatly over the poles, never varying his gait, until Alison's body relaxed and she posted smoothly through the obstacles. Next, Honey put the pole up to the first rung between posts, barely a foot off the ground. This was the momentous change, a jump. More of an elevated rocking motion than a departure from earth, as Willy took it, and Alison felt the surprised flush of success that Honey had meant her to. Her weight had been too far back, but Willy didn't care, and by the time she'd done it five more times, she'd gotten it right, felt the horse gather himself for the hop, and moved her weight to above the withers in sync with the animal.

"Ready for a notch up?" Honey asked.

Alison, who for quite a number of years hadn't had such sustained individual attention from an adult who wasn't angry at her, said, "Okay." She meant *No, that's enough,* but Honey was already moving the pegs up the posts and replacing the pole. At a signal from Honey, Alison moved Willy into a trot along the rail away from the fence, and then with a very small tug of the rein, turned him toward the jump. The horse did the rest. Broke into a loping canter, gathered himself, and popped over the fence, and never complained when Alison missed the moment and landed back on his kidneys as he hit the ground. Honey said nothing; she just motioned with the crop she carried that Alison should do it again. By the time she had really gotten into the rhythm, Honey was smiling at Alison. Honey's smile was a rare thing.

Alison walked the horse to cool him down, then followed Honey back to the stable and proudly went through the routine of untacking, grooming, and returning the horse to his stall as Honey did odd housekeeping jobs and kept an eye on her. When she was done, Honey said, "That wasn't so scary, was it?"

Alison, who had in fact been terrified through most of it, said, "No, it was great."

"Come back tomorrow and we'll raise the bar."

Alison ducked her head, meaning okay, or maybe. And she made no move to leave.

Honey said, "Want a Coke or something?"

After hesitation, Alison said, "Sure."

So Honey led the way upstairs.

This was actually not a practice she wanted to establish, the crossing of the line with a student into her private life, but she sensed something. At the top of the stairs, instead of inviting Alison in, she said, "I'll be right back." When she came back out, Alison was sitting on the top step, looking down the hill toward the campus. Honey sat beside her and showed her two cans of iced tea. "This is all we've got," she said. "Peach or lemon?"

When they both had their drinks open, they sat side by side and watched Main Street dozing in the afternoon light. Honey waited.

Finally Alison said, "I know something I should tell somebody."

"What would that be?"

Alison took a sudden interest in a burr that was caught in her jeans, above her barn boot. She studied it, then pulled it out and flicked it.

"A girl has a key to the pool."

Honey turned to look at her.

"Where the body was found?"

"Yes."

"What girl?"

"Lily Hollister."

Honey stared, then asked, "How do you know this?"

"I caught her coming out with her hair wet. I saw her lock the door outside Miss Scheinerlein's office."

"When was this?"

"Months ago."

"And you're sure she wasn't just locking up for Greta? Ms. Scheinerlein?"

"Yes, because the JV swim team was away at a meet. Coach wasn't there. No one was supposed to be in there."

After a beat, Honey asked, "And how did you happen to see her?"

Alison had hoped not to be asked that. But she answered after a pause, "I was coming back from the village. I took a shortcut."

Honey understood that this meant she was on that part of the campus at a time she should have been somewhere else and was hoping not to be seen herself.

"Lily Hollister is the girl who found the body," Honey said, after thought.

"Says she found it," said Alison. "She hated Mrs. Meagher." And with a sudden stab of alarm, Honey couldn't tell if Alison was frightened or was trying to ruin someone's life.

P*am Moldower was mooching around* the faculty lounge Tuesday evening, waiting for the signal to go up to the dining hall for dinner, when Honey Marcus came in. Pam was startled to see her in a skirt; it occurred to her she might never have seen Honey's bare legs before. Pam thought that if she had legs like that, she'd wear miniskirts at all times.

"Hello, stranger," she said as Honey took a seat at the central worktable and picked up the sports section of the paper. "You coming in to dinner?"

"I thought I would. Greta is off somewhere, and I don't really cook."

"You picked a good night for it. It's chicken fricassee."

Honey nodded, as if she hadn't registered. She turned the page of the paper. Then she put it down and said, "Actually, I wanted to talk to you."

"Me?"

"Yes. Is Lily Hollister in your dorm?"

"No, she's in Sloane Two. Her best friend is in mine, and I see a fair amount of her. Why do you ask?"

"You know. Greta works with her. Someone mentioned something about Lily the other day and I wondered if it was true. Thought I should ask someone who knows her."

Pam was well aware that this sentence meant "someone besides Greta." Interesting.

"What was it? About Lily?"

"That she didn't like Florence Meagher very much."

"Oh," said Pam. "Well, that's an understatement."

"This is some well-known fact?"

"A truth universally acknowledged," said Pam.

Honey sat with that. "I didn't really know Florence, but we— well you know. Lily and Greta. What did Florence ever do to Lily?"

"Poor Florence. She tried so hard. You'd have had to see her in action to get it, but . . . she had this laser instinct for the kids who were lost or wounded. She'd make special pets of them."

"Like the Goldsmith kid."

"Exactly. She tried it with Lily, and Lily *hated* her for it. The idea that Lily was in need of *anything* that Florence Meagher had to offer. That Lily was in the same category as Jesse Goldsmith or Gussie Spoonmaker. She has quite the ego, our Miss Hollister. Greta never told you?"

Honey shook her head. "She says she's driven."

"I'll say," said Pam. "I don't believe in spirit animals, but if I did, Florence would have been a cocker spaniel. Lily is more like a cave bear. Fine when it's hibernating down there at the back of the cave while you're up in the front eating your dinner, but Christ on a cracker, you don't want to see it on its hind legs coming at you out of the dark."

The five-minute bell rang and Pam stood up. "You coming?"

There was a pause, then Honey said, "In a minute."

Avis Metcalf couldn't exactly remember how she knew Maggie Detweiler. In her New York world almost everyone knew who Maggie was: legendary head of the legendary Winthrop School. Avis hadn't sent her daughter—her late daughter and only child—to Winthrop. It was coed and the most intellectual of the city's private schools, and the Winthrop girls had the reputation in some circles of being bullies in bloomers.

Bloomers. When her darling Grace had been in school, girls still played field hockey in tunics and fantastically unbecoming pouchy pull-ups over their undies. Those had finally gone the way of the bustle, thank god. But Grace had been a gentler, milder sort of girl than the Winthrop world beaters, and Avis had chosen one of the all-girls schools for her, where she had thrived but from which she had emerged unmarked by any particular drive or interest. The only clear vision she had had for her future was that she wanted to be married and she wanted it to be nothing like the marriage of her parents.

And she had been, and it hadn't been. And now there was nothing left but Avis's granddaughter. If Grace had gone to Winthrop instead, would. . . . No. Stop. That was not a permitted train of thought.

For her part, Maggie hadn't seen Avis since Grace Metcalf's funeral. Maggie had gone because her school community was so shocked at what had happened, because there were so many ties from Grace's family, and her husband's family, to Maggie's school community. She'd spoken to Avis at the reception after the service, which had been devastating, but distinctly felt that Avis's body was there, upright and muddling through, but her heart and mind were in a medically induced coma somewhere else.

Maggie had called Avis's gallery to make an appointment and learned that Avis mostly worked from home these days, since she was a single grandmother. Now Maggie was in the elevator of Avis's grand Park Avenue building, the doorman having announced her from below.

Avis was waiting at her open door. Her smile of welcome was warm and the color had returned to her austere face with its high-beaked nose and deep eyes. Her hair retained most of its dark natural color, though it was shot through with white. She wore, to Maggie's surprise, a long-sleeved T-shirt and blue jeans on her bony frame and laceless sneakers on her otherwise bare feet.

"Pardon the *déshabillé*," Avis said as she waved her in and led her to the living room. "My granddaughter and I take ceramics together on Wednesdays. I always come home spattered in mud."

"What a great idea," Maggie said.

"We've been at it for years. I've stuck with hand building but Lindy is on the wheel. She made me this," said Avis, picking up a small but beautifully shaped bowl, glazed a pure sky blue, with a red dot slightly off center in the bottom.

"That's lovely," said Maggie, who'd been to a lot of student art shows and meant it. "How old is Lindy?"

"Nine."

"I'm impressed."

"Will you have some tea? Coffee?"

"Coffee if it's no trouble."

Avis rang a little hand bell that sat on the table beside her chair, and a tiny woman in a gray uniform appeared, then bustled back toward the kitchen with her marching orders. It was like visiting someone's grandmother, Maggie reflected, but of course, Avis *was* someone's grandmother, and she had always been like someone from an earlier, more formal generation.

There was a silence in the living room. Avis said eventually, "Forgive me—are you connected to Paul Detweiler? Is that how we met?"

"He was my husband," said Maggie. "He bought me a very beautiful Rembrandt print from you for my birthday one year."

"Ah," said Avis. "Cows in a village lane? I remember. I hope you still have it."

"My prized possession."

"And—Paul?"

"He was killed in the Middle East. It's a long time ago now."

"That's right," said Avis thoughtfully. "That's right. I knew that. He was a lovely man. I was very fond of him."

"I was too," Maggie said, and smiled.

"Forgive me for losing track of the details."

"Don't worry. You are completely excused. Things get lost in the fire."

"Yes. Well—how can I help you? Are you interested in a purchase? Or a sale?"

"Neither at the moment. I need some art world education, if you're willing."

"Of course. I'll do my best," said Avis.

"I'm hoping you can tell me a little about Hugo Hollister."

Avis sat very still for just a beat too long to conceal her feelings although she was deeply averse to idle gossip. When she spoke, she said blandly, "He's a charmer, isn't he? Oh, thank you, Ursula. Put it right here. Bless you."

The tiny woman had come in with a tray bearing a coffee service and a plate of thin mints.

"He is charming, yes," said Maggie. "And very bright, I think."

"Yes," said Avis. She poured coffee, asked about sugar and cream, offered the mints. "How have you happened across him? I haven't seen him in years."

Interesting. If Avis liked him, and cared, Maggie would have expected her to ask how Hugo was. That she didn't ask suggested much.

"He's married to a very nice woman, and has a daughter at the Rye Manor School. You may have heard, they've had some trouble up there." She watched closely as Avis Metcalf digested this and worked at balancing some internal weights and counterweights.

"I had heard something," she said.

"Hugo is on the board of Rye Manor. I've been consulting with the young school head, coaching her while she gets the ship back on course."

"Ah," said Avis. "And whom has Hugo married?"

"A woman named Caroline Westphall. That was her maiden name."

Avis looked startled. "Angus Westphall's little sister?"

"Yes."

There was a silence. Maggie didn't want to rush Avis. It was better, when people were wrestling with principles, to let them work it out without distraction.

Eventually Avis said, in a different tone, "I do know Hugo Hollister. How can I help?"

"The trouble at the school is serious, and confusing. You know what schools are like; a million things going on at once. In this case, we're trying to sort out what's relevant and what's not. Hugo and Caroline have a daughter who is involved."

"Involved in what way?" Avis asked, perhaps more sharply than she meant to.

"We're not sure. Probably by mischance, but—I need to know whom I can trust."

"I'd bet you can trust Caroline Westphall from here to the moon," said Avis.

"I agree with you. And Hugo? He's been very helpful to us so far. Are they a pair?"

Avis rang her little bell and the tiny lady appeared again. "Ursula dear," Avis said, "I changed my mind about the coffee. Could you bring me some ginger ale?"

"The coffee isn't good, missus?" Ursula looked as if she was ready to rush back to the kitchen and fall on her sword.

"It's absolutely perfect, I'd just love some ginger ale with it. Thank you. Maybe Mrs. Detweiler would like—?"

"I'm fine," said Maggie.

After this diversion had given Avis the time she needed, she began again.

"I don't know if you knew my stepmother, Belinda Binney."

Maggie had. Belinda had been a beauty, and as a wealthy young-ish widow, a very well-known woman about town. A philanthropist, a fashion plate, a woman who loved a party, Maggie had known her mostly by reputation and liked everything she knew about her.

"Hugo walked Belinda for several years. You know what I mean?" Maggie did, of course. In Avis's parlance, a walker was a gentleman available for whatever reason to accompany a lady to performances and benefits her husband wouldn't or couldn't attend. A walker was a companion and friend, not a suitor. She provided the invitations, the expensive tickets, the social entrées; he provided company, amusement, and social cover. No one, no matter how beloved or secure, enjoyed walking alone into a crowded ballroom.

"He's from a good family, but not the branch with the money," Avis was saying.

"So he told me," said Maggie.

"He was younger than Belinda, but he was single and straight, mostly. He had beautiful manners, and he was fun. Belinda was having a grand time with him. He knows a lot about art and music;

Belinda loved all that. She introduced him to everyone she knew. Opened a lot of doors for him."

"What kind of doors?"

"He was a private art dealer. Probably still is, I guess that's why you're here. When I knew him, he was making friends with people who collected, or could afford to collect if they could be persuaded to, and then advised them. He made it seem as if he was just doing social favors, for the pleasure of being useful. Belinda's friends thought he was a marvelous resource."

"I sense a 'but' coming."

Avis fell silent again. One of her old-fashioned qualities, Maggie saw with interest, was a true dislike of speaking ill of someone. What a disruption *that* would cause in this reality TV world, if it ever came back in fashion.

"You said he was straight *mostly*," said Maggie, meaning a question.

"Oh, that part was all right. I think very few people are altogether one way or the other," Avis said. "I thought he had a right to his private life. At that point I didn't realize that he *was* paying court to Belinda."

Maggie was startled. Hugo was decades younger than Avis's stepmother had been. She had been a beautiful woman, but . . .

"With hindsight I think he'd been shopping for a rich wife for some time. Since his golden promise had failed to develop into whatever he thought the world owed him. No, the problem was that he was warning Belinda's friends against his competitors, totally trustworthy dealers. One of Belinda's cronies told me in hushed tones that he'd had to stop buying from Colnaghi in London because of irregularities Hugo had mentioned in a slip of the tongue. He thought I'd want to know. Colnaghi! It was ridiculous."

"So you . . ."

"I'm sorry to say, I did nothing at first except pay closer attention. Belinda was a grown-up. But." She got up and left the room, returning with a framed piece, which she handed to Maggie.

It was a sepia ink drawing of the head and torso of a woman, her arms outstretched, a filmy transparent cloth covering one shoulder and breast. Her hair was carelessly wound around her head, tendrils escaping, and the face was turned to the side, eyes downcast. The paper was pocked with age.

"It's absolutely beautiful," Maggie said, after careful study.

"It's a fake," said Avis.

Maggie was shocked.

"Hugo Hollister sold it to Belinda, for I don't want to know how much. He knew she wouldn't know the difference. What he didn't know was that she had bought it as a present for me. And I would."

"But . . . how did you . . . ?"

"It's a Claude Lorrain study. Date should be about 1640. The real one is in the Vatican. I've seen it. This frame is old—he gets the details right. But I had it unframed, and sure enough, the paper is nineteenth century."

"But did Hugo know it was a fake?"

"He knew, all right. This drawing has changed hands once before, in the 1960s. A Berlin dealer sold it to an American museum, I forget which one. They took it off its old mount, discovered the paper was wrong, and the dealer had to buy it back. Where Hugo got it I don't know, but no legitimate dealer would have sold it as anything but a decoration. The provenance was a crock. When I confronted him, he claimed he'd bought it from a Swiss family that had owned it for centuries. When I proved that he hadn't, we made a deal. He'd bow out of Belinda's life, I didn't care how, without hurting her feelings, and I wouldn't call the police."

Maggie was silent. Avis Metcalf seemed stunned at herself, that she had told the story. Wordlessly, she reclaimed the drawing and took it back to wherever she kept it.

"I hope Caroline Westphall is all right," she said when she returned.

After a moment, Maggie said, "I do too." She thanked her hostess and stood to leave, just as a lithe bouncing child with sleek dark hair in a ponytail charged through the door and headed for the kitchen. Avis called, "Hello, Lindy!"

"Hi, Birdy!"

"Could you say good afternoon to Mrs. Detweiler?"

Lindy could. She came and greeted Maggie prettily, then, dancing from one foot to the other, added, "May I be excused?"

Avis released her, and she charged off toward the kitchen. Avis smiled after her.

"Thank you," Maggie said, gathering her things. "May I call you again if I need to?"

Avis opened the drawer of a small antique desk in the corner of the room, and brought Maggie a card with her private contact information on it.

"Greet Caroline for me, if you see her."

"I will," said Maggie.

*   *   *

Greta Scheinerlein was sitting in her office in the pool building. The natatorium, the donor had wanted to call it. She had her grade book in front of her, and her laptop open; she wasn't a particularly fluent writer, so she tried not to leave her student comments to the last minute, as so many teachers did because they could. She knew the head read all of them, fixing grammar and spelling before they went to the parents, and she didn't want to embarrass herself.

She was stuck on Melissa Boardman, new to her class this semester. "Melissa has only chosen the breaststroke because she doesn't like getting her hair wet" was not the kind of thing either the parents or Christina wanted to hear, but what else could she say?

Not saying what was true was emerging as a theme in her life. It was almost six o'clock. She should have locked up and gone home an hour ago, but she hadn't. Now why, exactly? And if she admitted why, what was she going to do about it? She deleted what she had written about Melissa and was staring at the blank screen when she heard a door open and close somewhere out in the locker room.

A natatorium is a place of bright impervious surfaces. An echo chamber. There were footsteps now. Footsteps made by someone in leather shoes. No one wore leather shoes in the pool house. This was a place of athletes, or at least of athletics. The footwear here, if any, had rubber soles.

The footfalls were neither heavy nor light. The person walking was not trying to be quiet. Was that good or bad? She was alone here. That was obvious to any passerby who knew the school rhythms and saw her light burning. She looked around the office. There was a trophy on a shelf across the room. It had a heavy base. It would make a good club if she could get to it.

But she could not. The footsteps were right around the corner. She sat bolt upright with her eyes fixed on her open door when Honey Marcus stepped into the door frame. They looked at each other. It was months since Honey had been in this building.

"Were you hiding from me?" Honey asked. Her voice was cool. Maybe angry, Greta couldn't tell.

"Were you trying to give me a heart attack?" Greta answered, annoyed that she'd been frightened.

"I came to see if you were ever coming home for dinner, or should I make other plans."

"I didn't say I wasn't coming home."

"You haven't said much. I've hardly seen you."

Greta didn't reply. Sometimes their fights were sun showers, fierce bouts of rain from some localized cloud while the sun shone, the storm pelting and stinging but soon over. And afterward, the air had a cleaner, loamy smell and everything felt better.

But sometimes, the fights felt like the world coming to an end and she never knew which it would be until they were into it, teeth and claws bared. Neither of them wanted those, but neither seemed to know how to head them off, or stop them once they started.

Honey had still not relaxed her posture or stepped into the room.

"When were you going to tell me that Lily Hollister had a key to this building?"

Greta's heart moved in her chest, a sickening feeling.

"Who told you that?" It was a childish response. Diversionary, defensive. Though it often worked.

But not this time.

"Is that what you've really been afraid of all this time? Lily Hollister? Not Ray?"

Greta hadn't moved, but she felt as if she were backing away, soon to be flattened against the wall by the quiet force of what Honey was pushing on her.

"You used to talk about her all the time, but not anymore."

"It's been a terrible time," said Greta, suddenly fearing she would cry. Her emotional core had long since gone from solid to molten.

"Don't cry, it won't work. You told me more times than I can count that Lily is so driven you found it scary. *You.* Found it scary, you who competed with a cracked collarbone in Dubai and almost won."

"She's impulsive. It's different."

"*Reckless* is the word you used. More than once. So she has a key to the building. So she could come here and practice even when no one was here. Even though you'd have to kick her off the team if you found out? And you did find out?"

"I . . ."

"You what?"

"I . . ." Greta had heard the expression "tongue-tied" but thought it was just an expression. Now she was afraid of so many things, some of them mutually contradictory but all seeming equally terrifying, from losing Honey to being the next one found in the pool, that she couldn't speak. They stared at each other, and it wasn't softening Honey in the least.

"You what? You think she's not just reckless, she's a Bad Seed? You think *she's* the one who killed Florence? Then decided to put the body in the pool, to give you an idea of who could be next?"

"No! I mean—no, I don't think that, I thought that Ray must have taken the key from her!" Which was plenty scary enough, but now that she'd been asked point-blank, she had to admit that there was a tiny part of her—like the part of you that knows there isn't anything waiting for you in the dark when you're alone in the house but is terrified of it anyway—that believed reckless, driven, ambitious Lily might be capable of that, and that was so much worse . . .

Finally Honey came toward her. She stood about three feet from her, her eyes hot and focused on Greta's face.

"And were you ever going to tell me? What was really going on with you?"

"I didn't want to get Lily in trouble! I didn't really think she could . . ."

"Yes. You did. You didn't want to get her in trouble, or you're afraid of her?"

"I didn't want to get her in trouble!"

"When did you find out about the key?"

"Months ago. In the winter. I came in on a Sunday morning and caught her here. She swore the building was unlocked, and I knew it hadn't been."

"Then what?"

"I demanded the key and she dared me to search her."

Honey saw instantly why *that* was something Greta couldn't risk. The nervy little bitch.

"I told her I didn't want to know anything about it, I just didn't want her to drown or break her neck with nobody here and she said she was sorry. And I believe her! She never did it again!"

"That you know of. You knew this months ago and never mentioned it? Not even after what happened to Florence?"

Honey stood watching Greta's face for what seemed like hours. Finally she said, softer, "You didn't want to get your star in trouble. But how about the trouble we're in?"

Greta, fearing tears again, said, "I don't know what you mean. Ray, the threats, or . . ."

"This. I mean this. How did you think it was going to help if you didn't talk to me? If you stopped coming home, if you tried to handle this like a fucking twelve-year-old?"

Greta gave a kick and spun her chair so her back was to Honey. She sat like that staring out the window at the darkening lot where Honey's car was parked next to hers. After a long time, she said, "Go on home. I'll lock up and meet you there."

Honey said after a beat, "Jesus, Greta." But she didn't sound angry anymore. Greta listened to the sound of Honey's loafers on the tile floor as she left the office and walked away.

Maggie and Hope, bundled against the unusual chill of the early May morning, were race-walking along the track that skirts the Central Park Reservoir. The sun was just beginning to warm the world, and there were plenty of fiercely fit New Yorkers running as if pursued, or loping, or pushing jogging strollers before them. Hope wore a navy-blue fleece tracksuit, a visor, and a pashmina looped around her neck. Maggie wore mismatched sweat clothes from the Winthrop School lost and found and was thankful to have recovered from an earlier charley horse.

Hope was looking for real estate in the city. "Just to see what's out there," she said as they chugged along, arms pumping. What she had found were staggeringly high prices, but also new neighborhoods in what used to be fringes of civilization, now home to wonderfully built-out conversions with soundproofing and central a/c that the prewar buildings in more fashionable neighborhoods often lacked, and new buildings surrounded by interesting new restaurants. There was a Frank Gehry building down on the edge of Chinatown that looked as if it had been partly melted, with fantastic views of the East River, the downtown bridges, and Brooklyn. Maggie didn't even want to tell Hope how pleased she was.

"Won't Lauren be sad if you move back?"

"The twins might be, but Lauren is so busy I doubt she'd notice. How was Avis Metcalf, speaking of grandchildren?"

Maggie told her about Hugo and Belinda, and the fake Claude Lorrain.

"Damn," said Hope.

"Yes. So he found his rich wife. Poor Caroline. Now what do we do?"

"I think my man Angus should be our next stop."

"I do too. My impression is that Avis won't go looking for dirt, but she'd confirm or deny what we find out on our own."

"Angus won't mind looking for dirt, if Hugo is making his sister unhappy. Or blotting the family copybook. You said you had other news."

"I do. I talked with young Christina last night. She said things are going pretty well, except for the Goldsmith nightmare."

"Explain." A young woman ran by, sideswiping Hope and shouting on her cell phone.

"You know how people are about school shootings," Maggie said. "We did our best to make it underwhelming, but good luck with that. When Marcia tried to go home from the hospital, she found her house was a designated crime scene. Yellow tape all around the property, the police inside tossing everything, looking for weapons, looking for bombs. They completely trashed the living room and all the bedrooms, confiscated computers and notebooks no matter who they belonged to. Some tabloid published an aerial photo of the house—you've seen that house, it's a handyman special in a failed development, but from the air it looks big and the press called it a mansion, so people are demonizing these 'rich' people who screwed up their kid."

"God."

"The place was surrounded by the media that night and for days afterward. She had to go hide out with Todd's sister in Connecticut, and that wasn't so comfortable, because Todd's family has blamed her for years for spoiling Jesse. As they see it."

"People are so sure they'd know what to do with other people's children. You should have heard Hank's family on the subject of Buster. If I was such a bad mother, how did Lauren turn out so well?"

"And Buster turned out fine too."

"Right. So screw them."

"So the police escorted Marcia into her house a couple of days ago just to get a change of clothes and some meds she needed, and she saw what they'd done to the place."

"Where is she now?"

"Still with the sister-in-law, I guess. She can't even go to see Jesse, for fear the press will tail her back to her hidey-hole. She isn't looking at social media at all, thank god, but Christina sends someone to pick up her snail mail and screen it, and it is horrible. People saying they hope Jesse dies. NRA people blame her for bad gun publicity and say she should be shot, or shoot herself. Antigun people, who are even worse."

"I had no idea," Hope said.

"But you see the problem this causes for Christina."

"Are the papers all over the campus again?"

"They are, but surprisingly, they don't seem to be getting much traction. The girls claim they weren't there, or didn't see anything."

"Go Christina."

"Yes. That was a teaching moment. No, her problem is, she's down one French department. Marcia was all she had. Finding a qualified sub this late in the year, for what they can pay, is next to impossible. She got some responses to her ad, mostly bored house-wives who were good at French thirty years ago but have never taught. The first three people who interviewed for the job all turned out to be reporters. For Pete's sake. Didn't they think we'd check?"

"Who is this 'we'? Oh wait. Christina hired *you*," Hope crowed, proud to have figured it out before she was told. "Do you even speak French?"

"I haven't since I was twenty-three except when I had to take the French lunch table once or twice a year."

"Oh, that sounds good enough. I remember everything I knew when I was twenty-three."

"I'm glad you approve."

"Approve? I'm thrilled. It's a perfect cover. What is she paying you?"

"I'm not telling."

"When are you leaving?"

"This afternoon. The girls have exams to study for, and I have some brushing up to do." They passed the woman who had been yelling into her cell phone. She was sitting on the verge beside the path, with her face stained with tears and one cheek abraded by gravel, examining an ankle that was beginning to swell. Maggie slowed. Hope sensed that she was about to go back to offer help and with a firm grip on her elbow, moved her on. "Don't," she said. "It's another teaching moment."

Detective Bark was on Ray detail. Detective Phillips was working on Jesse. She had interviewed him several times, with his father present, and knew a great deal more than she had before about his inner life. He'd used his brother's ID and money he stole from his mother to buy the shotgun at a gun show. He didn't look much like his brother, but still, it hadn't been that hard. The dealer was stupid. Almost everybody was stupid, full of themselves and easy to fool, if you were Jesse.

Forensic IT guys had gone through his computer and phone. There was a rich harvest of ranting, much of it obscene, against girls who ignored him or laughed to each other behind their hands if he spoke to them. Skanks who swarmed around his fuckboy brother. Girls who didn't answer when he asked for noods on Snapchat but sent pictures of their boobs and their butts to their "boyfriends," who laughed at them and posted screenshots of pictures the moron girls thought were private, which he never would but they never bothered to get to know him. He had a permanent front-row seat plus a backstage pass to the parties he wasn't invited to, the dramas and romances of the teenagers around him, all of whom were morons, all of whom would be amazed someday. And very, very sorry.

His mother was a moron. It was her fault he had to wear her long blue raincoat to hide his shotgun. It should have been a trench coat. Black. Or his father's tan one would have been all right. Phillips's eyes had flicked to Jesse's father when the boy said this. Todd sat slump-shouldered in his stiff chair beside the hospital bed, his face a blank as his son described how stupid his mother was, how she'd wrecked the family. He blamed her for his father moving out.

But this contrasted with the tone of his messaging with Florence Meagher, who called him Jamie, short for Jesse James and whom he called Floro, as her husband did. With her he was almost unguarded. She "got" him. He told her about a girl he was in love with. No one else knew. He was going to ask her out soon. He was going to bring her to his house and show her his room, and let her play with his hamsters. They would be in the musical together. Florence wasn't laughing at him. Until it turned out she was.

But Phillips couldn't put any of this together with Florence's murder. Strangling someone takes heft and physical strength. Jesse couldn't weigh more than a hundred pounds soaking wet. And moving the body required a car. Jesse could drive; his father confirmed that he knew how; Marcia had taught him. But he didn't have a license and he didn't have a car. Usually.

"How did he get to the gun show?" Bark asked, at this point in Phillips's reporting.

"Marcia's car. She'd gone to a wedding in Hartford with a couple of friends. This was in March sometime. Left the keys in the car. His mother is very stupid, remember."

"Without a license?"

"He knew he couldn't afford to be pulled over, so he drove super carefully. No one was going to notice. Cops are morons too."

"I see," said Bark.

Ray was eating a sandwich in the deli on Main Street when a shadow fell across the paper he was reading. The shadow belonged to Charlie Bark, who had a chai latte in his hand.

"Mind if I sit?" Bark said, sitting.

Ray stared at him. There was an alfalfa sprout in the corner of his lips. When Bark didn't say anything more, Ray took another bite of his sandwich and went back to reading his paper.

Except that focusing his attention was now a problem. He turned a page and stared at it for a while, then looked up. Bark was regarding him steadily.

"You wanted something?" Ray asked, with an air of delivering a remark of cutting wit.

"Just in the neighborhood," Bark said.

Ray ostentatiously turned in his chair to observe the other tables in the deli. At least three were empty. He turned back to look at Bark, his eyebrows raised.

"How'd you get into the pool house, Ray?" Bark asked.

Ray gaped at him, suddenly totally focused, his eyes slightly bulging.

"I don't know what you're talking about."

"The building where your wife's body was found. How'd you get into it?"

"I didn't! What the fuck?" Ray was the kind of man who, when he felt anything he didn't want to feel, like fear or guilt or pity, transformed it to anger. Bark could feel it radiating from him.

"You've got no alibi, Ray. You had plenty of time to get back from the Poconos and dump the body. I'm not sure yet where it was, the body, before you dumped it, but I'm working on it."

"You are just fishing, asshole. You've got *nothing* on me, because I'm innocent. This is harassment!"

"We found her purse. The purse you dumped in the Wallenpaupack Lake on the way back to the casino that night. It had the key to the pool house in it."

Ray stood up. "I'm not talking to you without a lawyer." And he stalked out of the deli. Bark reached across to the untouched half of his sandwich to see what was in it. Salami, cheese, tomatoes, sprouts. He liked salami. He ate.

*A*ngus *Westphall stood* as Hope approached the table for two he'd reserved in the Members Dining Room at the Metropolitan Museum. He'd been on the board so long the table practically had his name on it; he loved the midday view of Cleopatra's Needle and Central Park. Rain spattered against the glass wall that slanted over them as the captain pulled out a chair for Hope and waited as she and Angus kissed each other on each cheek.

"This is very grand, Angus," said Hope, settling her napkin in her lap.

"My canteen. The food is fine, but I think it's the best view in New York," he said happily. His pink complexion glowed, and she smiled to see that he still favored bow ties. She liked that in a plutocrat.

The captain was back with an ice bucket holding a bottle of Taittinger, followed by a waiter with champagne flutes. The captain presented the bottle for Angus's inspection, which he performed by sliding his glasses a little way down his nose and peering at the label.

"Angus, how nice!" said Hope.

The cork popped with a discreetly muffled thunk into the waiter's white cloth.

"We're celebrating."

"Would you like to taste, sir?" the wine waiter asked.

"No, just pour, please," said Angus without looking away from Hope.

"Celebrating what?" asked Hope.

"That you're moving back." He lifted his glass to hers and they clinked as Hope said, "*Thinking* of moving back."

"Oh, I have faith," said Angus. "New York spoils you for anything else."

Well, it certainly would if every stitch of clothing you own is custom-made, and you eat lunch at this table every day, Hope thought.

"Now tell me where you're looking," Angus said. There is nothing New Yorkers enjoy more than contemplating real estate, even if, like Angus, they've lived in the same Park Avenue triplex since before the first moon shot.

"Let's decide what to eat," said Hope, "then we can concentrate on conversation."

"Good idea," said Angus. He would never have thought of suggesting it because he ordered the same thing every day, poached asparagus followed by the Gruyère Soufflé. If the chef absolutely could not recommend the asparagus, he sent out a salad.

When she had accepted the waiter's recommendation of grilled octopus to start, and Angus had persuaded her to have the soufflé as well, Hope said, "I'm thinking of downtown."

"Really! Why?" And Hope described the fresh views, the surprising street life, the sense of newness and experiment. Angus looked at her smiling as if he'd never heard anything so original, and perhaps he hadn't.

"To be honest, though," said Hope, "I wanted to talk with you about something else. I'm a little worried about Caroline."

Instantly, Angus's demeanor changed.

"I know he's your brother-in-law, so forgive me if this is out of bounds, but could we talk about Hugo?"

Angus took a slug of champagne, as if for once he wasn't noticing that he was savoring the best of everything.

"We could. It's high time someone did."

Hope raised her glass to him and they clinked again, to the start of a new understanding.

"Tell me this," she said. "What does Caroline know? How does she feel about her marriage? She totally stonewalled me on the subject, I thought she was happy as a clam with him." Her grilled octopus was put in front of her and she added, "Why do people say that? There must be something happier than clams."

"Larks," said Angus. He began, perfectly correctly, to eat his perfectly cooked asparagus with his fingers.

"I thought she was as happy as a lark."

"Yes. She's good at that," said Angus. "You know about her first divorce."

"I do."

"That was a mess, embarrassed her and the rest of us and cost her a lot of money. She hated it. Well, I mean. No one enjoys being divorced, we both know that. I know it a little better than you, even," he said, alluding bravely to the fact that he'd been through it three times. "But she took it harder than most. Inside herself. You remember what Mother was like with Caroline, always implying she never got things right, wanting her to be perfectly groomed and to spend her life at the dressmaker's, and Caroline wanted . . . well I think, Hope, that she wanted to be like you."

"Like me!" Hope knew absolutely when someone was trying to snooker her, and could hear the champagne talking, but this was interesting.

"Someone like you, someone who wasn't afraid to be unconventional. I've always thought she'd have liked to have a career. Or, you know, move downtown, live in a loft . . . I don't know."

If Angus's idea of unconventional in this day and age was living in a three-million-dollar loft in Tribeca, Hope thought, good luck to all of them, but she knew what he was trying to say, no matter how limited his perspective. Their mother had worshipped her son and been endlessly carping toward Caroline.

"Never too late for a career," Hope said, since she was just now contemplating beginning her first one.

"No, no . . . I mean yes, you're right, but that's not the issue at the moment. She couldn't admit that her first marriage was a mistake for so long because of what Mother would say, and in the event Mother *was* horrible about it. But that's all changed now."

"How, exactly?"

"Our parents are dead," said Angus. "And besides, Hugo is *such* a shit."

Hope might have spilled her wine, if her glass hadn't been empty. People drink more than they mean to in the throes of emotion, she knew, and she and Angus noticed at the same time that their bottle was empty, upside down in the bucket.

"Shall we have another?" Angus asked.

"Why not."

While Angus finished his asparagus, and the wine waiter bustled about them, Hope told him what they'd learned from Avis Metcalf.

"You know her, of course?" Hope asked. To her surprise, Angus blushed.

"I adored her at one time," he said eventually. "This was after you threw me over. But Harrison Metcalf got in before me."

"I didn't throw you over."

"What would you call it?"

"I wandered off."

"Oh. Well in any case I do know Avis. Did, at least. She's very busy these days."

"You're in the art world. Had you ever heard that story? That Hugo sold Belinda Binney a phony Lorrain?"

Angus liked to call himself a "collector, in a small way." As with so much in Angus's worldview, "small" was relative. "I hadn't heard it and I'm glad; Belinda would have been mortified. But I do know that his reputation among the better dealers isn't good. What you heard is true; he'd move in on another dealer's client and let slip disparaging things about the first dealer, then start selling to the client himself, sometimes work that wasn't the best. And there's the other issue. A man's private life is his own, but not when he's married to my sister."

"Meaning?"

"In Europe, in certain circles, it's believed that theirs is a white marriage."

"You mean that . . ." Hope was beginning to feel the bubbles and had to pause to ponder the right way to put it.

"They think Caroline is a beard, that the marriage is sexless. Abroad, he's known as a gay man. Or at least seriously bi."

"Then where do they think Lily came from?"

"I have no idea. But here's the shameful part; I know my sister. She's a loving, generous woman. If only he was honest with her, she would have understood. But he lies for the fun of it."

"Is she in love with him?"

"Is. Was. I don't know, we can't talk about it."

"You've tried?"

"Yes, but I made a hash of it."

"Tell me."

"It was early in the marriage. He asked to borrow some money from her. Quite a lot. It worried her and surprised her because he'd led her to believe he *came* from money. She came to ask me what I thought."

"What's quite a lot?"

"A million? A mill five? Something like that."

Hope whistled. It took her two tries, but she managed.

"So I asked around and found out that he had a client in Europe who was building a collection, one of those deals where she wanted at least one work from every great old master, even if it's a second-rate piece. Was planning to build a museum with her name all over it and leave the whole thing to the nation. She was shopping for something specific, old and fairly rare. A Cranach. The Elder.

"Cranach's *Sybille of Cleves* was coming to auction and Hugo had promised it to his collector for such and such a price. He knew there wouldn't be heavy interest in the piece; it had been offered two years before and withdrawn when it didn't meet its reserve. But he thought Madame Collector would never know that. Not surprisingly, Hugo had poached Madame Collector from the dealer in Paris who had shaped her holdings. Hugo met her somewhere socially, I forget the details. He romanced her and convinced her that the Paris dealer had been overcharging or self-dealing or something. I'm trying not to name names here, you understand."

"I do."

"Dealers are a competitive lot, but they don't like it when someone is spitting in the common soup. So they made a pact to bid the piece up. Hugo couldn't figure out what was happening. He was in the room, but the bids were coming in by phone. Clearly he had to make a good show of fighting for the piece, even as his margin of profit got smaller and smaller. He had quoted Madame Collector a much higher price than he thought he'd buy it for. He just had to choose the right moment to drop out, when he'd be able to say he'd done it to protect Madame from overpaying. But they played him. They dropped out while he still had his paddle up. The selling price was way more than he had. Someone put Madame wise and she refused to advance him the money, and he couldn't settle his account with the auction house and the sale had to be canceled. You don't get to do that twice in this lifetime; he'd have been barred. He was pretending it wasn't a big deal, but he desperately needed that loan."

"What did you do?"

"I made the mistake of telling Caroline what I just told you. She got angry at me, and protective of Hugo, and that was the last time she asked me for advice."

"Dessert? Coffee, monsieur, madame?" said the waiter, dropping new menus on the table.

"Coffee, please," said Hope with a bright smile. She noticed that the champagne bottle was upside down in the bucket again.

"Dessert?"

"Just the fruit for me," said Angus.

"Madame?"

"A double espresso, please," said Hope, wondering if they served a triple.

"Dessert wine, monsieur?"

"What about a little port?" Angus asked her. "Or the late harvest Sémillon from the North Fork, that's very nice."

Hope pretended to think about it, then said, "Just the coffee, please." She wanted to add "and a pillow and a blanket and I'll just lie down over there, under the piano," but she made it through to their parting at the curb where Angus kissed her on the cheek and put her into a taxi. He was looking after her, wistfully waving as the car pulled away.

*   *   *

Hope and Maggie had agreed to Skype at nine o'clock that evening.

On her computer screen, Hope could see that Maggie was in a room she didn't recognize. It had French toile wallpaper that must have cost a king's ransom when it was new, which was not at all recently.

"Where are you?"

"Christina's house. In the second-best guest room."

"Who got the best one?"

"Pinky."

"That's right, I forgot."

"I thought staying here would be easiest. And certainly cheapest, and I can be more help to Christina from here. Also her French is much better than mine, so she can help me stay a step ahead of the class. Why do you keep putting that spoon against your eye?"

"When was the last time you drank a whole bottle of champagne at lunch?" Hope asked.

Maggie looked startled. "I don't think ever."

"Well I have, but not lately. I had no idea how much difference thirty or forty years would make in my capacity."

"Where on earth did you have lunch?"

"Members Dining Room. The Met. With Angus Westphall. Oh, my god, that man has a hollow leg."

"This was very noble service, you. I'll see that you get the department's commendation."

"You better. I've never had such a headache in my life. My eye feels like it's going to explode."

"Was it worth it?"

"To who?"

Maggie would have said "whom," but she couldn't bring herself to torture an ailing colleague. "I'll rephrase. Did you learn anything useful?"

"Did I ever. Let's see if I have enough brain cells left to repeat it."

Hope then did a creditable job of reporting Angus's story.

"Well, that is very very interesting," Maggie said.

"I know," said Hope, making a piteous sound as she laid the cool spoon against her other eye. "How are things there?"

"Jesse Goldsmith is out of the hospital."

"Did they let him go home?"

"Oh no. He's in custody. Probably good; he'd need massive protection if he wasn't under arrest. It's gotten really ugly here."

"In what way?"

"Someone painted a swastika on the front of Marcia's house.

There's a thing trending on social media here. People keep retweeting 'A loaded gun in a crowded church? Hashtag Jewsneedtoleave.'"

"I don't even understand what you just said."

Maggie wrote it on a piece of paper, as it would look as a tweet, and held it up for Hope to read.

A loaded gun in a crowded church? #Jewsneedtoleave.

"Yes but . . . Oh, wait. I think I have it. If he took a loaded gun to a crowded church that means he's Jewish?"

"That's the gist."

"Oh god. Is it just me, or is there something really evil slouching around out there?"

"But wait. Did I tell you about my conversation with Hugo, the first night I met him?"

"A little bit. You told me something about that way he stammers . . ."

"Yes. I remembered who he reminds me of. A father of one of my students in Washington, a politician. He used to do that exact stammering thing when he was controlling the conversation. This was some time ago, when—"

"Darling, please don't tell me a story, I'm not a well woman."

"Oh. Sorry. It's interesting, though."

"Punch line, please."

"He was a total liar. He's in jail now. My theory is he did that stammering thing to give himself time to come up with the right lie for the right person."

After a pause, Hope said, "That *is* interesting."

"But that wasn't what I meant to tell you. In that first conversation, do you remember, Hugo told me he had flown to Europe with Caroline on their honeymoon, but his back went into spasm and they had to turn around and come right back on the *QE2*? Something about claustrophobia on planes and boats."

"The *QE2* is a boat," said Hope.

"You're missing the point. Isn't it convenient that he never can go to Europe with his wife, where he has a reputation he'd rather she didn't hear about?"

After a long silence, Hope said, "Oh poor Caroline. I'm beginning to have a really creepy feeling about this guy. And now, I am going to bed."

As will happen in spring, especially in a year of El Niño, the rain had cleared off by Saturday morning in Rye-on-Hudson and the temperature had risen into the seventies. Maggie and Pinky Tyson sat in the shade of the front porch of the head's house after breakfast, each studying French for different reasons. Pinky was wearing a newsboy hat over her moth-eaten hair and she was chewing gum. This was technically not allowed on campus, but since it helped her concentrate, Christina had declared a dispensation within her walls, and this morning extended the boundary to include the porch.

Maggie looked up to ask Pinky a question about irregular verbs and found that Pinky was not reading but watching the street in front of Sloane House. A silver Mercedes-Benz SUV had pulled up to the curb, and Maggie followed Pinky's gaze in time to see Hugo Hollister get out, wearing green linen pants and a short-sleeved polo shirt showing off his tanned and muscular arms. In a very few minutes, Lily Hollister, Steph Ruhlman, and two other girls whose names Maggie didn't know came out chattering among themselves, wearing shorts and flip-flops and pulling roller suitcases. They stopped and posed close together, sporting huge smiles, wide open eyes, and raised eyebrows while Steph took a selfie of them all with her phone and Hugo loaded their luggage. When everyone was in and belted down, the car drove off.

"What's all that?" Maggie asked.

"They're going to Lily's country house overnight," said Pinky.

"That sounds like fun."

"Yes," said Pinky neutrally.

Both were still looking at the street where the SUV had been.

"Have you ever been there?" Maggie asked.

"No. I've seen the pictures though. Lily takes friends, and they post about it all weekend."

"I know Lily and Steph. If the other two are in my classes I haven't met them yet."

Pinky picked up her phone from the table between them and opened Instagram. She showed Maggie the screen, on which glowed the picture they'd just seen taken.

"The one in the red hat is Melanie Meek. Ann Semple is this one."

Pinky's phone made a noise, and she saw that she'd gotten another picture, this one taken inside the SUV.

"Here," she said, showing it to Maggie. "That's Ann."

Ann was holding a cellophane bag of licorice allsorts up to her cheek, beaming and pointing to the candy.

* * *

Detective Phillips paused outside the Frigate Bookshop on Main Street, in Rye-on-Hudson. Inside, all was quiet. She could see a small colorless man sitting behind the counter, head bowed, so still she wasn't entirely sure he was breathing. But the sign in the window read OPEN, so she did.

A bell tinkled above the door as she stepped in, and the man came to life, closed his book, and said, "Good morning."

"Good morning."

After a pause, the man asked, "Are you looking for something particular? Or just kicking the tires?"

"Neither, really. Detective Phillips, White Plains PD."

"Well, welcome," said Mattias Benes. "We live to serve."

Phillips walked farther into the shop, looking around with genuine curiosity. The last time she'd been in a shop selling nothing but books—no cards, no chocolate, no cappuccinos, no calendars—she'd been about ten. She inhaled, remembering something from childhood, maybe to do with libraries.

"I didn't know stores like this still existed," she said.

Mattias made a small laugh-like sound. "All swept away in the Amazon? Not quite. At least not yet."

Detective Phillips had wandered toward the vintage children's books. After a while she pulled out a worn hardcover copy of *Curious George*. She opened it in the middle, and Mattias watched her read. Without realizing it, she'd begun to smile.

"That's just a readers' copy," he offered. "Hardly pristine, and priced accordingly."

She put it back and pulled out a book entitled *The Roosevelt Bears,* featuring the illustrated adventures of Teddy B (for brown) and Teddy G (gray). She turned the pages. Then she looked at the price penciled on the flyleaf and whistled.

"It's a first," said Mattias. "I should keep it in the locked case, but I like looking at it myself."

Phillips put the book back in the shelf with care.

"I came to town to talk to Todd Goldsmith," she said. "His office is closed."

"There's a lot of feeling in town about what his boy did. There were some incidents."

"So I've gathered. Do you know where I can find him?"

"He had a little apartment in the Pendleton building, but I think he's left town. His son, the other one, was here for a little while yesterday morning, helping him pack. I haven't seen either of them since. Kate Curtin in The Wooly Bear would know more."

"That's Ellie Curtin's mother?"

Mattias nodded.

"She's next on my list. Thank you."

She left the shop, bell tinkling. Mattias watched from behind his desk as she crossed the street midblock and went into the yarn shop opposite.

Detective Bark stood in the open door to the firehouse, getting his eyes adjusted to the dark interior. The town firetruck stood facing out and ready. It was far from a new model, but the hardware was polished. He began to walk in, his hard soles sounding on the concrete floor. By the time he reached the back of the building, where four men sat around a folding table with cards in their hands, the game had stopped and four heads were turned toward him, staring. There was a wiry little one with a belly that hung out over his belt like a plaid beach ball. There was a dark-haired unshaven one whose T-shirt said LIPSEY PLUMBING on the front. There was a fair-haired one with a toothbrush mustache, and there was the one with the butternut squash head. Ray Meagher was glaring at him.

"Good morning, gentlemen," said Bark.

"You can't just follow me around and barge in here," Ray said aggressively.

"Pretty sure this is a municipal facility, Ray. Anyone with business here can come in."

"What's your business then?"

"You gentleman all auxiliary police, are you?"

"I'm not," said the Lipsey Plumbing man.

"Uh-huh. So the rest of you are. I have a few questions. Would I be right, that you all act as watchmen for the school up there on the hill, Rye Manor?"

There was a pause.

"We patrol the town when needed," said the mustache man, quoting some job description or employment contract.

"That a full-time job?" the detective asked, eyeing the playing cards.

"When needed," the same man said again, a little louder, as if Bark were deaf or slow.

"I see. And when are you needed?"

They kept nervously exchanging glances, as if they would coach each other if anyone knew what to say, or what not to.

Mustache said, "Parades. Concerts. Night patrol at the campuses. That type of thing."

"I see. And this is on foot, in a car, what?"

"Foot. Car. Bicycle. It depends."

Mustache was doing the talking but Bark kept his eyes on Ray. Who was not enjoying it.

"You wear uniforms, the whole deal?"

"Sometimes just the badge at night."

"If it's too much trouble to put on the whole kit?" Bark asked.

"That type of thing," said Mustache.

"And you have firearms, do you? When you're on duty?"

The three who were not Ray shifted or twitched in various ways. Ray narrowed his eyes.

"Nah," said Mustache.

"Sometimes I take a baseball bat, if I'm in the car," said the belly.

"Dangerous job?"

"You never know."

Then everyone looked at Ray. "Auxiliary police are not armed," he said coldly, knowing that Bark knew the answer before he asked.

"But what about you, Ray? You were an air marshal. You had a weapon with the marshals, didn't you?"

"Of course."

"You still got it?"

"What's it to you? It's licensed. What are you trying to say here?" He suddenly raised his voice, rising from his chair.

"Whoa," said Bark. "Just asking questions. Why, is there a problem?"

"There's a problem and you know it! You are harassing me! I am an innocent man and you keep inferring something . . ."

"I think you mean *implying,* Ray," said Bark. He'd been helping his youngest study for the SATs. "Or maybe *insinuating.*" Ray's face began to turn red.

Mustache said softly to Ray, "Sit down, Ray. We got this."

Ray had a hard time downshifting, but after a minute, still bristling, he sat.

Mustache said, "Is there something you needed, detective?"

"Yeah, one more thing. When you patrol say, down at the junior high at night, do you have keys to the buildings?"

Mustache said after a beat, "No, we don't."

"What about up at Rye Manor, do you have keys to the buildings up there?"

"No. We just watch for things that don't look right, and if we see something we call the police."

"The real police."

"The police in White Plains," said Mustache, exactly as offended as he was meant to be, but resisting the bait.

"What about you, Ray? You have a set of keys to the buildings there?"

Everyone had seen this coming. They all looked at Ray to see how he'd field it.

Ray looked levelly at Bark. "The dorms have keypad systems. I don't have the codes. There's a set of keys in the office if I need them. Why don't you ask Sharon Comfort if she put Florence in the swimming pool? She's got the keys to the whole shebang. Or those dykes at the stable, or Carlos, the maintenance guy? He's got keys to everything. He's got a wife and nine kids but hey, maybe he and Florence were having a thing, you check that out?" He did not add "asshole," but everyone heard it hanging in the air.

The three other guys at the table were looking at their cards or their laps. They knew that Ray was not doing himself any favors.

"What makes you think we haven't?" Bark asked, genially. He stood for a long minute, his eyes locked on Ray's until Ray looked away. Then Bark turned and left the firehouse.

In the car on the way back to White Plains, Phillips said, "You get anything from the poker boys?"

"Nope. I keep thinking if I keep Ray rattled, he'll eventually make a mistake."

"What kind of mistake?"

"Contradict himself. Try to get rid of something. Lose his temper and blow."

Phillips drove in silence. "You talk to the DA?"

"Yep. Still no. She wants more than circumstantial."

"And they want us on the home invasion in Scarsdale?"

"Yeah."

A burglary had gone way wrong. A toddler was shot, and a father beaten nearly to death. So far, no suspects.

*   *   *

"I don't know who you had to kill to get those tickets," Hope said, "but it was worth it." Angus Westphall, his sister Caroline, and Hope had just seen the Saturday matinee performance of *Hamilton* at the Public Theater.

"Money should be fun," said Angus, beaming. They were all exhilarated from the show. Angus spotted his driver across Lafayette Street, and signaled to him to stay where he was, they would come to him.

"I am *not* gonna give up my . . . shot," Hope chanted as they crossed the street.

"Oh, how Hugo would have *hated* it," said Caroline happily. She was climbing into the backseat as the chauffer held the door. Hope's and Angus's eyes met over her head.

"He would have?" Hope asked, settling into the seat beside her. Angus was in front. "What is *wrong* with him?"

"He hates perspiration," Caroline said. And then, as if she had just heard what she herself had said, let out a peal of laughter.

"He *what*?" Hope would have been galvanized by this even had she not had a hidden agenda.

"Hates it," Caroline said happily, as if she had just noticed how ridiculous it was. "I think it's one of the reasons he loves that Lily is a swimmer. No matter how hard she works out he doesn't see her sweat."

"Calling Doctor Freud—can you explain that?"

"He has his little quirks," said Caroline. She was still too happy to be baited.

"I'll say," said Angus.

"Angus, don't be mean."

"At least be honest—he'd hate to see Jefferson played by a black man."

Caroline just looked out the window, smiling. She turned to Hope and chanted, "*Nobody else* was in the *room* where it happened."

"Where *is* Hugo, by the way?" Angus asked.

"He took Lily and some friends to the country for the weekend," Caroline said. "He'd rather be up there than in the city anyway. And Lily loves it now that it's warm enough for swimming out-doors. At school she can only practice when the coach is there and she gets so frustrated. For a while she had her own key to the pool building but someone found out."

"She dives alone?" Hope asked. "We were never allowed to do that when I was young." What she meant was, *You let her dive alone? Are you out of your mind?*

"No, she wasn't supposed to either. She confessed to her father before anyone could turn her in, and he took the key away from her. Secretly he was proud I think. His little Olympian, he likes to call her. His little chip off the old block."

"Not if the old block hates perspiration," Angus said, turning in his seat to join the conversation.

"So he promised her he'd take her to the country every weekend he could when the weather got warm."

"Is she allowed to practice all alone up there?" Hope asked, deeply skeptical.

"There's always someone around. But you don't know what it's like to try to stop Lily. She's relentless. I've known her to go out there in the pitch-dark, turn on the pool lights, and go to work. It drives her crazy to go to sleep when she's tried something new that day but not nailed it. I'll be in the bathroom, brushing my teeth for bed, and I'll hear the boiing of the springboard." She shrugged. "At some point, you just have to let them make their choices."

The car had arrived at Angus's building.

"Come up for a cocktail, ladies?" Angus said, turning to them hopefully.

Caroline looked at Hope. Who said "Oh, why not?" and they all climbed out of the car.

The Hollisters' country place had been a simple Dutchess County farmhouse when they bought it. Over the years, they'd redone the kitchen, added porches and a swimming pool, and eventually built a guesthouse. Hugo spent more and more time working from there until eventually Caroline built him his own separate studio. It was designed to look like a farm structure from the outside, except for the bank of windows high up the wall, under the eaves. Inside it resembled nothing used in agriculture. It was climate controlled, with a full bath in the back, high-speed Internet, racks for storing framed artwork, and flat cabinets for drawings and prints. Another wall held a built-in desk and worktable, and shelves and shelves of art books.

"My father's kingdom," said Lily, leading her friends into the room. Her father, at his desk, whirled around in his chair to see four girls in tiny bathing suits backlit by brilliant sunlight at the open door.

In the far side of the central room, there was a door that might have led to a bedroom or study. Hugo stood up from his desk as Lily led her friends through to it across the studio. "My father's favorite child," said Lily drily, opening it.

The room was more like a den than a garage. It had wainscoting on the walls and three small windows high above eye level, and at the back, a broad Dutch door like the door to a luxurious box stall. In the middle of the room there was a polished concrete pad set into the wood floor. On it sat a gleaming powder blue 1954 Berlinetta Maserati.

"Just giving the tour, Dad," said Lily as he followed them. An expression that might have been annoyance had become a proud smile of welcome. "Isn't she gorgeous?" he said to the girls. "There were only . . . only . . . only four made."

"Does it, like, run?" asked Ann, who hadn't been to the house before.

"Like a dream."

"Wow," said Ann. She was hoping to be offered a ride, but Hugo said nothing.

"We better let Dad get back to work," Lily said to her friends.

"Wait, I wanted a picture of you with the car," said Steph. Lily leaned against the car, and with an arm draped across the hood she pursed her lips and made a duck face.

"Hot," Steph said. She snapped the shot and posted it on Instagram tagged *@LilyHollister with her sister.*

"Does he really drive it, though?" Ann asked as Hugo closed the door behind them and they walked back to the pool.

"He does. He likes to drive eight hundred miles an hour over the Newburgh-Beacon Bridge because once you're on it, the police can't do a thing to you till you get to the other side."

"Cool," said Ann wistfully.

"I wish it was a convertible," said Lily.

*   *   *

Hope and Caroline had ended up having supper with Angus. He had produced a very creditable spaghetti carbonara with his own lily-white hands, and Caroline made a salad. After Caroline went home Hope had stayed for a nightcap, because there was something she wanted to discuss with him alone, and if she didn't do it tonight she'd have to see him again, and she feared her liver couldn't take it unless she made a trip to the Betty Ford Center first.

After he had finished telling her the provenance of the Armagnac he had poured for her, Angus settled down beside Hope on the plush sofa. He stretched his arm along the back of it, inches from her shoulders, and said wistfully, "Ah Hopie—it's been a lovely evening, hasn't it?"

"Lovely. I can't thank you enough."

"You can thank me by promising we can do it again," he murmured. He was gazing at her, which she could tell without looking at him. Hope tested the fumes in her snifter, then swirled the liquid and watched it thoughtfully as the silence stretched.

"Did I say something wrong?" Angus purred. His fingers behind her head flicked a lock of her hair. She knew these moves—she'd first encountered them at a drive-in movie outside of Bar Harbor when she was fifteen, and they hadn't been any more welcome then.

She said, "Angus, what are we going to do about Caroline?"

He suddenly straightened, and his arm came back to his side as he took a slug of Armagnac. That was not the conversation he'd thought they were having.

"I thought we just did it," he said.

"It was a lovely evening, yes. But I mean about Hugo."

Angus cracked his knuckles and took a handful of chocolate-covered coffee beans from a dish on the table. When he had crunched and swallowed them, he said, "I've been down that road. You can't tell my sister something she doesn't want to hear."

"Are you so sure she doesn't want to hear it?"

"Who knows what goes on behind closed doors? Maybe he makes her happy," Angus said. "Maybe he's great in the sack. If she doesn't bring it up, I'm not going to."

Soon afterward they both realized it was later than they thought and Hope was on her way back to her club and to bed.

H*ope's plan had been* to collect her car after breakfast and head back to Boston, with a stop in Rye-on-Hudson to see Maggie and Christina. When her mobile rang as she was getting out of the bath, she assumed it would be Maggie, or possibly Angus, or even perhaps her Realtor. She'd seen a rental she loved in the melted Frank Gehry building on Spruce Street. The last person she expected was her son, Buster. Buster never called her. Was it Mother's Day?

"Hi, Ma," said Buster.

"Greetings, sweet pea. Is everything all right?"

"Fine. How are you?"

"Good. I'm just getting ready to go back to Boston and see if all my plants are dead."

"Where are you?"

"New York. Didn't I tell you?"

"You might have."

There was a pause.

"Work going well?" she asked.

"Yuh, fine. I'm studying for the detective exam."

"Yes." She already knew that.

Another pause. She was *not* going to ask him about the weather. Not.

"How's Brianna?" she asked finally.

"She's good," said Buster. "She's pregnant."

Hope sat down and tried not to scream or burst into tears. Finally she said, relatively calmly, "Well darling, that is just wonderful news."

After another pause, Buster said, "Yeah?" He sounded relieved.

"Yes of *course* it's wonderful news, I couldn't possibly be happier. How long have you known?"

"About a month," said Buster.

Once again she managed not to say anything she should not. "Oh how lovely. Then she's seen a doctor and everything?"

"Yuh."

"When is she due?"

"Uh—"

"Darling, is Brianna there?"

"Yuh."

"May I talk to her?"

Buster lived in perpetual dread that his mother would mortify him or otherwise shatter his hard-won self-esteem, but Brianna, who had been raised in a school of hard knocks, had apparently formed some effortless bond with his mother, which he had seen with his own eyes and yet still not believed. Brianna had tattoos on both arms and worked at a nursing home doing things with bedpans.

"Hi, Hope," Brianna said.

"My dear girl, you have made me unbelievably happy. When are you due?"

"Doc thinks November sometime."

"And how do you feel?"

"Not too bad."

"I just have a million questions. Do you know yet, boy or girl?"

"Not yet."

"And is your mother thrilled?"

"That's not a word you'd really use about my mother."

"But you've told her . . ."

"Not yet. We thought we'd tell you first."

Hope was so pleased by this that she started to cry.

"Well, darling, I'm just as happy as I can be. Will you keep me posted and let me know what I can do for you both?"

"Will do," said Brianna, sounding happy. She handed the phone back to Buster and after a few more exchanges of burbling, they ended the call. Hope could not wait to tell Maggie how proud she was to have gotten all the way through it without asking if they planned to get married.

Lily was up early Sunday morning. Although she had her own bedroom in the house, she slept in the guesthouse with her friends. She was sharing the king-size bed with Steph, glad it was so big because she didn't really like to be touched. Ann and Melanie had the twin beds in the room down the hall. Steph snored a little, then turned over and was silent, breathing deeply. Lily slid out of bed without jiggling the mattress.

The living room of the guesthouse smelled like popcorn and looked like a frat house after a football weekend. Clothes and backpacks were all over the room. Half-empty cans and bottles of soft drinks and juices and eight kinds of water stood on every horizontal surface. She crossed the room, silently slid the glass door on the pool side open, and stepped out into the morning.

It was cooler than she'd expected and the grass was wet under her bare feet. The scent from the lilac hedge outside the door was fresh and spicy and heavy with spring. Her bare feet left wet prints on the bluestone apron around the pool as she passed. She turned once to look at the main house. All was silent and dark. Not even the lights on automatic timers had come on yet. Lily was wearing only the T-shirt and gym shorts she slept in and didn't have her phone, so she didn't know what time it was, but early. She went on to the studio.

The front door to the studio was locked, but not the wide Dutch door at the back for the Maserati. She slipped in quietly and stood stock-still, waiting to be sure the alarm system hadn't been armed. It never used to be, when someone was at home, but.

When all remained quiet, she padded to the car and peered in. Front seat. Backseat. Nothing that shouldn't have been there. In fact, there was nothing in the car at all except a lap robe in the backseat in a tartan her father liked to say belonged to the Caldwells. Who knows, maybe it really did. After a moment's pause, she opened the trunk. Though the light was dim she could see that it was pristine and empty. She closed it again as quietly as she could and went on into the studio. Again stood listening. She padded across the room to her father's desk and turned on the arc lamp that lit his work area. Then she sat down in his chair and studied what was before her.

The desktop was orderly to the point of fussiness. The papers on the blotter were neatly stacked and carefully aligned in a pile with the edge of the desk. Anything that couldn't be made to line up or match was banished to drawers. She checked the shallow top drawers first. She knew she wasn't going to find anything. She knew that. So there was no reason not to look. Just to see if he still had it, after all these months. Why should anyone care if she wanted to know?

The next drawers had been built to hold hanging files, but now Hugo scanned papers and stored them digitally, the files discarded. One now held a pair of running shoes and socks, and a bottle of single malt scotch, half-empty. The other held a Rolleiflex camera she'd never seen her father use, an old-fashioned answering machine, its cord wrapped around it, and an assortment of empty eyeglass cases. Weird, what people couldn't seem to throw out.

She moved on to the other side. Pencils, boxes of rollerball pens, rubber bands, paper clips. A bottle of clear nail polish. Really? Why? Some random unlabeled thumb drives. An old external hard drive.

An antique silver magnifying glass, black with tarnish, on which she could just barely discern the words STERLING and DENMARK in tiny letters. Some Caldwell family thing? She'd never seen it before. On the other side of the handle was the monogram **BB**. Who was BB?

"You're up early," said her father.

Lily jumped visibly and thought for one second that her heart might not restart. She spun around in the chair. He was close enough to touch her.

"You scared me," she said, when she was able to.

"I can see that," he said softly. "You were looking for something?"

She took a deep breath to calm herself, but it shuddered on the inhale.

"Nothing particular. I was awake, and I—didn't want to disturb anybody."

"I see," he said, regarding her steadily, thoughtfully. She'd seen this look before but not combined with that creepy soft uninflected voice. They stared at each other. If the thoughts flying between them had been visible the air would have been thick with colliding currents of them, curtains of words. At last, he shifted his weight to one foot, extended a hand toward her, and cocked his head toward the door.

"Why don't you come up to the house now. I'll put the coffee on."

It was not a suggestion. Lily rose and walked past him to the front door. Outside, he pulled it carefully closed behind them, making almost no noise. Then he followed her across the lawn to the kitchen door. Once inside, he indicated wordlessly where she should sit. She sat. He turned on the lights and pushed the button on the coffeemaker. Then he turned, crossed his arms, and quietly looked at her. She looked back. It went on a long time as the coffee machine began to pop and gurgle behind them.

Hope was so excited about Buster and Brianna that she drove straight toward Boston, forgetting to stop in Rye. Maggie called her in the car and found her halfway across Connecticut instead of pulling into Christina's driveway. Maggie laughed, and they had a long talk about whether Hope should call Brianna's formidable mother, and decided no. Ditto no calling Buster's sister; that was for Buster or Brianna to do. Hope said she would just pack a new suitcase, go to see Lauren and get her grandbaby fix, then be back down, either to Rye or back to the city, depending. She was hoping Maggie would at least let her send Brianna a layette, and a Pack 'n Play, and a Maclaren stroller, and a thousand Onesies.

With her day suddenly open, Maggie went to find Pinky. A grateful parent had given Maggie an iPad as a retirement gift. She didn't use it much except for doing jigsaw puzzles on the subway, but she decided to grasp the nettle. With Pinky's coaching she had managed to transfer the contents of the thumb drive Florence's sister had given her into the iPad. She felt guilty that she hadn't even looked at Florence's book, let alone been in touch with Suzanne since the memorial service. On the other hand, she couldn't bear to sit indoors on a beautiful afternoon in May or to spend it staring at a computer screen. Instead, she was on her way to the weeping birches with a book bag and a lightweight lounge chair.

It didn't take long to discover that Florence's exuberant teaching style did not translate well to fiction. Her prose was sentimental and florid, and the plotting creaked with the weight of her research, which she was as much in love with as she had been with Velázquez himself. The scenes were about the wrong things, and she had the fatal tendency of writers who don't trust their readers to tell you what she was going to tell you, then telling it, then summing up what she'd told. Maggie wanted badly to like it, both because of what it had meant to Florence and because she was going to have to say something about it to Suzanne. And that was before she suddenly understood that Florence might actually have died for it.

Maggie had begun to swipe rapidly through the electronic pages, assessing chapter breaks, getting a feel for length and structure. This was to distract herself, if briefly, from a lifeless sequence introducing the young Velázquez to the studio of the Seville master Pacheco, who employed him, taught him, and finally became his father-in-law. There were exhaustive lists of the equipment and furnishings of the studio, the names and personalities of the other apprentices, the trouble one of the lesser talents had in painting a still life of a bowl of eggs.

Then the story stopped. What Maggie had thought were many more pages of text were instead camera rolls of photographs that Florence had taken during her research.

First came Madrid. There were endless shots of *Las Meninas,* Velázquez's complex portrait of the little infanta Margaret Theresa and her ladies-in-waiting. Florence had taken it from every angle she could, always including the crowds surging around it and the backs of a lot of heads. Then of other works in the Prado, and elsewhere in Madrid. Then Seville, where Florence had concentrated on genre pictures. There were many that were familiar and many more that were not, and Maggie relished the art history lesson, especially as Florence, the good teacher, had carefully annotated the images. She could see that the genre paintings were invaluable sources of information and detail for the historical setting Florence had tried to paint in words. The clothes. The food. The pictures practically included the smells.

At the Met Museum in New York she'd captured the court portraits, of course, but especially focused on the heart-stopping portrait of Juan de Pareja, Velázquez's slave and studio assistant. Was Florence planning a plotline about the Moors in Spain? And then the pictures from the Boston MFA. There were more portraits of Philip IV, with his giant Hapsburg jaw, and other members of the family. But then the transfixing picture of the poet Góngora, so like a Manet or Eakins. And then, Maggie turned the page.

There was the John Singer Sargent picture *The Daughters of Edward Darley Boit*. Such an homage to *Las Meninas,* such a masterpiece in its own right. Maggie could see what Florence would do with that as a teacher. It was almost as hard to get a clear shot of *The Daughters* as it had been of *Las Meninas* at the Prado. Of course, you could pull professional pictures from the Internet, but here Florence was making visual notes to herself, taking details of the girls' faces, of their dresses, of the beautiful vases as tall as the children. There were six or eight pictures from different distances and angles. Maggie was fully enjoying her ability to enlarge the pictures with a flick of her fingers and zoom in on different parts of the image when she saw, standing at the edge of one frame and before a different picture entirely, a couple kissing. The man's back was sideways to the camera, his body stocky, his coarse hair ash blond. His arms were around the young lady, one hand in her hair. She was mostly out of frame, but Maggie could see that the hair was dark and worn loose and long in the manner of the young.

She swiped to the next picture. Florence had moved; her angle on the picture was such that she must have come closer to the amorous couple, who had now broken from each other. By enlarging the picture and moving as far to the edge of it as she could on the screen, Maggie could see that the man had turned and was looking directly at Florence. It was Hugo Hollister.

Angus Westphall had almost forgotten that he had a landline when he took the first phone call he'd had from Avis Binney Metcalf in some forty years. Not that they hadn't seen each other *en passant;* that happened quite frequently in certain seasons, or had until the terrible thing happened to her daughter. Since then she'd been raising her grandchild and was not as often on the social circuit, though she still turned out from time to time for a cause she cared about, and once in a while appeared at the auctions, though she was shy and preferred to bid by phone.

He would have loved to think that her call meant she had remembered she had a yen for him after all these years, but reason suggested that the impulse more likely sprang from something else. True to her natural reserve, apparently unchanged from the young woman he remembered, she had not wanted to say much on the phone, so his curiosity was unabated as he arrived at her club for their lunch date.

"Thank you for coming," she said to him as he crossed the reception room toward where she sat on a narrow couch upholstered in yellow striped silk. She rose to kiss him on the cheek with cool, dry, slightly chapped lips.

"It's my pleasure," he said with a little bow. He followed her to the elevator, which they rode to the top floor where the terrace was newly open after the winter. Angus had plenty of opportunity to notice how well she had maintained her figure. She was wearing a charcoal gray cashmere skirt with matching sweater, and a dark silk scarf knotted in some attractive way. He liked well-dressed women. He wondered if she thought he had changed much. And why she wanted to see him. A board or committee she wanted him to serve on, was his best guess. But maybe a letter to some club or co-op board on someone's behalf . . .

Or maybe an escort to the Costume Gala? That would be fun . . .

"You're sure you're happy eating outdoors?" she asked.

He was.

"You don't mind that it's buffet?"

He didn't.

When they had filled their plates, or half-filled in Avis's case, and were seated face-to-face at a table in dappled sun, and had said all there was to say about the view and the weather, Avis said, "I hope . . ."

And paused so long that Angus finally had to smile at her and say, "You hope what?"

Avis said, "I hope I'm not about to offend you."

What on earth was she going to say? That his breath was the talk of Park Avenue? That he needed to lose fifteen pounds?

"We've been friends a long time, Avis," he said, smiling.

She pushed some salmon mousse around on her plate. Finally she said, "Do you know a woman named Maggie Detweiler?"

Angus felt as if his brain were a kaleidoscope and it had just refocused itself in an entirely unexpected design.

"Maggie Detweiler. Winthrop School, is that the one?" Hope had mentioned her too, he thought.

"It is. Nice woman. She's retired now. Apparently doing some consulting for the Rye Manor School. She came to see me about something that"—she hesitated, then plunged on—"that affects your sister Caroline."

"Caroline's daughter goes to Rye Manor."

"So I understand. How is she, by the way? Caroline? She was so appealing when I first knew her."

"Still is. She'd love to see you, I know."

Avis gave a brief smile but returned to her topic.

"Maggie told me something I hadn't known, that Caroline is married to Hugo Hollister."

Angus sat up straight. Anything to do with Hugo had that effect on him.

"She is, yes."

"I'm not going to ask if you and he are close, because the answer might make it hard for me to say what I feel I have to say."

"Put your mind at ease then," said Angus seriously. "Hugo is good company and I love my sister, but . . . put it this way, I haven't put him up for any of my clubs, and I'm not likely to."

Avis smiled briefly. This she understood perfectly, and it answered her question.

She paused, reassured, and ate a spear of asparagus with her fingers. Angus felt himself beginning to adore her.

"Maggie Detweiler needed some background information, which I happened to have, because Hugo was once close to my stepmother, Belinda Binney. You knew her, I'm sure. Oh yes, I know you did. You wrote me that very nice letter when she died."

"She was a treasure. So kind, and so much fun."

"Yes. Well, Hugo agreed with you, but if you don't mind, I'll skip that story. It doesn't reflect well on anyone involved, and you don't really need to know."

Angus said only, "Then there's something else that I do need to know?"

"I think so. Yes."

A waitress came to take their plates and offer coffee. That settled, Avis went on.

"This came to me more or less by accident. It reminded me of Maggie Detweiler's questions and I found myself thinking that you or Caroline might . . . that you should probably be aware. In case you are not already."

Angus watched her with complete attention. He wasn't even blinking.

"You know I'm an art dealer. Mostly my partner minds the store these days, but he had an appointment out of the gallery. Something we'd bought in London was being delivered to the shop; we were trying a new shipper and someone had to be there to watch the uncrating. While I was there, an old client of ours came in. Dutch, a brewery heir. We hadn't seen him in some years. He was hoping to talk with my partner, but there he was and there I was. He wanted our advice on a 'situation.' To be brief, he'd met Hugo Hollister somewhere, maybe Newport or the Cape or somewhere like that, the client's a great sailor. Hugo did what Hugo does best, and soon they were going to exhibitions together. And Hugo was letting innuendos slip about who had been badly advised in the art market and how Hugo had saved the day.

"Eventually, Hugo told our client that he knew of a Bierstadt that might be available for the right price, a particularly desirable one. Sioux encampment or some such subject, big scale, dramatic sky, had never been publicly exhibited. It would cause a fuss if it came to auction but the owner didn't want it known that he was deaccessioning."

"I have a feeling I know what's coming."

"Well, our client—he's a little sheepish, as you can imagine—was nervous about the piece, although it looked gorgeous in snapshots. Hugo was pressuring; he said the word was getting around to other collectors that it might be available."

"Had he seen the actual painting?"

"Once. It was at the owner's house out on the Island somewhere, Hugo got him in on the quiet. He couldn't stay long, he couldn't touch it or examine the frame or the back or any of that sort of thing, but he said it was magnificent. He'd been looking for just such a thing for years."

"Which Hugo had known perfectly well, of course."

Avis didn't respond to that, but the line of her mouth suggested what she felt about it.

"So he bought it," said Angus.

"Yes."

"And now there are problems with the provenance."

"Yes. But our client is no fool and something was making him nervous. He bought on the condition that if he changed his mind, Hugo would buy it back."

"For the same money."

"Yes."

They sat in silence for a minute. Angus ate a macaroon.

Avis shifted a little in her seat. By barely moving a finger, Angus signaled a waiter, and Avis, grateful, asked for more coffee. Then she resumed.

"The Hudson River School is not my field, so my partner went to see the canvas."

"Where is the picture now?"

"In Delaware, where the client has a house. You really don't need the details. But the chit has been called in. He's lost confidence in the piece and wants Hugo to take it back and make him whole."

"For how much?"

Avis named a figure, and Angus whistled.

"So far, Hugo is stalling. I thought you should know, in case . . . I have no idea about how Hugo runs his business or if cash flow might be a problem, but . . . a man with that kind of money pressure. I just thought you ought to know."

"Thank you," said Angus.

"It's not a tale I enjoyed bearing."

"No. But you did the right thing. Thank you."

He wondered if she *would* go to the Costume Gala with him if he asked, and decided that now would not be the time.

It wasn't until Tuesday that Bark and Phillips could get over to Rye to talk to Maggie Detweiler. They had a pair of suspects in the Scarsdale home invasion case in custody and they had been working all Sunday night and most of Monday on trying to get them to rat each other out. A disgusting pair of grifters, one of whom had been out on parole for only six weeks. They'd had to let them go, only to get a tip from the prison cell mate of one of the suspects, still in Comstock. He said the suspect's brother mowed lawns in the neighborhood of the break-in and had told the pair which family would be out of town until Memorial Day. Bark and Phillips still weren't sure if the tip had been wrong or these mental giants had hit the wrong house, but now they had to find and catch them again. And now Mrs. Detweiler had a bee in her hairnet about the Meagher case.

Maggie was down at Greenleaf Field watching her girls play soft-ball when they found her. Pinky Tyson was catcher and the Rye girls were ahead by three runs. Not at all unhappy to be outside in sunlight with no one in the immediate vicinity bleeding, the detectives sat down beside Maggie and watched with her until the end of the inning. Bark had coached his older daughter's high school team, and he even started cheering for plays he liked, in spite of not knowing which team was which. Maggie had the distinct impression he'd rather have stayed there to see how the game turned out than follow her to the library where they could talk in private.

They talked about the book Florence Meagher had been working on as they walked. In the Katherine Jones room two senior girls were doing calculus homework, but they politely gathered their books and skittered off when the grown-ups came in. Maggie took her tablet from her book bag and scrolled to the pictures that had been haunting her. First she showed them the Sargent the way Florence probably saw it, then enlarged the image and moved to the edge of the frame, where a couple embraced. She let them study it. Then she moved to the next picture on the roll, in which the man has turned to face the camera.

Phillips enlarged the face even more than Maggie had. "He was at the funeral," she said. "I saw him talking to Ray Meagher."

"He's a trustee here. His daughter is in the junior class. Lily Hollister."

"The girl who found the body?"

"The same. This is Hugo Hollister. Married to a woman named Caroline, maiden name Westphall. From a prominent midwestern family, newspaper fortune, from back when newspapers made money."

"Currently married, you mean?"

"I do."

"He have money himself?" asked Bark.

"Champagne taste, for sure, but I very much doubt the money to pay for it."

"So it would put quite a spoke in his wheels if someone showed this picture to his wife?"

"I presume it would," said Maggie.

There was a silence while the detectives pondered what Maggie had been thinking about from all angles for days.

"Any idea when this picture was taken?"

"The pictures are in date order," said Maggie. "The Madrid ones are from her trip last summer. She went to New York in late fall, her sister says. The Boston ones are quite recent, maybe as late as mid-April. She might not even have really sorted through them. She had just sent this file to Suzanne the week before she died."

"Are you thinking," Bark said at last, "that this picture could be a motive for murder?"

"He's seen Florence aiming the camera toward him. He's got to assume that she's seen him already, or would eventually find his picture on her camera roll."

"And would he have reason to think she wouldn't keep it to herself?" Phillips asked.

"With Florence I think the question is whether she *could* keep it to herself. The woman could not shut up. He'd have had to expect that with the best will in the world she'd spill it to someone sooner or later."

"But she hadn't yet, as far as we know," Phillips said.

Maggie agreed. "Which probably means she hadn't seen him in the pictures yet. She was teaching a full schedule plus preparing for the evaluation during the time between her Boston trip and the murder."

After a long silence, Bark said, "Well, this throws a new light on things."

"Yes. Would you like to hear my theoretical, while you're adjusting?"

Both would.

"Hugo and his wife have a weekend house up the Hudson. A village called Hatfield. He was up there the morning Florence was found; I remember that he was one of the first from the outside world to arrive on the scene because he was relatively close."

Phillips and Bark both took out their notebooks.

"Florence disappeared Wednesday morning. Hugo and his wife were on campus, or had been the night before."

"You know that how?" Bark interrupted.

"I was here evaluating the school. My team had arrived that afternoon, and the trustees were all here to meet us. There was a reception Tuesday evening. Hugo must have been nervous as a fox with his wife and Florence in the same room."

"Florence was there?"

"Very much so," said Maggie and thought of Florence rattling on about olives in her cereal in Madrid. Then she had a flicker of a memory of Hugo going to intercept his wife when . . . ? Then she lost it.

"Go on."

"From what I've learned, Florence was a creature who loved routine. She left the house about the same time on school mornings, drove into the village for a coffee and the paper, then got to campus about eight. Morning prayers start at eight-thirty. She'd spend a half hour in the faculty room, then begin her day. Wednesday morning, she never showed up."

"She was last seen at the coffee shop at her usual time," said Phillips, who had done the legwork.

Maggie knew that. Presumably she'd left the house at her usual time, with phone and laptop and all her usual stuff, since those things were now gone.

"So, between about seven-forty and eight A.M., she disappeared, car and all. Suppose Hugo meets her in the village that morning with some story. He needs a ride somewhere. His car has a flat tire, he has something to show her, I don't know. She's a kind soul, and she's got a half hour to spare. He gets in the car with her. Neither she nor her car is seen again until Thursday morning."

"Okay, wait. Where is *his* car?"

Maggie said, "For instance—Hugo and his wife stayed over in the village Tuesday night. Went to dinner with their daughter; something like that. In the morning he drops his wife at the station and she goes back to New York. He puts his car someplace where it won't attract attention and waits for Florence in the village. Once he's in the car with her, I can only guess, but I'd like very much to know whether her car can be traced heading north up the Hudson Valley. Can you check? Are there cameras at the toll stations? E-ZPass records?"

Bark and Phillips were making notes, tapping texts.

"I don't know what the autopsy showed about time of death,"

Maggie went on. "It could be that he killed her immediately, it could be that he hadn't really worked out what would happen once he had her. Maybe he started out thinking he would threaten her or bribe her. But the more time that passed without his getting what he wanted, the more desperate or angry he would have gotten.

"Let's say he takes her to Hatfield. He wants to work something out with her, make her an offer she can't refuse, but she is frantic. It's evaluation day, she's been preparing for weeks, she has to get back to school. He can't calm her down or make her listen, and it all goes wrong. He strangles her. On purpose or by mistake. Why doesn't he bury the body or dump it somewhere nearby? My guess would be that it's not that easy to get rid of a body, and if he screwed up and it was found, the location could cause people to wonder who in the area had a connection to her."

"But why bring her back to the school?"

"To throw suspicion on someone else in the school community. Ray, leading the pack."

"Why the pool?"

"I'm not sure, but I think that points to Ray too. You should talk to Greta and Honey, the swimming coach and her partner. Ray and Lyndon McCartney have been trying to buy their property. Pretty aggressively."

"McCartney. That guy keeps showing up in this story."

"I saw Hugo and McCartney together having an intense powwow shortly after the body was found," Maggie said, "probably about McCartney's outing with Ray the night the body was dumped. If my theory is right, the news that Ray was out of town Thursday night would have come as a bad surprise to Hugo. I also saw Ray arguing with Honey Marcus the first day I was on campus. Honey and Greta weren't selling and they're afraid of something; you should see the locks on their doors. If I've got it right so far, a body in the pool would be threatening as hell to them, if they thought Ray put it there."

"You know we found Florence's handbag," said Bark.

Maggie had not known that.

"It was on the route Ray would have driven back to the casino, if he'd been the one to dump the body. A key to the pool house was in the bag."

"But it could just as well have been Hugo who dumped the purse. Again, to point toward Ray."

"How would Hollister get into the pool building, if it was him?" Phillips asked.

"I think you should talk again to Marcus and Scheinerlein."

Bark and Phillips were looking at each other.

"Okay, wait," said Bark. "You're suggesting that Hollister took Florence, or her body, to his country house and had her there for two days without anybody finding out. Was he alone up there? No one works for him on the place? Does he have any neighbors? Didn't anybody at least see Florence's car?"

"I'm hoping you can find out. What I can add to the pot goes to moral compass."

"Make your case," said Bark.

"Hugo Hollister is a private art dealer," Maggie began.

"What does that mean, exactly?" Phillips asked.

"He presents himself as a gentleman consultant, only available to people he knows socially. In theory he helps out of friendship and passion for the subject. Say you're a collector who wants elite access to special works, things not on the market yet, or at all, things in private hands that no one knows about. Hugo comes along and offers you that, plus the benefit of his big brain, his very expensive education, and his social graces. You think you're getting an insider's deal; he takes his cut without you ever noticing."

"How?"

"He persuades you to buy a piece for a certain price. He buys it on your behalf but for less than what you've promised to pay, sometimes a lot less. You never feel the fee leaving your pocket; for all you know, he did it as a favor. He can pose as a gifted dilettante, proud to have had a hand in shaping your collection. You feel smart for having bypassed all those expensive commissions that go with buying and selling art at auction, or through a regular dealer."

"Is it illegal?"

"Not at all, if the piece is really what he says it is and you're content with the price you paid for it. You may have overpaid, but you may not know or care if you don't mean to sell. If you find out he misled you, you won't be happy, but you know it means you should have done your homework better and you'll probably be embarrassed to talk about it. It isn't what I'd call ethical, but he's far from the first to play the game."

"Huh," said Bark.

Phillips said, "Doesn't sound like a prince of a guy, but it's a long way from rooking the One Percent to murdering schoolteachers."

"Does he really have the fancy education or is that a con?" Bark asked.

"He has it," said Maggie. "His relatives are who they say they are and he really did graduate from Harvard, magna and Phi Beta Kappa. The things that are hard to accomplish, he really accomplished. It's the things he chooses to fake that interested me. He lies for the thrill of it. He enjoys fooling people. It makes him feel omnipotent and confirms that the rest of us are fools and deserve to be conned."

Phillips looked at Bark. Bark was giving Maggie the thousand-yard stare, both listening and thinking, and chewing the inside corner of his lip. He began imperceptibly to nod his head.

"I've seen it before," he said.

"So have I," said Maggie. "Hugo Hollister has a very rich wife who appears to love him. He has brains and backing; he could easily be an honest dealer. Being legit doesn't interest him. People like him need the danger, they need the rush of getting away with things. But the rush doesn't last, and soon he needs to do it again, whatever *it* is. Cheat the customers, cheat on the wife, and it's never enough. He doesn't believe honest people resist lying and stealing out of principle; he believes we're just scared. He's simply braver than we are, and that's what makes him so much better than the rest of us. And that's why I don't have much trouble imagining him moving on to murder. Because he really doesn't feel anything for anybody else, he has to keep escalating his game in order to feel anything at all."

Phillips said to Bark, "What do you think?"

After a pause he said, "I'm thinking of Florence, sitting in her car with her cappuccino in her hand, seeing that face at the car window, smiling. The handsome rich guy from the city, just wanting an easy favor."

Phillips said, "Two days is a long time to hide a body. Let alone drive it around the countryside. Why didn't anyone see anything?"

"I'm hoping someone did see something but didn't know what it meant. There are a lot of ways it could have worked. And I understand that though it *could* have worked doesn't mean that it did. But look at this."

She swiped through to another picture, this one of Lily Hollister in a bikini, with her arm draped over a little blue car.

"Wow," said Bark, taking the tablet so he and Phillips could see it better.

"What is this?" Phillips asked.

"Looks like a vintage Maserati."

"No, what is this picture? What kind of building is that? When was it taken?"

"Saturday. At the Hollisters' country house. This is Hugo's studio. One of the girls posted it on Instagram and my housemate took a screenshot."

"Your housemate?"

"Yes, she's seventeen. She's my tech consultant."

After a silence, Bark said, "Well. We've got some work to do.

We'll check the E-ZPass thing, and take a drive up to Hatfield and ask some questions. That garage would certainly be a nice private place to do your dirty work."

"If it happened that way, there will be traces. Fibers, DNA, something. Not to mention that some people like to take little keepsakes," Phillips said.

Bark looked at her. "Trophies."

Phillips nodded.

After they had gone, Maggie tried calling Hope, but it just went to voice mail.

Hope *was a moving target* because, after a packed visit to Boston, she had hurried back to New York, summoned in stereo by her Realtor, who had an appointment to show her a two-bedroom on a high floor in the Gehry building she liked, and by Angus, with whom she was now on a mission.

"We're catching her between board meetings," Angus said to Hope as they waited for the maid to open Caroline Hollister's door on Wednesday afternoon. "Good afternoon, Marie."

"Afternoon, Mr. Westphall," said the young woman. "Mrs. Hollister is just changing. Would you like some tea?"

Angus looked at his watch as Marie led them to the den, a small room dominated by a large flat-screen TV on the wall opposite the windows, with their slatted view of a leafy Carnegie Hill side street. The room was lined floor to ceiling with books, but many were behind horse and dog paintings that hung by nearly invisible wires from hidden hooks in the ceiling. The room was very manly, very English country gentleman.

"Tea, or something stronger, Hope?"

"Tea, please."

"Tea and a bucket of ice, Marie," said Angus. He opened a door that was cunningly concealed behind what looked like a wall of books to reveal a wet bar lined with fox-hunting prints. He rustled around in the cabinet below the counter and found a bottle of gin and some tonic. He adjusted his glasses and peered at the "best by" date on the tonic label. "Caroline's not much of a drinker," said Angus. "Usually this stuff is from the last ice age." He twisted the cap and was rewarded with a satisfying hiss of carbonated pressure. "Sure you won't change your mind?"

Hope said, "Tea will be fine." Marie reappeared with his ice bucket and tea things for one on a tray.

Angus poured his drink, and raised it to salute her. She waited for him to say "Sun's over the yardarm *somewhere*."

He said, "Sun's over the yardarm *some*where," and took his first happy swallow.

Caroline came in, dressed in a simple shift and dangerous-looking heels, still putting on her second earring.

"Hope! Angus didn't tell me you were coming!" She gave her a kiss on the cheek, then air-kissed her brother.

"Have a drink?" he asked.

"Too early for me," she said, sitting down beside Hope.

"You're dressy for a board meeting," Hope said.

"The executive committee is going on to dinner. Somewhere rather grand, I think. How are you? This is such a nice surprise."

You won't think so in a minute, Hope thought, but said only, "I'm very well. And you look blooming."

"Thank you," said Caroline. She wasn't a beauty and never had been, but she did have the attractive polish of a healthy human enjoying her day.

Then there was a silence, in which Caroline's good cheer lost some of its buoyancy. She said to her brother, "What was it you wanted to talk about?"

"Where's Hugo?" Angus asked.

"In the country." Her tone was now wary. It was always wary

when her brother wanted to talk about Hugo. "He has something big cooking and needs to be at command central, but I think he'll be back tomorrow. Did you want him to be here?"

"No. Very much not."

Caroline stopped trying to pretend this was a pleasant social occasion. She became very still, and waited.

"I heard a very disturbing story a couple of days ago. I've discussed it with Hope, who loves you as much as I do, and she agrees with me that you have to hear it."

"Oh, does she," said Caroline flatly, not looking away from Angus.

Hope had the feeling she was looking at two oft-tested combatants, strapping on their armor, maneuvering their chargers into the lists. Visors down, lances up.

"I didn't go looking for this, Caroline. Someone very discreet and very knowledgeable thought the family needed to know."

"That horrible dealer friend of yours? Who's always telling you awful things about Hugo?"

"It is not Dick Trimble. And why do you think people like that have awful things to say about Hugo in the first place?"

The emotional temperature in the room was rising quickly, and Hope could see this turning into a bout of nursery hair pulling. She said, "It's someone without a mean bone in her body. This is not a time to shoot the messenger, Caddy."

Caroline turned and gave Hope a look that said, *Et tu, Brute?*

"I want to know who," she said stubbornly.

Hope and Angus looked at each other. Angus said to his sister, "Avis Metcalf."

Caroline was taken aback. Some moments passed, feeling much longer to all three than they probably were. Eventually Caroline said, "Okay, tell me what you came to say. I doubt you've got the whole story, but, go to town."

Angus gave her Avis's account, which he'd already told to Hope.

When he had finished, Caroline just stared at him. Hope, beside her on the sofa, reached a hand to her, and Caroline pulled away from her touch as if she'd been burned.

"You've always had it in for him, Angus. You never liked him. You never think there can be two sides where Hugo's concerned."

Before Angus could speak, Hope said, "Well, *I* liked him. I found him absolutely charming. I see exactly why you would think him so, and I know how loyal and loving you are, Caroline. I do."

"I don't want to hear any more of this," Caroline said. "You're ganging up on me. There are things you don't know, there are—"

"Caddy, there are always things in a marriage that nobody knows," said Angus. "I know that better than anyone. The point is, nobody's bad childhood, or hurt feelings, or whatever it is you love about him, excuses slimy behavior. This is not the first event of this kind that you know about. It's not a one-time misstep, although this time he may be in further over his head than usual. You can operate the way Hugo does for a while, but over time you run out of luck. You run out of rope. The art world's too small."

"You only know one side of it."

"What other side can there be?"

"I don't *know,*" she said angrily. "But you're talking about my husband. I want to hear it from him, and then it's our business. Thank you for telling me, I'm sure you think you were doing the right thing. You can go now."

She stood up. Angus did not, so Hope did not.

"Just tell me one thing," he said. "Tell me that Hugo hasn't asked to borrow money, or mortgaged the country house, or this apartment. Tell me you know that for sure."

"He can't mortgage anything. It's all in my name," said Caroline. She seemed pleased to have trumped him, then not so pleased as she realized what she'd revealed.

Angus looked at her. He took a sip of his drink. So Caroline *had* somewhere along the line gotten some legal advice, and taken precautions.

"Are you missing any jewelry?"

"Stop it, Angus."

"Just asking. I hope Mummy's diamonds are at the bank."

"Look, I'll give you the goddamn diamonds right now if that's what this is about. The older two can buy their own diamonds, and Lily won't want them anyway."

"You know that *isn't* what this is about."

And she did. Which was not to say, there was not a bone of contention there. Angus had daughters who would have loved the diamonds and Angus was sentimental about their mother.

"How about asking you for a loan? Can you tell me he hasn't done that in the last little while?"

Hope, closer to Caroline than her brother was, could see tears start in her eyes. No, she apparently could not tell him that. Hope wondered if Caroline hadn't been feeling uncomfortably alone with this information, knowing as she did that it had happened before. Maybe more than once or twice. What did Hugo do, Hope wondered, to keep Caroline so loyal? What excuses could he give, what appeals did he make?

Angus let the silence stretch even longer this time. Finally he said, "Caroline, why do you put up with this? With all you have to offer?"

Hope knew it was a misstep. The thick-skinned older brother telling his not-pretty-enough little sister that she had a great personality. The fact that he didn't mean it that way didn't change the way she would hear it.

Caroline marched to the door and opened it. Then she closed it again and turned to face them. She was deeply upset, and it was turning into anger at both of them.

"You don't know," she said.

"We know we don't," Hope said. "Tell us."

"You don't know how he feels inside. What it's like for him. He *feels* like a bankrupt. He—"

"Caroline, he *is* bankrupt!" said Angus. Hope wished he would shut up.

"I meant emotionally! He feels empty inside, if it weren't for me and Lily, he'd . . ." She didn't want to say this to her brother but she did want to say it to Hope, so she turned to her. "He'd kill himself," she finished simply. "He'd kill himself. I know him. You don't. It would be like leaving him in an empty room with a gun and a box of bullets. How could I live with that? What would it do to Lily?"

Behind her, Angus said without a trace of doubt, "Caddy, if you left him alone in an empty room with a gun and a box of bullets, he'd pawn them. And turn up in a year in Cape Town or Brasília with a whole new raft of Harvard-hugger friends and a whole new string of rich women who haven't heard his excuses yet."

Hope and Caroline just looked at each other. Hope could see the grief and anger in Caroline's eyes, hurt in so many ways by this conversation that Hope couldn't even count them. And she was far less convinced than Angus that Caroline was wrong.

*   *   *

Maggie's hunch about the E-ZPass records went nowhere. There was no record of Florence's car on the Taconic at the right dates and times. But Phillips said, when Bark's spirits sagged at the news, "It's easy enough to pop those suckers off the windshield. Let's see if Hollister's E-ZPass made the trip."

This also required some time to sort out, since at first NY State Motor Vehicles could not find that Hugo Hollister *had* an E-ZPass, or even a car. Phillips said, "See about in his wife's name." That rang the bell. Registered to Caroline Hollister were an Audi sedan, a Mercedes-Benz SUV, and a vintage Maserati. All had E-ZPasses. But there was still no record of payments on the relevant days.

Bark and Phillips looked at each other. "He could have stayed off the toll roads. Would have, in fact, if this thing was premeditated."

"Shit."

"He had to have taken Florence's car. Once she turned up missing, we scoured the town for that car. His own could be parked anywhere and not excite suspicion."

"We need to find someone who saw Florence's car in Hatfield over those two days, and we need to find some proof that Florence was there. Road trip tomorrow? If we can place the car there, we'll get a forensics team in to scour the place."

"I'll pick you up at seven," said Phillips.

But that night there was a breakthrough on the Scarsdale case. A man stopped for a broken taillight in Glens Falls, New York, proved to be drunk and extremely disorderly, not to mention unwashed and half starved, and the Saturday night special in his sock matched the ballistics of one of the weapons used in the break-in. One way or another, as Phillips and Bark had the prisoner transferred to them and then went to work on him to find out where his partner in crime was, where the stolen goods were, and where he'd been since the attack, it would be days before they were able to return to the cooling trail leading to Hugo Hollister.

H*ugo, barbered and polished* and wearing a new summer-weight cashmere jacket from Paul Stuart, stood to greet his wife as she followed the dining room captain to join him at their table at the new Tribeca epicurean mecca on White Street. The restaurant had recently held a soft opening in the form of a $10,000-a-plate dinner for President Obama, and it had caused a sensation among food snobs. Reservations were impossible to get, but Hugo knew the chef-owner. He'd explained all this to Caroline last week and again this morning. He hoped it had registered. Caroline had had to postpone a committee meeting to join him, and it was important to him that the evening be a success.

"You look delicious," he said to her, kissing the cheek she offered. "And that's a new scent for you—what is it?" He didn't like it when people wore fragrance at dinner, especially not when the food was important, but when you came right down to it, Caroline wasn't very sensitive. Fortunately, Hugo was a forgiving soul. He had to be.

"Something I found in Lily's bathroom. I'm out of Joy," Caroline said. "Tell me about this place again? It's a nightmare getting down here. The cab got lost three times."

He began yet another iteration of why it was a coup that he'd gotten a table, but she was looking at the menu and again, didn't seem to be listening. When at last they had ordered cocktails, he took her hand and said, "Your pinfeathers are all ruffled. What's the matter?"

Caroline drew a deep breath, sighed, and smiled, and seemed to refocus on the here and now.

"Oh, I'm worried about Lily. And Angus has been annoying me. For a change."

"Tell me," murmured Hugo sympathetically. He always enjoyed a good Angus-bashing.

"He's pressing me to give a major gift to the ASPCA, and he just won't understand that it isn't a good time," she said.

"He never seems to remember that you have your own causes."

"It's not that; I completely agree on this one, but you remember, I moved a lot of money out of my IRA into a Roth, for Lily, to try to get her evened up with her siblings, and my tax bill is just stupendous this year. My banker says if I spend one extra penny he'll call the trustees. One of whom is Angus, of course." She made a face.

The cocktails arrived. After the ritual of smelling and tasting and passing judgment, Hugo said casually, "This must have slipped my mind, the wroth thing. Tell me again?"

"You know. The IRA is tax-deferred until you start to spend it; for a Roth IRA, you pay the tax when the money goes in, so it will be tax-free on the other end, for whoever inherits. So I haven't an extra sou. Someday Lily will thank me, except I'll be dead. And except that 'thank you' doesn't seem to be in her vocabulary these days."

The waiter arrived and took their food orders. Hugo was unusually fussy, asking what the chef recommended and wanting half portions of things so he could taste more dishes. The waiter bowed and scraped. When they were alone again, he said, "Do you really think it's a good idea to leave her so much? She already has enough to ruin her."

Caroline looked at him. "Well I must have thought so, or I wouldn't have done it. Why, don't you?"

"No, yes, I just-just-just . . . I don't want you to beggar yourself."

Caroline laughed. "I wouldn't worry about it. Why, is this dinner about money?"

Hugo looked wounded. "Sweetie, of course not. I've just been missing you."

For the rest of dinner, he seemed jangled, even coming close to overturning his wineglass as he twisted on his chair to signal their waiter, to say that although he had been assured—twice—that there was no cilantro in his soup, there definitely was. The waiter apologized and asked if he would accept instead a portion of the sautéed foie gras, which was prepared very simply, with no herbs at all. Caroline on the other hand seemed to enjoy the meal and the evening very much, and appeared genuinely sorry the next morning that she couldn't go with him to Hatfield for the weekend.

P*hillips and Bark were delayed* on the morning of May 19 by a GPS snafu. Just outside of Hatfield their device directed them up a suspiciously unkempt woods road that narrowed until they reached a sign saying PRIVATE PROPERTY; KEEP OUT. Below it, another sign, hand-lettered on cardboard, said YOUR GPS IS WRONG, and it certainly was. Good God, Bark thought. What hope was there, really, for self-driving cars?

Phillips backed gingerly down the way she had come, hoping not to skid off the mush of pine needles and loose gravel into the boggy woods at either side of the track. When she was able to turn around they drove back to the village and Bark went into the post office to ask for directions.

When he got back into the car, he said, "She told me how to get there, and then she said, 'The excitement's about over, though.'"

Phillips looked at him and said, "Don't tell me." Bark just shrugged, and gave her the directions.

As they drove up the neatly tended drive of Glimmer Glen Farm, they could see from afar that the excitement was indeed over, although the fire trucks were still there. Before them stood a smartly appointed farmhouse-like residence, white with gray shutters and trim, up-to-the-minute skylights and windows, and an extension that Phillips guessed was the new eat-in kitchen with a screened porch dining/living room for summer days. That's what it would be if it was hers, anyway. She was quite a consumer of shelter magazines.

There was no garage or car barn at the house. Beyond the main house was a guesthouse or something, plus a swimming pool with what looked like an equipment shed and changing rooms. These they glimpsed, noting it would all have to be investigated; for now their business was with the smoking black mess across the lawn beyond the pool. The firefighters were still playing hoses on it, waterlogging any possible remaining hot spots. Partial blackened walls still stood to about shoulder height in places. Some of the roof could be recognized where it had fallen in on all that was below. Because he knew what he was looking for, Bark could just see a squashed and blackened bit of metal the size of an omelet pan that he guessed was what remained of the Maserati.

They had left their car in front of the house and walked down to the disaster site. A firefighter with smoke-blackened skin leaned against a hose truck with her helmet off, drinking vitamin water from a plastic bottle. On the fender of the truck sat the man they were looking for. He was in pajamas and a blue dressing gown and he clearly hadn't looked at a mirror since before daylight. His hair stood up in tufts, as if he had just gotten out of bed. His face was gray with fatigue and streaked from tears.

"Hugo Hollister?" Phillips said.

Hugo looked up. His blue-gray eyes were bloodshot and he broadcast a mixture of bewilderment and despair. His expression said, How could this be happening? Who are you? Can you help?

"Detective Phillips, White Plains. This is Detective Bark. We were at the service for Florence Meagher?"

Hugo climbed to his feet and shook their hands, still looking dazed and uncomprehending. "Related to Jed?" he said to Bark.

"Jed who?"

Hugo shook his head. "Nothing, sorry."

"Who's Jed?"

"Jed Bark. A famous art framer. Never mind."

Phillips noticed that his feet were bare. They were long and narrow and bluish white, as if he had been out here a long time and they were freezing. The nails needed clipping. Strangers' bare feet creeped her out.

"What happened here?" Bark asked him.

Hugo turned toward the wreckage and looked at it, a small wrinkle of bewilderment between his eyebrows, as if he'd been struggling with that question for some time.

"I was asleep and I heard a . . . heard a boom. A *boom,* and I felt the building shake. I went to the window and I saw this, like, a fireball blazing up out of the studio."

"You were sleeping where?"

He gestured toward the house. "In my bedroom. I ran outside and I . . . I . . . I couldn't believe what I was seeing, it didn't seem real, but it was so *loud* . . . so I ran back and called 9-1-1."

"And as far as you know, what caused the fireball?"

"They seem to think something blew up. Maybe the water heater? Ask them." With his shoulder he indicated the firefighters with the hoses.

"I will. How was the building heated, Mr. Hollister?"

"Baseboard. Electric. And I have—had—a woodstove."

"And what other appliances were in there?"

"Gas range. Gas water heater. Microwave. Coffee machine."

"And what was the building used for?"

Hugo Hollister started to cry. He put his hand over his face and wept, his shoulders shaking. Neither detective moved. After a while he took some deep breaths and took a lump of used tissue from his pocket and tried to wipe his nose with it.

"Ah . . . sorry," he said. "It was my principal place of business.

I'm an art dealer. And collector. I had my whole inventory here, except for a few pieces in the house, here and in New York. All my records, correspondence. My library. Mementos . . . a lifetime. My whole career."

He took some deep breaths, and they were relieved to see that his crying jag seemed to have passed.

"Did you do art restoration here?" Bark asked.

"What? Oh, no. No. I have professionals do that."

"So you don't store any flammables in the studio?"

Hugo stood still, seemingly looking inward, struggling with some emotion. Then he said, "Besides art, I had a vintage car. I'd had it completely restored." He put a hand over his mouth, as if he thought he might come apart again, but he didn't.

"Was it drivable, this car?"

"Oh yes."

"And you did drive it?"

"Yes. Only in perfect weather of course."

"So it was filled with gas and oil."

"Probably not filled with. But it ran."

"And was this car valuable, Mr. Hollister?"

Bark could see a glint of unholy pride flash in his expression.

"Very," he said. "It was a Maserati, Berlinetta, '54. Very rare."

"It must be quite a blow, losing a thing like that."

Hugo nodded, but said, "It's not a human life or anything. Thank god no one was hurt. I just had my daughter here with some friends, the other weekend. It could have happened when they were here. God, they could have been in the building."

The two detectives stood quietly, looking concerned, hoping the silence would make him uncomfortable.

"It was a dream of mine, that car," he said. "I had an uncle who had one when I was a kid."

The detectives left him and went to the firefighters. They showed their badges and said to the nearest one, "Talk to you?"

A very young man turned to them. His huge boots and water-proof overalls and the various kinds of equipment hanging from his belt made him monumental, though his pipe-stem neck suggested he was slight inside his regalia.

"You probly want Jerry," he said. "He's the chief. Hey, Jerry!"

An older firefighter with a day-old beard who'd been leaning against the front end of the lead engine doing some paperwork put his clipboard aside and came to join them.

Bark said, "Looks as if it was intense. Any idea what caused it?"

"It was a hot one," Jerry agreed. "Hydrocarbons plus a lot of wood and paper. It went up so fast it's hard to tell much about where it started or why, the blaze just ate everything."

"The owner said he thought something like the water heater blew up."

"Could have. Faulty installation or something. I suppose it could be."

"He had a car in there," said Bark.

"Yeah, we saw that just before the roof fell in. Didn't help matters."

"So you don't have any idea what caused the explosion? If it was an explosion?"

"Not yet. I imagine the insurance guys will be all over it, we'll know more in a couple of days. He said his inventory was worth four or five mill."

"When you have an idea, would you get in touch?"

"Got a card?"

Bark gave Jerry his card, and Jerry went back to his clipboard.

Hugo Hollister was still sitting where they'd left him. "We need to look around the rest of the property," said Phillips. Hugo just looked up at her as if he didn't exactly speak English.

"Okay with you?"

"Sure," he said, as if he couldn't think why they'd want to but didn't care one way or the other.

They walked over to the pool. A plastic cover was unrolled over the water, keeping out flying debris like leaves and insects and now ashy detritus. Five or six chaise longues with turquoise upholstery stood on the bluestone apron around the pool. Two small changing rooms made of cedar or redwood stood opposite the low and high diving boards. Behind that was a bunker-like structure within which machinery hummed. Bark looked in. The machinery filled the space except for some chlorine supplies and a long-handled net for skimming things out of the water. A couple of bathing suits in various sizes hung from pegs in the changing rooms, and there was a long low storage chest with an unlocked padlock hanging from the hasp. Inside the box Phillips found inflatables, web mitts and flippers, a couple of face masks, kickboards and pool noodles. Nothing that didn't belong, no storage spaces surprisingly empty.

They went on to the guesthouse that stood between the pool and the main house. It had a terrace outside with a picnic table and benches, and a vast outdoor grill under a fitted cover. Phillips took the cover off.

"I always wanted one of these," Bark said.

"Propane tank is missing," said Phillips.

"Stored somewhere for the season, maybe. We'll ask." He made a note.

Inside, the guesthouse looked exactly as it had when Lily and her friends had left it. There was a tennis sock lying under the breakfast table, and a pair of bikini underpants with polka dots partly hidden behind a cushion on the sofa. Milk was spoiling in the refrigerator, and there were pizza boxes in a stack on the counter, as if someone thought that putting them in one place was the same as cleaning up. Recyclable cans and bottles were all in a special blue can in the corner; at least they gave some thought to the environment. The trash was filled with empty ice cream cartons.

Upstairs there was a master bedroom with a king-size bed, and a small dark bedroom with twin beds. The twin beds in the middle room had been stripped; they found the sheets in a hamper in the hall bathroom. The king-size bed was unmade, and the hamper in the master bath was full of teenage-girl clothes they assumed to be Lily's. The bathrooms were a monument to the number of different hair and skin products that could be considered necessary to one's happiness. There was aspirin and Midol in the cabinets, and an old prescription vial of Xanax in Lily's name. It looked untouched.

They walked up to the main house. They walked all the way around the outside before going in, considering lines of sight. At the far end outside what must have been the original kitchen, there was a vegetable and flower garden. In a shed they hadn't seen when they arrived they found gardening tools, rough shelves for bags of potting soil, fertilizer, and bug sprays, and a small riding lawn mower. Bark stood looking around for long minutes after Phillips had exhausted her curiosity. Eventually he said, "Wouldn't you expect to see a gas can here for the lawn mower?"

Phillips hadn't thought about it. She didn't do yard work.

"Could be somewhere else?"

"Like the studio?"

"Maybe the basement." She pointed to the back of the house, where there was a basement hatch.

"Good thought," said Bark, making another note.

They went into the house through a side door and found themselves in a quiet sunroom. It was neat and bright and looked unused, at least in this season. The rooms here were relatively small, with low ceilings, typical of a farmhouse designed to be heated with wood. There was a small but cozy front parlor that also looked unused. Across the entry hall was a formal dining room, and beyond it the new kitchen, with (as Phillips had expected) a table that looked to be where the family really ate, a state of the art cooking theater, and at the far end, cushiony furniture arranged around the huge screen against one wall.

They heard a toilet flush and a door open, and a small woman with iron gray curls, wearing jeans and a T-shirt, walked into the room, jumped and yelped in surprise. Then she laughed and put a hand over her heart.

"Sorry," said Phillips. "We didn't know anyone was here. Detective Phillips, and this is Detective Bark."

The woman was still laughing at her fright and taking deep breaths to calm herself.

"I'm Jean. Mrs. Hollister's housekeeper." She waved her hand in front of her face, as if to cool herself down. "Mercy Maude. Okay, I'm going to live."

"We've been down at the fire, and talked to Mr. Hollister. He said we were welcome to come in."

"Oh, I'm sure you are, I just . . . Whew. Well tell me how I can help. If I can. I'm just about to go down to the cottage to get to work. I understand Lily had a sleepover down there."

"We've been there," said Phillips.

"Looks like a pack of wolverines been through?"

Phillips laughed. "Pretty much."

"Terrible about the fire," said Bark.

"I heard the fire bell ring in the town before dawn," said Jean. "I said to my husband, 'bad news for somebody,' but I never thought . . . I was just that shocked when I come up the driveway."

"Any idea what caused it?"

"Mr. Hollister said something blew up. He was crying, he was so upset."

"I gather he had all his artwork and records in there," said Bark.

"And his car. He just loved that car. My brother has an old Mustang convertible he restored himself. We all go to the car show over in Rhinebeck every year and he won a prize for it once. But it's nothing like that car of Mr. Hollister's. It's Italian. You could see your face in the chrome, he took such care of it."

"So he drove it regularly?"

"I wouldn't say regularly. But in good weather."

"Has he had it out this spring?"

"Yes, he had it out a couple of weeks ago."

"Do you remember when?"

Jean suddenly stopped. Up to now, they'd been talking about what everyone was talking about. The fire. Mr. Hollister's car. Why would they want to know when the car was driven?

"I'm sorry—tell me who you are, again?"

"We're detectives with the White Plains police," said Bark.

"White Plains?" That wasn't very near here. They could see the question marks begin to form above her head.

"We met Mr. Hollister when we were investigating a case down where Lily goes to school. We came up to talk to him about it."

"So you're not here because of the fire?"

"No."

"He said we were welcome to come in and look around," said Bark.

After a tiny beat, Jean said, "All righty then. I just finished in here, and I haven't done upstairs yet, if you don't mind. I thought I ought to tackle the guesthouse while I still have the courage."

"Don't let us keep you. We'll find you before we leave, if we have questions."

"Okey dokey," said Jean.

"This the door to the basement?" Bark asked.

Jean said, "That's my broom closet. Basement stairs are around here." She opened the door to a long, dank, nineteenth-century flight of wooden stairs. A stale smell of earth and mold rose from below.

"Anything we should know about what's down there?"

Jean flipped on the light for them. "It's a cellar."

"Right. Thanks for your help," Phillips said. Jean went back to the broom closet and they heard her gather her cleaning supplies as they went down the stairs.

"She has to ask Hollister if she should talk to us," Phillips said.

"Yes. Good jobs not thick on the ground in this neck of the woods."

They found no gas cans in the basement, but nothing else that aroused suspicion. There were some old paint cans containing, it appeared from the drips, a supply of the shade on the outside trim of the house. Someone kept the grounds looking shipshape; they should find out who. There were some old clothes racks probably from before the farmhouse boasted a washer and dryer. There was a dark low corner that looked as if it had once been a root cellar. A new furnace, oil burning. Cross-country skis and snowshoes hung neatly from one wall. A heap of packing boxes and old suitcases. The usual. They opened them all.

They went back upstairs and walked slowly through the first floor, studying family photographs, looking at outgoing mail in the bowl on the kitchen table. Nothing jumped out. They went up to the second floor. There they found two guest bedrooms that shared a bathroom at the end of the hall. Another room with its own bath, clearly Lily's. There were swimming and diving ribbons on a cork board, and a couple of trophies on the bookshelves, along with pictures of Lily at various ages, often wearing a competition swimsuit. The room was neat, though the bathroom showed signs that teenagers had recently been through. Various kinds of makeup lay on the sink counter, and the makeup mirror's light had been left on. A half-empty bottle of peach schnapps stood on the toilet tank.

"You think they let her drink that?" Bark asked.

"Probably a trophy of some kind. I once kept a half pack of cigarettes for a couple of years some boy had dropped."

"Really? Some random boy?"

"Some guy I thought was hot. He had five o'clock shadow and a motorcycle."

The master bedroom was definitely occupied. It was a larger room than the others; with its huge bathroom and two dressing rooms, it occupied the entire upstairs space of the new addition. The bed was unmade, and by the side of the bed that they guessed was Hugo's there was a box of tissues, a thermometer, and a bottle of cough syrup. They opened drawers and went through closets. The bedroom windows overlooked the pool and studio; Hugo would have had a front row seat for the fireball.

In the bathroom, Bark took extra care with the cabinet that held the shaving gear and manly toiletries. He took pictures of the labels on a couple of vials of pills.

"Guy has a massive case of acid reflux," he said.

"Good," said Phillips. "Any other interesting meds?"

"Some I don't recognize. We'll check it out."

"Are we done here?"

"I am. Let's go see what Jean has for us."

Downstairs, they went out by the kitchen door and met Hugo trudging toward them. He looked exhausted and ill.

"You okay?" Bark said.

"No," said Hugo.

"I'm sorry for your loss."

"Thank you. I'm going back to bed."

He passed them and stepped up to the kitchen door.

"We're just going to have a word with your housekeeper and then we'll be on our way," said Bark. Hugo nodded without looking at them and went inside. They watched through the window as he moved heavily through the kitchen and out of sight, heading for the stairs.

"Is it illegal to burn down your own studio?" Phillips asked.

"Not unless you claim on the insurance or blame someone else."

They looked at each other.

Jean had the guesthouse kitchen transformed. The refrigerator shone; the small range was spotless, the pizza boxes were gone, and there were three large black garbage bags by the door along with cans and bottles in clear plastic. There were a lot of weekenders in town who had gotten the dump rules all changed and now you had to sort everything or pay a fine. They kept changing the rules too. Whiteboard was recyclable but not dirty pizza boxes, although they were made of whiteboard, as far as she could tell. She did her best.

She was just about to get upstairs to the bedrooms when those two detectives sidled in.

"You find what you needed?" she asked.

"For now. We just came down to finish up what we were talking about before."

"What was that?"

"About the Maserati. Mr. Hollister's car. You said he had it out recently."

"Yes, he did. He always does when the weather turns warm."

"Do you remember when that was?"

"Oh, I couldn't tell you. A couple of weeks ago."

"I see. And was this on a weekend?"

"I work on Tuesdays or Wednesdays off-season, depending."

"Depending on what?"

"My other jobs. I help an older lady when she needs me, take her to doctor visits or shopping."

"I see. So, midweek."

"You don't work on weekends?" Phillips asked.

"I *do,* but not here. I clean at the church on Saturdays. I only come in on Sundays if Mrs. Hollister is here with a party. That doesn't usually happen until summer. I wasn't here at all last week

314 ♦ BETH GUTCHEON

because we went to my niece's wedding in New Hampshire, so I came today."

"So you saw the Maserati in the driveway when you got to work on a Wednesday? Three weeks ago, maybe? A month? Less?"

"Yes." She was not liking this.

"It was out when you got here."

"I said yes."

"And it was still out when you left?"

"Yes."

"And where was Mr. Hollister?"

"He was in and out."

"You mean he left the property?"

"I mean in and out between here and the studio. Like always."

"And do you clean the studio?"

"No, he does that himself. He has his art in there."

"So he didn't leave the property that day."

"I didn't say that. I think he went off in the afternoon."

"In the Maserati?"

"Yes. I think he did. I remember seeing it buzzing down the driveway. I think it was that day."

"Was his own car in the driveway too?"

"What?"

"His SUV. Was it in the driveway that day? When you got here?"

"It must have been."

"But you don't remember for sure?"

"No. But how else would he have gotten here?"

"Good question. You're sure you can't remember which Wednesday it was."

She looked at him, then briefly at Phillips. "Or Tuesday. They all blend together."

After a long pause, Bark said, "Thank you very much for your time. If we need to, can we talk to you again?"

She shrugged.

"Could we have a number?"

She gave him one, then started up the stairs, carrying empty trash bags and a vacuum cleaner.

They drove south in silence. Finally, Phillips said, "So he drives Florence's car from Rye to Hatfield, with Florence in it, dead or alive. He pulls out the Maserati, parks Florence's car in the car hole, and does whatever he has to do. Plenty of time to clean up whatever he has to. Plenty of time to wipe prints off everything. Then he drives the car back in the dead of night Thursday morning and dumps the body."

"But we can't prove it."

"If Florence was here, dead or alive, there would have been traces somewhere."

"Not anymore."

"What the hell would have tipped him off? Why burn the studio now?"

"Maybe it was a coincidence," Bark said.

Phillips looked at him, even though she was driving seventy miles an hour.

"Kidding," said Bark glumly.

After a beat she said, "So now what do we do?"

"I have no idea. Wait to hear what the arson squad makes of the fire, I guess."

As they approached their exit, Phillips said, "We should let Maggie Detweiler know, shouldn't we?"

Bark nodded.

But Maggie already knew. Lily's mother had called the school during lunch to tell her what had happened, and Lily had returned to the dining hall looking as if she'd seen a ghost. She had told Steph, who told Ann and Melanie, and soon it was all over the room. Oh, the schadenfreude, the thrill of disaster that happened to somebody else. A terrible fire! At Lily's country house! Steph and Ann and Melanie were just there! Nobody died, but they *could* have, and her dad's whole office is gone, his Ferrari burned up, all these masterpiece paintings he had in there . . .

Maggie was sitting with Pam Moldower when the news blew through the dining hall. It was interesting to watch it spread. Maggie watched the way the girls sorted themselves, Friends of Lily displaying sympathy and shock, and others who weren't so close to Lily leaning their heads together, buzzing about how *they* would feel if *their* country houses burned down. Pools of alarm and excitement eddied in the wider sea of adolescents to whom the news was of milder interest, or none.

Maggie's attention was snagged by the sight of Alison Casey. She was sitting with some younger girls who suddenly buzzed with excitement. One of them got her phone out, though this was not supposed to happen at meals, and was passing it around the table. Maggie could guess what was on it; the photographs posted by Lily's friends this past weekend. The pool, the glamorous car, the studio. LILY WITH HER SISTER Steph had titled the picture of Lily with the car.

What interested her particularly was the stricken expression on Alison's face. She had turned to look at Lily. And Lily was sitting very quietly, her face drained of color. Steph said something to her, and it took her two tries to get Lily's attention. Then Lily briefly shook her head, stood, and walked out of the dining hall without busing her dishes. Maggie and Pam watched her go.

After a thoughtful pause, Maggie asked, "By the way, who are the girls Alison Casey is with?"

"Freshmen," said Pam. "They're horse kids. Alison's turned into a stable rat. Honey's making a project of her."

"I wouldn't have thought that Honey Marcus was the maternal type," said Maggie.

"People surprise you," said Pam.

When Maggie left the dining room and checked her silenced phone, she found a voice mail from Hope, whom she'd been trying to reach for days.

"Hey—just wanted you to know I'm still breathing. My phone died. The nice man at the Town Club is having it fixed or cloned or something. From here I'm going to Maine because, hold your hat, Buster and Brianna are getting married on Saturday! Damn, I wish you'd pick up. Okay, I'll call you when I can." And she signed off.

Maggie immediately went to one of the phone booths outside the dining hall where you could either use a landline or make a call from your mobile in private. The woman on the desk at the Town Club said, "I think she's checked out, Mrs. Detweiler, hold on a minute." After an interval, the woman returned to say, "She checked out, but her luggage is in the cloakroom. When she comes back we can give her a message." Maggie left word that Hope should keep calling until she reached her, that it was important.

Hope meanwhile was at the New York Society Library. Without her phone, she needed to use her computer to pick up e-mail, and the library offered much nicer places to sit than her tiny bedroom at the club. Computer use was naturally not allowed in the club's public rooms at any time. Hope was grateful that she had the laptop with her at all; she had almost left it in Boston this trip, she'd gotten so good at typing on her phone with her thumbs. But there it was in the hold-everything chicken bag, and at the last minute, she'd slung it over her shoulder.

She'd settled herself in the Hornblower Room on the fifth floor, where computers were allowed, as long as they didn't make any noises. Around her, library members were beavering away at their novels or memoirs or histories of Malta. She loved the atmosphere and was a paying member on principle, since it was a cultural jewel of the city, though she'd rarely used it when she lived in New York because she really wasn't that kind of reader. But now, here she was, and she wondered what she'd done with her computer glasses; she rooted through her purse and then the clever pockets of the chicken bag. No glasses. She did find a favorite pen she'd been looking for, and then the thumb drive that held her checkbook program backup, which would be fatal to lose. And another thumb drive. She took it out and studied it. She'd never bought that brand, that she could remember. What the hell was it? What was it doing in her purse? Then she discovered that her computer glasses were on top of her head, holding her hair out of her eyes, although she had no memory of putting them there. It was disconcerting bordering on scary how many habitual behaviors these days seemed to bypass the conscious mind altogether. No wonder people in their sunset years seemed to spend half their waking hours looking for things.

She popped the mystery thumb drive into a USB port and opened its directory. The folders were: London, Paris, Florence, Madrid, Seville, Toledo, NYC, BMFA. This definitely wasn't hers, but whose was it? She opened London. It seemed to be someone's backup of a picture roll. She clicked an image: a painting of a man in a loincloth, his hands tied together and roped to a tree, with a little blue angel-like figure gazing at him. Everyone looking miserable. Then a picture of an old woman and a younger one, the younger one also looking miserable, and on the table before her a bowl of dead fish and another of eggs. The fishes were pretty terrific. Then a lugubrious portrait of, unmistakably, Philip IV of Spain, with his big jaw and his head shaped like a shoe box, and she knew. Velázquez. This had been on Florence Meagher's desk. She had just picked it up when Ray caught her and Maggie snooping. She must have dropped it into the chicken bag when they fled. That she had no memory of it proved less than nothing.

She clicked through to the pictures from the Prado. They were all Velázquez, all the time. The pictures from the Thyssen-Bornemisza were more of a mixed bag, and there were more of them. She decided to see if, as she hoped, the BMFA folder was for the Boston

Museum of Fine Arts. It was shocking but Hope had only been there twice since she had moved to Boston, and both times for special exhibitions. She hadn't explored the permanent collection since she was in college and their history of art teacher made them go as an assignment. Most of what she remembered about *that* day was the bus ride with her friends.

She expected more Spanish portraits in the Boston collection, but instead Florence had dwelt on four or five Rembrandt canvases. Well, why not, who doesn't love Rembrandt. Then, inevitably, another Philip IV. When had the man had time to rule? He must have spent every day being fitted for clothes and then painted in them. She was more struck by another Velázquez portrait of a man in a high white soft collar, not the starched disk of the royals, with a long skinny head and a fierce expression who looked very much like Hope's gynecologist. Then, a bounce forward in time, to a great big picture she was pretty sure was John Singer Sargent. She loved Sargent. Hope's husband had once had a famous portrait guy try to do Hope as Madame X, but he couldn't pull it off, which proved that what Sargent did was way harder than it looked. Her husband had refused to pay for the commission; that was embarrassing. Hope paid the man secretly in installments with money she siphoned out of her household cash allowance, and it took two years.

This was a picture of young girls of different ages, sisters they must be, in a big room with a complicated Oriental carpet, and huge blue-and-white vases. Florence had taken a lot of pictures of this painting, moving around it, trying to get details that were otherwise obscured by other art lovers' heads. Hope wondered if this was for a class Florence was preparing. Hope clicked through them, wishing for her phone so she could biggify the parts that were too small here. She whizzed past one wide shot, felt something snag her attention almost below the level of consciousness, and she clicked back. There they were, a couple sharing a passionate kiss at the edge of the frame. Strange museum behavior. Then the next shot. In which the girl was in profile, looking moony-eyed at the man, who had turned and was looking directly at the camera.

Steph found Lily in the gymnastics room at the gym. Lily had her earbuds in and was on the balance beam, standing on one leg with her eyes closed.

"Lily," Steph called quite loudly. Lily opened her eyes and looked annoyed. When she was upset it helped to disappear into her body, submerging feeling beneath the effort of forcing her physical self to ever greater mastery of strength, balance, precision.

Steph said, "Lily, don't be a dick. Get down."

Lily immediately had to put her foot down to keep from falling. She pulled the earbuds out of her ears and sat down on the bar, saying fiercely, "What is your problem?"

"You should see your face. And you shouldn't be doing that in those clothes, it isn't safe."

"Oh, *safe*," said Lily nastily.

"Jesus Christ! What'd I do to *you*?"

Lily said, "God, nothing! But you need to mind your own business!"

"I would, but you've been a total freak for like, weeks now!"

"No, I—"

"*Yes*, Lily. You have. And I just wanted to tell you I'm so sorry about the fire. It's—"

"Do you know how it feels to have your father be a total fucking liar?"

Steph still had her mouth open. "What?"

Lily was now on the edge of tears, a state Steph knew she hated more than most people. Her lips were pressed together in a clench that looked painful.

"Your . . . what?"

"Nothing. Forget it. Just leave me alone."

"No. Tell me what you're talking about."

Lily suddenly dropped from the balance beam to the floor and came at Steph so aggressively that it felt like an attack. She stood eye to eye with her friend as if she could convey with mental telepathy how angry she was.

Steph stood her ground. She was actually quite startled at what she'd unleashed, but having started, she meant to finish.

Lily said, "The day we found Mrs. Meagher, Daddy came to get me. He wanted to take me into the city, but I really wanted to go to Hatfield, so we went, but he was weird the whole time."

"Weird how?"

"He seemed mad at me, at least until Mummy came. And the whole time we were there, his studio was locked."

"What? I mean . . . why?"

"I don't know. I don't *know*. But I went out there to look for something I'd lost, and I couldn't get in. When I asked him why he did this." Lily stepped closer to Steph, practically nose to nose, and stared into her eyes, her unblinking gaze an unveiled threat.

Steph tried to sustain the look, but stepped back.

"Jesus," she said. She tried to imagine her own cheerful father, an allergist, doing anything remotely like that, and couldn't. "But I don't understand."

"So don't."

"Did you tell your mother?"

"You are *not* getting it. He's a total fucking liar and she pretends not to know it. I just need to get out of there."

What Steph was getting was that her friend was upset out of all proportion to what she understood of the situation. What she should do about it, if anything, she had no idea.

Caroline was just saying good-bye to her yoga instructor when Hope arrived at the apartment. She was still in her tights and T-shirt, but she'd put on a big cardigan and a pair of loafers. She urged the yoga teacher to give Hope her number, so Hope could make an appointment when she was settled back in the city. This was better than the reception Hope had feared. And after the door closed behind the yogini, as Hope said, "I'm so sorry to come on such short notice . . ." Caroline was saying "I'm so glad you're here, something terrible has happened."

Then they looked at each other. "Let's go into the den," Caroline said, and they did, closing the door.

"Tell me," Hope said.

"Just tell me first, are you in a tearing hurry?"

"I'm heading out this afternoon, but I'm driving, so my own schedule. What's happened?"

"Hugo's studio, in the country. Where he kept all his business records, and inventory. His holy of holies. It blew up in the middle of last night."

Hope stared at her. "Blew up?"

"Burned down. Blew up then burned down. He's such a mess I couldn't get a clear story. He says he heard a tremendous boom in the night, and when he got to the window there was this fireball streaming into the sky from the roof of his studio. It's lucky he was there or it might have spread to the house. The studio's a total loss. Tremendously hot fire, devoured everything."

Hope's mind was going at a rapid tilt. How does a man's business studio just blow up? In a fire so hot it destroys all traces?

"I'm shocked," Hope said.

"Yes. It makes you feel completely . . . naked. Unprotected. Which we all are, really, aren't we?"

"Did you have anything of your own in the building?"

"No, it was Hugo's domain. He needs that, a kingdom of his own. He's a proud man." Tears started in Caroline's eyes. "I don't think I've ever known him to cry before, he just seems shattered."

"Were you insured?"

"Oh yes. But most of it is irreplaceable. His inventory. The car."

"Wait—the car? Was this a garage apartment?"

Caroline smiled briefly at the thought of Hugo running his kingdom from a garage apartment. "No, a custom building, everything he ever wanted. Art storage, his office and library, and a little palace for his Maserati. He worshipped that car. It meant something mystical to him. His Rosebud."

Hope had questions, but they could wait. If Hugo owned an expensive Maserati, couldn't he have sold it to pay his debts? Only if it was in his name . . . well, now was not the time. Angus could find out if it was important. Feelings were more important than things, at the moment, and she had something to do that was not going to be easy.

"Is Hugo still in the country?" she asked instead.

"Yes, he wasn't feeling well to begin with, and then he got no sleep, and also he thought he ought to stay there to see what they can learn about the fire. The insurance people are coming this afternoon. I know how you feel about him, but honestly, Hope, this breaks my heart for him."

Hope could not think of a single thing to say that wouldn't be false, so she said nothing for a long stretch. When Caroline stopped twisting her fingers and imagining Hugo's distress and turned to look at her, Hope said, "I'm afraid what I feel for Hugo has gotten more complicated."

Caroline said, "Oh." She seemed to shift gears visibly as she remembered that Hope had asked to see *her;* she hadn't merely appeared as an angel of sympathy. More bad news was coming her way. She composed herself and turned an expression toward Hope that in another era might have been called haughty.

"I'm truly sorry, Caroline," said Hope.

"I doubt you, but do what you've got to do."

The atmosphere was suddenly like the noise of chalk on a blackboard between them as Hope got out her laptop and fired it up. When it had sung its little welcome song, she plugged in the thumb drive, opened the BMFA directory, and scrolled through to the picture of the Sargent with the amorous couple at the edge of the frame. She turned the screen toward Caroline, who looked at it steadily. She showed no emotion at all; Hope couldn't even tell for sure if she'd seen what she was being shown.

Hope opened the next image, in which Hugo has turned and is looking at the photographer. Again she couldn't tell if Caroline was seeing what was before her, she sat so still. Finally Hope said, "This is not a good man, Caroline."

Caroline said flatly, "This is cruel, Hope."

Hope hung her head. Maybe it was. She hated moral murk.

"You should go," Caroline added.

Hope went. Caroline's demeanor as she stood watching her retreat was so coldly angry that as Hope pulled the door shut behind her, she thought she might well never see her friend again.

Lily *had been working on a dive* from the three-meter board with a degree of difficulty rarely seen in competition in her age group. The diving coach from Fordham, an old friend of Greta's from her days in competition, had made a special trip to see her workout. Lily and Greta had worked on the dive list for the visit all spring. Steph had been watching the two of them closely, hoping for some sign that Lily had talked to Coach about what was going on with her, but Lily had totally closed her out.

Bobby Chiang arrived on Friday night in time for dinner. Greta had all her best swimmers and divers at the table. She sat at the head, with Chiang on her left and Lily on her right. The young athletes listened in avid silence as the two Olympians talked about old times, laughing nervously if Chiang turned his attention to any of them. They found his accent difficult to penetrate, though Greta apparently did not. The meal was chicken pot pie, Lily's favorite, but Steph noticed she put almost none of it into her mouth. Instead she concentrated on cutting a chunk of carrot into smaller and smaller pieces with the side of her fork. Lily seemed manic to Steph, talking too much and using her hands a lot, which wasn't like her. Only once did she seem to focus—when Chiang began to describe to

Greta the trip he was leading to Shanghai in the summer. Promising young divers would get to see the Chinese national competition and then train in the center used by the Shanghai team. Beautiful facilities with springboards and platforms at the pool and gymnastics practice rooms. There would be trips to see the sights as well, the Jade Buddha Temple, the Yu Garden—

Lily interrupted. "Is it too late to sign up?"

Chiang was surprised but recovered himself. The trip had been filled for some months now, but next year—

Lily interrupted again and asked with some urgency, "Is there a waiting list? If anyone drops out, can you let me know?"

Chiang looked at Greta, who smiled mildly, looking puzzled. Lily's manners were usually better than this.

Chiang said, "I have your information, I think?" He turned to Greta again.

In the morning, when Greta arrived at the pool house, Lily was already there, in her sweats with her gym bag, waiting on the bench outside the door nearest to Greta's office. She had a pinched look around her nose, and mauve shadows under her eyes.

"You're up early," Greta said. She herself was a little late because she and Honey had sat up with Chiang in the bar at his hotel, telling war stories.

"Couldn't sleep," said Lily.

"Did you have any breakfast?"

Greta could tell from her hesitation that she had not. "Well come in and get warmed up. I'll make some coffee and I've got some cheese and biscuits. You have to eat something."

By the time Chiang arrived with Honey, a cheering section had drifted in to sit in the bleachers. Everyone hoped that Lily was going to be an Olympian. Or least a star on the national level. It was thrilling to think of one of their own being great, becoming famous.

Chiang sat with Honey, and Greta stood with Lily at the deep end of the pool. Ms. Liggett came in with Mrs. Detweiler. Everyone in the hot moist pool room wanted to be uplifted, to see something that would white out the taint of what had happened here. Steph, sitting high in the bleachers, kept wondering if Lily's parents would appear. Normally they showed up for everything, at least her father did. If they weren't here, it was because Lily hadn't told them about it.

Lily, wearing a black tank suit, took her position on the three-meter board. Greta announced the first dive. Lily started with a relatively easy dive for her, and did it impeccably. Smooth upward spring to impressive height, a tidy perfectly calibrated forward twist, and an entry to the water so clean that she barely made a splash. Steph saw Chiang exchange a look with Greta. He sat waiting for the next dive with a little smile on his face.

The second dive, an inward straight dive, had a higher degree of difficulty but happened to be one that was easier for Lily than most. Greta announced it as Lily stood on the tip of the three-meter board, back to the water. She looked solemn as she went into her lift, turned her extended body upside down, and entered the water again in perfect form, toes pointed, with hardly a splash.

The third dive, a reverse tuck, was the one most in Lily's wheelhouse, the one she hadn't missed in years, chosen so the visceral experience of perfection would carry her into the big challenge, number four. Oddly, something went slightly wrong in her liftoff, and she wasn't quite in position when she hit the water. There was some splash and her feet were not touching when they disappeared below the surface.

Maggie clapped enthusiastically until she realized that Christina had recognized something less than perfection. Diving was not a sport Maggie had ever followed and it had looked dazzling to her, but Maggie's hands were folded in her lap as Lily's head broke the surface of the water, and she stayed for a moment treading water, looking blankly toward Greta, before she began to swim to the ladder.

Lily fussed with her suit, drank some water, fussed with her suit again before Greta whispered something to her and gave her a gentle pat on the rump, and she climbed back up the three-meter.

"Back one and a half somersault, one and a half twist," Greta announced, and immediately Lily called, "Back one and a half pike." She looked at Greta with something pleading in her expression. Greta looked dumbfounded.

"Did Greta make a mistake?" Maggie asked Christina in a whisper.

"No, Lily is trying to change the dive. It's really not done; a dive list is decided well in advance."

She broke off as Greta firmly announced the original dive.

Lily was now looking straight ahead. She took several deep breaths. She shook her arms. She rolled her feet so as to loosen her ankles, first one, then the other.

Then she began to move. She flung herself straight upward, revolving rapidly, then spun as she hurtled downward and was late by much too much to extend her arms to break the water before she hit it with her head and shoulder.

There was a ripple in the audience of fear for her. You could hit the water as if it were pavement if you didn't break it right.

Lily surfaced and swam for the ladder, climbed out without pausing to clear her eyes or answer Greta's whispered question, and climbed the ladder. Before she had quite taken her position she called, "Redive."

Greta, looking shocked, firmly announced the last dive, but Lily said, "Someone made a noise. I need a redive."

If there had been an unusual noise no one else had heard it. This would never be allowed in competition, but then, this wasn't competition. Lily stood, looking straight ahead, gathering herself as Greta looked to Chiang, who shrugged.

Lily took her place at the tip of the board and without stopping to gather herself, bounced upward. As she finished her somersault and plunged downward, spinning, and hit the water even worse than before, her timing completely wrong, and there were gasps throughout the small audience in fear that she could have really broken something. Like her neck.

She surfaced. She swam to the ladder and called, before she was fully out, "Redive!"

Greta called, "Lily, that's enough! Go get dressed!"

Chiang was putting away his clipboard, looking at no one. Greta and Lily faced each other. Greta's back was to the bleachers but her posture registered her anger and disappointment. She was relentless on the subject of sportsmanship and Lily had mortified her. Lily, meanwhile, was looking back with a ferocity that was almost feral. She looked like a cornered animal.

C*aroline was wearing leggings* and a long silk jacket with a mandarin collar and the apartment was filled with the smell of chicken with forty cloves of garlic, Hugo's favorite meal. She was waiting in the living room, looking out at lush green trees along the street and the beginnings of orange-pink dusk reflected in the windows opposite. Hugo hadn't been sure what time he'd get in; evidently there was still much to do with the insurance adjusters and the fire people, and then all the mess of replacing the computer he'd lost and finding someone to help him with the cloud backup that he hoped was in place. At least his cold sounded better. To put the cherry on top, he'd had a flat tire on the Mercedes when he got up this morning, but lovely Jean and her husband had come right over to help. They'd changed to the temporary spare, then followed him into the village, where the gas station man came in to help him even though it was Memorial Day. He didn't have a new tire in the right size but could repair the old one well enough to at least get Hugo safely back to New York.

She heard the key rattling in the front door and called, "It's unlocked, love."

Hugo walked in and dumped his bags in the front hall and stood there, like a cart pony taken out of its traces that doesn't know where to go unless it's being led or driven. She went to him and folded him in her arms and he gave a long shuddering sigh of relief and gratitude. She patted his back and he kissed her neck. Even in the embroidered flats she usually wore when they were together, she was taller than he. They stood together, breathing the scent of each other's skin. Then Caroline turned back toward where she had been waiting and said, "I was sitting out here, so I could see the light."

"Perfect," he said, and let her lead him toward the windows. He took his favorite chair with a sigh, and she went to the cocktail table and made him a vodka gimlet. She'd opened a fresh bottle of Rose's lime juice, knowing he claimed he could taste staleness if it had been opened more than a week.

He took his first sip, closed his eyes, and looked as if he were at prayer. She had resumed her seat and picked up her glass of wine. When he opened his eyes he looked straight at her. He held her gaze for a long time, then said, "I am so grateful for you. For your goodness and your kindness. With your love, I can face all of it."

She took a sip of wine and said, "Thank you, darling. You've had a hard time."

He shuddered and drank more deeply before saying, "So hard. I just can't . . . can't . . . can't tell you what it felt like to see that pillar of fire and picture all my work, all that . . . that . . . that . . . all that turning into ash."

She nodded. They had already said all this to each other over many phone calls.

"Tell me what they say, the fire people, now that they've had time to study it."

"They seem to agree with me that it must have been arson. There's just not another way to explain why it went up so fast, and burned so hot. And that boom. But who, and why, they're just . . . just . . . just at the start of their inquiries."

"You told them about the Black brothers?"

This was a pair of town outlaws, decidedly bad hats, according to Jean, whose family had once owned part of the farm that was now Glimmer Glen. A couple of generations back, but down in the scrub beyond the creek, there was a Black family graveyard on the property. It was all falling to ruin, only one of the headstones unbroken, but you could read some of them, and at least one ancestor had been killed in the Civil War. Somewhere in there in the scrub there were some cellar holes, where the houses had been and the family had farmed. Hugo had seen one of the Black women, Roberta he thought her name was, a slattern in shorts and a wife-beater, sunburned and tattooed, coming out of the woods carrying bags of things one September when she thought there was no one home. Hugo had surprised her and pointed out she was on private property. She had replied, not at all politely, that she was gathering apples from trees her family had planted and that he didn't even know where the trees were and without she picked them the apples would just rot, and he said that be that as it may, she was trespassing on his land and she said be *that* as it may he could fuck himself, and the relationship with the family had not improved since. The brothers liked to get a snootful and drive up onto his land with shotguns pointing out the windows of their truck. And similar. Hugo believed, and he had let it be known, that if anyone wanted to know who would burn his studio down, they should start by questioning the Blacks. And he strongly suspected that one of them had put a shiv into his tire sometime last night. The garage man said it was a suspiciously clean cut.

After a time, Caroline said, "We have to keep remembering that no one was hurt, and we're insured." She rose and took his glass to refill his drink.

When she sat back down she said, "Darling, we need to get away from this. I've made a plan that I hope you're going to be pleased about."

Hugo looked up expectantly.

"Linda Beemis is giving a surprise birthday party for Randy. She's asked us to come, and I said yes."

Linda was a lifelong friend of Caroline's who lived in Santa Barbara. She was married to a man that no one outside of the family circle called anything but Randolph, who had been under secretary of the treasury in the second Bush administration and was by most accounts worth many many millions. Hugo had always wanted to meet him, and tended to refer to him as Randy in conversation, even though up to now they were merely rumors to each other.

His eyes lit up. "When?"

"The weekend after school gets out."

"Here?"

"Oh no . . . at their ranch."

"But . . ."

"I know, you can't fly there, but you can take the train, and I'll fly out and meet you. You've always wanted to see the ranch."

That was absolutely true, he had.

"She asked us to stay with them too, but I know you don't like being a houseguest. I booked us at the Santa Barbara Biltmore. You will love it."

Actually he wouldn't have minded at all staying at the ranch with Randy Beemis, but he suppressed his flare of irritation at her for getting it wrong. "I'm just . . . I'm just . . . just . . . just . . . having trouble switching gears. Do you really think we should be away, with the . . . the . . . you know, the fire people needing to talk to us, and insurance people, so much to sort out?"

"They'll be able to reach us, and we won't be gone that long. It will be good for us. Say yes."

Caroline was smiling at him so hopefully.

He thought about meeting Randy and being able to say afterward, "When we were out at Randy Beemis's ranch for his birthday . . . ," and Linda was a nice woman, he liked her very much . . .

"Yes."

"Oh good!" Caroline crowed. "We are going to have so much fun. I booked you on a train that leaves on Wednesday at three P.M. and gets you into L.A. at eight in the morning Saturday. I'll have a car pick you up. You'll have a longish layover in Chicago, but it was the only train with a private room available, and I figured you could go to the Art Institute or something."

Hugo smiled. He quite loved trains. Except for the food, but he could pack his own. He took a big slug of his drink, relaxed into the plan, smiled, and said simply, "Thank you."

"You're welcome. And we're having chicken with forty cloves of garlic tonight and I made you a tarte tatin."

P*hillips and Bark were in the office* of the assistant DA. Again.

The report on the fire at Glimmer Glen was clear on the finding of arson, but how exactly it was set, and by whom, seemed to have gone up in the fireball.

They laid out their case against Hugo.

"And you want me to do what with this?"

"Take it to a grand jury."

"Weren't you just in here wanting me to take a circumstantial case against Ray Meagher for this same crime to the grand jury?"

It had been several weeks ago, but still.

"Hollister is a man of means," said Bark. "The arson is a clear destruction of evidence. He could afford to disappear. We need him held without bail until we can get the rest of the physical evidence."

"The rest of the physical evidence? Do you have *any* physical evidence?"

"As I said, we found his DNA in Florence's car."

"Along with Ray's, and how many other individuals, twelve was it? Including Jesse Goldsmith and about eight unknowns?"

"Yes, but those are explainable. Explain what Hugo was doing in Florence's car."

The assistant DA shrugged.

"The motive is powerful," Bark bore down. "Hugo relies completely on his wife's money. We know he was under financial pressure, and—"

"What do you mean, you *know*? Are you bringing me proof?"

"We are, but we need to make sure he doesn't leave the jurisdiction."

Country is what he meant. "We can make this case."

The assistant DA looked at him for a long time over his glasses. He was fairly new to the job, and he didn't want to start his work for the DA by swinging for the fences when a series of singles would look more solid. It was embarrassing to fail at the grand jury level.

"You seem to me to be flailing here, detective. The sheriff in Dutchess County likes a local family called Black for the fire. And a lot of men have cheated on their wives and not felt the need to murder anyone. How did he get into the pool house and why did he bother? Why didn't he just dig a hole and bury her in the woods? I have to tell you, I liked your case against the husband better."

"He burned up his prized possession! His own Maserati! Doesn't that tell you that he's desperate?"

"I get the feeling *someone* is, Bark. But you've got to convince *me* before I can convince a grand jury, and so far you're not even close."

Hope drove into Rye-on-Hudson early Tuesday evening. She'd come straight through from Bergen, Maine, after breakfast with the newlyweds. Maggie was waiting for her at Le Bistro. She was buying Hope a congratulatory Mother of the Groom dinner.

It was a warm night, but drizzly, and the room was full, the mood jolly. When they were settled at a table by the window, with a bottle of rosé between them, Maggie said, "Tell me everything, M.O.G."

"It's a whole lot easier than being mother of the bride," said Hope. "At least, when the bride is Lauren."

Hope's daughter, Lauren, had had nine bridesmaids and a dinner dance for 250, which was to say nothing of showers and bachelorette parties and postwedding brunches.

"Where was the ceremony?"

"Bergen Town Hall. The town clerk is a justice of the peace, and a pal of Buster's."

"Who was there?"

"Cherry was the maid of honor. Brianna's parents were the witnesses, and I was the best man."

"And what did you all wear?"

"Brianna rented a bridal gown."

"Virginal white?"

"Camo. Buster wore his uniform. The formidable Beryl wore a Hillary pantsuit, and Roy had had a shower. He got quite teary during the ceremony." Beryl and Roy were Brianna's parents, long divorced and still barely speaking to each other.

"And then what happened?"

"Gabe up at the inn gave the bridal luncheon. It was lovely to have the staff bowing and scraping over Beryl. She was so pleased."

Beryl worked in the kitchen at the inn, and at one time Brianna's sister, Cherry, had worked for Gabe there too, but it had ended badly. Maggie thought it was a lovely gesture, in the circumstance, for Gabe to give everyone lunch.

"It saved any worry that Beryl and Roy would feel they had to give a lunch party," Hope said.

"Which Beryl would have had to cook herself," said Maggie. "Did you give a rehearsal dinner the night before?"

"Oh, I did! Well, I mean, not as such." Hope suddenly looked ever so slightly as if she thought they maybe should glide over the details.

"Hope? You gave a dinner?"

"Well we *had* dinner . . ."

"Where?"

"At the bowling alley. It was more beer and cheese dogs than dinner in the way you mean."

"That sounds like great fun," said Maggie, who thought it sounded deadly.

"It was! I am excellent at bowling it turns out. It was me and Brianna against Buster and Cherry. We won."

"Well done!"

"Yes! And then we all got tattoos."

"Hope!"

"I may have had a little more beer than was strictly good for me."

"Where?"

"In Ainsley."

"No, where on your body?"

"Ankle. I'm not going to show you because they don't look very nice at first."

"What will it look like when it's unveiled?"

"Buster and Brianna both got bees—"

"Initial or insect?"

"Insect. Bumble. And I got two bees and Cherry got a skull and crossbones. My treat."

"This should startle your grandchildren," said Maggie, drily.

"It will be good for them. Tell me what's happened here."

"Oh dear. Well, you sure know how to ruin a party."

"That doesn't sound good."

"It isn't. The state finds Bark's case completely resistible. First they stonewalled us the whole time we were making a case against Ray and wouldn't indict."

"But they were right not to."

"Yes, but now they won't bring the case against Hugo because the defense will just make the trial about how Ray should be on trial instead. All our evidence that Florence was at the studio, assuming there was any, was destroyed in the fire. Hugo pulled the Maserati out into the driveway and parked Florence's car in the car hole and no one remembers seeing Hugo drive it through Hatfield. No one ever found her computer or phone, and now we never will. And Hugo was in some final club at Harvard with the state attorney general. So *that's* not going to speed the wheels of justice. A high-profile murder trial costs a fortune and it only makes the prosecutors look good if they win."

"Pretty risky, setting a fire like that. He's got a nerve on him, little Hugo."

"I don't think he had any choice, unless Caroline was about to lend him a huge chunk of money. He has to buy back that painting or he'll be sued right down to his underpants."

"I'm sorry to tell you, I wouldn't put odds on Caroline one way or another. She was very angry when I showed her Florence's pictures, but I couldn't tell if it was at him or at me."

"Are we missing something?" Maggie asked.

"Like what?"

"I don't know. The one piece of the circle I can't close is how he got into the pool house."

"But we *do* know that! Lily had a key and he took it away from her! I told you!"

"You certainly did not!"

"Caroline told me and Angus, the day we saw *Hamilton.* She said that Lily is so driven that she got a key to the building somehow and went to practice by herself, but someone caught her. Saw her using it. She confessed to her father, before he could find out some other way and blow a gasket, and Hugo took the key away from her. I'm sure I told you."

"*Hamilton.* That was the weekend you forgot to stop here on your way to Boston. Then you went back to New York and then to Maine. All I got from you for a week were texts about Onesies."

There was a silence. Hope looked thoughtful, then said, "That's sort of true, isn't it."

"Well it doesn't matter, I just wanted to know I hadn't known

it and forgotten." Hope understood. At their age, they were constantly running Alzheimer's drills on themselves. Maggie went
on, "So that very bad girl had a key to the pool, and nobody did
anything? If an athlete did that at my school, I'd have her off the
team in a hot minute!"

"Yes, so the coaches wouldn't tell you and neither would the parents. Why do athletes get away with rape all over the place? The
coaches' jobs depend on their stars and their winning teams."

"I'm calling Charles N. Bark," said Maggie, for once taking her
mobile out at the table.

"Will this help?"

"I doubt it. But we can hope."

The *morning of the Rye Manor School's* 126th commencement dawned hot and bright. Every hotel room and bed-and-breakfast in the area was booked, with parents, siblings, aunts, and uncles of graduating girls come to celebrate. Most of the trustees were in town as well, to witness the fact that against all odds, the school had survived the year. Maggie had been right; school pride had revived at Christina's handling of the shooting, plus the news that the school's accreditation was secure had quelled defeatist rumors. Of course, this morning the press was back in force to rehash the traumas of the spring. There was a profile of the Meaghers on the front page of the local paper, full of unattributed quotes from anonymous sources and "no comments" from the police, the DA's office, and the school. But on this sunlit morning, there was a sense that what had not broken the school had made it stronger.

Not so for the Goldsmith family, which was back in the spotlight with an update on the charges against Jesse, who was still in a psychiatric facility. There were pictures of the locked and abandoned house on Violet Circle with its graffiti and overgrown lawn, and quotes and reprinted posts and tweets from angry neighbors and random strangers about Jesse, his parents, the gun lobby, the antigun lobby, and the school.

Christina had decided not to hold the ceremony in the Congressional church, as had been the tradition for a hundred years. No one wanted to be reminded of Florence's funeral. Instead the Hollisters had generously offered to pay for an enormous tent, which was now pitched on one of the athletic fields beyond the weeping birches.

Hope had arrived the night before and was staying at Christina's house, along with Pinky Tyson and Maggie. Pinky had resumed taking her meals with her friends in the dining hall, so the three veterans of one of the strangest springs any of them would ever experience had breakfast together in the sunroom, quietly reading the papers and bracing themselves for the day.

The campus around them was full of dressed-up families strolling in the sun. The seniors were mostly still in their dorms, trussed into their white dresses and sobbing in one another's arms at parting, writing in each other's yearbooks and pledging eternal devotion. Hope and Maggie left Christina to attend to a million last-minute crises and went to find Pam Moldower.

The faculty was to be seated at the side of the dais, and they went in early to find seats and watch the assembling crowd. It was an odd moment for Maggie, so familiar and yet so changed from her years as a young teacher. She'd grown fond of many of her girls in the weeks she'd been with them. They wouldn't remember her in years to come, but she would be keeping track of them out in the world. And she had found an entertaining ally in sardonic Pam.

The families of seniors began to claim their seats. The Hollisters came in, led by a pretty student usher. Hugo kept a proprietary hand on the back of his wife's waist as they walked down the center aisle. Lily walked a little behind them. Suddenly a beaming young woman with swinging dark hair rushed toward them, tapped Lily on the shoulder, and embraced her. She was embraced with warmth and surprise in return as Maggie grabbed Hope's hand to be sure she had seen this. Hugo turned now and joined his daughter, also smiling widely, as he and the young woman exchanged a hug. Caroline, who had already taken her seat, looked up briefly from her program, smiling and waving her fingers at the newcomer.

"Who is that with the Hollisters?" Maggie demanded of Pam Moldower.

"Her name is Connie Pierce."

"Is she a student here?"

"She was Lily's Old Girl. She's at Amherst now, I think. I have no idea what she's doing here today, though."

But Maggie did. Connie Pierce was the girl with Hugo in the photograph on Florence's thumb drive. Lily's Old Girl, her assigned senior mentor and protector the year she first arrived. Well, wasn't that special.

As eleven o'clock drew near, most of the seats were filled with women and girls in flowered dresses and men in blazers and ties already fanning themselves in the heat. Hope nudged Maggie and gestured with her head toward the far side, where Detectives Phillips and Bark had come in and found seats with good views of the stage and especially of Hugo Hollister. Hugo was pink with contentment, flush with that special pleasure of cuckolding someone who is right there, unsuspecting, missing what's right under her nose. He was spoken to often by fellow trustees, sharing a joke with one, making a note and nodding after a request from another. Caroline mostly read her program.

Christina and Emily George took their seats on the dais, along with other dignitaries, and a mildly distinguished alum who was to give the commencement address. Greta and Honey came in together and found seats with the rest of the faculty, and around the edges there were flashes from big professional cameras, though what the press found to interest them at this juncture, Maggie couldn't guess. The sound system began to broadcast "Pomp and Circumstance."

The senior girls, all in white and arranged in pairs according to height, began to march down the center aisle. The underclassmen were now weeping as they watched their senior favorites prepare to leave them. The invocation, the speeches of welcome, the Bruce Springsteen song performed by the school a cappella group, all went smoothly. The mildly distinguished alum maundered on too long to not much purpose, but Maggie had heard worse. No one tripped ascending to receive her diploma or tottering back to her seat on spongy grass in too-high heels, and the seniors didn't scratch or woolgather too obviously when the school videographer was recording them. All the while, Maggie hoped against hope that Bark would rush down the aisle and clap Hugo into handcuffs, but instead the whole performance ground uneventfully to its conclusion, the senior girls were once again weeping in the arms of their friends or their parents, and the tent began to empty as the whole crowd straggled out toward whatever came next.

Alison Casey was making her way toward the faculty seats. As Maggie had predicted, her furious parents had withdrawn her from school when they dropped their lawsuit, but to everyone's surprise Alison had asked to finish the year. Now she edged down the aisle against the flow of traffic to where Honey Marcus stood with Greta and a young math teacher in a bow tie who was telling them a joke.

Honey laid a hand on the man's arm and stepped a little away as she saw Alison's expression. Alison stopped before her and began to cry. She took a blue box out of the pocket of her skirt and held it awkwardly toward Honey. Greta watched in surprise as Honey paused for a moment, then folded the girl in her wiry arms. When Alison pulled back, she pressed the blue box into Honey's hands, then turned and walked away. Still weeping, it looked like. Maggie's eyes followed the girl out of the tent to where her father, perpetually fuming at the school and also his daughter, waited to drive Alison away from here forever.

Maggie and Hope moved toward the sunlight, looking now for Bark and Phillips. They found themselves close enough behind the departing Hollisters to see a reporter pounce on them, and Hugo smoothly steering Caroline away without breaking stride, interrupting his sentence, or seeming to notice at all.

"That guy writes for Gawker," Hope said.

"How on earth do you know things like that?" Maggie asked.

"I've seen him at parties. I'm going to have a word with him," Hope said.

Maggie found the two detectives at the edge of the crowd, wearing their Sunday best and looking as if they were both battling severe attacks of nausea. They looked at each other. Each one was hoping the other had something to say, to add, that would change things. None did. Finally Bark held out his hand and Maggie shook it. With Phillips she did the same. And they parted.

Greta Scheinerlein, alone in the emptying tent with Honey, who was looking after Alison, said, "Well? What did she give you?"

Honey looked at the box in her hand as if she'd just remembered it, then untied the white ribbon and pried off the lid. Inside was a silver bracelet with gold screws, and a tiny gold screwdriver.

"Wow," said Greta. "That's not your box of homemade fudge."

"Proof that these girls get entirely too much allowance," said Honey. She looked in the direction that Alison had gone, as if she thought to follow her and thank her, but there was no sign of the Caseys.

"You going to put it on?"

"I don't know. Should I?"

"Do you like it?"

"I kind of do," said Honey, a note of surprise in her voice, as she was not a dressy woman. "But no. I can't be bothered taking it on and off when I'm working."

"Are you kidding? Once you put it on, you need a tool kit to get it off."

Honey stared at it, not sure how it worked.

Greta said, "Come out where we can sit down and I'll do it for you."

It was a while before Hope and Maggie found each other again.

"Was the Gawker guy after Hugo?" Maggie asked.

"No. Some Wall Street guy I never heard of."

"Damn," said Maggie.

They said their good-byes to Christina and to Pinky Tyson and Pam Moldower.

"I just want to stop and see Margot McCartney," Hope said. "Okay with you?"

"Fine."

"She's divorcing Lyndon," Hope added.

"I guess that's for the best."

"Very much so."

"I wish this whole thing hadn't ended in such a mess," Maggie said. "It's colossally frustrating."

"The world is full of bullies and liars getting away with disgusting things."

"I know. But I've lived my whole life telling young people that there is justice."

"And the world is a better place if we behave as if that's true," said Hope, "even when it isn't. Oh, I'll tell you one good thing—"

"I'm ready."

"Avis Metcalf is going to the Costume Gala with Angus."

"You're kidding!"

"Not. He just called me, he wanted to tell someone, and his sister isn't speaking to him. He was so pleased. I felt like his mother."

———

The night before he left on his train journey to California, Hugo made love to Caroline. He had always prided himself on his finesse in that department but he took special care on this occasion to treat her with passion and tenderness. As they lay in a postcoital embrace, he whispered, "You are *so* good for me."

Caroline kissed him on the forehead and murmured wordlessly. As he drifted toward sleep, he felt particularly content with his performance.

Hugo's train pulled into Chicago Thursday in time for him to have a leisurely breakfast in the city, then make his way to the Art Institute. He spent a good long time with the Frederic Remingtons (a style of art he'd never liked) because he knew Randy Beemis was a fan. Then he devoted himself with pleasure to the Sargents and Whistlers in the permanent collection, and paid an homage visit to the Monet haystacks. In the museum shop he bought a pair of Murano glass earrings for Caroline. They were cheap, but she would treasure them because they were from him, and because he'd spin her a tale about the glass blowers of Venice. He chose a set of Georgia O'Keeffe note bricks as a hostess present for Linda. He didn't know what they were taking to Randy for his birthday, but he was sure Caroline was on top of it.

He had slept well, and he enjoyed a stroll in the sun after a light lunch with a very acceptable half bottle of chenin blanc in the museum café. He stopped in a bookstore to stock up on magazines for the rest of the trip, and by two-thirty in the afternoon, he was once again rolling west, feeling sleepy and content.

When the train pulled into L.A.'s Union Station Saturday morning, he was showered, carefully dressed, and wearing the Hermès aftershave he knew Caroline liked. He hadn't eaten; supper on the train had been quite enough, but he could have brunch when he got to the hotel, before they left for the ranch. He had slept well and long, and as he felt and heard the miles receding, all that had seemed to have him in a death grip had loosened and relaxed and fallen far behind. Before him was bright weather, a day of pleasures, and a new world to conquer.

He walked up the platform toward the station with his monogrammed suitcase rolling obediently behind him. He felt like a million bucks as he scanned the handful of drivers holding signs, seeking his name and wondering if he would have time for a dip in the Pacific before they left this afternoon.

He couldn't see his driver, but here was a man in a shirt and tie who was waving to him.

"Hugo Hollister?" said the man, and smiling, Hugo agreed that that was he and tried to give the man his suitcase.

Instead the man handed him a thick document and said, "You are being sued for divorce in the state of New York by Caroline Westphall Hollister. You have been served." While Hugo was still speechless, the man turned and wove himself into the crowd of arriving passengers and disappeared.

He looked at the thing in his hand. He could hardly adjust his sense of what was possible to take it in, but there didn't seem to be any doubt about it. Part of his mind was still eyeing the crowd, expecting a limo driver to appear, tug the forelock, and drive him off to Santa Barbara.

He needed to sit down. He walked into the station, feeling the need to hurry but with no idea toward what. He stood in line for a cup of coffee at an outpost of one of the more reliable chains, though no coffee you bought on the street was as good as the coffee he ground fresh and brewed himself at home.

There was a small sticky table available in a corner and he took it. He found his reading glasses and applied himself. There it was in officialese: he was being sued for divorce on the grounds of mental cruelty, spousal abuse, and adultery.

WTF?

Spousal abuse? What was she thinking? Mental cruelty? Really? And adultery, didn't you have to prove that? She couldn't prove that. She knew nothing about his dalliances, never had a clue, the patsy. New York was not a no-fault divorce state. He could fight this, and he could get her back. That, or countersue and get a big fat alimony settlement. That would be second best and wouldn't go down well with Lily the snoop, but putting a little distance between himself and Lily might not be a bad idea just at the moment.

He drank his coffee. He got out his phone and called a lawyer friend back in New York, someone he'd gone to Harvard with and played squash with a couple of times a year. But of course, New York was at lunch or out in the Hamptons right this minute.

He should just go back there. He went to the ticket wicket, took out his travel envelope, and said to a weary black woman who needed to lose about fifty pounds, "I've had some bad news and I have to change this ticket. I have to go back to New York right away. What is available?"

The ticket had been issued by their travel agency, and he hadn't really looked at it, just handed it to the conductor when he was asked. The woman in the cage looked at it back to front, and said, "What is it you want to change?"

"The return itinerary. I need to go back today, not on Monday."

She handed it back to him. "Your itinerary is complete. This is a one-way ticket."

"It's a what? No." He took it back, still in its reassuring jacket from Caroline's travel agent, and flipped through, looking for the return ticket. There was no sign of one. He was so used to traveling on the Westphall magic carpet that he hadn't even noticed.

He felt a rising bilious desire to ruin the fatso's day for disrespecting him, although she had only pointed out what he should have discovered himself.

He tamped down the feeling and reached for his wallet. "All

right, I'd like to book my return for the next train out with a private room."

She looked at the schedule and said, "There's one in two hours that will get you into New York on Monday at noon."

"How much?"

"Sixteen hundred dollars."

"Fine."

He took out the black American Express card that always got him such attentive service. The fatso took it and swiped it. She swiped it again. Then she stepped away from the wicket and made a phone call. When she returned she said, "I'm sorry, sir, that card has been canceled."

"What? No. That's impossible. Give it back, I'll give you another."

"I can't do that, sir," she said as she took a pair of scissors from her drawer and cut the card in half. Hugo was now quite red, as if an attack of some kind might be imminent. He handed her a platinum Visa card. The fatso went through the whole routine again, up to and including the scissors; all his high-credit-line cards were actually companion cards on Caroline's accounts. But he had his own. He had about fourteen of his own. Every time a credit card company offered him one, he accepted, even though they were charging sky-high interest rates and had credit limits in very low ranges, given that he used them to pay the interest on previous cards. When you kept kiting like that, it didn't do much for your credit rating.

None of the cards he had could make a dent in the price of the ticket. Even when he had downgraded to a coach seat and an itinerary that would get him home on Tuesday, he couldn't cover the price, even if he combined cards. And how was he going to eat for the next four days? He left the woman, throwing his one-way ticket into a trash can like so much used tissue and went to look for someplace where he could talk on the phone in private. He tried to call his bank, but of course it was Saturday. His private banker wasn't available, and the weekend gum chewers couldn't seem to understand the problem. He needed them to wire money, or extend him a line of credit, or whatever your banker does in an emergency, but they said his card wasn't linked to the savings account that used to guarantee his overdrafts and there wasn't enough in his checking to . . . he hung up.

He found a locker, stowed his luggage, and walked out of the station. He walked all the way around it, feeling distinctly out of place and out of his depth. He needed a pawnshop. This ought to be the right kind of neighborhood. Counting his clothes and his shoes and his watch he was worth a couple of thousand on the hoof; he could deal.

He wanted to find a pawnshop by coming upon it; he didn't want to have to explain to a stranger what he needed, but finally he went into a betting parlor and said he needed to raise some fast cash; did they know a place? They did. They didn't even seem very interested. Apparently guys wearing clothes like his needed to raise ready cash as often as the guys with the pint bottles of Thunderbird in paper bags.

At the pawnshop he offered his wedding ring. The pawn broker laughed. Reluctantly, he offered his watch, a Patek Philippe. A present from Caroline; he didn't know what she paid for it, but he expected at least a thousand. The guy laughed again. Finally he left the shop with enough cash to cover a coach ticket home and food if he ate only hot dogs and yogurt.

Luis was on the door Tuesday evening when Mr. Hollister got out of a taxi. Luis was surprised to see him. Hugo looked tired and ill and as if he hadn't had a proper shower in days.

"Need help with your bags, sir?" Luis asked, standing very straight in his uniform, holding the heavy outside door. Mrs. Missirlian on twelve, with the three Maltese fluffballs, was just going out, and Hugo had to stand aside to let her pass.

"No thank you, Luis," Hugo said. He couldn't wait to get out of these clothes, brush his teeth, and have a long hot bath, and he didn't want to talk to anybody until he had done that. He wondered if Caroline would be home. Would she have stayed in California with her friends? Laughing at her little joke with Linda and Randy? Probably. She wouldn't be here, she wouldn't have the nerve, because she knew he could work her. He could always get her back. This was Angus's trick; Caroline would never do this to him. He'd had a very long couple of days to think about how he'd get around her, and he knew he could do it. First a bath, clean clothes, and a drink, and then he'd find her and go to work. Then tomorrow he'd get with his lawyer and see where they were.

Of course, to find her, he'd have had to know that Caroline and Lily were at the Hotel Phoenix in Copenhagen, a city Caroline loved and that Lily had never seen. Lily had not been abroad in her life, since her father didn't travel and didn't like her that far out of his orbit. They were going to make a leisurely tour of the continent, drifting wherever the fancy took them.

But how to find his wife and daughter was far from Hugo's thoughts as the front door of the apartment swung inward with his keys still in the lock. He could see . . . and hear and feel . . . that the place was as empty as the day they bought it. Every painting, every carpet, every stick of furniture, every book on the shelves was gone.

He dragged his suitcase in and took his keys from the lock. She must have hired the best to empty the place so fast. It looked exactly as they had first seen it as newlyweds nineteen years ago: empty, scarred, and lifeless.

He walked into the powder room. There wasn't a hand towel. Even the toilet paper was gone. He relieved himself, rinsed his hands without soap, and dried them on his pants.

He walked into the living room, where they'd sat together watching the sunset and planning the California trip. He flipped on the light switches and nothing happened. The floor lamps were gone and so was the chandelier.

The den. There was recessed light in there. They wouldn't have taken the bulbs. And indeed they had not. He flipped the switch and the lights came on. This room too was empty of books, art, everything. The glasses and bottles were gone from the wet bar, whose door stood open, but in the middle of the room there was a folding lawn chair, metal tubes with nylon strapping that the cook had sat in to watch television in her tiny room at the back of the apartment. Beside it on the bare floor was a Charter Arms revolver and a box of bullets.

ACKNOWLEDGMENTS

I *am grateful to Vicky Bijur* and Franny Taliaferro for their assistance with various research questions, and even more for their friendship. Lauren Belfer, Molly Munn, David Gutcheon, Lucie Semler, and Kitty Clements read and commented on the manuscript in ways that were incredibly helpful. Frank Richardson, Tom Clements, Page Bond, Shelley Kehl, and Tom "Boaty McBoatface" Richardson all contributed in invaluable ways. I thank them all. Benny Chan and Tai Vardi provided vital tutorials on IT matters and social media, and Michael W. Taylor readily shared a tiny fraction of his encyclopedic knowledge of classic and antique cars. Well, of anything with wheels and engines, really. And as always, everything I know about the world of school I learned from Robin Clements. For that and for so much more for which no words suffice, he has my gratitude and my heart.

I am so lucky to have Emma Sweeney for a friend and literary agent and am also grateful to her cheerful and helpful assistant, Kira Watson. To my wise editor and comrade in arms Jennifer Brehl, and to Kaitlin Harri and the rest of the team at William Morrow, my utmost thanks for their enthusiasm and support.

About the author

About the book

Read on . . .

Insights,
Interviews
& More . . .

Meet Beth Gutcheon

Sigrid Estrada

BETH GUTCHEON is the critically acclaimed author of ten previous novels: *The New Girls, Still Missing, Domestic Pleasures, Saying Grace, Five Fortunes, More Than You Know, Leeway Cottage, Good-bye and Amen, Gossip,* and *Death at Breakfast.* She is the writer of several film scripts, including the Academy Award nominee *The Children of Theatre Street.* She lives in New York City. ∾

Reading Group Guide

1. In a society that includes great social, cultural, and economic differences, what case would you make for private schools, pro or con? Would we be better off without them?

2. The French teacher, Marcia Goldsmith, says that some of the girls' parents "see their kids the way they see their cars and jewelry, advertisements for themselves. They think that raging at these girls, or at us, will change what they got in the delivery room." Have you seen this to be true of today's parents? What is Marcia really talking about here?

3. Cheating, in school and in life, is one of the themes of the book. Who cheats, and why?

4. Have you ever known a sociopath? A person incapable of empathy? Who in the novel fits the category? How do we deal with such people in private and public life? How should we?

5. Have you or someone you are close to had experience with anonymous online bulletin boards? What is the case for them, pro or con?

6. Maggie wonders, "Did society undervalue teachers *because* they were underpaid? Or did it underpay them because what they did seemed less valuable to a civil society than running a hedge fund?" What's the answer? ▶

7. There are a number of unhappy marriages in this story. How are they the same, and how are they different?

8. At least three damaged or difficult young people turn the gears of the plot of *The Affliction*. What is the pattern here? What can you say about how their teachers and parents handle them?

9. Several characters are particularly skillful at compartmentalizing, mentally or emotionally. Which characters are they, and is this a useful skill, or a danger sign, or both? Is it related to empathy?

10. Do you think that Pam Moldower serves a special function in the book? If yes, what is it? ∿

Excerpt from
Death at Breakfast

DAY ONE, SUNDAY, OCTOBER 6

Maggie Detweiler, *new-minted woman of leisure* and not at all sure she was going to like it, had no sense of impending tragedy as she posed in front of the broad stone veranda of the Oquossoc Mountain Inn that bright October morning. She didn't really know what made her say to Hope, "When your picture's being taken, don't you always wonder if it's the one that will run with your obituary?"

"Well, that one won't be," Hope Babbin said, consigning the image to the digital trash can. "Hold still and smile, will you?"

Maggie did.

"And no, of course I don't. What a strange woman you are." Hope showed Maggie her cheerful image now glowing on the screen of her iPad, of a smallish pleasant-looking woman with a warm smile, intense blue eyes, and a halo of feathery white hair.

"Oh, am I? I think it's much better to keep in mind that it's waiting for all of us than to have it come as a surprise," said Maggie.

FOR MAGGIE, IT was probably something to do with retirement, which already was not at all the way she had once pictured it. To begin with, in the time it took you to get to Bergen, Maine, you could have flown to London. When her husband was alive ▶

5

they had dreamed of retiring to a bedsit in the West End. But in this first unstructured autumn of the rest of her life, she had instead taken a train to Boston to meet her friend Hope who had recently left New York for a Beantown suburb. Together they had trailed out to Logan Airport and after a longish wait for "a piece of equipment," which turned out to be the plane (there had been fog somewhere along its puddle-jumping route), they had flown to Bangor. There Hope insisted on being the one to rent a car, because it was her treat, this whole trip. They drove another hour and a half through the early dusk, past a stark northern moonscape of blueberry barrens studded with vast boulders dropped by haphazard glaciers in the last ice age, then on narrow roads that felt like tunnels cut through blue-black evergreen forests pressing in on them from both sides. By the time they reached Bergen, Maggie had come to fear that Hope had no peripheral vision at all. When you lived in New York, you didn't know what kind of drivers your friends were. Hope never actually hit anything, but Maggie thought it a miracle that the car still had both side mirrors when they finally found the Oquossoc Mountain Inn, the late Victorian stone pile that hulked at the head of Long Lake.

So it wasn't London, but the inn was charming, and it made sense for Maggie and Hope to see if they traveled well together. They'd been friends for years. They made each other laugh. They shared a penetrating curiosity about how people had chosen to live their lives, now and in the past. Maggie's life list of things to do before the rocking chair and the ear trumpet was heavier on museums and medieval ruins than Hope's, and Hope's was longer on palaces and gardens than Maggie's, but both had a yen to see sites of ancient civilizations in uncomfortable parts of the world, which Maggie's much mourned late husband would have loved, and Hope's unlamented ex would have hated.

Hope could afford to travel in far grander style than Maggie, thanks to having years earlier caught the father of her children, a hedge fund monster, in an extremely compromising position with the children's nanny, indeed a position worthy of the Kama Sutra. The husband did not wish the details of their ensuing divorce aired in the New York scandal rags, let alone the *Wall Street Journal,* so he had made a generous settlement with Hope on the condition that she never talk about it, and she never had, which was more than could be said for his next three wives.

So the Oquossoc outing was a trial run. Here, it would be easier to pull the plug than if they were halfway up the Andes when they discovered that it wasn't working out. Hope had signed them up for a cooking course being given by the inn's resident chef, whose food was winning some attention on luxury travel blogs. Maggie remained agnostic about the amusement value of this, since her culinary skills were mostly confined to working the microwave. But retirement is a time to learn new things. They'd been given rooms in the original part of the inn with lake views as recommended by TripAdvisor and had ▶

enjoyed a late and excellent dinner in
the dining room the night before, where
they got a chance to take the measure of
their fellow inmates. They had spent this
morning canoeing and been thrilled when
an enormous blue heron, hidden among
some rushes they were plashing toward,
had suddenly erupted from its hiding place
with a crashing of water and great paddling
of wings.

And now, they were happily heading
back down the mountain to the village of
Bergen, dimly seen the night before, with
its two white-steepled churches on opposite
sides of the main drag and its interesting
Richardson Romanesque public library.
Someone in Bergen had had a good deal
of money 150 years ago.

ON THE OTHER hand, Buster Babbin,
the deputy sheriff of Bergen, Maine,
was not happy this morning. His mother
was one of those women with the impact
of a battleship; you could see her coming
like the prow of the USS *Nimitz*. Hope was
tall and slim, with carefully coiffed and
blonded hair, an altogether dressier person
than her dread friend Mrs. Detweiler.
Watching the two of them advancing
toward him up Main Street was like being
an involuntary spectator at Fleet Week. It
mattered little that he knew the objects of
his terror thought of themselves as good-
natured middle-aged women, salt of the
earth and beloved of the young.

Hope and Maggie enjoyed making
their way along the uneven leaf-spangled
sidewalk, its concrete slabs buckled here
and there by the roots of the mighty oaks

and maples that lined the streets of the village. There was something so majestic about big trees; you missed that in the city. The sun was bright, and Hope wore huge sunglasses and a broad-brimmed hat. Maggie, who had as usual forgotten her hat, squinted into the sun, shading her eyes with her hand, which made her look to Deputy Babbin as if she thought she was Sacajawea, the Bird Woman, gazing over some rushing gorge, to discern the safest route along which to lead her charges.

"Here they come," said Sandra. She was looking out the front window of Just Barb's, the village diner, which she ran with her mother-in-law. "Man your stations." Sandra had greatly looked forward to this visitation, which would be the town's first sighting of anyone from Buster's heretofore storied family of origin. He had for years prevented his mother and sister from showing up in his life and taking over everything by paying just enough home visits to them at birthdays and holidays to keep them pacified. Some of us are content and at ease in the worlds we are born to, and some of us know we've been raised by wolves and take decades to find our true native landscapes. There is no point in trying to explain this to the wolves.

Buster Babbin stood up from his counter stool and checked to see that his shirt was tucked in. He was wearing his holster and gun, just to make a point. Sandra took her place behind the counter.

A glittering burst of bright fall air came into the room with the ladies.

"Well, don't you look official!" Hope exclaimed, moving to kiss her son, whose ▶

9

given name was Henry, but had been nicknamed by his father, then everybody, because of his genius for breaking things. Buster leaned into Hope with his shoulders and head, keeping his body well out of embracing range, and managed to connect his cheek with his mother's ear.

"Mrs. Detweiler," he said, turning to Maggie with his hand extended. The idea that *she* might try to kiss him as well had presented itself as a possibility.

"Oh, let me be Maggie now, please," said Mrs. Detweiler, in a voice that was far gentler than the sort of prison guard Klaxon tone he thought he remembered. She was now shorter than he was. She wore her hair in a neat no-nonsense cut and had gained a little weight around the middle, but her warm smile and watchful blue eyes were utterly the same, dreadful as that was to contemplate.

Sandra had appeared in their midst, holding menus, and somehow herded all three of them toward the corner booth.

How the hell was he supposed to call this figure of menace by her first name? The last time he had seen her he'd been thirteen years old, his uniform was torn and his nose was bleeding, and Mrs. Detweiler was on the phone to Hope, explaining that everyone at the Winthrop School felt that Buster would really be happier in a setting where he could get more individual support and would not have to take higher math or a foreign language. Afterward his mother had sent him off for a Wilderness Attitude Adjustment Experience in Nevada and he hadn't come back to live on the East Coast for seventeen years.

While he was gone, his mother and Mrs. Detweiler had bonded over the perfections of Buster's younger sister Lauren, who was currently finishing her residency in obstetrics at Brigham and Women's Hospital in Boston and was also mother of twins. This trip to Bergen, he'd been told, was a present from Hope to Mrs. Detweiler, on her retirement after twenty-three years as Winthrop School head and all-around rhinoceros. In addition to the thrill of seeing Buster in situ, they were staying up at the inn, which, though struggling, was by far Bergen's biggest remaining employer. It was, in fact, pretty much the town's reason for being at this point. Once there had been farming and fishing, copper mining and a small factory that made toothpicks, but now there was leaf peeping in the fall, followed by hunting season, followed by old-fashioned Christmas follies with sleigh rides and taffy pulls and caroling, plus skating and cross-country skiing that lasted if they were lucky until mud season. At least this dreaded visit was boosting the local economy.

"Is that thing loaded?" asked Hope. She had her napkin tucked into her pearls.

"No, Ma," he said, with heavy sarcasm, "I just wear the holster belt to keep my pants up."

Hope looked up from the menu at him to see if he was being fresh. Under the table, his knees were jiggling the way they always had since he was small. (He had just remembered it drove his mother crazy, which made them want to jig more.)

"Well how exciting," said Hope. ▶

Excerpt from *Death at Breakfast* (continued)

Sandra appeared and took their orders. When that diversion was over, Hope returned, as he knew she would, to Inquisitor mode, her version of showing motherly enthusiasm.

"And do you have a jail?"

After a pause, Buster said with dignity, consciously holding his knees still, "We have a chair."

The women looked at each other.

"It's pretty heavy. We can handcuff them to the arms until someone comes to take them to Ainsley."

"Well, I'd love to see the chair," said Hope.

"It's over in the town hall," said Buster, gesturing at the squat stone building across the street. "In the selectmen's office." He was not going to spend the week leading these two on a tour of the civic arrangements of Bergen. Sandra arrived with their plates, two on one arm and one on the other.

The large black radio on Buster's belt began to crackle. Buster struggled to get it out from under the table.

"Deputy Babbin here—" He got up and walked outside, where they could see him pacing back and forth on the sidewalk with the zest of a prisoner let out of an oubliette. After he finished his transmission he strode back inside, all business.

"Gotta go," he said. His mother and Mrs. D looked up from their plates. Buster put on his hat, fastened his radio back in place, and hitched his pants as Sandra, with practiced motions, whisked over to their table with a huge roll of aluminum foil, wrapped his lunch, and handed it to him.

"Cow on the road out by Laskey's farm. Get to it before there's an accident," he said. Sandra nodded, as if she knew he rarely finished a meal without an emergency, and Buster strode out. They watched him swing into the driver's seat of the patrol car out by the curb as if he were mounting a horse, perfectly aware that the ladies were watching; then he was off with what seemed like an unnecessary and declarative burst of speed.

"Does he have an office?" Hope asked Sandra.

"Well, here," said Sandra. "Or his car. We all know how to find him."

"I had no idea he knew anything about cows."

"He's real good with 'em," said Sandra. "Goats too. If it's pigs, though, he calls for backup."

"Pigs can be mean," said the one that wasn't Buster's mother. She had a nice smile.

THAT EVENING, HOPE and Maggie had declined the gentle yoga class that was offered after the opening session of their cooking course. Several of their classmates could be seen at this moment out on the lawn saluting the setting sun, but the ladies were instead contemplating the cocktail menu in the lounge while they waited for dinner.

"I think an apple martini sounds sufficiently in the harvest bounty spirit," Hope declared. They had spent the afternoon learning about the importance of using seasonal produce with an emphasis on the wonders of root ▶

vegetables and a spice they'd never heard of, called za'atar.

"I only hope the gin is locally sourced and artisanal," said Maggie as they ordered two.

"You know, it might be," said Hope. "When I was a girl, Poland Spring up here made gin that came in a green glass bottle shaped like a little old man. My father drank it like water. Took me forever to figure out why he didn't make any sense after lunch until he'd had his nap."

Around them, the lounge was slowly filling with gastronomes bathed and dressed for dinner. A couple from Cleveland called Homer and Margaux Kleinkramer was across the room drinking something beige and disturbing-looking from coupe champagne glasses. Albie Clark, a long thin grayish man nursing a secret grief or grievance, or both, was sitting by himself reading his Nook book and pulling at a beer.

"I used to hide my cigarette butts in one of those little old man bottles. I loved to smoke," Hope said dreamily. "It was so glamorous. My friends and I used to spend the afternoon in my brother's tree house, smoking Kents and reading *True Romance* magazines aloud to each other. Do romance magazines even exist anymore?"

"I doubt it. I think it's all sexting and Internet porn these days."

The chicest members of the cooking group, Martin and Nina Maynard, materialized beside them. They both had wet hair, fresh from showers. Nina's dress was covered in printed hibiscus and she wore a bright lipstick that matched the flowers and nicely emphasized her bright smile.

"May we join you?" Martin asked. He was a well-buffed African American with the build of a recently retired football player. He was dressed as if for golf, which showed off his physique nicely. "It sounded as if you might know something about D.C. schools. We need advice."

"Definitely," said Maggie. "And we were hoping to ask you what you are doing in a cooking class."

Martin laughed as they settled themselves. "My wife thinks I don't know how to find our kitchen."

"Well, do you?" asked Nina. She was a beauty, elfin, with caramel-colored skin.

"I'm sorry," said Martin, "I'm not allowed to talk about it."

"He works for the FBI," said Nina.

"I told my wife she could have anything she wanted for her birthday and she said she wanted me to come to this class with her. Believe me, I tried to talk her into a mink."

He scanned the room for a waiter as Hope, turning in her chair, asked, "Now what do you think that's all about?"

Across the lobby, some kind of fuss was building at the front desk. A huge man in a rust-colored cashmere tweed jacket was leaning over the counter speaking loudly to the village girl who was trying, apparently, to check him into the hotel. Off to the side, a pair of glossy bottle-blondes who were certainly sisters, maybe even twins, stared into space as if this was nothing to do with them. There was a small stack of matched luggage beside them, and one of the women had a tiny white dog in her arms. ▶

"Don't those women look familiar?" Maggie asked.

Hope took off her glasses so she could see them better across the room.

"Are they from one of those reality TV shows?"

The large man had now turned his back to the girl behind the counter, who was tapping fruitlessly at her computer and making eye contact with nobody. She looked very young in her unbecoming moss green hotel uniform.

The man said something contemptuous to the woman with the dog, who was ignoring him. He leaned back with his elbows on the counter behind him and stared furiously across the lounge, as if daring anyone in it to notice that he had not been served.

GABRIEL GURRELL WAS closeted that evening with Zeke, his head of maintenance. The riding mower was broken again, this time probably fatally. Zeke's brother had already rebuilt it once and he never had got it running quite right after that, though Zeke was in favor of trying his brother again. Gabriel was spared making a decision about it by the call from Cherry downstairs on the front desk. Yet again, she seemed unable to deal with a check-in. Cherry was trying hard but, Gabriel admitted to himself, probably wasn't going to work out. Too bad; he dreaded having to tell her formidable mother. He apologized to Zeke and took off for the stairs at a trot.

"Good evening," he said as he crossed the lobby to the vast man who was blocking all sight of Cherry. "I'm so sorry to learn there's a problem. How can I help you?"

"You the manager?" the huge man roared. Gabriel could see that every stitch he was wearing was hand-tailored; they didn't make clothes out of fabric like that at the Large and Tall shops.

"Manager slash general factotum. Gabriel Gurrell." He offered the man his hand. The man ignored it.

"My secretary made reservations for me for dinner and the night and this idiot . . ."

"I'm so sorry, let me see if I can help." Gabriel whisked behind the counter and took Cherry's place at the computer. "Your name?"

The man slapped the driver's license and gleaming black credit card that were lying on the desk.

After more tapping, Gabe looked up and asked, "Did she reserve by e-mail, Mr. Antippas? Or by telephone?" He had unluckily emphasized the first syllable of the name.

"It's AnTIPPas, and how the hell do I know!" bellowed the man, so that even the Kleinkramers, far across the room, stopped their conversation and turned to look.

"I'm sorry for your inconvenience, and I'm sure I can accommodate you."

"That's what this idiot said, but she was wrong, weren't you?" he turned to Cherry, who shrank back a step.

"Just tell me what you're looking for."

"I reserved a suite with a California king bed and separate sitting room, smoking, and another room for my sister-in-law, nonsmoking, and we want views of the lake." ▶

Excerpt from *Death at Breakfast* (continued)

"I'm afraid all our rooms are nonsmoking, sir . . ."

"Well couldn't you have fucking told me that when I reserved?" he yelled.

Gabriel's eyes flicked toward the lounge. Had they all heard the *F*-bomb? By the l ook of the raised heads and startled-looking eyes all over the room, they had. Not what his clientele came to Oquossoc for.

After a moment he said, "It's stated clearly on our website, sir, that we are a nonsmoking facility, but I understand your disappointment."

"You think I have time to read your fucking website? Who owns this place, Mike Bloomberg?"

"I can offer you a very nice suite on the mountain side of the building, with a terrace you can smoke on. It's just here," said Gabriel, producing a map of the hotel and grounds and making an *X* with his pen.

"You think I drove for seven hours for a view of the fucking parking lot?"

The woman with the dog in her arms, presumably his wife, came to join him.

"Alex," she said wearily, "I'm sure it's fine."

The huge man turned to look at her, as if to say *you* think it will be fine?

To Gabriel he snapped, "Is your supervisor here? Who can I talk to? How about the owner?"

Gabriel said, "I am the owner." He was trying not to look as if he'd be glad if they just took their luggage and went out the way they came. In flush times, you could choose whom not to accommodate, but since the crash of '08, he needed every bit of trade he could get and keep.

"Why don't we just go up and have a look

at the suite he's got?" said Mrs. Antippas. "I'm tired, and Colette needs her dinner."

"Yes of course," Gabriel said. "I'll phone the dining room and tell them you'll need a table for three in what, fifteen minutes?"

"Colette is the dog," said the second blond woman, who delivered this news, then returned to her woolgathering. Behind him Cherry was whispering a long self-justifying explanation of the problem she'd been trying to solve. Which involved the dog.

Gabriel seemed to refocus. The woman with the huge man had a dog in her arms.

"Ah. I see." He went back to the computer, as the woman with the dog said with a warning note in her voice, "*I* read the website and it expressly said that this is a dog-friendly hotel."

"Yes it is, madame," said Gabriel. "But we are bound by health department rules. Dogs are only permitted in this wing here; we have guests who are allergic, and all animals have to be kept away from food service."

"Don't you clean the rooms between guests?"

Gabriel was close to losing it. "Yes of course we clean between guests," he said through tight lips. "These are not my rules."

"Then give us a suite in the dog wing."

"I'm afraid I don't have a suite in that wing, madame. I have only one room open there, and it has twin beds and no sitting room."

"Do you mean there are no suites in that wing?"

"There are two, madame, but they are both occupied." ▶

Excerpt from *Death at Breakfast* (*continued*)

"Well, tell someone they have to move to the one over the fucking parking lot," said Antippas.

"I can't do that, sir. They are booked for the week by people here for the cooking class."

"The chef is giving a cooking class?" asked the sister-in-law, suddenly seeming to come back to earth.

"Well that takes the fucking cake," bellowed Antippas. "I drove nine hours just to have dinner here, and I get to sleep over the parking lot and my wife has to kill her dog."

"I'd like to know more about this cooking class," said the sister-in-law.

"You'll have to leave her in the car," said Antippas to his wife.

The wife said to Gabriel, "You know what? It's fine. I'll sleep with my sister in the dog wing and my husband will take the suite with the balcony. Could you just take us to our rooms now? If I can't get out of these panty hose soon and take a leak, I'm going to wet myself right here. Alex, get the dog's suitcase and just shut up."

"What did you just say to me?"

"The dog is not spending the night in the car. *You* sleep in the car, if you think that's so nice." Gabriel had summoned a bellman without seeming to move a muscle and in spite of his high dudgeon the man mountain had picked up a pet carrier bag and a large tote, in which Maggie could see a red leather leash, and a tiny Burberry plaid dog overcoat. ◠